SARAH MACLEAN

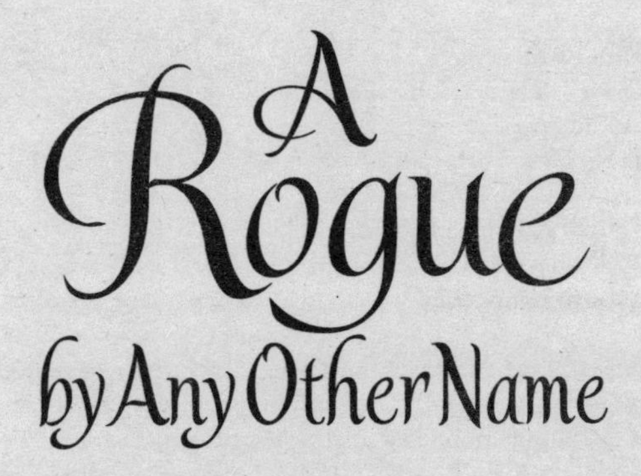

AVON
An Imprint of HarperCollins*Publishers*

This is a work of fiction. Names, characters, places, and incidents are products of the author's imagination or are used fictitiously and are not to be construed as real. Any resemblance to actual events, locales, organizations, or persons, living or dead, is entirely coincidental.

AVON BOOKS
An Imprint of HarperCollins*Publishers*
10 East 53rd Street
New York, New York 10022-5299

ISBN 978-0-06-206852-1
www.avonromance.com

First Avon Books mass market printing: March 2012

Printed in the U.S.A.

10 9 8 7 6 5 4 3 2 1

Four scandals,
whispered about in
ballrooms across London.

Four aristocrats,
exiled from society,
now royalty in the
London underworld.

Four loves,
powerful enough
to tame the darkness . . .

and bring these fallen angels
back into the light.

Here's Book I.

Romances by Sarah MacLean

A Rogue by Any Other Name
Eleven Scandals to Start to Win a Duke's Heart
Ten Ways to Be Adored when Landing a Lord
Nine Rules to Break when Romancing a Rake
The Season

For Meghan,
sister where it counts.

A
Rogue
by Any Other Name

Bourne

London
Winter 1821

The eight of diamonds ruined him.

If it had been the six, he might have saved himself. If it had been the seven, he would have walked away with triple his holdings.

But it was the eight.

The young Marquess of Bourne watched the card fly across the lush green baize and slide into place next to the seven of clubs that lay face up on the table, teasing him. His eyes were already closing, the air was already leaving the room in a single, unbearable rush.

Vingt et deux.

One more than the *vingt et un* on which he had wagered.

On which he had wagered everything.

There was a collective gasp in the room as he stayed the movement of the card with the tip of one finger—as bystanders watched the horror unfold with the keen pleasure of those who had narrowly escaped their own demise.

The chatter started then.

"He wagered it all?"

"Everything that wasn't entailed."

"Too young to know better."

"Old enough now; nothing makes a man faster than this."

"He's really lost all of it?"

"Everything."

His eyes opened, focusing on the man across the table, meeting the cold grey gaze he had known his whole life. Viscount Langford had been a friend and neighbor to his father, handpicked by the former Marquess of Bourne as guardian to his only son and heir. After Bourne's parents' death, it had been Langford who had protected the Marquessate of Bourne, who had increased its holdings tenfold, ensured its prosperity.

And then taken it.

Neighbor, perhaps. Never friend.

Betrayal scorched through the young marquess. "You did this on purpose." For the first time in his twenty-one years, he heard the youth in his voice. Hated it.

There was no emotion on his opponent's face as he lifted the mark from the center of the table. Bourne resisted the urge to wince at the arrogant scrawl of his signature across the white page—proof that he'd lost everything.

"It was your choice. Your choice to wager more than you were willing to lose."

He'd been fleeced. Langford had pressed him again and again, pushing him farther and farther, letting him win until he couldn't imagine losing. It was an age-old ploy, and Bourne had been too young to see it. Too eager. Bourne lifted his gaze, anger and frustration choking the words. "And your choice to win it."

"Without me, there would have been nothing to win," the older man said.

"Father." Thomas Alles, the viscount's son and Bourne's closest friend, stepped forward, his voice shaking. "Don't do this."

Langford took his time folding the mark and rising from the table, ignoring his son. Instead, he leveled Bourne with a cool look. "You should thank me for teaching you such a valuable lesson at such a young age. Unfortunately, now you've nothing but the clothes on your back and a manor house empty of its contents."

The viscount cast a glance at the pile of coins on the table—the remainder of his winnings from the evening. "I shall leave you the money, how's that? A parting gift, if you will. After all, what would your father say if I left you with nothing?"

Bourne shot up from his chair, knocking it back from the table. "You aren't fit to speak of my father."

Langford raised an eyebrow at the uncontrolled display, and he let silence reign for a long moment. "You know, I believe I shall take the money after all. And your membership to this club. It is time for you to leave."

Bourne's cheeks flamed as the words washed over him. His club membership. His land, servants, horses, clothes, everything. Everything but a house, a few acres of land, and a title.

A title now in disgrace.

The viscount lifted one side of his mouth in a mocking smile and flipped a guinea through the air toward Bourne who instinctively reached out, catching the gold coin as it glinted in the bright lights of White's card room. "Spend it wisely, boy. It's the last you'll have from me."

"Father," Tommy tried again.

Langford turned on him. "Not another word. I won't have you begging for him."

Bourne's oldest friend turned sad eyes on him, lifting his hands in a sign of helplessness. Tommy needed his father. Needed his money. His support.

Things Bourne no longer had himself.

Hatred flared hot and bright for the briefest of moments, before it was gone, extinguished by cold resolve, and Bourne placed the coin in his pocket and turned his back on his peers, his club, his world, and the life he had always known.

Vowing revenge.

Chapter One

Early January 1831

He did not move when he heard the door to the private room open and close quietly.

He stood in the darkness, silhouetted by the painted window overlooking the main room of London's most exclusive gaming hell. From the club floor, the window appeared as nothing but a stunning work of art—a massive piece of stained glass depicting the fall of Lucifer. In brilliant hues, the enormous angel—six times the size of the average man—tumbled toward the pit floor, cast into London's dark corners by Heaven's Army.

The Fallen Angel.

A reminder, not simply of the name of the club, but of the risk that those who entered took as they set their marks to the plush baize, as they lifted the ivory dice, as they watched the roulette wheel turn in a blur of color and temptation.

And when The Angel won, as it always did, the glass reminded those who lost of how far they had fallen.

Bourne's gaze flickered to a piquet table at the far end of the pit. "Croix wants his line increased."

The pit manager did not move from his place just inside the door to the owners' suite. "Yes."

"He owes more than he will ever be able to repay."

"Yes."

Bourne turned his head, meeting the shadowed gaze of his most trusted employee. "What is he willing to place against an extended line?"

"Two hundred acres in Wales."

Bourne watched the lord in question, who was sweating and twitching nervously as he waited for judgment to be passed.

"Extend the line. When he loses, see him out. His membership is revoked."

His decisions were rarely questioned, and never by the staff of The Angel. The other man headed for the door as quietly as he had entered. Before he could leave, Bourne said, "Justin."

Silence.

"The land first."

The soft click of door meeting jamb was the only indication that the pit manager had been there at all.

Moments later, he came into view on the floor below and Bourne watched the signal travel from boss to dealer. He watched as the hand was dealt, as the earl lost. Again.

And again.

And once more.

There were those who did not understand.

Those who had not gambled—who had not felt the thrill of winning—who had not negotiated with themselves for one more round, one more hand, one more shot—*just until he hit one hundred, one thousand, ten thousand . . .*

Those who had not known the luscious, euphoric, unparalleled feeling of knowing that a table was hot, that a night was theirs, that with a single card, everything could change.

They would never understand what kept the Earl of Croix in his chair, betting over and over and over again, fast as lightning, until he'd lost everything. Again. As though nothing he had wagered had ever been his to begin with.

Bourne understood.

Justin approached Croix and spoke discreetly into the ruined man's ear. The peer shot to his unsteady feet, outrage furrowing his brow as anger and embarrassment propelled him toward the manager.

A mistake.

Bourne could not hear what was said. He did not need to. He'd heard it hundreds of times before—watched as a long list of men had lost first their money, then their temper with The Angel. With him.

He watched Justin step forward, hands raised in the universal sign of caution. Watched as the manager's lips moved, attempting—and failing—to settle and calm. Watched as other players took note of the commotion and as Temple, Bourne's massive partner, headed into the fray, eager for a fight.

Bourne moved then, reaching toward the wall and pulling a switch, activating a complex combination of pulleys and levers, triggering a small bell beneath the piquet table and drawing the attention of the dealer.

Notifying him that Temple would not have his fight that evening.

Bourne would have it instead.

The dealer stayed Temple's impossible strength with a word and a nod toward the wall where Bourne and Lucifer watched, each willing to face whatever came next.

Temple's black gaze fell on the glass, and he nodded once before leading Croix through the throngs of people below.

Bourne descended from the owners' suite to meet them in a small antechamber set apart from the main floor of the club. Croix was cursing like a dockside sailor when Bourne opened the door and stepped inside. He rounded on Bourne, gaze narrowed with hatred.

"You bastard. You can't do this to me. Can't take what is mine."

Bourne leaned back against the thick oak door, crossing his arms. "You dug your grave, Croix. Go home. Be thankful I don't take more than my due."

Croix lunged across the small room before he had a chance to reconsider, and Bourne moved with an agility that few ever expected, clasping one of the earl's arms and twisting until his face was pressed firmly against the door. Bourne shook the lean man once, twice before saying, "Think very carefully about your next action. I find I am not feeling so magnanimous as I was mere moments ago."

"I want to see Chase." The words were slurred against the oak.

"Instead, you'll see us."

"I've been a member of The Angel since the beginning. You owe me. *He* owes me."

"On the contrary, it is *you* who owes *us*."

"I've given enough money to this place . . ."

"How generous of you. Shall we call for the book and see how much you still owe?" Croix went still. "Ah. I see you are beginning to understand. The land is ours now. You send your solicitor round in the morning with the deed, or I come looking for you myself. Is that clear?" Bourne did not wait for an answer, instead stepping back and releasing the earl. "Get out."

Croix turned to face them, panic in his gaze. "Keep the land, Bourne. But not the membership . . . don't take the membership. I'm a half a tick away from marrying. Her dowry will cover all my losses and more. Don't take the membership."

Bourne hated the keening plea, the undercurrent of anxiety in the words. He knew that Croix couldn't resist the urge to wager. The temptation to win.

If Bourne had an ounce of compassion in him, he'd feel sorry for the unsuspecting girl.

But compassion was not a trait Bourne claimed.

Croix turned wide eyes on Temple. "Temple. Please."

One of Temple's black brows rose as he crossed his massive arms across his wide chest. "With such a generous dowry, I'm sure one of the lower hells will welcome you."

Of course they would. The lower hells—filled with murderers and cheats—would welcome this insect of a man and his terrible luck with open arms.

"Bollocks the lower hells," Croix spat. "What will people think? What will it take? I'll pay double . . . triple. She's plenty of money."

Bourne was nothing if not a businessman. "You marry the girl and pay your debts, with interest, and we shall reinstate your membership."

"What do I do until then?" The sound of the earl's whine was unpleasant.

"You might try temperance," Temple offered, casually.

Relief made Croix stupid. "You're one to talk. Everyone knows what you did."

Temple stilled, his voice filled with menace. "And what was that?"

Terror removed the minimal intelligence from the earl's instincts, and he threw a punch at Temple, who caught the blow in one enormous fist and pulled the smaller man toward him with wicked intent.

"What was that?" he repeated.

The earl began to mewl like a babe. "N-nothing. I'm sorry. I didn't mean it. Please don't hurt me. Please don't kill me. I'll leave. Now. I swear. Please . . . d-don't hurt me."

Temple sighed. "You're not worth my energy." He released the earl.

"Get out," Bourne said, "before I decide that you *are* worth mine."

The earl fled the room.

Bourne watched him go before adjusting the line of his waistcoat and straightening his frock coat. "I thought he might soil himself when you took hold of him."

"He would not be the first." Temple sat in a low chair and stretched his legs out in front of him, crossing one booted ankle over the other. "I wondered how long it would take you."

Bourne brushed a hand across the half-inch linen cuff that peeked out from underneath his coat, making certain the swath of white fabric was even before returning his attention to Temple and pretending not to understand the question. "To do what?"

"To restore your clothing to perfection." One side of Temple's mouth curled in a mocking smile. "You're like a woman."

Bourne leveled the enormous man with a look. "A woman with an extraordinary right hook."

The smile became a grin, the expression showing off Temple's nose, broken and healed in three places. "You aren't honestly suggesting that you could beat me in battle, are you?"

Bourne was assessing the condition of his cravat in a nearby mirror. "I'm suggesting precisely that."

"May I invite you into the ring?"

"Anytime."

"No one is getting into the ring. Certainly not with Temple." Bourne and Temple turned toward the words, spoken from a hidden door at the far end of the room, where Chase, the third partner in The Fallen Angel, watched them.

Temple laughed at the words and turned to face Bourne. "You see? Chase knows enough to admit that you're no match for me."

Chase poured a glass of scotch from a decanter on a nearby sideboard. "It has nothing to do with Bourne. You're built like a stone fortress. No one is a match for you." The words turned wry. "No one but me, that is."

Temple leaned back in his chair. "Anytime you'd like to meet me in the ring, Chase, I shall clear my schedule."

Chase turned to Bourne. "You've paupered Croix."

He stalked the perimeter of the room. "Like sweets from a babe."

"Five years in business, and I remain surprised by these men and their weakness."

"Not weakness. Illness. The desire to win is a fever."

Chase's brows rose at the metaphor. "Temple is right. You are a woman."

Temple barked in laughter and stood, all six and a half feet of him. "I have to get back to the floor."

Chase watched Temple cross the room, headed for the door. "Haven't had your brawl tonight?"

He shook his head. "Bourne snatched it out from under me."

"There's still time."

"A man can hope." Temple left the room, the door closing firmly behind him, and Chase moved to pour another glass of scotch, walking it to where Bourne stood staring intently into the fireplace. He accepted the offering, taking a large swallow of the golden liquor, enjoying the way it burned his throat.

"I have news for you." Bourne turned his head, waiting. "News of Langford."

The words washed over him. For nine years, he'd been waiting for this precise moment, for whatever it was that would come spilling from Chase's mouth next. For nine years, he'd been waiting for news of this man who had stripped him of his past, his birthright.

His history.

Everything.

Langford had taken it all that night, all the lands, the funds, everything but an empty manor house and a handful of acres of land at the center of a larger estate—Falconwell. As he'd watched it all slip away, Bourne hadn't understood the older man's motives—hadn't known the pleasure of turning an estate into a living, thriving thing. Hadn't understood how much it would smart to turn it over to a mere boy.

Now, a decade later, he did not care.

He wanted his revenge.

The revenge he'd been waiting for.

It had taken nine years, but Bourne had rebuilt his fortune—doubled it. The money from the partnership in The Angel, along with several lucrative investments, had given him the opportunity to build an estate that rivaled the most extravagant in England.

But he'd never been able to reclaim what he'd lost. Langford had kept it all in a tight grip, unwilling to sell it, no matter how much he was offered, no matter how powerful the man who offered. And very powerful men had offered.

Until now.

"Tell me."

"It is complicated."

Bourne turned back to the fire. "It always is." But he hadn't worked every day to build his fortune for land in Wales and Scotland and Devonshire and London.

He'd done it for Falconwell.

One thousand acres of lush green land that had once been the pride of the Marquessate of Bourne. The land that his father and grandfather and great-grandfather had amassed around the manor house, which had been passed down from marquess to marquess.

"What?" He saw the answer in Chase's eyes before the words came, and he swore once, long and wicked. "What has he done with it?"

Chase hesitated.

"If he's made it impossible, I'll kill him."

As I should have done years ago.

"Bourne . . ."

"No." He slashed one hand through the air. "I've waited for this for *nine years*. He took everything from me. *Everything*. You have no idea."

Chase's gaze found his. "I have every idea."

Bourne stopped at that, at the understanding in the words. At the truth in them. It had been Chase who had pulled him from his lowest moment. Chase who had taken him in, cleaned him up, given him work. Chase who had rescued him.

Or, who had at least tried to rescue him.

"Bourne," Chase began, the words laced with caution. "He didn't keep it."

A cold dread settled deep within. "What do you mean, he didn't keep it?"

"Langford no longer owns the land in Surrey."

He shook his head, as though he could force understanding. "Who owns it?"

"The Marquess of Needham and Dolby."

A decades-old memory flashed at the name—a portly man, rifle in hand, marching across a muddy field in Surrey, trailed by a gaggle of girls sized small to smallest, the leader of whom had the most serious blue gaze Bourne had ever met.

His childhood neighbors, the third family in the holy trinity of the Surrey peerage.

"Needham has my land? How did he get it?"

"Ironically, in a game of cards."

Bourne could not find the humor in the fact. Indeed, the idea that Falconwell had been casually wagered and lost in a card came—again—set him on edge.

"Get him here. Needham's game is *écarté.* Falconwell will be mine."

Chase leaned back, surprised. "You would wager for it?"

Bourne's reply was instant. "I will do whatever is required for it."

"*Whatever* is required?"

Bourne was instantly suspicious. "What do you know that I do not?"

Chase's brows shot up. "Why would you think that?"

"You always know more than I know. You enjoy it."

"I merely pay closer attention."

Bourne's teeth clenched. "Be that as it may . . ."

The founder of The Fallen Angel feigned interest in a spot on one sleeve. "The land that was once a part of Falconwell—"

"*My* land."

Chase ignored the interruption. "You cannot simply retrieve it."

"Why not?"

Chase hesitated. "It has been attached to . . . something else."

Cold hatred coursed through Bourne. He'd waited a decade for this—for the moment when he would finally reconnect Falconwell Manor with its lands. "Attached to what?"

"To *whom*, more like."

"I am in no mood for your riddles."

"Needham has announced that the former lands of Falconwell are to be included in the dowry of his eldest daughter."

Shock rocked Bourne back on his heels. "Penelope?"

"You know the lady?"

"It's been years since I saw her last—nearly twenty of them."

Sixteen. She had been there on the day he'd left Surrey for the last time, after his parents' burial, fifteen years old and shipped back to a new world with no family. She'd watched him climb into his carriage, and her serious blue gaze had not wavered in tracking his coach down the long drive away from Falconwell.

She hadn't looked away until he had turned onto the main road.

He knew because he'd watched her, too.

She'd been his friend.

When he had still believed in friends.

She'd also been the eldest daughter of a double marquess with more money than one man could spend in a lifetime. There was no reason for her to have remained a spinster for so long. She should be married with a brood of young aristocrats to care for.

"Why does Penelope need Falconwell for a dowry?" He paused. "Why isn't she married already?"

Chase sighed. "It would serve me well if any one of you would take an interest in Society at large rather than our meager membership."

"Our *meager membership* is more than five hundred men. Every one of them with a file thick as my thumb, filled with information, thanks to your partners."

"Nevertheless, I have better things to do with my evenings than educating you on the world into which you were born."

Bourne's gaze narrowed. He'd never known Chase to spend evenings in any way other than entirely alone. "What things?"

Chase ignored the question and took another pull of scotch. "Lady Penelope made the match of the season years ago."

"And?"

"The engagement was overshadowed by her fiancé's love match."

It was an old tale, one he'd heard countless times, and still Bourne felt an unfamiliar emotion at the idea that the girl he remembered might have been hurt by her broken engagement. "Love match," he scoffed. "A prettier or wealthier prospect more like. And that was it?"

"I am told she has been pursued by several suitors in the years since. And yet, she remains unmarried." Chase appeared to be losing interest in the tale, continuing on a bored sigh. "Though I imagine not for long, with Falconwell to sweeten the honey pot. The temptation will have suitors swarming."

"They'll want a chance to lord it over me."

"Probably. You are not high on the list of favorite peers."

"I'm nowhere on the list of favorite peers. Nevertheless, I shall have the land."

"And you are prepared to do what it takes to get it?" Chase looked amused.

Bourne did not miss his partner's meaning.

A vision flashed of a young, kind Penelope, the opposite of what he was. Of what he'd become.

He pushed it aside. For nine years, he'd been waiting for this moment. For the chance to restore that which had been built for him.

That which had been left to him.

That which he had lost.

It was the closest he would ever get to redemption. And nothing would stand in his way.

"Anything." Bourne stood and carefully straightened his coat. "If a wife comes with it, so be it."

The door slammed shut after him.

Chase toasted the sound and spoke to the empty room. "Felicitations."

Chapter Two

Dear M—

You absolutely must come home. It's dreadfully boring without you; neither Victoria nor Valerie makes for a sound lakeside companion.

Are you very sure that you must attend school? My governess seems fairly intelligent. I'm sure she can teach you anything you need know.

Yrs—P
Needham Manor, September 1813

Dear P—

I'm afraid you're in for dreadful boredom until Christmas. If it is any consolation, I don't even have access to a lake. May I suggest teaching the twins to fish?

I'm sure I must attend school . . . your governess is not fond of me.

—M
Eton College, September 1813

Late January 1831
Surrey

Lady Penelope Marbury, being highborn and well-bred, knew that she should be very grateful indeed when, on a frigid January afternoon well into her twenty-eighth year, she received her fifth (and likely final) proposal of marriage.

She knew that half of London would think her not entirely out of bounds if she were to join The Honorable Mr. Thomas Alles on one knee and thank him and her maker for the very kind and exceedingly generous offer. After all, the gentleman in question was handsome, friendly, and had all his teeth and a full head of hair—a rare combination of traits for a not-so-young woman with a broken engagement and only a handful of suitors in her past.

She also knew that her father, who had no doubt blessed the match at some point prior to this moment—as she stared down at the top of Thomas's well-appointed head—liked him. The Marquess of Needham and Dolby had liked "That Tommy Alles" since the day, twenty-some-odd years ago, when the boy had rolled up his sleeves, hunkered down in the stables of her childhood home, and assisted in the whelping of one of the marquess's favorite hunting dogs.

From that day on, Tommy was a good lad.

The kind of lad that Penelope had always thought her father would have liked for his own son. If, of course, he'd had a son, instead of five daughters.

And then there was the fact that Tommy would someday be a viscount—a wealthy one, at that. As Penelope's mother was no doubt saying from her place beyond the drawing-room door, where she was no doubt watching the scene unfold in quiet desperation:

Beggars cannot be choosers, Penelope.

Penelope knew all this.

Which was why, when she met the warm brown gaze of this boy-turned-man she'd known all her life, this dear friend, she realized that this was absolutely the most generous offer of marriage she would ever receive, and she should say yes. Resoundingly.

Except she didn't.

Instead, she said, "Why?"

The silence that followed the words was punctuated by a dramatic "What does she think she is *doing*?" from beyond the drawing-room door, and Tommy's gaze filled with amusement and not a little bit of surprise as he came to his feet.

"Why not?" he replied, companionably, adding after a moment, "We've been friends for an age; we enjoy each other's company; I've need of a wife; you've need of a husband."

As reasons for marrying went, they weren't terrible ones. Nevertheless, "I've been out for nine years, Tommy. You've had all that time to offer for me."

Tommy had the grace to look chagrined before he smiled, looking not a small bit like a Water Dog. "That's true. And I haven't a good excuse for waiting except . . . well, I'm happy to say I've come to my senses, Pen."

She smiled back at him. "Nonsense. You'll never come to your senses. Why me, Tommy?" she pressed. "Why now, Tommy?"

When he laughed at the question, it wasn't his great, booming, friendly laugh. It was a nervous laugh. The one he always laughed when he did not wish to answer the question. "It's time to settle down," he said, before cocking his head to one side, smiling broadly, and continuing, "Come on, Pen. Let's make a go of it, shall we?"

Penelope had received four previous offers of marriage

and imagined countless other proposals in a myriad of fashions, from the glorious, dramatic interruption of a ball to the private, wonderful proposal in a secluded gazebo in the middle of a Surrey summer. She'd imagined professions of love and undying passion, profusions of her favorite flower (the peony), blankets spread lovingly across a field of wild daisies, the crisp taste of champagne on her tongue as all of London raised their glasses to her happiness. The feel of her fiancé's arms around her as she tossed herself into his embrace and sighed, *Yes . . . Yes!*

They were all fantasy—each more unlikely than the last—she knew. After all, a twenty-eight-year-old spinster was not exactly fighting off suitors.

But surely she was not out of line to hope for something more than, *Let's make a go of it, shall we?*

She let out a little sigh, not wanting to upset Tommy, who was very clearly doing his best. But they'd been friends for an age, and Penelope wasn't about to introduce lies to their friendship now. "You're taking pity on me, aren't you?"

His eyes went wide. "What? No! Why would you say such a thing?"

She smiled. "Because it's true. You pity your poor, spinster friend. And you're willing to sacrifice your own happiness to be certain that I marry."

He gave her an exasperated look—the kind of look that only one very dear friend could give another—and he lifted her hands in his, kissing her knuckles. "Nonsense. It's time I marry, Pen. You're a good friend." He paused, chagrin flashing in a friendly way that made it impossible to be annoyed with him. "I've made a hash of it, haven't I?"

She couldn't help herself. She smiled. "A bit of one, yes. You're supposed to profess undying love."

He looked skeptical. "Hand to brow and all that?"

The smile became a grin. "Precisely. And perhaps write me a sonnet."

"*O, fair Lady Penelop-e . . . Do please consider marrying me?*"

She laughed. Tommy always made her laugh. It was a good quality, that. "A shabby attempt indeed, my lord."

He feigned a grimace. "I don't suppose I could breed you a new kind of dog? Name it the Lady P?"

"Romantic indeed," she said, "but it would take rather a long time, don't you think?"

There was a pause as they enjoyed each other's company before he said, suddenly very serious, "Please, Pen. Let me protect you."

It was an odd thing to say, but he'd failed at all the other parts of the marriage proposal process, so she did not linger on the words.

Instead, she considered the offer. Seriously.

He was her oldest friend. One of them, at least.

The one who hadn't left her.

He made her laugh, and she was very, very fond of him. He was the only man who hadn't utterly deserted her after her disastrous broken engagement. Surely that alone recommended him.

She should say yes.

Say it, Penelope.

She should become Lady Thomas Alles, twenty-eight years old and rescued, in the nick of time, from an eternity of spinsterhood.

Say it: Yes, Tommy. I'll marry you. How lovely of you to ask.

She *should.*

But she didn't.

Dear M—

My governess is not fond of eels. Surely she's cultured enough to see that simply because you arrived bearing one does not make you a bad person. Loathe the sin, not the sinner.

Yrs—P

post script—Tommy was home for a visit last week, and we went fishing. He is officially my favorite friend.

Needham Manor, September 1813

Dear P—

That sounds suspiciously like a sermon from Vicar Compton. You've been paying attention in church. I'm disappointed.

—M

post script—He is not.

Eton College, September 1813

The sound of the great oak door closing behind Thomas was still echoing through the entryway of Needham Manor when Penelope's mother appeared on the first-floor landing, one flight up from where Penelope stood.

"Penelope! What have you done?" Lady Needham came tearing down the wide central staircase of the house, followed by Penelope's sisters, Olivia and Philippa, and three of her father's hunting dogs.

Penelope took a deep breath and turned to face her mother. "It's been a quiet day, really," she said, casually, heading for the dining room, knowing her mother would follow. "I did write a letter to cousin Catherine; did you know she continues to suffer from that terrible cold she developed before Christmas?"

Pippa chuckled. Lady Needham did not.

"I don't care a bit about your cousin Catherine!" the marchioness said, the pitch of her voice rising in tune with her anxiety.

"That's rather unkind; no one likes a cold." Penelope pushed open the door to the dining room to discover her father already seated at the table, still wearing his hunting clothes, quietly reading the *Post* as he waited for the feminine contingent of the household. "Good evening, Father. Did you have a good day?"

"Deuced cold out there," the Marquess of Needham and Dolby said, not looking up from his newspaper. "I find I'm ready for supper. Something warm."

Penelope thought perhaps her father wasn't at all ready for what was to come during this particular meal, but instead, she pushed a waiting beagle from her chair and assumed her appointed seat, to the left of the marquess, and across from her sisters, both wide-eyed and curious about what was to come next. She feigned innocence, unfolding her napkin.

"Penelope!" Lady Needham stood just inside the door to the dining room, stick straight, her hands clenched in little fists, confusing the footmen, frozen in uncertainty, wondering if dinner should be served or not. "Thomas *proposed*!"

"Yes. I was present for that bit," Penelope said.

This time, Pippa lifted her water goblet to hide her smirk.

"Needham!" Lady Needham decided she required additional support. "Thomas proposed to Penelope!"

Lord Needham lowered his paper. "Did he? I always liked that Tommy Alles." Turning his attention to his eldest daughter, he said, "All right, Penelope?"

Penelope took a deep breath. "Not precisely, Father."

"She did not accept!" The pitch at which her mother spoke was appropriate only for the most heartbreaking of mourning or a Greek chorus. Though it apparently had the additional purpose of setting dogs to barking.

After she and the dogs had completed their wails, Lady Needham approached the table, her skin terribly mottled, as though she had walked through a patch of itching ivy. "Penelope! Marriage proposals from wealthy, eligible young men do not blossom on trees!"

Particularly not in January, I wouldn't think. Penelope knew better than to say what she was thinking.

When a footman came forward to serve the soup that was to begin their evening meal, Lady Needham collapsed into her chair, and said, "Take it away! Who can eat at a time like this?"

"I am quite hungry, actually," Olivia pointed out, and Penelope swallowed back a smile.

"Needham!"

The marquess sighed and turned to Penelope. "You refused him?"

"Not exactly," Penelope hedged.

"She did not *accept* him!" Lady Needham cried.

"Why not?"

It was a fair question. Certainly one that everyone at the table would have liked to have answered. Even Penelope.

Except, she did not have an answer. Not a good one. "I wanted to consider the offer."

"Don't be daft. Accept the offer," Lord Needham said, as though it were as easy as that, and waved the footman over for soup.

"Perhaps Penny doesn't *wish* to accept Tommy's offer," Pippa pointed out, and Penelope could have kissed her logical younger sister.

"It's not about wishing or otherwise," Lady Needham said. "It's about selling when one can."

"What a very charming sentiment," Penelope said dryly, trying her very best to keep her spirits up.

"Well it's true, Penelope. And Thomas Alles is the only man in society who appears willing to buy."

"I do wish we could think of a better metaphor than purchase and sale," Penelope said. "And, truly, I don't think he wants to marry me any more than I want to marry him. I think he's just being kind."

"He isn't just being kind," Lord Needham said, but before Penelope could probe on that particular insight, Lady Needham was speaking again.

"It's hardly about *wanting* to marry, Penelope. You're far beyond that. You *must* marry! And Thomas was willing to marry you! You've not had a proposal in *four years*! Or had you forgotten that?"

"I had forgotten, Mother. Thank you very much for the reminder."

Lady Needham lifted her nose. "I gather you mean to be amusing?"

Olivia's brows rose, as though the very idea of her eldest sister being amusing was unbelievable. Penelope resisted the urge to defend her sense of humor, which she liked to think was very much intact.

Of course she hadn't forgotten it. Indeed, it was a difficult fact to forget, considering how often her mother reminded her of her marital state. Penelope was surprised that the marchioness did not know the number of days and hours that had passed since the proposal in question.

She sighed. "I am not aiming for humor, Mother. I'm simply . . . not certain that I *want* to marry Thomas. Or anyone else who isn't certain that he wants to marry *me*, honestly."

"Penelope!" her mother barked. "Your *wants* are not paramount in this situation!"

Of course they weren't. That wasn't how marriage operated.

"Really. How very ridiculous!" There was a pause as the marchioness collected herself and attempted to find her words. "Penelope . . . there is *no one* else! We've searched! What will become of you?" She collapsed elegantly back in her chair, one hand to her brow in a dramatic gesture that would have made any one of the actresses on the London stage proud. "Who will *have* you?"

It was a fair question, and one that Penelope should probably have considered more carefully before she revealed her uncertainty about her marital future. But she hadn't exactly *decided* to make such an announcement, at least, not until she'd made it.

And now, it seemed like the best decision she'd made in a very long while.

The thing was, Penelope had had plenty of opportunity to be "had" in the past nine years. There had been a time when she was the talk of the *ton*—passably attractive, well behaved, well-spoken, well-bred, perfectly . . . perfect.

She'd been betrothed, even. To a similarly perfect counterpart.

Yes, it had been a perfect match, except for the fact that he had been perfectly in love with someone else.

Scandal had made it easy for Penelope to end the engagement without being jilted. Well, at least, not *precisely.*

She would not describe it as a *jilt,* exactly. More of a *jolt,* really.

And not an unwelcome one.

Not that she would tell her mother that.

"Penelope!" The marchioness straightened again, her anguished gaze on her eldest daughter. "Answer me! If not Thomas, then *who*? Who do you suppose will *have* you?"

"I shall have myself, it seems."

Olivia gasped. Pippa paused, her soup spoon halfway to her lips.

"Oh! Oh!" The marchioness collapsed once more. "You cannot *mean* it! Don't be *ridiculous*!" Panic and irritation warred in Lady Needham's tone. "You are made of stronger stuff than *spinsters*! *Oh!* Don't make me think of it! A *spinster*!"

Penelope thought that it was in fact the spinsters who were made of stronger stuff than she, but she refrained from saying such a thing to her mother, who looked as though she might topple from her chair in a state of utter desperation.

The marchioness pressed on. "And what of me? I was not born to be a *spinster's mother*! What will they *think*? What will they *say*?"

Penelope had a very good idea of what they already thought. What they already said.

"There was a time, Penelope, when you were to be the very opposite of what you have become! And I was to be the mother of a *duchess*!"

And there it was. The specter that loomed between Lady Needham and her eldest daughter.

Duchess.

Penelope wondered if her mother would ever forgive her for the dissolution of the engagement . . . as though it had been Penelope's fault somehow. She took a deep breath, attempting a reasonable tone. "Mother, the Duke of Leighton was in love with another woman—"

"*A walking scandal!*"

Whom he loves beyond measure. Even now, eight years later, Penelope felt a twinge of envy . . . not for the duke, but for the emotion. She pushed the feeling aside. "Scandal or no, the *lady* happens to be the Duchess of Leighton. A title, I might add, that she has held for eight years, during which time she's birthed the future Duke of Leighton and three additional children for her husband."

"Who should have been *your* husband! *Your* children!"

Penelope sighed. "What would you have me do?"

The marchioness popped up once more. "Well! You could have *tried* a bit harder! You could have accepted any number of proposals after the duke's." She flopped back again. "There were *four of them*! Two earls," she recounted, as though proposals of marriage might have slipped Penelope's mind, "then George Hayes! And now *Thomas!* A future viscount! I could *accept* a future viscount!"

"How very magnanimous of you, Mother."

Penelope sat back in her chair. She supposed that it was true. Lord knew that she had been trained to try very hard to land a husband—well, as hard as one could try without appearing to be trying too hard.

But in the past few years, her heart hadn't been in it. Not really. For the first year after the broken engagement, it was easy to tell herself that she did not care to marry because she was shrouded in the scandal of a broken engagement, and no one showed much interest in her as a potential bride.

After that, there had been a few proposals, all men with ulterior motives, all eager to marry the daughter of the Marquess of Needham and Dolby, either for their political careers or their financial futures, and the marquess hadn't minded much at all when Penelope had politely declined those offers.

It hadn't mattered to him why she'd said no.

Hadn't occurred to him that she might have said no because she'd had a glimpse of what marriage could be—because she'd seen the way the Duke of Leighton had gazed, lovingly, into the eyes of his duchess. She'd seen that there might be something more to come from a marriage if she only had enough time to find it.

But somehow, during that time when she told herself she was waiting for more, she'd lost her chance. She'd become too old, too plain, too tarnished.

And today, as she'd watched Tommy—a dear friend, but not much else—offer to spend the rest of his life with her, despite his own utter disinterest in their marriage . . . she simply couldn't say yes.

She couldn't ruin *his* chances at something more.

No matter how disastrous her own were.

"Oh!" The keening began once more. "Think of your *sisters*! What of *them*?"

Penelope looked to her sisters, who were watching the conversation as though it were a badminton match. *Her sisters would be fine.* "Society shall have to make do with the younger, prettier Marbury daughters. Considering the fact that the two married Marbury daughters are a countess and a baroness, I should think all will be well."

"And thank goodness for the twins' excellent matches."

Excellent was not precisely the description Penelope would use to describe either Victoria or Valerie's matches—made for title and dowry and little else—but their husbands were relatively innocuous and at least discreet with their activities outside the marriage bed, so Penelope did not argue the point.

No matter. Her mother was plunging onward.

"And what of your *poor father*? It's as though you have forgotten that he was plagued with a houseful of girls! It would be different if you'd been a boy, Penelope. But he is positively *sick with worry* over you!"

Penelope turned to look at her father, who dipped a piece of bread in his bisque and fed it to the large black water dog seated at his left hand, staring up at him, long pink tongue lolling out of the side of her mouth. Neither man nor beast seemed particularly sick with worry. "Mother, I . . ."

"And Philippa! Lord Castleton has shown interest in her. *What* of Philippa?"

Now Penelope was confused. "What *of* Philippa?"

"Precisely!" Lady Needham waved a white linen napkin in a dramatic way. "*What of Philippa?*"

Penelope sighed and turned to her sister. "Pippa, do you feel that my refusing Tommy will impact your suit from Lord Castleton?"

Pippa shook her head, eyes wide. "I can't imagine it would. And if it did, I honestly wouldn't be devastated. Castleton's a bit . . . well, uninteresting."

Penelope would have used the word *unintelligent*, but she allowed Pippa her politeness.

"Don't be so silly, Philippa," the marchioness said, "Lord Castleton is an *earl*. Beggars cannot be choosers."

Penelope gritted her teeth at the adage, her mother's favorite when discussing her unmarried daughters' prospects. Pippa turned her blue gaze on her mother. "I was not aware that I was *begging*."

"Of course you are. You all do. Even Victoria and Valerie had to beg. Scandal does not simply *disappear*."

Penelope heard the meaning of the words even if it wasn't articulated. *Penelope's ruined it for all of you.*

A pang of guilt thrummed through her, and she tried to

ignore it, knowing that she shouldn't feel guilty. Knowing that it wasn't her fault.

Except, it might have been.

She pushed the thought away. It wasn't. He'd loved another.

But why hadn't he loved her?

It was a question she'd asked herself over and over during that long-ago winter, when she'd been holed up here, in the country, reading the scandal sheets and knowing that he'd chosen someone more beautiful, more charming, more exciting than she. Knowing that he was happy, and she was . . . unwanted.

She hadn't loved him. She hadn't thought much at all about him.

But it smarted nonetheless.

"*I've* no intention of begging," Olivia entered the conversation. "It's my second season, I'm beautiful and charming, and I've a very large dowry. Larger than any man can overlook."

"Oh, yes. Very charming," Pippa said, and Penelope looked down at her plate to hide her smile.

Olivia caught the sarcasm. "Laugh all you like, but I know what my value is. I'm not going to let what happened to Penelope happen to me. I'm landing myself a true aristocrat."

"A fine plan, darling." Lady Needham beamed with pride.

Olivia smiled. "Thank goodness I've learned my lessons from you, Penny."

Penelope could not help defending herself. "It's not as though I chased him away, Olivia. Father ended the engagement because of Leighton's sister's scandal."

"Nonsense. If Leighton had wanted you, he would have fought for you, scandal be damned," her youngest sister said, lips pursed, a born ingénue. "But he didn't. Want you, that is. Though I suppose he didn't fight for you, either. And I can only imagine that he didn't do those things because you didn't work hard enough to keep his attention."

Being the youngest, Olivia had never had to think much

about the way her words, always a touch too forthright, might sting. Now was no exception. Penelope bit the inside of her cheek, resisting the urge to scream, *He loved another!* But she knew an exercise in futility when she found one. Broken engagements were the woman's fault, always. Even when the woman in question was your older sister, apparently.

"Yes! Oh, Olivia, only one season out and already you are so astute, darling," Lady Needham chirped, before moaning, "And don't forget the others."

They had all appeared to have forgotten that she didn't wish to marry the others. But Penelope still felt she should defend herself. "I received a proposal of marriage this afternoon if you'll recall."

Olivia waved one hand dismissively. "A proposal from *Tommy.* That's not a *good* proposal. Only a henwit would think he asked because he *wanted* to marry you."

One could always count on Olivia to speak the truth.

"To that end, why *did* he ask?" Pippa interjected, not meaning for the question to be cruel, Penelope was certain. After all, she'd asked herself—and Tommy—that very question not an hour earlier.

She would like to say, *Because he loves me.*

Well, that wasn't precisely true. She'd like to say the words. But not about Tommy.

Which was why she hadn't said yes.

In all her years, she'd never once imagined marrying Tommy.

He'd never been the one of whom she dreamed.

"It's not important *why* he asked," Lady Needham interjected. "What's important is that he was willing to take in Penelope! That he was willing to give her a home and a name and care for her as your father has for all these years!" She leveled Penelope with a look. "Penelope, you must *think,* darling! When your father dies! What then?"

Lord Needham looked up from his pheasant. "I beg your pardon?"

Lady Needham waved one hand in the air as though she

hadn't time to think about her husband's feelings, instead prodding, "He shan't live forever, Penelope! What *then*?"

Penelope could not think of why this was in any way relevant. "Well, that shall be very sad, I imagine."

Lady Needham shook her head in frustration. "Penelope!"

"Mother, I honestly have no idea what you are implying."

"Who will take care of you? When your father dies?"

"Is Father planning to die soon?"

"No," her father said.

"One never knows!" Tears were welling in the marchioness's eyes.

"Oh, for God's—" Lord Needham had had enough. "I'm not dying. And I take no small amount of offense in the fact that the thought simply rolled off your tongue." He turned to Penelope. "And as for you, you'll marry."

Penelope straightened her shoulders. "This is not the Middle Ages, Father. You cannot force me to marry someone I do not wish to marry."

Lord Needham had little interest in the rights of women. "I've five daughters and no sons, and I'll be damned if I leave a single one of you unmarried and fending for yourself while that idiot nephew of mine runs my estate into the ground." He shook his head. "I will see you married, Penelope, and married well. And it's time you stop dickering around and accept yourself a suit."

Penelope's eyes went wide. "You think I've been dickering around?"

"Penelope, language. Please."

"To be fair, Mother, he did say it first," Pippa pointed out.

"Irrelevant! I didn't raise you girls to speak like common . . . common . . . oh, you know."

"Of course you've been dickering around. It's been eight years since the Leighton debacle. You're the daughter of a double marquess with the money of Midas."

"Needham! How crass!"

Lord Needham looked to the ceiling for patience. "I don't know what you've been waiting for, but I do know I've coddled you too long, ignoring the fact that the Leighton debacle cast a pall over the lot of you." Penelope looked to her sisters, who were both staring down at their laps. Guilt whispered through her as her father continued, "I'm through with it. You'll marry this season, Penny."

Penelope's throat was working like mad, struggling to swallow against the knot of sawdust that appeared to have become lodged there. "But . . . no one but Tommy has proposed to me in four years."

"Tommy's just the beginning. They'll propose now." She'd seen the look of complete certainty in her father's eyes enough times in her life to know that he was right.

She looked her father straight in the eye. "Why?"

"Because I've added Falconwell to your dowry."

He said it in the manner in which one would say things like, *It's a bit cold.* Or, *This fish needs more salt.* As though everyone at the table would simply accept the words as truth. As though four heads would not turn to him, eyes wide, jaws dropped.

"Oh! Needham!" Lady Needham was off again.

Penelope did not take her gaze from her father. "I beg your pardon?"

A memory flashed. A laughing, dark-haired boy, clinging to a low branch of a massive willow tree, reaching down and urging Penelope to join him in his hiding place.

The third of the trio.

Falconwell was Michael's.

Even if it hadn't belonged to him in a decade, she'd always think of it that way. It did not feel right that it was somehow, strangely, hers now. All that beautiful, lush land, everything but the house and immediate grounds—the entail.

Michael's birthright.

Now hers.

"How did you get Falconwell?"

"How is not relevant," the marquess said, not looking up from his meal. "I can't have you risking your sisters' successes on the marriage mart any longer. You need to get yourself married. You shan't be a spinster for the rest of your days; Falconwell will ensure it. Already has, it looks like. If you don't like Tommy, I've already a half dozen letters of interest from men across Britain."

Men who wanted Falconwell.

Let me protect you.

Tommy's strange words from earlier made sense now. He'd proposed to keep her from the mess of proposals that would come for her dowry. He'd proposed because he was her friend.

And he'd proposed for Falconwell. There was a small parcel of land belonging to Viscount Langford on the far side of Falconwell. Someday, it would be Tommy's and, if she married him, he'd have Falconwell to add to it.

"Of course!" Olivia interjected. "That explains it!"

He hadn't told her.

Penelope had known he wasn't really interested in marrying her, but the proof of it wasn't exactly a pleasant discovery. She remained focused on her father. "The dowry. It is public?"

"Of course it's public. What good is it tripling the value of your daughter's dowry if you don't make it public?" Penelope ran a fork through her turnip mash, wishing she were anywhere but at that table, at that moment, when her father said, "Don't look so miserable. Thank your stars you'll finally have yourself a husband. With Falconwell in your dowry, you could win yourself a prince."

"I find myself tiring of princes, Father."

"*Penelope!* No one *tires* of *princes*!" her mother interjected.

"I should like to meet a prince," Olivia interjected, chewing thoughtfully. "If Penelope doesn't want Falconwell, I should happily have it as part of my dowry."

Penelope slid her gaze to her youngest sister. "Yes, I imagine you would, Olivia. But I doubt you will need it." Olivia had the same pale hair and pale skin and pale blue eyes that Penelope had, but instead of making her look as Penelope did—like tepid dishwater—Olivia was breathtakingly beautiful and the kind of woman who could snap her fingers and bring men to her side.

Worse, she knew it.

"You *do* need it. Especially now," Lord Needham said pragmatically before turning back to Penny. "There was a time when you were young enough to capture the attention of a decent man, but you're well past that."

Penelope wished that one of her sisters would enter into the fray to defend her. To protest their father's words. To say, perhaps, *Penelope doesn't need it. Someone wonderful will come along and stumble into love with her. At first sight. Obviously.*

She ignored the pang of sadness that flared at the silent acceptance of the words. Penelope saw the truth in her father's gaze. The certainty. And she knew, without a doubt, that she would be married as her father willed, as though it *were* the Middle Ages, and he was carving off a little piece of his fiefdom.

Except he wasn't carving off anything. "How is it possible that Falconwell now belongs to the Marquess of Needham and Dolby?"

"That shouldn't worry you."

"But it does," Penelope pressed. "Where did you get it? Does Michael know?"

"Don't know," the marquess said, lifting his wineglass. "Imagine it's only a matter of time before he does."

"Who knows what *Michael* knows," her mother scoffed. "No one in *polite* society has seen the Marquess of Bourne for years."

Not since he disappeared in scandal. Not since he'd lost everything to Tommy's father.

Penelope shook her head. "Did you try to return it to him?"

"Penelope! Don't be ungrateful!" the marchioness trilled. "The addition of Falconwell to your dowry is a shining example of your father's generosity!"

An example of her father's desire to rid himself of his troublesome daughter.

"I don't want it."

She knew the words were a lie even as she said them. Of course she wanted it. The lands attached to Falconwell were lush and vibrant and filled with memories of her childhood.

With memories of Michael.

It had been years since she'd seen him—she'd been a child when he'd left Falconwell, and barely out when his scandal had been the talk of London aristocrats and Surrey servants. Now, if she heard of him at all, it was in snippets of gossip from more experienced women of the *ton*. He was in London running a gaming hell, she'd once heard from a particularly chatty group of women in a ladies' salon, but she'd never asked where, seeming to know instinctively that ladies like herself did not frequent the place where Michael had landed when he'd fallen from grace.

"You don't have a choice, Penelope. It's mine. And soon it will be your husband's. Men from across Britain will come for a chance to win it. Marry Tommy now or one of them later, if you like. But you'll marry this season." He leaned back in his chair, spreading his hands over his wide girth. "One day, you'll thank me."

You'll marry this season.

"Why didn't you return it to Michael?"

Needham sighed, throwing down his napkin and rising from the table, through with the conversation. "He was careless with it in the first place," he said simply before quitting the room, Lady Needham fast on his heels.

It might have been sixteen years since she'd seen him last, but a part of her still considered Michael Lawler, Marquess of Bourne, a dear friend, and she did not like the way her father spoke of him, as though he were of little value and less import.

But then, she really didn't know Michael—not the man. When she allowed herself to think of him, more often than she'd like to admit, he was not a twenty-one-year-old who had lost everything in a silly game of chance.

No, in her thoughts, Michael remained her childhood friend—the first she'd ever made—twelve years old, leading her across the muddy landscape on one adventure or another, laughing at inopportune moments until she could not resist laughing with him, muddying his knees in the damp fields that stretched between their houses and throwing pebbles at her window on summer mornings before he headed off to fish in the lake that straddled Needham and Bourne lands.

She supposed the lake was part of her dowry, now.

Michael would have to ask permission to fish there.

He would have to ask her husband permission to fish there.

The idea would be laughable if it weren't so . . . wrong.

And no one seemed to notice.

Penelope looked up, meeting first Pippa's gaze across the table, wide blue eyes blinking behind her spectacles, then Olivia's, filled with . . . relief?

At Penelope's questioning glance, Olivia said, "I confess I did not like the idea of a sister who had failed at the marriage mart. It's much better this way for me."

"I'm happy someone can be satisfied with the events of the day," Penelope said.

"Well, really, Penny," Olivia pressed on, "you have to admit, your marrying will help us all. You were a significant reason for Victoria's and Valerie's settling for their boring old husbands."

It was not as though she'd planned it that way.

"Olivia!" Pippa said quietly, "that's not very nice."

"Oh, tosh. Penny knows it's true."

Did she?

She looked to Pippa. "Have I made it difficult for you?"

Pippa hedged. "Not at all. Castleton sent news to Father just last week that he was planning to court me in earnest, and it's not as though I'm the most ordinary of debutantes."

It was an understatement. Pippa was something of a blue-stocking, very focused on the sciences and fascinated by the insides of living things, from plants to people. She'd once stolen a goose from the kitchens and dissected it in her bedchamber. All had been well until a maid had entered, discovered Pippa up to her elbows in fowl entrails, and screamed as though she'd stumbled upon a Seven Dials murder scene.

Pippa had been scolded profusely, and the maid had been reassigned to the lower floors of the manor house.

"He should be named Lord Simpleton," Olivia said, frankly.

Pippa chuckled. "Stop. He's nice enough. He likes dogs." She looked to Penelope. "As does Tommy."

"This is what we've come to? Choosing our potential husbands because they like dogs?" Olivia asked.

Pippa lifted one shoulder simply. "This is how it's done. Liking dogs is more than most husbands and wives of the *ton* have in common."

She was right.

But it was not as it should be. Young women with the looks and breeding of her sisters should be choosing their husbands based on more than canine companionship. They should be darlings of the *ton,* with all of society in their hands, waiting to be molded.

But they weren't, because of Penelope, who, ironically, had been considered the most darling of darlings of the *ton* when she'd first been out—the chosen bride of the impeccably behaved, impeccably pedigreed Duke of Leighton. After their match had dissolved in a perfect storm of ruined young women, illegitimate children, and a love match for the ages, Penelope—tragically, for her sisters—had lost darling status. Instead, she'd been relegated to good friend of the *ton,* then welcome acquaintance and, more recently, guest, complete with long-overstayed welcome.

She wasn't beautiful. She wasn't clever. She wasn't very much of anything except the eldest daughter of a very rich, very titled aristocrat. Born and bred to be the wife of an equally rich, equally titled aristocrat.

And she'd almost been just that.

Until everything had changed.

Including her expectations.

Sadly, expectations did not make for good marriages. Not for her, and not for her sisters, either. And, just as it was not fair for her to suffer because of a near-decade-old broken engagement, it was not fair for her sisters to suffer for it either.

"I never intended to make it difficult for you to marry," she said, quietly.

"You are lucky, then, that you are able to rectify the situation," Olivia offered, obviously disinterested in her eldest sister's feelings. "After all, *your* chances of finding a quality husband may be slim, but mine are very good indeed. Even better if you're married to a future viscount."

Guilt flared, and Penelope turned to Pippa, who was watching her carefully. "Do you agree, Pippa?"

Pippa tilted her head, considering her options, finally settling on, "It can't hurt, Penny."

Not you, at least, Penelope thought under a wave of melancholy as she realized that she was going to accept Tommy's suit.

For the good of her sisters.

She could do much worse, after all. Perhaps, in time, she would love him.

Dear M—

They burned the Guy tonight in Coldharbour, and the entire Marbury clan headed out for the impressive display. I had to write, as I was quite distressed to discover that not one young man was willing to test his skill at climbing the woodpile to steal Mr. Fawkes's hat.

Perhaps at Christmas, you can teach them a thing or two.

Your loyal friend—P
Needham Manor, November 1813

Dear P—

They don't need me to teach them—not when you're there and perfectly capable of stealing that shabby cap yourself. Or are you too much of a lady these days?

I shall be home for Christmas. If you are very good, I shall bring you a gift.

—M
Eton College, November 1813

That night, when all the house was asleep, Penelope donned her warmest cloak, fetched her muff and a lantern from her writing desk, and took a walk on her land.

Well, not precisely *her* land. The land that was attached to her hand in marriage. The land that Tommy and any number of handsome young suitors would happily accept in exchange for plucking Penelope from her family fold and taking her to wife.

How very romantic.

She'd gone too many years hoping for more. Believing—even as she told herself not to—that she might be that lucky, too. That she might find something more, some*one* more.

No. She wouldn't think on it.

Especially not now that she was headed straight for precisely the kind of marriage she'd always hoped to avoid. Now, she had no doubt that her father was committed to marrying off his eldest child this season—to Tommy or someone else. She considered the unmarried men of the *ton* who were desperate enough to marry a twenty-eight-year-old with a broken engagement in her past. Not a single one seemed like a husband she could care for.

A husband she could love.

So, it was Tommy.

It would be Tommy.

She braced herself against the cold, ducking her face into her cloak and pulling her hood low over her brow. Well-bred ladies did not take walks in the dead of night, she knew, but all of Surrey was asleep, it was miles to the nearest neighbor, and the bitter cold matched her bitter irritation at the events of the day.

It was not fair that a broken engagement from the distant past made for such a challenging present. One would think that eight years would have made London forget the legendary autumn of 1823, but instead, Penelope was plagued with her history. In ballrooms, the whispers remained; in ladies' salons, the fans still fluttered like hummingbird wings, hiding the quiet conversations of which she caught snippets now and then—hushed speculation about what she'd done to lose the interest of her duke, or about why she thought herself high enough to turn down the other offers.

It wasn't that she thought highly of herself, of course.

It was that she thought highly of the promise of more.

Of a life filled with more than the husband she'd been trained to expect would be fond of her but not love her, and the child or two who she'd always assumed would love her but not know her.

Was that too much to ask?

Apparently.

She marched up a snowy rise, pausing briefly on the crest of the ridge, looking down toward the blackness of the lake below, the lake that marked the edge of Needham and Bourne lands . . . or, *former* Bourne lands. And, as she stood, staring into the darkness, thinking on her future, she realized just how little she wanted a quiet life of pastel colors and quadrilles and tepid lemonade.

She wanted more.

The word whispered through her thoughts on a wave of sadness.

More.

More than she would have, it turned out.

More than she ever should have dreamed.

It wasn't that she was unhappy with her existence. It was luxurious, really. She was well kept and well fed and wanted for very little. She had a family that was, for the most part, tolerable, and friends with whom she could spend an afternoon now and then. And, when it came right down to it, her days weren't that much different now than they would be if she were married to Tommy.

Why did it make her so sad to think of marrying Tommy, then?

After all, he was kind, generous, had a modicum of good humor and a warm smile. He was not so handsome as to attract attention and not so clever as to intimidate.

Those all seemed like suitable characteristics.

She imagined taking his hand and allowing him to escort her to a ball, to the theatre, to dinner. She imagined dancing with him. Smiling up at him. She imagined the feel of his hand in hers.

It was—

It was clammy.

There was no reason to believe that Tommy would have moist hands, of course, indeed, he likely had warm, perfectly dry hands. Penelope wiped her gloved palm on her skirts nonetheless. Weren't husbands supposed to have strong, firm hands? Especially in fantasy?

Why didn't Tommy?

He was a good friend. It wasn't very kind of her to imagine him with clammy hands. He deserved better.

She took a deep breath, enjoying the sting of the frigid

air, closed her eyes, and tried again . . . tried her very best to imagine being Lady Thomas Alles.

She smiled up at her husband. Lovingly.

He smiled down at her. *"Let's make a go of it, shall we?"*

She opened her eyes.

Drat.

She trudged down the rise toward the icy lake.

She would marry Tommy.

For her own good.

For the good of her sisters.

Except, it didn't seem at all good. Not really.

Nevertheless. It was what eldest daughters of good breeding did.

They did as they were told.

Even if they absolutely didn't want to.

Even if they wanted more.

And that was when she saw the light in the distance, in the copse of trees at the far edge of the lake.

She stopped, squinting into the darkness, ignoring the biting wind on her cheeks. Perhaps she'd imagined it. Perhaps it had been the moon glinting off the snow.

A reasonable possibility, if not for the falling snow blocking the moon from view.

The light flickered again, and Penelope gasped, taking one step back, eyes going wide as it moved quickly through the trees.

She squinted into the darkness leaning forward without moving her feet, fixated on the place where a faint yellow light flickered in the woods, as though the inch or two would make it easier to see the source of the light.

"There's someone . . ." she whispered, the words trailing off in the cold silence.

Someone was there.

It could have been a servant, but it seemed unlikely. Needham servants had no reason to be by the lake in the dead of night, and it had been years since the last of the servants had left Falconwell. After they'd gone, the contents of the estate had been collected and the enormous stone structure had been left empty and unloved. No one had been to the house in years.

She had to do something.

It could be anything. A fire. A trespasser. A *ghost.*

Well, likely not the latter.

But it was quite possible that it was a trespasser—soon to be intruder—ready to lay siege to Falconwell. If it was, someone had to do something. After all, intruders simply could not be allowed to take up residence inside the estate of the Marquess of Bourne.

If the man himself was not going to secure his estate, it seemed the task fell to Penelope. She had an equal investment in Falconwell at this point, did she not? If the manor house was taken over by pirates or brigands, that would certainly impact the value of her dowry, would it not?

Not that she had been excited about the prospect of using her dowry.

Nonetheless, it was a matter of principle.

The light flickered again.

It did not seem that there were very many brigands out there, unless they had come ill equipped with light sources.

Come to think of it, it was unlikely that either pirates or brigands were planning to take up residence in Falconwell, what with the ocean being rather far away.

Nevertheless.

Someone was there.

The question remained as to who.

And why.

But there was one thing of which Penelope was certain. Eldest daughters of good breeding did not inspect strange lights in the middle of the night.

That would be decidedly too adventurous.

It would be *more.*

And that made the decision for her, really.

She'd said she wanted more, and more had come.

The universe worked in marvelous ways, did it not?

She took a deep breath, squared her shoulders, and moved forward, excitement propelling her to a large cluster of holly bushes at the edge of the lake before she registered the stupidity of her actions.

She was outside.

In the middle of the night.

In the bitter cold.

Headed toward any number of nefarious, questionable creatures.

And no one knew where she was.

Suddenly, marriage to Tommy did not seem so very bad.

Not when it was very possible that she was about to be murdered by inland pirates.

She heard the crunch of snow nearby, and she stopped short, lifting her lantern high and peering into the darkness beyond the holly, toward the woods where she'd seen the earlier light.

Now, she saw nothing.

Nothing but falling snow and a shadow that could easily have been that of a rabid bear.

"What nonsense," she whispered to herself, the sound of her voice in the darkness a comfort. "There are no bears in Surrey."

She remained unconvinced, and she did not linger to discover if that black shadow was, in fact, a bear. She had things to do back at home. First among them, accepting Tommy's proposal.

And spending some careful time with her needlepoint.

Except, at the precise moment that she'd decided to turn tail and head back, a man came through the trees, lantern in hand.

Chapter Three

Dear M—

A gift! How extravagant. School is certainly turning you into a fine man; last year, you gave me a half-eaten piece of gingerbread. I shall be very excited to see what you've planned.

I suppose this means I shall have to find a gift for you as well.

Soonest—P
Needham Manor, November 1813

Dear P—

That was excellent gingerbread. I should have known that you wouldn't appreciate my generosity in the slightest. Whatever happened to the thought and how well it counts?

It will be good to be home. I've missed Surrey. And you, Sixpence (though it pains me to admit it).

—M
Eton College, November 1813

Flee!

The word echoed through her as though it had been shouted through the night, but Penelope's limbs seemed unable to follow the command. Instead, she crouched low, hiding behind the bushes and hoping wildly that the man would not see her. Hearing his footsteps in the snow nearby, she crept along the hedge toward the lake, preparing to make a mad dash away from him when she stepped on the edge of her cloak, toppled off-balance, and landed, squarely, in the holly bush.

Which was quite prickly.

"Oof!" She put out one hand to save herself from becoming tangled in the vicious plant, only to be stabbed by a rogue branch. She bit her lip and froze as the footsteps stopped.

She held her breath.

Perhaps he hadn't seen her. After all, it was very dark.

If only she were not holding a lantern.

She shoved the light into the bush.

It did not help, as she was almost instantly flooded with a different source of light.

His light.

He took a step toward her.

She pressed backward into the bush, sharp leaves preferable to his shadowed bulk. "Hello."

He stopped but did not reply, and they remained in long, unbearable silence. Penelope's heart was pounding, the only part of her that seemed to remember how to move. When she could not bear the silence a moment longer, she spoke from her position, unbalanced in a holly bush, trying for her most firm of tones. "You are trespassing."

"Am I?" For a pirate, he had a very nice voice. It rolled out from deep in his chest, making her think of goose down and warm brandy. She shook her head at the thought, obviously the product of the cold playing tricks with her mind.

"Yes. You are. The house in the distance is Falconwell Manor. Owned by the Marquess of Bourne."

There was a beat. "Impressive," the pirate said, and she had the distinct feeling that he was not at all impressed.

She tried to rise with haughtiness. Failed. Twice. On the third attempt, she brushed off her skirts, and said, "It is *quite* impressive. And I assure you, the marquess will be very unhappy to know that you are"— she waved her muffled hand in the air—"whatever you are doing . . . on his land."

"Will he?" The pirate seemed unconcerned, lowering his lantern, casting his upper half into shadow, continuing his advance.

"Indeed." Penelope squared her shoulders. "And I shall give you three pence worth of advice; he is not to be trifled with."

"It sounds as though you and the marquess are very close."

She lifted her lantern and began to edge away. "Oh, yes. We are. Quite close. Very, even."

It was not precisely a lie. They had been very close when he was in short pants.

"I don't think so," he said, his voice low and menacing. "In fact, I don't think the marquess is anywhere near this place. I don't think anyone is near this place."

She stopped at the threat in his words, a deer hesitating in advance of a rifle's report, and considered her options.

"I would not run if I were you," he continued, reading her mind. "It is dark, and the snow is thick. You would not get very far without . . ."

He trailed off, but she knew the end of the sentence.

Without him catching and killing her.

She closed her eyes.

When she'd said she wanted more, this was not at all what she had been asking for. She was going to die here. In the snow. And they would not find her until spring.

That was, if her corpse was not carried off by hungry wolves.

She had to do something.

She opened her eyes to find him much much closer.

"Sirrah! Do not come any closer! I . . ." she flailed for a decent threat. "I am armed!"

His response was unmoved. "Do you plan to smother me with your muff?"

"You, sir, are not a gentleman."

"Ah. Truth at last."

She took another step back. "I am going home."

"I don't think so, Penelope."

Her heart stopped at the sound of her name, then started again, pounding so loudly in her chest that she was certain this . . . this . . . scoundrel would hear it. "How do you know my name?"

"I know many things."

"Who are you?" She lifted her lamp, as if it could ward off danger, and he stepped into the pool of light.

He did not look like a pirate.

He looked . . . *familiar.*

There was something there, in the handsome angles and deep, wicked shadows, the hollows of his cheeks, the straight line of his lips, the sharp line of his jaw—in need of a shave.

Yes, there was something there—a whisper of recognition.

He wore a pin-striped cap dusted with snow, the brim of which cast his eyes into darkness. They were a missing piece.

She would never know from where the instinct came—perhaps from a desire to discover the identity of the man who would end her days—but she could not stop herself from reaching up and pushing the hat back from his face to see his eyes.

Only later would it occur to her that he did not try to stop her.

His eyes were hazel, a mosaic of browns and greens and

greys framed by long, dark lashes, spiked with snow. She would have known them anywhere, even if they were far more serious now than she'd ever seen them before.

Shock coursed through her, followed by a thick current of happiness.

He was not a pirate.

"Michael?" He stiffened at the sound of his name, but she did not take the time to wonder why.

She flattened her palm against his cold cheek—an action at which she would later marvel—and laughed, the sound muffled by the snow falling around them. "It is you, isn't it?"

He reached up, pulling her hand from his face. He wasn't wearing gloves, and still, he was so *warm.*

And not at all clammy.

Before she could stop him, he pulled her to him, pushing back the hood of her cloak, exposing her to the snow and the light. There was a long moment while his gaze roamed her face, and she forgot to be uncomfortable.

"You've grown."

She couldn't help it. She laughed again. "It *is* you! You beast! You scared me! You pretended not to *know*—! Where have you—? When did you—?" She shook her head, her smile straining her cheeks. "I don't even know where to begin!"

She smiled up at him, taking him in. The last time she'd seen him, he'd been a few inches taller than she, a gangly boy, arms and legs too long for his body. No longer. This Michael was a man, tall and lean.

And very, very handsome.

She still did not quite believe that it was he. "Michael!"

He met her gaze head-on, and a bolt of pleasure shot through her as though the look were a physical touch, warming her—catching her off guard before the brim of his cap shielded his eyes once more, and she filled his silence with her own words. "What are you doing here?"

His lips did not move from their perfect, straight line. There was a long pause, during which she was consumed with the heat of him. With the happiness of seeing him. It didn't matter that it was late and it was dark and he didn't seem nearly as happy to see her.

"Why are you traipsing through the darkness in the dead of night in the middle of nowhere?"

He'd avoided her question, yes, but Penelope didn't care. "It's not the middle of nowhere. We're no more than a half a mile from either of our houses."

"You could have been set upon by a highwayman, or a thief, or a kidnapper, or—"

"A pirate. Or a bear. I've already considered all the options."

The Michael she had once known would have smiled. This one did not. "There are no bears in Surrey."

"Pirates would be rather a surprise, too, don't you think?"

No answer.

She tried to rouse the old Michael. To coax him out. "I would take an old friend over a pirate or a bear any day, Michael."

Snow shifted beneath his feet. When he spoke, there was steel in his tone. "Bourne."

"I beg your pardon?"

"Call me Bourne."

Shock and embarrassment coursed through her. He was a marquess, yes, but she'd never imagined he'd be so firm about his title . . . they were childhood friends, after all. She cleared her throat. "Of course, Lord Bourne."

"Not the title. Just the name. Bourne."

She swallowed back her confusion. "Bourne?"

He gave a slight nod, barely there before it was gone. "I'll ask you one more time. Why are you here?"

She did not think of ignoring the question. "I saw your lantern; I came to investigate."

"You came, in the middle of the night, to investigate a strange light in the woods of a house that has been uninhabited for sixteen years."

"It's only been uninhabited for nine years."

He paused. "I don't remember your being so exasperating."

"Then you don't remember me very well. I was a very exasperating child."

"You were not. You were very serious."

She smiled. "So you do remember. You were always trying to make me laugh. I'm simply returning the favor; is it working?"

"No."

She lifted her lantern high, and he allowed her to free him from the shadows, casting his face in warm, golden light. He had aged marvelously, grown into his long limbs and angled face. Penelope had always imagined that he'd become handsome, but he was more than handsome now . . . he was nearly beautiful.

If not for the darkness that lingered despite the glow of the lantern—something dangerous in the set of his jaw, in the tightness of his brow, in eyes that seemed to have forgotten joy, in lips that seemed to have lost their ability to smile.

He'd had a dimple as a child, one that showed itself often and was almost always the precursor to adventure. She searched his left cheek, looking for that telltale indentation. Did not find it.

Indeed, as much as Penelope searched this new, hard face, she could not seem to find the boy she'd once known. If not for the eyes, she would not have believed it was him at all.

"How sad," she whispered to herself.

He heard it. "What?"

She shook her head, meeting his gaze, the only thing familiar about him. "He's gone."

"Who?"

"My friend."

She hadn't thought it possible, but his features hardened even more, growing more stark, more dangerous, in the shadows. For one fleeting moment, she thought perhaps she had pushed him too far. He remained still, watching her with that dark gaze that seemed to see everything.

Every instinct told her to leave. Quickly. To never return.

And still she stayed. "How long will you remain in Surrey?" He did not reply. She took a step toward him, knowing she shouldn't. "There's nothing inside the house."

He ignored her.

She pressed on. "Where are you sleeping?"

A wicked black brow rose. "Why? Are you inviting me into your bed?"

The words stung with their rudeness. Penelope stiffened as though she had received a physical blow. She waited a beat, sure he would apologize.

Silence.

"You've changed."

"Perhaps you should remember that the next time you decide to go on a midnight adventure."

He was nothing like the Michael she had once known.

She spun on her heel, heading into the blackness, toward the place where Needham Manor stood. She'd gone only a few feet before she turned back to face him. He had not moved.

"I really was happy to see you." She turned and headed away, back to her home, the cold seeping deep into her bones before she turned back, unable to resist a final barb. Something to hurt him as he'd hurt her. "And Michael?"

She couldn't see his eyes, but she knew undeniably that he was watching her. Listening.

"You're on my land."

She regretted the words the instant she spoke them, the product of frustration and irritation, laced with an edge of teasing that better suited a mean-spirited child than a woman of eight-and-twenty.

Regretted them even more when he shot toward her, a wolf from the night. "*Your* land?"

The words were dark and menacing. She stepped back instantly. "Y-yes."

She should never have left the house.

"You and your father think to catch you a husband with my land?"

He knew.

She ignored the pang of sadness that came with the realization that he was there for Falconwell. *And not for her.*

He kept coming, closer and closer, and Penelope's breath caught in her throat as she backed away from him, trying to keep pace with his strides. Failing. She shook her head. She should deny the words. Should rush to comfort him. To settle this great beast who stalked her through the snow.

But she didn't.

She was too angry. "It's not yours. You lost it. And I've already caught myself a husband." He needn't know she hadn't accepted the offer.

He paused. "You are married?"

She shook her head, moving away quickly, taking the chance to put distance between them as she slung her words at him. "No, but we will be . . . in no time. And we shall live quite happily here, on *our* land."

What was wrong with her? The words were out, quick and impetuous and they could not be taken back.

He advanced again, this time with complete focus. "Every man in London wants Falconwell, if not for the land, then to hold it over my head."

If she moved any more quickly, she would topple into the snow, but it was worth the attempt, for she was suddenly very nervous about what would happen if he caught her.

She stumbled, a hidden tree root sending her falling backward with a little screech, and she threw her arms wide, dropping her lantern in an awkward attempt to catch herself.

He beat her to it, his large, strong hands coming around her arms, catching her, lifting her, pressing her back against a large oak tree and, before she could regain her footing and escape, bracing against the wood to cage her in his arms.

The boy she remembered was gone.

The man in his place was not to be trifled with.

He was very close. Too close, leaning in, lowering his voice to a whisper, the breath of his words against the arch of her cheek heightening her nervousness. She did not breathe, too focused on the heat of him, on what he would say next. "They'll even marry an aging spinster to get it."

She hated him then. Hated the words, the way he spoke them with such simple cruelty. Tears threatened.

No. *No.* She *would not* cry.

Not for this beast of a man who was nothing like the boy she'd once known. The one she'd dreamed would one day return.

Not like this.

She struggled against him once more, irritated now, desperate to be free. He was stronger than her by half and refused to release her, pressing her back to the oak, leaning in until he was close—too close. Fear lanced through her, followed by quick, blessed anger. "Let me go."

He did not move. In fact, for a long moment, Penelope thought he had not heard her.

"No."

The refusal was emotionless.

She struggled again, kicking out, one booted foot connecting with his shin, hard enough to spur a very satisfying grunt. "Dammit!" she cried, knowing that ladies didn't curse, knowing that she would likely spend an eternity in purgatory for the transgression but not knowing how else to communicate with this brutish stranger. "What are you going to do, leave me here in the snow to freeze to death?"

"No." The word was low and dark at her ear as he held her, easily.

She did not give up. "Kidnap me then? Hold me for ransom for Falconwell?"

"No, though it wouldn't be a terrible idea." He was so close, she could smell him, bergamot and cedar, and she paused at the sensation of his breath brushing over the skin of her cheek. "But I've got something much worse in mind."

She stilled. *He wouldn't kill her.*

After all, they'd been friends once. Long ago, before he'd become handsome as the devil and twice as cold.

He wouldn't kill her.

Would he?

"Wh—what is it?"

He stroked the tip of one finger down the long column of her neck, leaving a trail of fire in its wake. Her breath caught in her throat at the touch . . . all wicked warmth and nearly unbearable sensation.

"You have my land, Penelope," he whispered at her ear, the sound low and liquid and altogether too distracting even as it sent tremors of anxiety spiraling through her, "and I want it back."

She should not have left the house that evening.

If she survived this, she would never leave the house again.

She shook her head, eyes closed as he wreaked havoc on her senses. "I can't give it to you."

He stroked one hand down her arm in a long, lovely caress, taking her wrist in his firm, warm clasp. "No, but I can take it."

She opened her eyes, met his, black in the darkness. "What does that mean?"

"It means, my darling"—the endearment was mocking—"that we are to be married."

Shock coursed through her as he lifted her arm, tossed her over his shoulder, and headed into the trees toward Falconwell Manor.

Dear M—

I cannot believe that you did not tell me that you were named head of class and I had to hear it from your mother (who is very proud indeed). I'm shocked and appalled that you would not share with me . . . and not a little bit impressed that you managed not to brag about it.

There must be masses that you haven't told me about school. I am waiting.

Ever patient—P
Needham Manor, February 1814

Dear P—

I'm afraid head of class isn't much of a title when you're a first-year; I'm still subject to the whims of the older boys when I am not at study. Fear not—when I am named head of class next year, I shall brag shamelessly.

There are masses to tell . . . but not to girls.

—M
Eton College, February 1814

Bourne had imagined a half dozen scenarios that ended in his ferreting Penelope away from her father and her family and marrying her to reclaim his land. He'd planned for seduction, and for coercion, and even—in the extreme—for abduction.

But not one of those scenarios had involved a snow-covered woman with a penchant for danger and less than the recommended allotment of sense approaching him in the bitter cold of a Surrey January in the dead of night.

She'd saved him quite a bit of work.

Naturally, it would have been wrong of him to look this particular gift horse in the mouth.

And so he'd taken her.

"You brute!"

He winced as she pounded her fists against his shoulders, her legs flailing about, their awkward angle the only thing that kept him from losing critical parts of his anatomy to a single well-placed kick.

"Put me down!"

He ignored her, instead capturing her legs with one arm, tilting her up until she squeaked and grasped the back of his coat for balance, then resettling her on his shoulder, taking no small amount of pleasure in her grunted "Oof!" as his shoulder found purchase in the soft swell of her stomach.

It seemed that the lady was not pleased with the direction of her evening.

"Is there a problem with your ability to hear?" she said archly, or, as archly as one could sound while tossed over a man's shoulder.

He did not reply.

He did not have to. She was filling the silence quite well with her muttering. "I should never have left the house . . . Lord knows if I'd known you would be out here, I would have locked the doors and windows and sent for the constable . . . To think . . . I was actually *happy* to see you!"

She had been happy to see him, her laughter like sunshine and her excitement palpable. He stopped himself from thinking about the last time someone had been so happy to see him.

From questioning if anyone had ever been so happy to see him. Anyone but Penelope.

He'd stripped the happiness from her, coolly, efficiently, with skill, expecting her to be cowed by it, to be weakened.

And she'd spoken, soft and simple, the words echoing across the lake, punctuated by the falling snow, the rushing of blood in his ears, and the biting knowledge of the truth.

You're on my land.

It's not yours.

You lost it.

There was nothing weak about this woman. She was strong as steel.

With a handful of words, she'd reminded him that she was the last thing standing in the way of the one thing he'd wanted for his entire adult life. Of the only thing that gave him purpose.

Falconwell.

The land from whence he had come, and his father before him, and his father's father before that, back generations—too many to count.

The land he had lost and vowed to regain.

At any cost.

Even marriage.

"You cannot simply carry me off like . . . like . . . a sheep!"

His stride broke for a split second. "A sheep?"

She paused, obviously rethinking the comparison. "Don't farmers carry sheep over their shoulders?"

"I have never seen such a thing, but you've lived in the country longer than I, so . . . if you say I am treating you like a sheep, so be it."

"You evidently do not care that I *feel* as though I have been ill-treated."

"If it is any comfort, I do not plan to shear you."

"It's no comfort at all, in fact," she said tartly. "I will tell you once more! Put. Me. Down!" She squirmed again, nearly slithering out of his grasp, one foot coming dangerously close to connecting with a valuable portion of his anatomy.

He grunted and tightened his grasp. "Stop it." He lifted one hand and spanked her once, firmly, on her bottom.

She went board stiff at the action.

"You did not . . . I cannot . . . You hit me!"

He flung open the rear door to the Falconwell kitchens and marched her inside. Placing his lantern on a nearby table, he set her down at the center of the dark room. "You're wearing half a dozen layers of clothing and a winter cloak. I'm surprised you felt it at all."

Penelope's eyes flashed with fury. "Nevertheless, a gentleman would never dream of . . . of . . ."

He watched her flounder for the word, enjoying her discomfort, finally offering, "I believe the word you are looking for is 'spanking.' "

Her eyes went wide at the word. "Yes. That. Gentlemen don't . . ."

"First, I thought we'd already established that I am not a gentleman. That ship sailed long ago. And second, you'd be surprised what gentlemen do . . . and what ladies enjoy."

"Not this lady. You owe me an apology."

"I would not hold my breath waiting for it." He heard her little gasp as he moved across the kitchen to the place where he'd left a bottle of scotch earlier in the evening. "Would you like a drink?"

"No, thank you."

"So polite."

"One of us should be, don't you think?"

He turned to face her, half-amused and half-surprised by her smart mouth.

She was not tall, barely the height of his shoulder, but at the moment she looked like an Amazon.

The hood of her cloak had fallen away, and her hair was in disarray, tumbling around her shoulders, gleaming pale blond in the dim light. Her chin was thrust forward in a universal sign of defiance, her shoulders were stiff and straight, and her chest rose and fell with harsh anger, swelling beneath her cloak.

She looked as though she'd like to do him no small amount of bodily harm.

"This is kidnapping."

He took a long pull on the bottle, enjoying her look of shock at his behavior as he wiped the back of his hand across his lips and met her gaze. He remained quiet, enjoying the way his silence set her on edge.

After a long moment, she announced, "You cannot kidnap me!"

"As I said outside, I have no intention of kidnapping you." He leaned forward until his face was on a level with hers. "I intend to marry you, darling."

She stared at him for a long moment. "I am leaving."

"No, you are not."

"I'm not restrained. I could leave if I tried."

"Restraints are for amateurs." He leaned back against the sideboard. "I encourage you to try."

She cast an uncertain look at him before shrugging one shoulder and heading for the door. He blocked her exit. She stopped. "I realize you've been out of society for quite some time, but you cannot simply abduct your neighbors."

"As I said, this is not an abduction."

"Well, whatever it is," she said peevishly, "it isn't *done*."

"I should think you would have noticed by now that I care very little for what is *done*."

She considered the words for a moment. "You should."

There was a hazy familiarity in the way she stood, stick straight, instructing him in proper behavior. "There she is."

"Who?"

"The Penelope from my childhood. So concerned with propriety. You haven't changed at all."

She lifted her chin. "That's not true."

"No?"

"Not at all. I'm quite changed. Entirely different."

"How?"

"I—" she started, then stopped, and he wondered what she was about to say. "I just am. Now let me go." She moved to push past him. When he did not move, she stopped, unwilling to touch him.

A pity. The memory of the warmth of her gloved hand on his cold cheek flashed. Apparently her behavior outside had been the product of surprise.

And pleasure.

He wondered what else she might do instinctively in response to pleasure. An image flashed—blond hair spread wide across dark, silken sheets, ice blue eyes alight with surprise as he gave prim, proper Penelope a glimpse of dark and heady pleasure.

He'd nearly kissed her in the darkness. It had started out as a way to intimidate her, to begin the systematic compromising of quiet, unassuming, Penelope Marbury. But he did not deny that as they stood in his barren kitchen, he wondered what she would taste like. How her breath would sound fluttering across his skin. How she would feel against him. Around him.

"This is foolish."

The words snapped him back to the present. "Are you sure you would not like a drink?"

Her eyes went wide. "I—no!"

She was so easy to frustrate. She always had been. "It is still polite to offer one's guests refreshment, is it not?"

"Not *whiskey*! And certainly *not* straight from the bottle!"

"I suppose I've made a hash of it, then. Perhaps you could remind me of what I *should* be offering my guests in such a situation?"

Her mouth opened, then closed. "I don't know, considering I'm not in the habit of being abducted in the middle of the night to barren country houses." Her lips pressed into an irritated straight line. "I should like to return home. To bed."

"That can be arranged without your having to return home, you know."

She made a little noise of frustration. "Michael . . ."

He hated the name on her lips.

No, he didn't. "Bourne."

She met his eyes. "Bourne . . . you've proven your point." He stayed quiet, curious, and she pressed on. "I understand that it was bad judgment to wander out into the woods in the middle of the night. I see now that I could have been overcome. Or abducted. Or worse, and I am prepared to admit that you have taught me a well-needed lesson."

"How very gracious of you."

She pressed on, as though he had not spoken, edging around him. He moved to block her exit. She stopped and met his gaze, her blue eyes flashing with what he imagined was frustration. "I am *also* prepared to ignore the fact that you have committed an egregious breach of etiquette by moving me—bodily—from a public location to an entirely inappropriate . . . altogether too private one."

"And don't forget spanking you."

"That, too. Utterly . . . completely . . . *beyond* inappropriate."

"Appropriateness seems not to have got you very far."

She stilled, and he knew immediately that he had struck a nerve. Something unpleasant flared deep within him. He resisted it.

He might be planning to marry her, but he was not planning to care for her.

"I'm afraid I've plans for you, Penelope, and you're not going anywhere tonight." He extended the bottle of whiskey toward her and spoke, all seriousness. "Have a drink. It will take the edge off until tomorrow."

"What happens tomorrow?"

"Tomorrow, we marry."

Chapter Four

Penelope reached out and took hold of the whiskey, snatching it from Michael's hand and considering, for a fleeting moment, drinking deep, for surely there was no better time than this to begin a life of drink.

"I will not marry you!"

"I'm afraid it's done."

Indignation flared. "It is most certainly *not* done!" She clutched the bottle to her chest and began to push past him toward the door. When he did not move, she stopped, a hairsbreadth away, her cloak brushing against him. She stared directly into his serious, hazel gaze, refusing to bend to his ridiculous will. "Step aside, Lord Bourne. I am returning home. You are a madman."

One irritating dark brow rose. "Such tone," he mocked. "I find I am not in a mood to move. You shall have to find another way."

"Do not make me do something I shall regret."

"Why regret it?" He lifted one hand, a single, warm finger tilting her chin up. "Poor Penelope," he said, "so afraid of risk."

Poor Penelope.

Her gaze narrowed at the hated name. "I am not afraid of risk. Nor am I afraid of you."

One dark brow arched. "No?"

"No."

He leaned in, close. Too close. Close enough to wrap her in bergamot and cedar. Close enough for her to notice that his eyes had turned a lovely shade of brown. "Prove it."

His voice had gone low and gravelly, sending a thrum of excitement down her spine.

He stepped closer, close enough to touch—close enough for the heat of him to warm her in the freezing room—and the fingers of his hand slid into the hair at the nape of her neck, holding her still as he hovered above her, threatening. Promising.

As though he wanted her.

As though he'd come for her.

Which, of course, he hadn't.

If it weren't for Falconwell, he wouldn't be here.

And she would do well to remember that.

He didn't want her any more than any of the other men in her life did. He was just like all the others.

And it wasn't fair.

But she'd be damned if he took the only choice she had in the matter away from her. She lifted her hands, the bottle of whiskey firmly clasped in the left, and shoved him with all her might—not enough to move a man of his size usually, but she had the element of surprise on her side.

He stumbled back, and she rushed past him, almost reaching the door to the kitchens before he regained his footing and came after her, catching her with an "Oh, no you don't!" and spinning her to face him.

Frustration flared. "Let me go!"

"I can't," he said simply. "I need you."

"For Falconwell." He didn't reply. He didn't have to. She took a deep breath. *He was compromising her.* As though it were the Dark Ages. As though she were nothing more than chattel. *As though she were worth nothing but the land attached to her hand in marriage.*

She paused at the thought, disappointment coursing through her.

He was worse than the others.

"Well, that is unfortunate for you," she said, "as I am *already spoken for.*"

"Not after tonight you're not," he said. "No one will marry you after you've spent the night alone with me."

They were words that should have held a hint of menace in them. Of danger. But instead, they were stated as simple fact. He was the worst kind of rogue; her reputation would be in tatters tomorrow.

He'd taken the choice from her.

As her father had earlier.

As the Duke of Leighton had all those years ago.

She was trapped by a man once again.

"Do you love him?"

The question interrupted her rising ire. "I beg your pardon?"

"Your fiancé. Do you fancy yourself very much in love?" The words were mocking, as though love and Penelope were a laughable combination. "Are you starry-eyed with happiness?"

"Does it matter?"

She surprised him. She could see it in his eyes before he crossed his arms and raised a brow. "Not in the slightest."

A gust of cold wind ripped through the kitchen, and Penelope wrapped her cloak tightly around her. Michael noticed and muttered harshly beneath his breath—Penny imagined that the words he used were not for polite company. He removed his greatcoat, then frock coat, carefully folding them and placing them on the edge of the large sink before confronting the large oak table that sat at the center of the kitchens. It was missing a leg, and there was an axe half-buried in its scarred top. She should be surprised by the mangled piece of furniture, but there was very little about the evening that was at all normal.

Before she could think of what to say, he grasped the axe and turned toward her, his face a mass of angles in the lanternlight. "Step back."

This was a man who expected to be heeded. He did not wait to see if she followed his direction before he lifted the axe high above his head. She pressed herself into the corner of the dark room as he attacked the furniture with a vengeance, her surprise making her unable to resist watching him.

He was built beautifully.

Like a glorious Roman statue, all strong, lean muscles outlined by the crisp linen of his shirtsleeves when he lifted the tool overhead, his hands sliding purposefully along the haft, fingers grasping tightly as he brought the steel blade down into the age-old oak with a mighty *thwack,* sending a splinter of oak flying across the kitchen, landing atop the long-unused stove.

He splayed one long-fingered hand flat on the table, gripping the axe once more to work the blade out of the wood. He turned his head as he stood back, making sure she was out of the way of any potential projectiles—a movement she could not help but find comforting—before confronting the furniture and taking his next swing with a mighty heave.

The blade sliced into the oak, but the table held.

He shook his head and yanked the axe out once more, this time aiming for one of the remaining table legs.

Thwack!

Penelope's eyes went wide as the lanternlight caught the way his wool trousers wrapped tightly around his massive thighs. She should not notice . . . should not be paying attention to such obvious . . . maleness.

But she'd never seen legs like his.

Thwack!

Never imagined they could be so . . . compelling.

Thwack!

Could not help it.

Thwack!

The final blow ended with the splintering of wood, the leg

twisting under the force as the massive tabletop tilted, one end dropping to the floor as Michael tossed the axe aside to grasp the leg with his bare hands and wrench it free from its seat.

He turned back to her, tapping one end of the leg against the empty palm of his left hand.

"Success," he announced.

As if she had expected anything less.

As if he would have *accepted* anything less.

"Well-done," she said, for lack of anything better.

He rested the wood on his wide shoulder. "You didn't take the opportunity to escape."

She froze. "No. I didn't." Though she couldn't for the life of her say why.

He moved to set the table leg in the wide sink and carefully lifted his frock coat, shook out any possible wrinkles, and pulled it on.

She watched as he rolled his shoulders into the exceptionally well made clothing, underscoring the perfect fit—a fit she no longer took for granted now that she had seen hints of the Vitruvian Man beneath.

No.

She shook her head. She would not think of him as a Leonardo. He was already far too intimidating a character.

She shook her head. "I'm not marrying you."

He straightened his cuffs, buttoned his coat carefully, and brushed a dusting of moisture from the sleeves of the coat. "It is not up for discussion."

She tried for reason. "You would make a terrible husband."

"I never said I would make a good one."

"So you would condemn me to a life of unhappy marriage?"

"If needs be. Though your unhappiness is not a *direct* goal, if that's any consolation."

She blinked. He was serious. This conversation was honestly occurring. "And this is supposed to endear me to your suit?"

He lifted one shoulder in a careless shrug. "I do not fool myself into thinking that the goal of marriage is happiness for one or both of the parties involved. My plan is to restore Falconwell's lands to its manor and, unfortunately for you, it requires our marriage. I shan't be a good husband, but I also haven't the slightest interest in keeping you under my thumb."

Her jaw dropped at his honesty. He did not even feign kindness. Interest. Concern. She closed her mouth. "I see."

He went on. "You can do or have whatever you wish, whenever you wish it. I've enough money for you to fritter it away doing whatever it is women of your ilk like to do."

"Women of my *ilk*?"

"Spinsters with dreams of more."

The air left the room on a *whoosh.* What a horrible, unpleasant, entirely apt description. *A spinster with dreams of more.* It was as though he had stood in her receiving room earlier that evening and watched as Tommy's proposal had filled her with disappointment. With hopes of something more.

Something different.

Well, this certainly was different.

He reached for her, stroking one finger down her cheek, and she flinched from the touch. "Don't."

"You're going to marry me, Penelope."

She snapped her head back, out of his reach, not wanting him to touch her. "Why should I?"

"Because, darling," he leaned in, his voice a dark promise as he trailed that strong, warm finger down her neck and across the skin above her dress, setting her heart racing and turning her breath shallow, "no one will ever believe that I didn't utterly compromise you."

He grasped the edge of her gown and with a mighty tug, rent her gown and chemise in two, baring her to the waist.

She gasped, dropping the bottle to clutch her gown to her chest, whiskey sloshing down the front of her as it fell. "You . . . you . . ."

"Take your time, darling," he drawled, stepping back to admire his handiwork. "I shall wait for you to find the word."

Her gaze narrowed. She didn't need a word. She needed a horsewhip.

She did the only thing she could think to do. Her hand flew of its own volition, connecting with a mighty *crack!*—a sound that would have been immensely satisfying if she hadn't been so utterly mortified.

His head snapped around at the blow, his hand coming instantly to his cheek, where a red splotch was already beginning to show. Penelope stepped backward again, toward the door, her voice shaking. "I will never . . . *never* . . . marry someone like you. Have you forgotten everything you were? Everything you could have been? One would think you had been raised by *wolves*."

She turned then, and did what she should have done the moment she'd seen him come around the house.

She ran.

Yanking open the door, she plunged into the snow beyond, heading blindly toward Needham Manor, getting only a few yards before he caught her from behind with one, steel-banded arm, and lifted her clean off the ground. It was only then that she screamed. "Let me go! You beast! Help!"

She kicked out, her heel coming in direct contact with his shin, and he swore wickedly at her ear. "Stop fighting, you harpy."

Not on her life. She redoubled her efforts. "Help! Somebody!"

"There's no one alive for nearly a mile. And no one awake for farther than that." The words spurred her on, and he grunted when her elbow caught him in the side just as they returned to the kitchens.

"Put me down!" she screamed, as loudly as she could, directly into his ear.

He turned his head away and kept walking, lifting the lantern and the leg he'd hacked from the table as he passed through the kitchen. "No."

She struggled more, but his grip was firm. "How do you intend to do it?" she asked. "Ravish me here, in your empty house, and return me to my father's home slightly worse for wear?" They were headed down a long hallway, lined on one side with a series of wooden slats that marked the landing of a servants' stairwell. She reached out and clasped one of the slats, hanging on for all she was worth.

He stopped walking, waiting for her to release her grip. When he spoke, there was immense patience in his tone. "I don't ravish women. At least, not without them asking *very* nicely."

The statement gave her pause.

Of course he wouldn't ravish her.

He'd likely not had a single moment of considering her as anything more than plain, proper Penelope, the only thing standing between him and the return of his familial right.

She wasn't sure if that made the situation better or worse.

But it did make her heart ache. He didn't care for her. Didn't want her. Didn't even think highly enough of her to pretend those things. To feign interest. To *attempt* to seduce her.

He was using her for Falconwell.

Wasn't Tommy?

Of course he was. Tommy had looked deep into her gaze and saw not the blue of her eyes but the blue of the Surrey sky above Falconwell. Certainly, he'd seen his friend, but that wasn't why he'd offered for her hand.

At least Michael was honest about it.

"This is the best offer you'll get, Penelope," he said softly, and she heard the edge in his tone, the urgency.

The truth.

Her grip loosened. "Your reputation is deserved, you know."

"Yes. It is. And this is not at all the worst thing I've done. You should know that."

The words should have been prideful. If not that, unemotional. But they weren't. They were honest. And there was something in them, there and then gone, something that she wasn't entirely certain she'd heard. Something she would not allow herself to recognize.

But she released the rail of the banister, and he set her down several steps above him.

She was actually considering it. Like a madwoman.

Actually imagining what it would be to marry this new, strange Michael. Except, she couldn't imagine it. Couldn't even begin to conceive of what it would be like to marry a man who took an axe to a kitchen table without a second thought. And carried screaming women off into abandoned houses.

It would not be a normal marriage of the *ton,* that was certain.

She met his gaze, straight on, thanks to the step upon which he'd deposited her. "If I marry you, I'll be ruined."

"The great secret of society is that ruination is not nearly as bad as they make it out to be. You'll have all the freedoms that come with a ruined reputation. They are not inconsiderable."

He would know.

She shook her head. "It's not simply me. My sisters will be ruined as well. They'll never find good matches if we marry. All of society will think they're as . . . easily scandalized . . . as I was."

"Your sisters are not my concern."

"But they are *my* concern."

He raised a brow. "Are you certain that you are in a condition to be making demands?"

She wasn't. Not at all. But she soldiered on nonetheless, squaring her shoulders. "You forget that no vicar in Britain will marry us if I refuse."

"You think I would not spread it across London that I thoroughly ruined you this evening if you did so?"

"I do."

"You think wrong. The story I would concoct would make the most hardened of prostitutes blush."

It was Penelope who blushed, but she refused to be cowed.

She took a deep breath and played her most powerful card. "I don't doubt it, but in ruining me, you would also ruin your chances at Falconwell."

He stiffened. Penelope was breathless with excitement as she waited for his reply.

"Name your price."

She had won.

She had *won.*

She wanted to crow her success, her defeat of this great, immovable beast of a man. But she retained some sense of self-preservation. "Tonight must not affect my sisters' reputations."

He nodded. "You have my word on it."

She clenched the torn fabric of her dress in a tight fist. "The word of a notorious scoundrel?"

He took a step up, coming closer, crowding her in the darkness. She forced herself to remain still when he spoke, his voice at once danger and promise. "There is honor among thieves, Penelope. Doubly so for gamblers."

She swallowed, proximity squelching her courage. "I—I'm neither of those."

"Nonsense," he whispered, and she imagined she could feel his lips at her temple. "It appears you are a born gamer. You simply require instruction."

No doubt he could teach her more than she had ever imagined.

She pushed the thought—and the images that came with it—from her mind as he added, "Do we have an agreement?"

Triumph was gone, chased by trepidation.

She wished she could see his eyes. "Do I have a choice?"

"No." There was no emotion in the word. No hint of sorrow or guilt. Just cold honesty.

He offered her his hand once more, and the wide, flat palm beckoned.

Hades, offering pomegranate seeds.

If she took it, everything would change. Everything would be different.

There would be no going back. Though, somewhere in her mind, she knew there was no going back anyway.

Clutching her dress together, she took his hand.

He led her up the stairs, his lantern the only refuge from the pitch-blackness beyond, and Penelope could not help but cling to him. She wished that she'd had the courage to release him, to follow under her own control, to resist him in this small thing, but there was something about this walk—something mysterious and dark in a way that had nothing to do with light—that she could not force herself to let him go.

He turned back at the foot of the stairs, his eyes shadowed in the candlelight. "Still afraid of the dark?"

The reference to their childhood unsettled her. "It was a *fox hole*. Anything could have been down there."

He started to climb the stairs. "For example?"

"A fox, perhaps?"

"There were no foxes in that hole."

He had checked it first. That had been the only reason why she'd allowed him to convince her to enter it at all. "Well . . . something else then. A bear, perhaps."

"Or perhaps you were afraid of the dark."

"Perhaps. But I am not any longer."

"No?"

"I was out in the dark tonight, wasn't I?"

They turned down a long hallway. "So you were." He released her hand then, and she did not like the way she missed his touch as he turned the handle of a nearby door and pushed it open with a long, ominous creak. He spoke low in her ear. "I will say, Penelope, that while it is unnecessary for you to be afraid of the dark, you are quite correct to be afraid of the things that thrive in it."

Penelope squinted into the darkness, trying to make out the room beyond, nervousness coiling deep within. She hovered on the threshold, her breath coming fast and shallow. Things that thrived in the dark . . . like him.

He pushed past her slowly, the movement simultaneously a caress and a threat. As he passed, he whispered, "You're a terrible bluff." The words were barely a sound, and the feel of his breath on her skin counteracted its insult.

Lanternlight flickered across the walls of the small, unfamiliar room, casting a golden glow across the once-elegant, now hopelessly faded wall coverings in what must have once been a lovely rose. The room was barely large enough to hold them both, a fireplace nearly taking up one wall, across from which two small windows looked out on the copse of trees.

Michael bent to build a fire, and Penelope went to the windows, watching a sliver of moonlight cut across the snowy landscape beyond. "What is this room? I don't remember it."

"You very likely never had a chance to see it. It was my mother's study."

A memory flashed of the marchioness, tall and beautiful, with a wide, welcoming smile and kind eyes. Of course this room, quiet and serene, had been hers.

"Michael," Penelope turned to face him, where he crouched low at the fireplace, laying a bed of straw and kindling. "I never had a chance to . . ." She searched for the right words.

He stopped her from finding them. "No need. What happened, happened."

The coolness in his tone seemed wrong. Off. "Nevertheless . . . I wrote. I don't know if you ever . . ."

"Possibly." He remained half-inside the hearth. She heard the flint scrape across the tinderbox. "Many people wrote."

The words shouldn't have cut, but they did. She'd been devastated by the news of the deaths of the Marquess and Marchioness of Bourne. Unlike her own parents, who seemed to have little more than a quiet civility between them—Michael's parents had seemed to care deeply for one another, for their son, for Penelope.

When she'd heard of the carriage accident, she'd been overcome with sadness, for what had been lost, for what might have been.

She'd written him letters, dozens of them over several

years before her father had refused to mail any more. After that, she'd continued to write, hoping that he would somehow know that she was thinking of him. That he would always have friends at Falconwell . . . in Surrey . . . no matter how alone he might have felt. She'd imagined that one day, he'd come home.

But he hadn't returned. Ever.

Eventually, Penelope had stopped expecting him.

"I'm sorry."

Tinder flashed; straw ignited.

He stood, turning to face her. "You'll have to do with firelight. Your lantern is in the snow."

She swallowed back her sadness, nodding. "I will be fine."

"Don't leave this room. The house is in disrepair, and I have not married you yet."

He turned and left the room.

Chapter Five

She woke in the dim light of the fire with an unbearably cold nose and an unbearably warm everything else.

Disoriented, she blinked several times, taking in the unfamiliar surroundings before the glowing embers in the fireplace and the rose-colored walls brought clarity.

She was lying on her back in the nest of blankets she had arranged before she'd fallen asleep, and she was covered with a large and warm one that smelled wonderful. She buried her frigid nose in the fabric and inhaled deeply, trying to place the smell—a blend of bergamot and tobacco flower.

She turned her head.

Michael.

Shock flared, then panic.

Michael was asleep next to her.

Well, not exactly *next* to her. Against her, more like.

But it *felt* like he was all around her.

He was turned on his side, head on one bent arm, his other arm draped across her, hand firmly clasping the far side of her person. She inhaled abruptly as she realized just how close his arm was to certain . . . parts of her . . . that were not to be touched.

Not that there were many parts of her that were open for reasonable touching, but that was not the point.

His arm was not the only problem. He was pressed to her quite thoroughly, his chest, his arm, his legs . . . and other parts as well. She couldn't decide if she should be horrified or utterly thrilled.

Both?

It was best that she not explore the question too thoroughly.

She turned toward him, trying to avoid unnecessary movement or sound and unable to ignore the feel of his arm stroking across her midsection in a steady caress as she rotated beneath it. When she faced him, she let out a long, careful breath and considered her next course of action.

It was not, after all, every day that she awoke in the arms of—well, *under* the arm of—a gentleman.

Not much of a gentleman anymore, was he?

While awake, he was all angles and tension—the muscles of his jaw were strung tight as a bow, as though he were in a perpetual state of holding himself back. But now, in slumber, in the glow of the fire, he was . . .

Beautiful.

The angles were still there, sharp and perfect, as though a master sculptor had had a hand in creating him—the tilt of his jaw, the cleft of his chin, his long, straight nose, the perfect curve of his brows, and those eyelashes, just as they were when he was a boy, unbelievably long and lush, a black, sooty caress against his cheeks.

And his lips. Not pressed in a firm, grim line at the moment, instead lovely and full. They had once been so quick to smile, but . . . they had become dangerous and tempting in a way they'd never been when he was a boy. She traced the peak and valleys of his upper lip with her gaze, wondering how many women had kissed him. Wondering what his mouth would feel like—soft or firm, light or dark.

She exhaled, temptation making the breath long and heavy.

She wanted to touch him.

She stilled at the thought, the idea so foreign and still so *true.*

She *shouldn't* want to touch him. He was a beast. Cold and rude and selfish and absolutely nothing like the boy she'd once known. Like the husband whom she'd imagined. Her thoughts flickered back to earlier in the evening, to imagining her plain, boring old husband.

No. Michael was nothing like that man.

Perhaps that was why she wanted to touch him.

Her gaze lingered at his mouth. Maybe not there, on his tempting, terrifying lips . . . maybe she wanted to touch his hair, dark and curly the way it had always been, but devoid of its youthful unruliness. The curls behaved now, even as they brushed against his ears and fell against his brow, even as they recovered from a day of travel and snow and caps.

They knew better than to rebel.

Yes. She wanted to touch his hair.

The hair of the man she would marry.

Her hand was moving of its own volition, heading for those dark curls. "Michael," she whispered, as her fingertips touched the silken strands, before she could think better of it.

His eyes snapped open, as though he had been waiting for her to speak, and he moved like lightning, capturing her wrist in one strong, steel hand.

She gasped at the movement. "I beg your pardon . . . I did not mean . . ." She tugged at her hand once, twice, and he let her go.

He returned his arm to where it had been quite inappropriately draped across her midsection, and the movement reminded her of every place where they touched—his leg pressed distractingly against her own, his gaze, a mosaic of color that hid his thoughts so very well.

She swallowed, hesitated, then said the only thing she could think to say. "You're in my bed."

He did not reply.

She pressed on. "It's not . . ." She searched for the word.

"Done?" Sleep made his voice rough and soft, and she could not stop the shiver of excitement that coursed through her at the word.

She nodded once.

He slid his arm away from her, all too slowly, and she ignored the pang of regret that flared at the loss of the weight. "What are you doing here?"

"I *was* sleeping."

"I mean, why are you in my bed?"

"It's not your bed, Penelope. It's mine."

Silence fell, and a shiver of nervousness slipped down Penelope's spine. What did she say to that? It did not seem at all appropriate to discuss his bed in detail. Nor hers, for that matter.

He rolled to his back, unfolding the long arm that had been under his cheek and stretching long and luxurious before he turned away from her.

She tried to sleep. Really, she did.

She took a deep breath, studying the way his shoulders curved, pulling the linen of his shirt taut. She was in a bed. With a man. A man who, though he would soon be her husband, did not yet hold the title. The situation should have been devastatingly scandalous. Wickedly exciting. And yet . . . no matter what her mother would think when she heard of it, the situation did not seem at all scandalous.

Which was a bit of a disappointment, really. It seemed that even when she was face-to-face with the prospect of adventure, she couldn't get it right.

It did not matter how scandalous her future husband was . . . she was not the kind of woman who compelled him to scandal. That much had been made clear.

Even now, alone in an abandoned manor house, she wasn't enough to capture a gentleman's attention.

She exhaled audibly, and he turned his head toward her, giving her a view of one perfectly curled ear.

She'd never noticed anyone's ears before.

"What is it?" he said, his voice a low gravel.

" 'It'?" she asked.

He rolled to his back again, jostling the blanket and baring one of her arms to the cold air in the room. When he replied, it was to the ceiling. "I know enough about women to know that sighs are never simply sighs. They indicate one of two things. That particular sigh represents feminine displeasure."

"I am not surprised that you recognize the sound." Penelope could not resist. "What does the other indicate?"

He pinned her with his beautiful hazel gaze. "Feminine pleasure."

Heat flared on her cheeks. She supposed he would easily recognize that, too. "Oh."

He returned his attention to the ceiling. "Would you care to tell me what it is, precisely, that has made you unhappy?"

She shook her head. "Nothing."

"Are you uncomfortable?"

"No." The blankets beneath her provided ample padding against the wooden floor.

"Are you frightened?"

She considered the question. "No. Should I be?"

He slid her a look. "I don't hurt women."

"You draw the line at abducting and spanking them?"

"Are you hurt?"

"No."

He turned his back to her once more, through with the conversation, and she watched the back of him for long moments before, whether from exhaustion or exasperation, she blurted, "It's just that when a woman is kidnapped and forced into agreeing to marriage, she hopes for a bit more . . . excitement. Than this."

He rolled slowly—maddeningly—to face her, the air between them thickened, and Penelope was instantly aware of their position, scant inches apart, on a warm pallet in a small room in an empty house, beneath the same blanket—which happened to be his greatcoat. And she realized that perhaps she should not have implied that the evening was unexciting.

Because she was not at all certain that she was prepared for it to become any more exciting. "I didn't mean—" She rushed to correct herself.

"Oh, I think you did an excellent job of meaning." The words were low and dark, and suddenly she was not so very sure that she wasn't afraid after all. "I am not stimulating enough for you?"

"Not *you* . . ." she was quick to reply. "The whole . . ." She waved one hand, lifting the greatcoat as she thought better of finishing. "Never mind."

His gaze was on her, intent and unmoving and, while he had not moved, it seemed as though he had grown larger, more looming. As though he had sucked a great deal of air from the room. "How can I make this night more satisfying for you, my lady?"

The soft question sent a thrum of feeling through her . . . the way the word—*satisfying*—rolled languid from his tongue set her heart racing and her stomach turning.

It seemed the night was becoming very exciting very quickly.

And everything was moving much too quickly for Penelope's tastes. "No need," she said, at an alarmingly high pitch. "It's fine."

"Fine?" The word rolled lazily from his tongue.

"Quite thrilling." She nodded, bringing one hand to her mouth to feign a yawn. "So thrilling, in fact, that I find myself unbearably exhausted." She made to turn her back to him. "I think I shall bid you good night."

"I don't think so," he said, the soft words as loud as a gunshot in the tiny space between them.

And then he touched her.

He clasped her wrist, staying her movement, turning her

to face him, to meet his unflinching gaze. "I would hate for the evening to leave you so . . . unfulfilled."

Unfulfilled.

The word unfurled deep in her stomach, and Penelope took a deep breath, trying to settle her roiling emotions.

It did not work.

He moved then, his hand sliding away from her wrist, settling on her hip instead, and in that moment, all of her awareness was focused on that spot, beneath skirts and petticoat and cloak, where she was *certain* she could feel the searing heat of his massive hand. He did not tighten his grip, did nothing to bring her closer, nothing to move her in one way or another. She knew she could pull away . . . knew she *should* pull away . . . and yet . . .

She didn't want to.

Instead, she hovered there, on the brink of something new and different and altogether *exciting.*

She met his eyes, dark in the firelight, and begged him silently to *do something.*

But he didn't. Instead, he said, "Play your card, Penelope."

Her mouth dropped open at the words, at the way he gave her power over the moment, and she realized that it was the first time in her entire life that a man had actually given her the opportunity to make a choice for herself.

Ironic, wasn't it, that it was this man. This man who had taken all choice from her in the span of mere hours.

But now, there it was, the freedom of which he'd spoken. The adventure he'd promised. The power was heady. Irresistible.

Dangerous.

But she did not care, because it was that wicked, wonderful power that propelled her to speech.

"Kiss me."

He was already moving, his lips capturing the words.

Dear M—

It's utter misery here—hot as Hades even now, in the dead of night. I'm sure I'm the only one awake, but who can sleep in the worst of a Surrey summer? If you were here, I'm sure we would be mischief-making at the lake.

I confess, I'd like to take a walk . . . but I suppose that's something young ladies should not do, isn't it?

Warmly—P
Needham Manor, July 1815

Dear P—

Nonsense. If I were there, I would be mischief-making. You would be enumerating all the ways that we would soon be caught and scolded for our transgressions.

I'm not entirely sure what young ladies should or should not do, but your secrets are safe with me, even if your governess does not approve. Especially so.

—M
Eton College, July 1815

It should be said that Penelope Marbury had a secret.

It wasn't a very big secret, nothing that would bring down Parliament or dethrone the King . . . nothing that would destroy her family or anyone else's . . . but it was a rather devastating secret personally—one she tried very hard to forget whenever she could.

It should not be a surprise, as, until that evening, Penelope had led a model life—entirely decorous. Her childhood of good behavior had aged into an adulthood of modeling excellent behavior for her younger sisters and behaving in precisely the manner that young women of good breeding were expected to behave.

Therefore, it was the embarrassing truth that, despite the fact that she had been courted by a handful of men and even *engaged* to one of the most powerful men in England, who seemed to have no problem at all displaying passion when it moved him, Penelope Marbury had never been kissed.

Until then.

It really was ridiculous. She knew that.

It was 1831, for goodness sake. Young ladies were dampening their petticoats and revealing their skin, and she knew from having four sisters that there was nothing at all wrong with a chaste brush of the lips now and then from an avid suitor.

Except it had never happened before, and this did not feel at all chaste.

This felt utterly wicked and not at all like the kind of kiss one received from one's future husband.

This felt like something one *never discussed* with one's future husband.

Michael pulled back just barely, just enough to whisper against her lips. "Stop thinking."

How did he know?

It didn't matter. What mattered was that it would be rude to ignore his request.

So she gave herself up to it, this strange, new sensation of being kissed, his lips at once somehow both hard and soft, the sound of his breath harsh against her cheek. His fingertips stroking delicately, whisper-soft, along the column of her neck, tilting her chin to better access her mouth. "Much better."

She gasped as he realigned his lips to hers and robbed her of thought with a single, shocking . . . wicked . . . *wonderful* caress.

Was that his *tongue*?

It was . . . gloriously stroking along the seam of her closed lips, coaxing her open, then it seemed he was consuming her, and she was more than willing to allow it. He traced a slow path of fire along her lower lip, and Penelope wondered if it was possible for someone to go mad from pleasure.

Surely not every man kissed like this . . . else women would get nothing done.

He pulled back. "You're thinking again."

She was. She was thinking he was magnificent. "I can't help it." She shook her head, reaching for him.

"Then I am not doing it correctly."

Oh dear. If he kissed her any more correctly, her sanity would be threatened.

Perhaps it already was.

She really, honestly didn't care.

Just as long as he kept at it.

Her hands moved of their own volition, reaching up, stroking through his hair, pulling him closer, until his lips were on hers again, and this time . . . this time, she let herself go.

And kissed him back, reveling in the deep, graveled sound that rose from the back of his throat—the sound that spiraled straight to the core of her and told her, without words, that for all her lack of experience, she'd done something right.

His hands were moving then, up, up until she thought she might die if he didn't touch her . . . there, on the curve of her breast, sliding wickedly into the torn cloth of her dress, the cloth he'd ripped to save himself the trouble of seducing her.

Not that it seemed as though he would have had any trouble at all.

She stroked one hand down his arm until she was pressing his hand to her, stronger, more firmly, sighing his name into his mouth.

He pulled away at the sound, throwing his greatcoat back to reveal them to the waning firelight, pushing the cloth aside, baring her to his gaze, returning his hand to her, stroking, lifting until she arched toward him.

"Do you like that?" She heard the answer in the question.

He knew she'd never in her life felt anything so powerful. So tempting.

"I shouldn't." Her hand returned to his, holding him there, against her.

"But you do." He pressed a kiss to the soft skin at the base of her neck as his expert fingers found the place where she strained for his touch. She gasped his name. He scraped his teeth across the soft lobe of one ear until she shivered in his arms. "Talk to me."

"It's incredible," she said, not wanting to ruin the moment, not wanting him to stop.

"Keep talking," he whispered, peeling the fabric back as he pressed her breast up, baring one aching nipple to the cool room.

He stared at her then, watching the tip pucker at the air or his gaze or both, and Penelope was suddenly horribly embarrassed, hating her imperfections, wishing she was anywhere but there, with him, this perfect specimen of man.

She moved to grasp the greatcoat, afraid that he would see her. That he would judge her. *That he would change his mind.*

He was faster, clasping her wrists in his hands, staying her movement. "Don't," he growled, force in the words. "Never hide yourself from me."

"I cannot help it. I don't want . . . you should not look."

"If you think I'm going to avoid looking at you, you're mad." He shifted then, throwing the greatcoat back, out of her reach, making quick work of her destroyed dress, brushing the torn edges away.

He stared at her then, for long moments, until she couldn't bear watching him anymore for the fear that he might reject her. For it was rejection that she was most used to when it came to his sex. Rejection and refusal and disinterest. And she didn't think she could bear those things now. From him. Tonight.

She closed her eyes tightly, taking a deep breath, preparing for him to turn away at her plainness. Her imperfections. She was sure he would turn away.

When his lips settled on hers, she thought she might cry.

And then he was taking her mouth in one long kiss, stroking deep until all thought of embarrassment was chased away by desire. Only when she was clinging to the lapels of his coat did he release her from the devastating caress.

One wicked finger circled the tip of her breast lazily, as if they had all the time in the world, and she watched the movement, barely visible in the deep orange glow of the dying fire. Pleasure pooled there, at the tight, puckered tip . . . and in other scandalous places at the sensation.

"Do you like that?" he asked, low and dark. Penelope bit her lip and nodded. "Tell me."

"Yes . . . yes it's splendid." She knew it made her sound simple and unsophisticated, but she could not keep the wonder from her voice.

His fingers did not stop. "It should all feel splendid. You tell me if it doesn't, and I shall rectify the situation."

He kissed her neck, running his teeth across the soft skin there. He looked up. "Does that feel splendid?"

"Yes."

He rewarded her by pressing kisses down her neck, sucking at the delicate skin of her shoulder, licking down the slope of one breast before circling the hard, peaked tip, nipping and caressing—the whole time avoiding the place where she wanted him most. "I'm going to corrupt you," he promised her skin, one hand sliding down the swell of her stomach, feeling the way the muscles there tensed and quivered at his touch. "I'm going to turn you from light to dark, from good to bad. I'm going to ruin you." She didn't care. She was his. He owned her in this moment, with this touch. "And do you know how it will feel?"

She sighed the word this time. "Splendid."

More than that.

More than she'd ever imagined.

He met her eyes and, without breaking their gaze, he took the tip of one breast deep into his warm mouth, worrying the flesh with tongue and teeth before pulling in lush tugs that had her moaning his name and plunging her fingers into his hair.

"Michael . . ." she whispered, afraid that she might break the spell of pleasure. She closed her eyes.

He lifted his head, and she hated him for stopping. "Look at me." The words were a demand. When she met his gaze once more, his hand slid beneath the pooled fabric of her dress, fingers brushing against curls, and she snapped her thighs shut with a little cry of dismay. *He couldn't possibly . . . not there . . .*

But he returned his attention to her breast, kissing and sucking until her inhibitions were lost and her thighs parted, allowing him to slide his fingers between them, resting softly against her but not moving—a wicked, wonderful temptation. She stiffened again but did not refuse him access this time.

"I promise you shall like this. Trust me."

She gave a shaky laugh as his fingers moved, widening her thighs, gaining access to her core. "Said the lion to the lamb."

He tongued the soft skin at the underside of her breast before turning to the other, lavishing the same attention there as she writhed beneath him and sighed his name. His fingers were wicked, separating her secret folds with one finger and stroking gently, slowly, until he found the warm, wet entrance to her.

He lifted his head, finding her gaze as he slid one long finger slowly into the heart of her, sending a bolt of unexpected pleasure through her. He pressed a kiss to the skin between her breasts, repeating the motion with his finger before whispering, "You're already wet for me. Gloriously wet."

It was impossible to stem her embarrassment. "I'm sorry."

He kissed her long and slow, sliding his tongue deep in her mouth as his finger mirrored the action below, before he pulled back, placed his forehead to hers, and said, "It means you want me. It means that, even after all these years, after everything I've done, after everything I am, I can make you want me."

Later, she would reflect on the words, wish that she'd said something to him, but she couldn't, not when he slid a second finger in with the first, his thumb circling as he whispered at her ear. "I am going to explore you . . . to discover your heat and softness, every bit of your decadence." He stroked against her, feeling the way she pulsed around him, loving the way she rocked her hips against him as his thumb worked a tight circle at the straining nub of pleasure he had uncovered. "You make my mouth water."

Her eyes went wide at the words, but he did not give her time to consider them as he moved his hand again, lifting her hips and sliding her gown down, over her legs and off until she was utterly bare, and he was between her legs, parting them slowly, saying the most wicked things as his hands slid along her legs. He stalked her on his knees as he parted them, pressing long, soft, lush kisses to the soft skin of her inner thighs just above her stockings. "In fact . . ." He paused, swirling his tongue in a slow, stunning circle. " . . . I don't think I can go another moment . . ." Again, on the opposite thigh. " . . . Without . . ." Slightly higher, closer to the ache. " . . . Tasting you."

And then his mouth was on her, his tongue stroking in long, slow licks, curling almost unbearably at the place where pleasure pooled and strained and begged for release. She cried out, sitting up straight before he lifted his head and pressed one large hand to her soft stomach. "Lie back . . . let me taste you. Let me show you how good it can be. Watch. Tell me what you like. What you need."

And she did, God help her. As he licked and sucked with his perfect tongue and his wicked lips, she whispered her encouragement, learning what she wanted even as she was not sure of the end result.

More, Michael . . .

Her hands slid into his curls, holding him close to her.

Michael, again . . .

Her thighs widened, willing and wanton.

There, Michael . . .

Michael . . .

He was her world. There was nothing beyond this moment.

And then his fingers joined his tongue, and she thought she might die as he pressed more firmly, rubbed more deliberately, giving her everything for which she did not know to ask. Her eyes flew open, his name on a gasp.

His tongue moved faster, circling at the place where she needed him, and she moved, all inhibition gone, lost to the rising, cresting pleasure . . . wanting nothing more than to know what lay beyond.

"Please, don't stop," she whispered.

He didn't.

With his name on her lips, she threw herself over the edge, rocking against him, pressing to him, begging for more even as he gave it to her with tongue and lips and fingers until she lost awareness of everything but the bold, brilliant pleasure he gave her.

As she floated back from her climax, he pressed long, lovely kisses to the inside of her thighs until she sighed his name and reached for his soft mahogany curls, wanting nothing more than to lie next to him for an hour . . . a day . . . a lifetime.

He stilled at her touch as her fingers sifted through his hair, and they remained that way for long moments. She was limp with pleasure, her whole world in the feel of his silken curls in her hands, in the scrape of his beard at the soft skin of her thigh.

Michael.

She stayed quiet, waiting for him to speak. Waiting for him to say what she was thinking . . . that the experience had been truly remarkable, and that if this evening was any indication, their marriage would be far more than he'd ever imagined it could be.

All would be well. It had to be. Experiences like this one did not come along every day.

He finally shifted, and she sensed the unwillingness in the movement as he pulled the greatcoat up around her, surrounding her in the scent and heat of him before he rolled away and came to his feet in a single, fluid movement, lifting his wool frock coat from where he must have placed it, carefully folded, earlier in the evening.

He pulled it on, quick as lightning. "You're well and truly ruined now," he said, the words cold.

She sat up, clutching his greatcoat to her as he opened the door and turned back to her, his wide shoulders fading into the blackness beyond. "Our marriage is no longer a question."

He left then, the door closing firmly behind him, punctuating his words, leaving Penelope seated in a pool of fabric, staring at the door, sure that he would return, that she had misheard him, that she had mistaken his meaning.

That all would be well.

After long minutes, Penelope pulled on her dress, her fingers shaking at the feel of the torn fabric. She returned to her pallet, refusing to allow tears to come.

Chapter Six

Dear M—

You may think that since you've returned to school, I've been in a constant state of ennui (note the use of French), but you would be entirely wrong. The excitement is nearly overwhelming.

The bull got loose from Lord Langford's pasture two nights ago, and he (the bull, not the viscount) had a fine time knocking down fences and making the acquaintance of the cattle in the area until he was captured this morning, by Mr. Bullworth.

I wager you wish you were home, don't you?

Always—P
Needham Manor, September 1815

Dear P—

I believed you until the bit about Bullworth capturing his namesake. Now, I'm convinced you're merely attempting to lure me home with your extravagant tales of attempted animal husbandry.

Though, I would be lying if I told you it wasn't working. I wish I'd been there to see the look on Langford's face. And the smile on yours.

—M

post script—I am happy to see that your governess is teaching you something. Très bon.

Eton College, September 1815

Dawn had barely broken when Bourne paused outside the room where he had left Penelope the night before, the cold and his thoughts joining forces to keep him from rest. He'd paced the house, haunted by the memories of the empty rooms, waiting for the sun to rise on the day when he would see Falconwell restored to its right and proper owner.

There was no doubt in Bourne's mind that the Marquess of Needham and Dolby would relinquish Falconwell. The man was no fool. He had three unmarried daughters, and the fact that the eldest had spent the evening with a man in an abandoned house—with *Bourne* in an abandoned house—would not endear the remaining unwed ladies Marbury to potential suitors.

The solution was marriage. A quick one.

And with that marriage, the passing of Falconwell.

Falconwell, and Penelope.

A different man would feel remorse at the unfortunate role Penelope was forced to play in this game, but Bourne knew better. Certainly, he was using the lady, but was that not how marriage worked? Were not all marital relations devised on that very premise—mutual benefit?

She would gain access to his money, his freedoms, and anything else she wished.

He would gain Falconwell.

That was that. They were not the first to marry for land, nor would they be the last. It was a remarkable offer, the one he'd made her. He was rich and well connected, and he was offering her a chance to trade her future as a spinster for one as a marchioness. She could have anything she wanted. He'd give it to her with pleasure.

After all, she was giving him the only thing he'd ever really wanted.

Not quite. No one *gave* Bourne anything. He was *taking* it.

Taking her.

A vision flashed, large blue eyes set wide in her plain face, pleasure and something more blazing there. Something too close to emotion. Too close to caring.

That was why he'd left her, strategically. Coolly. Calculatingly.

To prove the marriage would be a business arrangement.

Not because he had wanted to stay.

Not because removing his mouth and hands from her had been one of the most difficult things he had ever done. Not because he'd been tempted to do just the opposite—to sink into her and revel in her, soft where women were meant to be soft and sweet where they were meant to be sweet. Not because those little sighs that came from the back of her throat while he kissed her were the most erotic things he'd ever heard, or that she tasted like innocence.

He forced himself to move away from her door. There was no reason to knock. He'd be back before she woke, ready to take her to the nearest vicar, present the special license for which he'd paid a handsome sum, and get her married.

Then, they would return to London and live their separate lives.

He took a deep breath, enjoying the sting of the crisp morning air in his lungs, satisfied with his plan.

That was when she screamed, the heart-stopping sound punctuated with the sound of shattering glass.

He responded instinctively, unlocking the door and nearly tearing it from its hinges to get it open. He pulled up short just inside the room, heart pounding.

She stood unharmed at the side of the broken window, back against the wall, barefoot, wrapped in his greatcoat, which hung open to reveal her ruined gown, gaping wide, baring an expanse of peach-colored skin.

For one fleeting moment, Bourne was arrested by that skin, by the way a single blond curl cut across it, drawing his attention to the place where a lovely rose-colored nipple stood peaked and proud in the cold room.

His mouth went dry, and he forced himself to return his gaze to her face, where her wide eyes blinked in shock and disbelief as she stared at the great glass window next to her, now missing a pane, shattered by . . .

A bullet.

He was across the tiny room in seconds, shielding her with his body and pushing her from the room into the hallway beyond. "Stay here."

She nodded, shock apparently making her more agreeable than he would have expected. He returned to the room and the window, but before he could inspect the damage, a second gunshot shattered another pane of glass, missing Bourne by a distance with which he was not at all comfortable.

What in hell?

He swore once, harshly, and pressed himself against the wall of the room, next to the window.

Someone was shooting at him.

The question was, *Who?*

"Be careful—"

Penelope stuck her head back into the room, and Bourne was already moving toward her, sending her a look that had sent the worst of London's underground into retreat. "Get out."

She did not move. "It is not safe for you to stay in there. You could be—" Another shot sounded from outside, interrupting, and he leapt for her, praying he could get to her before a bullet did. He barreled into her, pushing her back out the door until they were both pressed up against the opposite wall.

They were still for a long minute before she continued, her words muffled by his bulk. "You could be hurt!"

Was she out of her mind?

He grasped her shoulders, not caring that his ordinarily tightly reined temper was beginning to fray. "Idiot woman! What did I say?" He waited for her to answer the question. When she didn't, he couldn't help himself. Shaking her once by the shoulders, he repeated, "*What* did I say?"

Her eyes went wide.

Good. She should fear him.

"Answer me, Penelope." He heard the growl in his voice. Didn't care.

"You—" The words caught in her throat. "You said I should stay here."

"And are you somehow unable to understand such a simple direction?"

Her gaze narrowed. "No."

He'd insulted her. Again, he did not care. "Stay. The bloody hell. Here." He ignored her wince and returned to the room, inching around toward the window.

He was just about to risk looking out onto the grounds to attempt a glimpse at his would-be assassin when words floated up from below. "Do you surrender?"

Surrender?

Perhaps Penelope had been right. Perhaps there were indeed pirates in Surrey.

He didn't have much time to consider the question, as Penelope cried out, "Oh, for heaven's sake!" from the hallway and rushed back into the room, clutching his coat around her and heading straight for the window.

"Stop!" Bourne lunged to block her progress, catching her

around the waist and hauling her back. "If you get anywhere near that window, I'll paddle you. Do you hear me?"

"But . . ."

"No."

"It's just—"

"*No.*"

"It's my father!"

The words coursed through him, remaining hazy for longer than he would care to admit.

She couldn't be right.

"I came for my daughter, ruffian! And I shall leave with her!"

"How did he know the room at which to shoot?"

"I—I was standing at the window. He must have seen the movement."

Another bullet sent glass splintering across the room, and Bourne pressed closer to her, shielding her with his body. "Do you think he is aware that he could shoot you?"

"It does not appear to have occurred to him."

He swore again. "He deserves to be hit in the head with his rifle."

"I think he might be overcome with the fact that he's hit his target. Thrice. Of course, considering the target was a *house,* it would have been something of a surprise if he *hadn't* hit it."

Was she amused?

She couldn't be. Another shot rang out, and Bourne felt the final thread of his temper snap. He strode to the window, not caring that he might get shot in the process. "Dammit, Needham! You could kill her!"

The Marquess of Needham and Dolby did not look up from where he was aiming a second rifle, a nearby footman reloading the first. "I could also kill you. I like my odds!"

Penelope came up behind him. "If it's any consolation, I sincerely doubt that he could kill you. He's a terrible shot."

Michael leveled her with a look. "Get away from this window. Now."

Miracle of miracles, she did.

"I should have known you'd come for her, you ruffian. I should have known you'd do something worthy of your foul reputation."

Bourne forced himself to appear calm. "Come now, Needham, is that any way to speak to your future son-in-law?"

"Over my dead body!" Fury made the other man's voice crack.

"It can be arranged," Bourne called out.

"You send the girl down here. Immediately. She won't marry you."

"After last night, there's little question she will, Needham."

The rifle cocked below, and Bourne ducked away from the window, pressing Penelope back into the corner as the bullet flew through another pane of glass.

"Scoundrel!"

He wanted to rail at her father for the lack of caution he exhibited for his daughter. Instead, he turned to the window, affected a tone of utter disinterest, and called out, "I found her. I'm keeping her."

There was a long pause, so long that Michael could not help but lift his head around the window frame to see if the marquess had left.

He had not.

A bullet lodged itself in the exterior wall, several inches from Michael's head. "You're not getting Falconwell, Bourne. Nor are you getting my daughter!"

"Well, I'll be honest, Needham . . . I've already had your daughter—"

The words were cut off by Needham's bellow. "Blighter!"

Penelope gasped. "You did *not* just tell my father you've *had* me."

He should have seen this potential outcome. Should have known that it would not be so easy. The whole morning was spiraling out of control, and Bourne did not like being out of control. He took a long, slow breath, trying for patience. "Penelope, we are holed up inside a house as your irate father fires numerous rifles at my head. I should think you'd forgive me for doing what I can to ensure we both survive this event."

"And our reputations? Were they to survive as well?"

"My reputation is rather shot to hell," he said, pressing his back to the wall.

"Well, mine isn't!" she cried. "Have you taken leave of your senses?" She paused. "And your language is atrocious."

"You'll have to get used to my language, darling. As for the rest, when we marry, your reputation will be shot to hell, as well. Your father may as well know it now."

He couldn't stop himself from turning to face her, to watch the way the words affected her . . . the way the light went out of her eyes . . . the way she stiffened as though he'd struck her. "You're horrible," she said, simply. Honestly.

In that moment, as she looked at him, all calm accusation, he hated himself enough for both of them. But he was a master at hiding his emotions. "It seems that way." The words were flippant. Forced.

Her distaste showed. "Why would you do this?"

There was only one reason—only one thing that had ever guided his actions. Only one thing that had turned him into this cold, calculating man.

"Does Falconwell mean so much?"

Silence fell outside, and something dark and unpleasant settled in the pit of his stomach, the feeling all too familiar. For nine years, he'd taken every measure to regain his land. To restore his history. To secure his future. And he was not about to stop now.

"Of course it does," she said with a little self-deprecating laugh. "I am a means to an end."

In the hours that had passed since he'd stumbled upon Penelope at the lake, he'd heard her irritated and surprised and affronted and impassioned . . . but he had not heard her like this.

He'd not heard her resigned.

He did not like it.

For the first time in a very long time—in nine years—

Bourne felt the urge to apologize to someone he'd used. He steeled himself against the inclination.

He turned his head toward her—not enough to meet her gaze—just enough to watch her from the corner of his eye. Enough to see her head bowed, her hands holding his greatcoat closed around her. "Come here," he said, and a small part of him was surprised when she did.

She crossed the room, and he was consumed with the sound of her—the slide of her skirts, the soft fall of her footsteps, the way her breath came in little uneven spurts marking her nervousness and anticipation.

She stopped behind him, hovering, as he played out the next few moves of this chess match in his mind. He wondered, fleetingly, if he should let her go.

No.

What was done was done.

"Marry me, Penelope."

"Just because you phrase it in such a way does not give me a choice, you know."

He wanted to smile at the irritated way she said the words, but he didn't. She watched him carefully for a long moment and he—a man who had made a fortune by reading the truth in the faces of those around him—could not say what she was thinking. For a long moment, he thought she might refuse him, and he prepared himself for her resistance, cataloging the number of clergymen who owed him and The Angel enough debt to marry an unwilling bride—preparing himself to do what needed to be done to secure her hand.

It would be one more wrongdoing to add to his ever-expanding list.

"You will keep your word from last night? My sisters will remain untouched by this marriage."

Even now, even as she faced a lifetime with him, she thought of her sisters.

She was legions too good for him.

He ignored the thought. "I will keep my word."

"I require proof."

Smart girl. Of course, there wasn't any proof. And she was right to doubt him.

He reached into his pocket and retrieved a guinea rubbed nearly bare over the nine years that he'd kept it with him. He held it out to her. "My marker."

She took the coin. "What am I to do with this?"

"You return it when your sisters are married."

"One guinea?"

"It's been enough for men across Britain, darling."

She raised her brows. "And they say men are the more intelligent sex." She took a deep breath, slipping the coin into her pocket, making him long for the weight of it again. "I shall marry you."

He nodded once. "And the fiancé?"

She hesitated, her gaze flickering past his shoulder as she considered the words. "He will find another bride," she said softly, fondly. *Too* fondly. Instantly, Bourne felt a perverse anger at this man who had not protected her. Who had left her alone in the world. Who had made it too easy for Bourne to step in and claim her.

There was movement in the doorway over her shoulder. Her father. Needham had obviously grown tired of waiting for them to exit the building, and so he had come in to fetch them.

Bourne took it as his cue to hammer the final nail into this marital coffin, knowing even as he did it that he was using her. That she didn't deserve it.

That it didn't matter.

He lifted her chin and pressed a single, soft kiss to her lips, trying not to notice when she leaned into the touch, when she breathed a little sigh as he lifted his head a touch . . .

A rifle cocked in the doorway, punctuating the words of the Marquess of Needham and Dolby. "Dammit, Penelope, look what you've done now."

Dear M—

My father thinks that we should stop writing. He's certain that "boys like him" (meaning you) haven't the time for "silly letters" from "silly girls" (meaning me). He says you're only replying because you're well-raised and you feel obligated. I realize you're nearly sixteen, and you've likely got more interesting things to do than write to me, but remember: I have no such interesting things. I shall have to make do with your pity.

Sillily—P

post script—He's not right, is he?

Needham Manor, January 1816

Dear P—

What your father doesn't know is that the only thing that breaks up the monotony of Latin, Shakespeare and the droning on about the responsibilities boys like me shall one day have in the House of Lords are silly letters from silly girls. You of all people should know that I've been very poorly raised, and I rarely feel obligated.

—M

post script—He's not right.

Eton College, January 1816

"You bastard."

Bourne looked up from his whiskey in the Hound and Hen and met the angry gaze of his future father-in-law. Leaning back in his chair, he affected the look of vague amusement that had thrown off far greater opponents than the Marquess of Needham and Dolby, and waved one hand at the empty chair across the pub table. "Father," he mocked, "please, join me."

Bourne had been seated in a dark corner of the tavern for several hours, waiting for Needham to arrive with the papers that would restore Falconwell. As evening gave way to night, and the lively room filled with laughter and chatter, he'd waited, fingers itching to sign the papers, dreaming of what came next.

Of revenge.

Trying very hard not to think about the fact that he was betrothed.

Trying even harder not to think of the woman to whom he was betrothed—so earnest and innocent and entirely the wrong kind of wife for him.

Not that he had any idea of the right kind of wife for him.

Irrelevant. He'd not had a choice.

The only way he'd had a chance at Falconwell was through Penelope. Which made her entirely the *right* kind of wife for him.

And Needham knew it.

The portly marquess sat, calling over a servant girl with the wave of one enormous hand. She was smart enough to bring a glass and the bottle of whiskey with her, leaving it quickly and hurrying away to brighter—and friendlier—climes.

Needham drank deep and slammed his glass onto the hard oak table. "You bastard. This is blackmail."

Michael affected a look of boredom. "Nonsense. I'm paying you handsomely. I'm taking your eldest, unmarried daughter off your hands."

"You'll make her miserable."

"Probably."

"She's not strong enough for you. You'll ruin her."

Bourne refrained from pointing out that Penelope was stronger than most women he'd encountered. "You should have considered that before you attached her to my land." He tapped the scarred oak. "The deed, Needham. I find myself disinclined to marry the girl without it in my possession. I want it now. I want the papers signed before Penelope stands before a vicar."

"Else?"

Bourne turned in his chair, extending his boots out from under the table, crossing one leg over the other. "Else Penelope doesn't stand before the vicar at all."

Needham's gaze was fast on his. "You wouldn't. It would destroy her. Her mother. Her sisters."

"Then I suggest you seriously consider your next course of action. It's been nine years, Needham. Nine long years during which I've longed for this moment. For Falconwell. And if you think I'm going to allow you to get in the way of my restoring those lands to the marquessate, you are sorely mistaken. I happen to be quite friendly with the publisher of *The Scandal Sheet.* One word from me, and no one of good *ton* will come near the young ladies Marbury." He paused and poured himself another drink, allowing the cold threat to settle between them. "Go on. Try me."

Needham's gaze narrowed. "So this is the way of it? You threaten everything I have in order to get what you want?"

Bourne smirked. "I play to win."

"Ironic, is it not, that you are famous for losing?"

The barb struck true. Not that Bourne would show it. Instead, he remained silent, knowing that there was nothing like quiet to unsettle an opponent.

Needham filled the silence. "You're an ass." With a curse, he reached into his coat and retrieved a large, folded piece of paper.

Bourne's triumph was heady as he read the document. Falconwell was his, upon the marriage, which would come tomorrow. His only regret was that Vicar Compton did not work at night.

When Bourne placed the document safely in his own pocket, imagining he could feel the weight of the deed against his chest, Needham spoke. "I'll not have her sisters ruined by this."

They were all so worried about her sisters.

What of Penelope?

Bourne ignored the question and toyed with Needham—the man who had tried so hard to keep Falconwell from him. Bourne lifted his glass. "I'm marrying Penelope. Falconwell is mine tomorrow. Tell me why I should bother caring even a bit about the reputation of your other daughters. They are your problem, are they not?" He threw back the scotch and set the empty glass on the table.

Needham leaned into the table, his tone all force. "You're an ass, and your father would be devastated to know what you've become."

Bourne snapped his gaze to Needham's, registering, oddly, that the marquess did not share Penelope's blue eyes. Instead, his eyes were deep brown and lit with a knowledge that Bourne knew all too well—the knowledge that he had wounded his opponent. Bourne stilled, a memory of his father coming unbidden, of him standing in the center of the massive foyer at Falconwell, in breeches and shirtsleeves, laughing up at his son.

The muscles in his jaw tensed. "Then we are lucky that he is dead."

Needham seemed to understand that he was treading dangerously close to ground that was out-of-bounds. He relaxed away from the table. "The details of your betrothal are never to be revealed. I've two other daughters who need marrying. No one can know Penelope went to a fortune hunter."

"I've three times the holdings you have, Needham."

Needham's gaze turned black. "You didn't have the holding you wanted, did you?"

"I have it now." Bourne pushed his chair back from the table. "You are in no position to make demands. If your daughters survive my entry into the family, it shall be because I condescend to allow it and for no other reason."

Needham followed the movement with his gaze, his jaw

clenching at the sound. "No, it shall be because I have the one thing you want more than the land."

Bourne considered Needham for a long moment, the words echoing in their dark corner before he brushed them aside. "You can't give me the only thing I want more than Falconwell."

"Langford's ruin."

Revenge.

The word shot through him, a whisper of promise, and Bourne leaned forward, slowly. "You lie."

"I should call you out for the suggestion."

"It won't be my first duel." He waited. When Needham did not rise to the bait, he said, "I've looked. There's nothing to be found that can ruin him."

"You haven't looked in the right places."

It had to be a lie. "You think that with my reach, with the reach of The Angel, I have not turned London inside out for a whiff of scandal on the stench of Langford?"

"Not even the files at your precious hell would have this."

"I know everything he's done, everywhere he's been. I know the man's life better than he himself. And I am telling you, he took everything I had and spent the last nine years living a pristine life *off my lands*."

Needham reached into his coat again. Withdrew another document, this one smaller. Older. "This happened far more than nine years ago."

Bourne's gaze narrowed on the paper, registered the Langford seal. He raised his eyes to his future father-in-law. His heart began to pound, something frighteningly akin to hope in his chest. He didn't like the way he hung on the silence that swirled between them. Willed himself calm. "You think to tempt me with some ancient letter?"

"You want this letter, Bourne. It's worth a dozen of your famous files. And it's yours, assuming you keep my girls' names out of your dirt."

The marquess had never been one to pull his punches. He said precisely what he thought, whenever he thought it—the product of holding two of the more venerable titles in the peerage—and Bourne couldn't help but admire the man for his straightforwardness. He knew what he wanted, aimed for it.

What the marquess did not know was that his eldest daughter had negotiated these precise terms the evening before. That document, whatever it was, would not require additional payment.

But Needham deserved his own punishment—punishment for ignoring Langford's behavior all those years ago. Punishment for using Falconwell on the marriage mart.

Punishment that Bourne was more than willing to mete out. "You are a fool if you think I will agree without knowing what is inside. I built my fortune on scandal, thieved it from pockets of sin. I shall be the judge of whether that document is worth my effort."

Needham opened the letter, laid it on the table, slowly. Turned it to face Bourne and held it down with one finger. Bourne couldn't help himself. He leaned forward more quickly than he would have liked, his eyes scanning the page.

Dear God.

He looked up, met Needham's knowing gaze. "It's real?"

The older man nodded once. Twice.

Bourne reread the lines. Took in the scrawl across the bottom of the paper, unmistakably Langford's, though the paper was thirty years old.

Twenty-nine.

"Why would you share this? Why give it to me?"

"You give me little choice." Needham hedged. "I like the boy . . . I kept this close at hand because I thought that Penelope would marry him eventually, and he'd require protection. Now my girls need that protection. A father does what he must. You make sure that Penelope's reputation is unblemished by this match and that the others' are worthy of decent matches, and it is yours."

Bourne turned his glass in a slow circle, watching the

way it caught the candlelight of the pub for a long moment before lifting his gaze to Needham. "I shan't wait for the girls' weddings."

Needham dipped his head, suddenly gracious. "I shall settle for betrothals."

"No. Betrothals are dangerous indeed when it comes to your daughters, I hear."

"I should walk away from you right now," Needham threatened.

"But you won't. We are strange bedfellows, you and I." He sat back in his chair, tasting victory. "I want the other daughters in town as quickly as possible. I'll get them courted. They'll not be tarnished by their sister's marriage."

"Courted by decent men," Needham qualified. "No one with half his estate in hock to The Angel."

"Get them to town. I find I am no longer willing to wait for my revenge."

Needham's gaze narrowed. "I shall regret marrying her to you."

Bourne tossed back his drink and turned the glass upside down on the wooden table. "It is unfortunate, then, that you haven't a choice."

Chapter Seven

Dear M—

I've just seen you off, and I came inside straightaway to write.

I haven't anything to say, really, nothing that every other person in Surrey hasn't already said. It seems silly to say, "I am sorry," doesn't it? Of course, everyone is sorry. It's horrible, what's happened.

I am not only sorry for your loss, however; I am sorry that we were not able to talk when you were home. I am sorry that I could not attend the funeral . . . it's a stupid rule, and I wish I had been born a male so I could have been there (I plan to have a chat with Vicar Compton regarding that idiocy). I am sorry I could not be—more of a friend.

I am here now, on the page, where girls are allowed. Please write when you have time. Or inclination.

Your friend—P
Needham Manor, April 1816

No reply

Surely there had never been a longer carriage ride than this—four interminable, deathly silent hours from Surrey to London. Penelope would rather have been trapped in a mail coach with Olivia and a collection of ladies' magazines.

She slid a glance across the wide, dark interior of the conveyance, taking in her hours-old husband, leaning back against his seat, long legs extended, eyes closed, corpse-still, and attempted to quiet her rioting thoughts, which seemed to be focused on a handful of extraordinarily disquieting things. Namely:

She was married.

Which led to,

She was the Marchioness of Bourne.

Which explained why,

She was traveling in a conveyance that was stuffed to the gills with her possessions and would soon be in London, where she would live, with her new husband.

Which brought her to,

Michael was her new husband.

Which meant,

She would share her wedding night with Michael.

Perhaps he'd kiss her again. Touch her again.

More.

One would think he'd have to, wouldn't he? If they were married. It was what husbands and wives did, after all.

She hoped.

Oh, *dear.*

The thought was enough to make her wish she had the courage to throw open the door to the carriage and toss herself right out of the vehicle.

They'd been married so quickly and so efficiently that she barely remembered the ceremony—barely remembered promising to love, comfort, honor, and obey, which was probably for the best, as the love portion of the promise was something of a lie.

He'd married her for land and nothing else.

And it did not matter that he'd touched her and made

her feel things she'd never imagined a body could feel. In the end, this was precisely the kind of marriage she'd been raised to have—a marriage of convenience. A marriage of duty. A marriage of propriety.

He'd made that more than clear.

The coach bounced over a particularly uneven bit of road, and Penelope gave a little squeak as she nearly slid off the extravagantly upholstered seat. Regaining her composure, she rearranged herself, planting both of her feet squarely on the floor of the coach and throwing a glance toward Michael, who had not moved, except to open his eyes to slits—presumably to ensure that she had not injured herself.

When he was certain that she was not in need of a surgeon, he closed his eyes once more.

He was ignoring her, his silence easy and utterly off-putting.

He couldn't even feign interest in her.

Perhaps, if she weren't so consumed by nervousness at the events of the day, she might have been able to remain quiet herself—to match him silence for silence.

Perhaps.

Penelope would never know, because she was unable to remain silent for a moment longer.

She cleared her throat, as though preparing to make a public statement. He opened his eyes and slid his gaze to her but did not move otherwise. "I think it would be best if we took this time to discuss our plan."

"Our plan?"

"The plan to ensure that my sisters have a successful season. You do recall your promise?" Her hand moved to the pocket of her traveling dress, where the coin he'd given her two nights earlier weighed heavily against her thigh.

Something she couldn't recognize played across his face. "I recall the promise."

"What is the plan?"

He stretched, his legs extending even farther across the coach. "I plan to find husbands for your sisters."

She blinked. "You mean suitors."

"If you like. I've two men in mind."

Curiosity flared. "What are they like?"

"Titled."

"And?" she prompted.

"And in the market for wives."

He was exasperating. "Do they have sound, husbandly traits?"

"In the sense that they are male and unmarried."

Her eyes went wide. He was serious. "Those are not the qualities to which I refer."

"Qualities."

"The characteristics that make for a good husband."

"You are expert in the subject, I see." He dipped his head, mocking her. "Please. Enlighten me."

She pulled herself up, ticking the items off on her fingers as she went. "Kindness. Generosity. A modicum of good humor—"

"Only a modicum of it? Ill humor on say, Tuesdays and Thursdays would be acceptable?"

Her gaze narrowed. "*Good humor,*" she repeated before pausing, then adding, "A warm smile." She couldn't resist adding, "Though, in your case, I would accept any smile at all."

He did not smile.

"Do they have these qualities?" she prodded. He did not reply. "Will my sisters like them?"

"I haven't any idea."

"Do you like them?"

"Not particularly."

"You are an obstinate man."

"Consider it one of my qualities."

He turned away, and she raised a brow in his direction. She couldn't help it. No one in her life had ever irritated her quite so much as this man. *Her husband.* Her husband, who had plucked her, without remorse, from her life. Her husband, whom she'd agreed to marry because she did not want her sisters to suffer another blow to their reputations at her hands. Her husband, who had agreed to help her. Only now did she realize that by *help,* he'd meant, arrange another loveless marriage. Or two.

She wasn't having it.

She couldn't do much, but she could make certain that Olivia and Pippa had their chance at happy marriages.

The chance she hadn't had.

"First, you don't even know if these men will have them."

"They will." He leaned back against the seat and closed his eyes once more.

"How do you know that?"

"Because they owe me a great deal of money, and I will forgive their debts in exchange for marriage."

Penelope's jaw dropped. "You will *buy* their fidelity?"

"I'm not certain that fidelity is part of the bargain."

He said it without opening his eyes—eyes that remained closed for the long minutes during which she considered the horrible words.

She leaned forward and poked him in the leg with one finger. Hard.

His eyes opened.

There was no room for triumph in her as she was too full of outrage. "No," she said, the word short and sharp in the small carriage.

"No?"

"No," she repeated. "You gave me your word that our marriage wouldn't ruin my sisters."

"And it will not. Indeed, marriage to these men would make them quite revered in society."

"Marriage to titled men who owe you money and might not be faithful will ruin them in other ways. In the ways that matter."

One of his dark brows rose in that irritating expression she was coming to dislike. "The ways that matter?"

She would not be cowed. "Yes. The ways that matter. My sisters will not have marriages built on stupid agreements related to gaming. It's bad enough that *I* have one of those. They shall choose their husbands. They shall have marriage built on more. Built on—" She stopped, not wanting him to laugh at her.

"Built on . . . ?"

She did not speak. Would not give him the pleasure of a reply. Waited for him to press her.

Oddly, he did not. "I suppose you have a plan to capture these men with qualities?"

She didn't. Not really. "Of course I do."

"Well then?"

"You reenter society. Prove to them that our marriage was not forced."

He raised a brow. "Your dowry included *my* land. You think they will not see that I forced you into wedlock?"

She worried her lip, hating his logic. And she said the first thing that came to her mind. The first, ridiculous, utterly insane thing that came to her mind. "We must feign a love match."

He showed none of the shock that she felt at the words. "How is it—I saw you in the village square and decided to mend my wicked ways?"

In for a penny, in for a pound. "That seems—reasonable."

That brow arched once more. "Does it? You think people will believe it when the truth is that I ruined you on an abandoned estate before your father stormed the house with a rifle?"

She hesitated. "I would not call it storming."

"He fired several rounds at my house. If that isn't storming, I don't know what is."

It was a salient point. "Fair. He stormed. But that is not the story we are going to tell." She hoped the words came out emphatically even as she silently pleaded, *Please, say it isn't.* "If they're to have a chance at real marriages, they need this. You gave me your word. Your *marker*."

He was silent for a long while, and she thought he might refuse, offering her marriage for her sisters or nothing at all. And what would she do? What could she do now that she was beholden to him and his will—his power—as her husband?

Finally, he leaned back once more, all mockery when he said, "By all means. Devise our magical tale. I am all attention." He closed his eyes, shutting her out.

She would have given everything she held dear for a single, biting retort in that moment—for something that would have stung him as quickly and deftly as his words. Of course, nothing sprang to mind. Instead, she ignored him and plunged ahead, building the story. "Since we have known each other all our lives, we might have become reacquainted on St. Stephen's."

His eyes opened, barely. "St. Stephen's?"

"It might be best if our story began prior to the announcement that Falconwell was . . . part of my dowry." Penelope pretended to inspect a speck on her traveling cloak, hating the fullness in her throat at the words, the reminder of her true worth. "I've always liked Christmas, and the Feast of St. Stephen in Coldharbour is quite . . . festive."

"Figgy pudding and the rest, I assume?" The question was not a question at all.

"Yes. And caroling," she added.

"With small children?"

"Many of them, yes."

"It sounds like precisely the kind of thing I would attend."

She did not miss his sarcasm, but she refused to be cowed by it. She gave him a firm look and could not resist saying, "If you were ever at Falconwell for Christmas, I imagine you would enjoy it very much."

He seemed to consider responding, but he held back the words, and Penelope felt a wave of triumph course through her at the crack in his cool demeanor—a minor victory. He closed his eyes and leaned back once more. "So, there I was, feasting on St. Stephen's Day and there you were, my childhood sweetheart."

"We weren't childhood sweethearts."

"Truth is irrelevant. What is relevant is whether or not they believe it."

The logic in the words grated. "The first rule of scoundrels?"

"The first rule of gambling."

"Six of one, half a dozen of the other," she said, tartly.

"Come now, you think anyone will care to confirm the part of our tale that began during our childhood?"

"I suppose not," she grumbled.

"They won't. And besides, it's the closest thing to the truth in the entire thing."

It was?

She would be lying if she said that she had never imagined marrying him, the first boy she'd ever known, the one who made her smile and laugh as a child. But he'd never imagined it, had he? It didn't matter. Now, as she stared at the man, she was unable to find any trace of the boy she'd once known . . . the boy who might have considered her sweet.

He moved on, pulling her from her thoughts. "So, there you were, all blue-eyed and lovely, veritably glowing in the flames of the figgy pudding, and I couldn't bear another moment of my unbridled, unsaddled, suddenly unwelcome state of bachelorhood. In you, I saw my heart, my purpose, my very soul."

Penelope knew it was ridiculous, but she couldn't stop the wash of warmth that flooded her cheeks at the words, quiet and low in the close quarters of the carriage.

"That—that sounds fine."

He made a noise. She wasn't sure what it meant. "I was wearing an evergreen velvet."

"Very becoming."

She ignored him. "You had a sprig of holly in your lapel."

"A nod to the holiday spirit."

"We danced."

"A jig?"

His mocking tone pulled her out of her little fantasy, reminding her of the truth. "Possibly."

He sat up at that. "Come now, Penelope," he said, chiding, "it was mere weeks ago, and you don't remember?"

She narrowed her gaze on him. "Fine. A reel."

"Ah. Yes. Much more exciting than a jig."

He was exasperating.

"Tell me, why was I there, in Coldharbour, celebrating the Feast of St. Stephen?"

She was beginning to dislike this conversation. "I don't know."

"You know I wore a sprig of holly in my lapel . . . surely you considered my motivation in this particular story?"

She hated the way the words oozed out of him, condescending, bordering on scathing. Perhaps that was why she said, "You were here to visit your parents' graves."

He stiffened at the words, the only movement in the carriage the slight sway of their bodies with the rhythm of the wheels. "My parents' graves."

She did not back down. "Yes. You do it every year at Christmas. You leave roses on your mother's marker, dahlias on your father's."

"I do?" She looked away, out the window. "I must have an excellent connection at a nearby hothouse."

"You do. My younger sister—Philippa—grows the loveliest flowers, year-round, at Needham Manor."

He leaned forward, mocking in his whisper. "The first rule of falsehoods is that we only tell them about ourselves, darling."

She watched the spindly birch trees at the road's edge fading into the white snow beyond. "It's not a falsehood. Pippa is a horticulturalist."

There was a long silence before she looked at him again, discovering him watching her intently. "If someone were to have visited my parents' gravesites on St. Stephen's, what would they have found there?"

She could lie. But she didn't want to. As silly as it was, she wanted him to know that she'd thought of him every Christmas . . . that she'd wondered about him. That she'd cared. *Even if he hadn't bothered to.* "Roses and dahlias. Just as you leave them every year."

It was his turn to look out the window, then, and she took the opportunity to study his features, his firm jaw, the hard look in his eyes, the way his lips—lips she knew from experience were full and soft and wonderful—pressed into a straight line. He was so guarded, the tension in him so unyielding, and she wished she could shake him into emotion, into some shift in his rigid control.

There had been a time when he had been so fluid, filled with unbridled movement. But watching him, it was nearly impossible to believe that he was the same person. She would have given everything she had to know what he was thinking in that moment.

He did not look at her when he spoke. "Well, you seem to have thought of everything. I shall do my best to memorize the tale of our love at first sight. I assume we will be sharing it a great deal."

She hesitated, then, "Thank you, my lord."

He snapped his head around. "*My lord?* My my, Penelope. You intend to be something of a ceremonial wife, don't you?"

"It is expected that a wife show deference to her husband."

Michael's brows pulled together at that. "I suppose that's how you've been trained to behave."

"You forget I was to be a duchess."

"I'm sorry you had to settle for a besmirched marquessate."

"I shall endeavor to persevere," she replied, the words dry as sand. They rode in silence for a long while before she said, "You will need to return to society. For my sisters."

"You have grown rather comfortable making demands of me."

"I *married* you. I should think you could make a sacrifice

or two, considering I gave up *everything* so you could have your land."

"Your perfect marriage, you mean?"

She sat back. "It wouldn't have been perfect." He said nothing, but his keen gaze made her add quietly, "I do not doubt that it would have been more perfect than *this,* however."

Tommy wouldn't irritate her nearly as much.

They rode in silence for a long while before he said, "I shall attend the requisite functions." He was looking out the window, the portrait of boredom. "We'll start with Tottenham. He is as close to a friend as I have."

The description was discomfiting. Michael had never been one to be without friends. He had been bright and vibrant and charming and filled with life . . . and anyone who knew him as a child had loved him. *She had loved him.* He had been her dearest friend. What had happened to him? How had he become this cold dark man?

She pushed the thought aside. Viscount Tottenham was one of the most-sought-after bachelors of the *ton,* with a mother who was above reproach. "A fine choice. Does he owe you money?"

"No." Silence fell. "We will dine with him this week."

"You have an invitation?"

"Not yet."

"Then how—"

He sighed. "Let's end this before it starts, shall we? I own the most lucrative gaming hell in London. There are few men in Britain who cannot find time to speak to me."

"And what of their wives?"

"What of them?"

"You think they won't judge you?"

"I think they all want me in their beds, so they will find room for me in their drawing rooms."

Her head snapped back at the words, at their indelicacy. At the idea that he would say such a thing to his wife. At the idea that he would spend time in other wives' beds. "I think that you mistake the value of your presence in a lady's bedchamber."

He raised a brow. "I think you will feel differently after tonight."

The specter of their wedding night loomed in the words, and Penelope hated that her pulse quickened even as she wanted to spit at him. "Yes, well, however you might ensorcel the women of the *ton,* I can guarantee you that they are far more discerning in their company in public than they are in private. And you are not good enough."

She couldn't believe she'd said it. But he made her so very *angry.*

When he looked at her, there was something powerful in his gaze. Something akin to admiration. "I'm happy you've discovered the truth, wife. It's best to remove any false hope that I might be a decent man or a decent husband early in our time together." He paused, brushing a speck from his sleeve. "I don't need the women."

"Women are the gatekeepers to society. You do, in fact, need them."

"That's why I have you."

"I'm not enough."

"Why not? Aren't you the perfect English lady?"

She gritted her teeth at the description and the way it underscored her once-and-future purpose. Her utter lack of value. "I'm inches from the shelf. It's been years since I was belle of the ball."

"You're Marchioness of Bourne now. I've no doubt you'll fast become a person of interest, darling."

She narrowed her gaze on him. "I'm not your darling."

His eyes widened. "You wound me. Don't you remember St. Stephen's? Did our reel mean nothing to you?"

She would not be sorry if he fell right out the side of the carriage and rolled into a ditch. Indeed, if he did that, she would not stop to retrieve his remains.

She didn't care if Falconwell were ever returned to him.

But she cared for her sisters, and she would not allow their reputations to be clouded by that of her husband. She took a deep breath, willing herself calm. "You'll need to prove your worth again. They'll need to see it. To believe *I* see it."

He cut her a look. "My worth is three times that of most respected men of the *ton*."

She shook her head. "I mean your *value*. As a marquess. As a man."

He went still. "Anyone who knows my tale can tell you that I haven't much value as either of those things. I lost it all a decade ago. Perhaps you hadn't heard?"

The words oozed from him, all condescension, and she knew the question was rhetorical, but she would not be cowed. "I have heard." She lifted her chin to meet his gaze head-on. "And you are willing to let one foolish, childhood peccadillo cloud your image for the rest of eternity? And mine as well, now?"

He shifted, leaning toward her, all danger and threat. She held her own, refusing to sit back. To look away. "I lost it all. Hundreds of thousands of pounds' worth. On one card. It was colossal. A loss for the history books. And you call it a peccadillo?"

She swallowed. "Hundreds of thousands?"

"Give or take."

She resisted the urge to ask precisely how much was to be given or taken. "On one card?"

"One card."

"Perhaps not a peccadillo, then. But foolish, to be sure." She had no idea where the words came from, but they came nonetheless, and she knew that her choices were to brazen it through or show her fear. Miraculously, she kept her gaze steady, trained upon him.

His voice went low, almost a growl. "Did you just call me a fool?"

Her heart was pounding—so hard that she was surprised he could not hear it in the close quarters of the carriage. She waved one hand, hoping it appeared nonchalant. "It isn't the point. If we're to convince society that my sisters are worth marrying, you must prove that you're a more-than-worthy escort for them." She paused. "You need to make amends."

He was silent for a long time. Long enough for her to think she might have gone too far. "Amends."

She nodded. "I shall help you."

"Do you always negotiate so well?"

"Not at all. In fact, I never negotiate. I simply give in."

He narrowed his gaze. "You haven't given in once in three days."

She'd certainly been less biddable than usual. "Not true. I agreed to marry you, didn't I?"

"So you did."

She went warm at the words, the way they made her so very *aware* of him.

Her husband.

"What else is there?"

Confusion flared. "My lord?"

"I find I do not like the constant surprises that come from our arrangement. Let us put the cards on the table, shall we? You want a successful season for your sisters, good matches for them. You want my return to society. What else?"

"There is nothing else."

A flash of something—displeasure, maybe?—crossed his face. "If your opponent makes it impossible for you to lose, Penelope, you should wager."

"Another rule of gambling?"

"Another rule of scoundrels. One that also holds true with husbands. Doubly so with husbands like me."

Husbands like him. She wondered what that meant, but before she could ask, he pressed on. "What else, Penelope? Ask it now, or not again."

The question was so broad, so open . . . and its answers so myriad. She hesitated, her mind racing. What did she want? *Really want.*

What did she want *from him*?

More.

The word whispered through her, not simply an echo

from that evening that already seemed so far away . . . that evening that had changed everything, but an opportunity. A chance to be more than a puppet on strings for him and for her family and for society. A chance to have remarkable experiences. A remarkable life.

She met his gaze, all golds and greens. "You might not like it."

"I'm certain I shan't."

"But, as you asked . . ."

"It is my own fault, I assure you."

She pursed her lips together. "I want more than a plain, proper life as a plain, proper wife."

That seemed to set him back. "What does that mean?"

"I've spent my life as a model young lady . . . edging into a model spinster. And it was . . . *Awful*." The words surprised her. She'd never thought it awful before. She'd never imagined anything else. Until now. *Until him*. And he was offering her a chance to change it. "I want a different sort of marriage. One where I'm allowed to be more than a lady who spends her days on needlepoint and charitable works and knows little more than her husband's favorite pudding."

"I don't care if you do needlepoint or not, and if I recall correctly, the activity and you do not exactly suit."

She smiled. "An excellent start."

"If you never give a moment of your time to charity . . . I honestly can't imagine I'd care a whit."

The smile widened. "Also promising. And I assume you haven't a favorite pudding?"

"Not one of note, no." He paused, watching her. "There is more, I imagine?"

She liked the way the word sounded on his lips. The liquid curl of it. Its promise.

"I hope so. And I should like very much if you would show it to me."

His gaze darkened almost instantly to a lovely mossy green. "I am not certain I follow."

"It's quite simple, really. I want the adventure."

"Which adventure?"

"The one you promised me at Falconwell."

He leaned back, a gleam of amusement in his eyes—a gleam she recognized from their childhood. "Name your adventure, Lady Penelope."

She corrected him. "Lady Bourne, please."

There was a slight widening of his eyes. Just enough for her to see his surprise before he tilted his head. "Lady Bourne, then."

She liked the sound of the name. Even though she shouldn't. Even though he'd given her no reason to.

"I should like to see your gaming hell."

He cocked a brow. "Why?"

"It seems like it would be an adventure."

"It would indeed."

"I suppose women don't frequent the place?"

"Not women like you, no."

Women like you.

She didn't like the insinuation in the words. The implication that she was plain and boring and unlikely to do anything adventurous . . . ever. She soldiered on. "Nevertheless, I should like to go." She thought for a moment, then added, "At night."

"Why should time of day matter?"

"Events of the evening are much more adventurous. Much more *illicit.*"

"What do you know about illicitness?"

"Not much. But I feel confident that I shall be a quick study." Her heart pounded as the memory of their first night together—of the pleasure she'd felt at his hands—flashed, before she recalled the way he'd left her that evening, having ensured their marriage. She cleared her throat, suddenly unsettled. "What luck that I've a husband who can give me a tour of these dark excitements."

"What luck, indeed," he drawled. "If only your desire for adventure did not run directly counter the respectability with which you insist I cloak myself, I would happily oblige. Unfortunately, I must refuse."

Anger flared.

His offer for more had not been a real offer at all. He was willing to entertain her whims, willing to pay a price for their marriage, for Falconwell—but only the price *he* set.

He was no different than any of the others. Than her father, than her fiancé, than any of the other gentlemen who had tried to court her in the ensuing years.

And she wasn't having it.

She had accepted being forced into marriage by events she had not been able to control. She had accepted a marriage to a notorious scoundrel. But she would not be made a pawn.

Not when he so tempted her to be a player.

"It was part of our agreement. You promised me on the night I agreed to marry you. You told me I could have whatever life I wanted, whatever adventures I desired. You promised me you'd allow me to explore, that assuming the besmirched title of Marchioness of Bourne might ruin my reputation, but it would give me the world."

"That was before you insisted on my respectability." He leaned forward. "You want your sisters respectably married. Do not bet what you are not willing to lose, darling. Third rule of gambling."

"And of scoundrels," she said, irritated.

"Those as well." He watched her for a long moment, as though testing her anger. "Your problem is that you do not know what you really want. You know what you *should* want. But it's not the same as the real desire, is it?"

He was an infuriating man.

"Such pique," he said, amusement in his tone as he leaned back.

She leaned forward and said, "At least tell me about it."

"About what?"

"About your hell."

He crossed his arms over his chest. "I imagine it would be very similar to a long carriage ride with a bride with a newfound taste for adventure."

She laughed, surprised by the jest. "Not that kind of hell. Your *gaming* hell."

"What would you like to know about it?"

"I want to know everything." She smiled at him, all teeth. "You wouldn't have to tell me about it if you brought me there to experience it firsthand." The corner of his lips lifted once, just barely. She noticed. "I see you agree."

He cocked a brow. "Not entirely."

"But you'll take me, nonetheless?"

"You are dogged." He stared at her for a long time, considering his answer. Finally, he said, "I'll take you." She smiled broadly and he hastened to add, "Once."

It was enough.

"Is it very exciting?"

"If you like to gamble," he said simply, and Penelope wrinkled her nose.

"I've never gambled."

"Nonsense. You've wagered every minute we have been together. First for your sisters and today, for yourself."

She considered the words. "I suppose I have. And I've won."

"That's because I've let you win."

"I gather that does not happen at your hell?"

He gave a little huff of laughter. "No. We prefer to allow gamers to lose."

"Why?"

He cut her a look. "Because their loss is our gain."

"You mean money?"

"Money, land, jewels . . . whatever they are foolish enough to wager."

It sounded fascinating. "And it is called The Angel?"

"The Fallen Angel."

She considered the name for a long moment. "Did you name it?"

"No."

"It seems appropriate for you."

"I imagine that's why Chase chose it. It's appropriate for all of us."

"All of you?"

He sighed, opening one eye and leveling her with a look. "You are voracious."

"I prefer curious."

He sat up, fiddling with the edge of one sleeve. "There are four of us."

"And you are all . . . fallen?" The last came on a whisper.

Hazel eyes found hers in the dim carriage. "In a sense."

She considered the answer, the way he said the words with neither shame nor pride. Just simple, unbridled honesty. And she realized that there was something very tempting in the idea of his being fallen . . . of his being a scoundrel. Of his having lost everything—*hundreds of thousands of pounds!*—and gained it all back in such a short time. He'd somehow restored it all. With no help from society. With nothing but his unflagging will and his fierce commitment to his cause.

Not only tempting.

Heroic.

She met his gaze, suddenly seeing him in an entirely new light.

He shot forward, and the carriage became instantly small. "Don't do that."

She sat back, pressing away from him. "Don't do what?"

"I can see you romanticizing it. I can see you turning The Angel into something it is not. Turning *me* into something I am not."

She shook her head, unnerved by the way he had read her thoughts. "I wasn't . . ."

"Of course you were. You think I haven't seen the same look in the eyes of a dozen other women? A hundred of them? Don't do it," he said firmly. "You shall only be disappointed."

Silence fell. He uncrossed his long, booted legs and re-crossed them, one ankle over the other, before closing his eyes again. Shutting her out.

She watched him quietly, marveling at his stillness, as though they were nothing more than traveling companions, this nothing more than an ordinary carriage ride. And perhaps he was right, for there was nothing about this man that felt husbandly, and she certainly felt nothing like a wife.

Wives were more certain of their purpose, she imagined.

Not that she had felt any more certain of her purpose the last time she'd come close to becoming a wife. The last time she'd come close to marriage to a man she hadn't known.

The thought gave her pause. He was no different than the duke, this new, grown-up Michael, who was not at all the boy she'd once known. She searched his face now for some hint of her old friend, for the deep-set dimples in his cheeks, for the easy, companionable smiles, for the wide-mouthed laughter that never failed to get him into trouble.

He wasn't there.

He was replaced by this cold, hard, unyielding man who cut a wide swath through the lives of those around him and took what he wanted without care.

Her husband.

Suddenly, Penelope felt very alone—more alone than she'd ever been before—here in this carriage with this strange man, far from her parents and her sisters and Tommy and everything she'd ever known, rattling toward London and what was bound to be the strangest day of her life.

Everything had changed that morning. *Everything.*

Forevermore, her life would be thought of in two parts—before she was married, and after.

Before, there was Dolby House and Needham Manor and her family. And after, there was . . . Michael.

Michael, and no one else.

Michael, and who knew *what* else.

Michael, stranger turned husband.

An ache settled deep in her chest, sadness perhaps? No. Longing.

Married.

She took a deep breath, and it shuddered out of her, the sound rattling around the close confines of the carriage.

He opened his eyes, capturing her gaze before she could pretend to be asleep. "What is it?"

She supposed she should be touched that he even asked, but in fact, she found she could feel nothing but annoyance at his insensitive tone. Did he not understand that this was a rather complicated afternoon as far as emotions went? "You may lay claim to my life, my dowry, and my person, my lord. But I am still keeper of my thoughts, am I not?"

He stared at her for a long while, and Penelope had the distinct, uncomfortable impression that he was able to read her thoughts. "Why did you require such a large dowry?"

"I beg your pardon?"

"Why were you unmarried?"

She laughed. She couldn't help it. "Surely you are the only person in Britain who does not know the story." He did not reply, and she filled the silence with the truth. "I was the victim of the worst sort of broken engagement."

"There are 'sorts' of broken engagements?"

"Oh, yes. Mine was particularly bad. Not the breaking part . . . circumstances allowed me to call it off. But the rest . . . marriage to a woman he actually loved within a week? That was not so complimentary. It took me years to learn to ignore the whispers."

"What could people have possibly had to whisper about?"

"Namely, why I—a perfect English bride, pampered and dowered and titled and all—was unable to retain control over a duke for even one month."

"And? Why couldn't you?"

She looked away from him, unable to say the words to his face. "He was madly in love with another. It seems that love indeed conquers all. Even aristocratic marriages."

"You believe that?"

"I do. I've seen them together. They're . . ." she searched for the word. "Perfect." He did not reply, so she pushed on. "At least, I like to think so."

"Why should it matter to you?"

"It shouldn't, I suppose . . . but I like to think that if they weren't perfect together . . . if they did not love each other so very much . . . then he would not have done what he did, and . . ."

"And you would be married."

She looked at him, a wry smile on her lips. "I'm married anyway."

"But you'd have the marriage you were raised to have instead of this one, a scandal waiting to be discovered."

"I did not know it, but that one was a scandal waiting to be discovered, too." At his questioning look, she said, "The duke's sister. She was unmarried, not even out, and with child. He wanted our marriage to ensure that there was more to the House of Leighton than her scandal."

"He planned to use you to cover up the scandal? Without telling you?"

"Is that any different than using me for money? Or land?"

"Of course it's different. I didn't lie."

It was true, and for some reason, it mattered. Enough to make her realize that she would not exchange this marriage for that long-ago one.

It was growing cold in the carriage, and she adjusted her skirts, trying to leech the very last of the heat from the warming brick at her feet. The action bought time to think. "My sisters, Victoria and Valerie?" She waited for him to recall the twins. When he nodded, she continued. "They had their first season immediately following my scandal. And they suffered for it. My mother was so terrified they'd be colored by my tragedy, she urged them to take the first offers they received. Victoria was matched with an aging earl, desperate for an heir, Valerie to a viscount—handsome, but with more money than sense. I'm not sure they are happy . . .

but I don't imagine they ever expected to be—not once marriage became a real possibility." She paused, thinking. "We all knew better. We weren't raised to believe that marriage was anything more than a business arrangement, but I made it impossible for them to have more."

She kept talking, not entirely understanding why she felt she should tell him the whole story. "My marriage was to be the most calculated, the most businesslike of them all. I was to become the Duchess of Leighton. I was to keep quiet and do my husband's bidding and breed the next Duke of Leighton. And I would have done it. Happily." She lifted one shoulder in a little shrug. "The duke—he had other plans."

"You escaped."

No one had ever referred to it in such a way. She'd never admitted it, the quiet comfort that had come in the dissolution of the engagement, even as her world had come crashing down around her. She'd never wanted her mother to accuse her of being selfish. Even now, she couldn't bring herself to agree with Michael. "I'm not sure that most women would call what happened to me an escape. It's funny how a little thing like a broken engagement can change everything."

"Not so little, I imagine."

She met his gaze again, realizing that he was paying close attention to her. "No . . . I suppose not."

"How did it change you?"

"I was no longer a prize. No longer the ideal aristocratic bride." She ran her hands over her skirts, smoothing out the wrinkles that had appeared during their journey. "I was no longer perfect. Not in their eyes."

"In my experience, perfection in the eyes of society is highly overrated." He was staring at her, his hazel eyes glittering with something she could not identify.

"That's easy for you to say; you walked away from them."

He ignored the shift of focus, refused to allow the conversation to turn to him. "All those things—everything you just said—that's how your broken engagement changed you for *them*. How did it change *you*, Penelope?"

The question gave her pause. In the years since the Duke of Leighton had caused the scandal of the ages and destroyed any chance of Penelope's becoming his duchess, she'd never once asked herself how it had changed her.

But now, as she looked across the carriage at her new husband—a man she'd approached in the dead of night and whom she'd wed only days later—the truth whispered through her.

It had made happiness a possibility.

She swallowed back the thought, and he leaned forward quickly, almost eager. "There. There—you just answered the question."

"I—" She stopped.

"Say it."

"It doesn't matter anymore."

"Anymore. Because of me?"

I was never destined to have what they have. She considered her words carefully. "It made me realize that marriage did not have to be an arrangement. The duke—he loves his wife madly. Their marriage . . . there is nothing quiet and sedate about it."

"And you wanted that?"

Only once I knew it was an option.

But it hadn't mattered.

She gave a little shrug. "It doesn't matter what I wanted, does it? I've got my marriage now."

Her teeth chattered on the last, and he muttered his disapproval at the sound, shifting and moving across the carriage to sit next to her. "You're cold." He wrapped one long arm around her shoulders, pulling her close to him, his heat pouring off of him in waves. "Here," he added, pulling a traveling blanket around them, "this will help."

She huddled against him, trying not to remember the last time she was this close to him. "It seems you are always sharing your blankets with me, my lord."

"Bourne," he corrected, cocooning them tightly together

in the rough wool, the words a rumble beneath her ear. "And it is either share my blankets or have you steal them."

She couldn't help it. She laughed.

They rode in silence for a long while before he spoke again. "So, all these years, you've been waiting for a happy marriage."

"I don't know if *waiting* is the word I would use. Hoping, more like." He did not reply, and she fiddled with the button of his coat.

"And your fiancé, the one from whom I stole you, would he have given it to you?"

Maybe.

Maybe not.

She should tell him the truth about Tommy. That they were never honestly engaged. But something held her back.

"It's not worth thinking about it now. But I won't be blamed for two more unhappy marriages. I don't fool myself into thinking that my sisters could find love, but they could be happy, couldn't they? They could find someone who suits them . . . or perhaps that's too much to ask?"

"I don't know, honestly," he said, one hand slipping around her, pulling her close as the carriage rattled onto the bridge that would take them over the Thames and into London. "I am not the kind of man who understands how people suit."

She should not enjoy the feel of his arm around her, but she could not help leaning into his warmth, pretending, for a fleeting moment, that this quiet conversation was the first of many. His hand was sliding slowly up and down her arm, transferring heat—and something more wonderful—to her with each lovely, warm stroke. "Pippa is virtually engaged to Lord Castleton; we expect he'll propose within a matter of days of her return to London."

His hand stilled for a moment before continuing its long, slow slide. "How did she and Castleton come to know each other?"

She thought of the plain, uninspiring earl. "The same way

it happens with anyone, really. Balls, dinners, dancing. He seems nice enough, but . . . I do not care for the idea of him with Pippa."

"Why not?"

"Some would say she's peculiar, but she's not. She's simply bookish, loves the sciences. She is fascinated by how things work. He doesn't seem to be able to keep up with her. But, honestly? I don't think she gives a fig one way or another about whether or whom she marries. As long as he has a library and a few dogs, she'll make a happiness of sorts for herself. I only wish she could find someone more . . . well, I hate to sound cruel, but . . . intelligent. "

"Mmm." Michael was noncommittal. "And your other sister?"

"Olivia," she replied, "is very beautiful."

"Then it sounds like she will suit most men quite well."

Penelope sat up. "It's that simple?"

He met her gaze. "Beauty helps."

Penelope was never going to be considered beautiful. Plain, yes. Passable, even, on a good day, in a new frock. But never beautiful. Even when she was set to become Duchess of Leighton, she wasn't beautiful. She was just . . . ideal.

She loathed the honesty in Michael's words.

No one liked to be reminded that she was outvalued by a prettier lady.

"Well, Olivia is beautiful, and she knows it—"

"She sounds delightful."

She ignored his wry tone. "—and she will need a man who treats her very very well. Who has a great deal of money and does not mind spending it to spoil her."

"That sounds like the very opposite of what Olivia needs."

"It's not. You'll see."

Silence fell, and she did not mind, instead turning into his warmth, loving the way he felt against her, the heat of him making the carriage infinitely more comfortable. Just as the rocking motion of the coach was about to lull her to sleep, he spoke. "And you?"

Her eyes flew open. "Me?"

"Yes. You. What kind of man would suit you?"

She watched the way the blanket rose and fell against his chest as he breathed, the long, even movements calming her in a strange way.

I would like for you to suit me.

He was her husband, after all. It was only natural for her to imagine that he might be more than a fleeting companion. More than an acquaintance. More of a friend. More than the cold, hard man she'd come to expect him to be. She did not mind this Michael, the one next to her, warming her, talking to her.

Of course, she did not say any of those things. Instead, she said, "It doesn't matter much anymore, does it?"

"If it did?" He was not going to let her avoid the question.

Whether because of the warmth or the quiet or the journey or the man, she answered. "I suppose I should like someone interesting—someone kind—someone who is willing to show me . . ."

How to live.

She couldn't say *that.* He would laugh her out of the carriage. "Someone to dance with—someone to laugh with—someone to care about."

Someone who would care about me.

"Someone like your fiancé?"

She thought of Tommy, considered for a fleeting moment telling Michael that the unidentified man to whom he referred was the friend they'd known all their lives. *The son of the man who took everything from him.* But she didn't want to upset him, not while they were quiet and warm, and she could pretend they enjoyed each other's company.

So instead she whispered, "I should like for it to be someone like my husband."

He was silent for a long time, long enough for her to wonder if he'd heard her. When she risked peering up at him through her lashes, she found that he was staring at her with an unsettling intent, his hazel eyes nearly golden in the fading light.

For one, fleeting moment, she thought he might kiss her.

She wished he would kiss her.

A flush spread high on her cheeks at the thought, and she turned away quickly, returning her head to his chest, closing her eyes tightly, and willing the moment gone—along with her silliness.

It wouldn't be so bad if they did suit.

Chapter Eight

Dear M—

Just a quick note today to tell you that we are all thinking of you, me most of all. I asked my father if we could come to Eton for a visit, and of course he told me that it wouldn't be appropriate, as we are not family. It's silly, really. You've always felt as much like family as some of my sisters. Definitely more like family than my Aunt Hester.

Tommy will be home for his summer holiday. I am crossing my fingers that you will join us.

Ever—P
Needham Manor, May 1816

No reply

On the evening of his wedding, Bourne exited his town house almost immediately after depositing his new wife inside and headed for The Fallen Angel.

He would be lying if he said that he didn't feel like something of an ass in leaving her so summarily, in a new home with a new staff and nothing familiar, but he had a single, immovable goal, and the faster he reached it, the better they all would be.

He would send the announcement of their marriage to the *Times*, get the young ladies Marbury matched, and have his revenge.

He did not have time for his new wife.

He certainly did not have time for her quiet smiles and her quick tongue and the way she reminded him of everything that he had lost. Of everything on which he'd turned his back.

There was no room in his life for them to talk. No room to be interested in what she had to say. No room to find her entertaining or to care even a bit about how she felt about her sisters or how she had coped with her broken engagement, now years behind her.

And there was definitely no room for him to wish to murder the man who had broken that engagement and made her doubt herself and her worth.

It did not matter that she put flowers on his parents' graves at Christmas.

Maintaining a distance from her was essential—it was distance that would establish the parameters of their marriage, namely, that he would retain his life, and she would build her own, and while they would see her sisters matched together, it was for their individual reasons.

So, he left her sleepy-eyed and wrinkled in her traveling cloak and headed to The Angel, doing his best to ignore the fact that she was alone on her wedding night, and that he'd likely suffer extra torture in hell for leaving her there.

Four hours in a coach, and he was already too soft with her.

He breathed deep, enjoying the frigid dampness in the evening air, yellow with thick January fog as he navigated through Mayfair to Regent Street, where a handful of peddlers remained in the waning light, rising up out of the mist only when they were an arm's length away. They did not speak to him, their well-honed instincts telling them that he was not in the market for what they were selling. Instead, they faded away as quickly as they appeared, and Bourne made his way to the great stone building atop St. James's.

The club was not open yet, and when he slipped through the owners' entrance and onto the pit floor, he was grateful for the lack of company in the cavernous room. There were lanterns lit around the floor, and a handful of maids were completing the day's work—scrubbing at carpet, polishing sconces, and dusting the framed art on the walls.

Bourne crossed to the center of the pit floor, stopping there for a long moment to take in this place—the place that had been home for the last five years.

Most afternoons, he was the first of the owners to arrive at The Fallen Angel and he liked it that way. He enjoyed the quiet of the pit at that hour, the silent moments before the dealers arrived to check the weight of the dice, the oil on the wheels, the slickness of the cards, preparing for the mass of humanity that would descend like locusts and fill the room with shouts and laughter and chatter.

He liked the club empty of all but possibility.

All but temptation.

He reached into the pocket of his waistcoat, feeling for the talisman that was always there, the coin that reminded him that it was temptation and nothing else that kept these tables full.

That it was temptation that ruined.

That one did not risk what one could not afford to lose.

The coin was gone. Another reminder of his unwanted wife.

He moved to the roulette table, brushing his fingers across the heavy silver handle of the wheel, spinning it, running the colors together, all speed and luxury, as he reached for the ivory ball on which so many hopes had been pinned—and lost. With a practiced flick of his wrist, he sent the ball spinning into the well, loving the sound of bone on metal, the way it shivered over him, all smoothness and sin.

Red.

The whisper echoed through him, unbidden, unstoppable. Unsurprising.

He turned away before the wheel slowed, before gravity and providence pulled the ball into its seat.

"You're back."

On the other side of the room, silhouetted by the open door to the bookkeeper's suite, stood Cross, the fourth partner in The Fallen Angel. Cross handled the club's finances, ensuring every penny that came through the door to the hell was well accounted for. He was a genius with numbers, but he neither looked nor lived like the unparalleled man of finance he was. He was tall, a half a foot taller than Michael, even taller than Temple. But where Temple was the size of a small house, Cross was long and slim, all angles and sinew. Bourne rarely saw him eat, and if the dark hollows beneath his eyes were any indication, it had been a day or two since the other man had slept.

"You're here early."

Cross rubbed one hand over his unshaven jaw at the words. "Late, really." He moved aside, allowing a beautiful woman to exit the room behind him. She flashed Bourne a shy smile before pulling the enormous hood of her cloak up to shield her face.

Bourne watched as the woman hurried to the entrance of the club, letting herself out with barely a sound, before he met Cross's gaze. "I see you were working very hard."

One side of Cross's mouth rose at the words. "She's good with the books."

"I imagine she is."

"We weren't expecting you back so quickly."

He hadn't expected to be back so quickly. "Things took a bit of a turn."

"For better or worse?"

The echo of the marriage vows he'd spoken with Penelope set Bourne on edge. "It depends on your view of the situation."

"I see."

"I doubt you do."

"Falconwell?"

"Mine."

"Did you marry the girl?"

"I did."

Cross let out a long, low whistle. Bourne couldn't agree more.

"Where is she?"

Too near. "At the town house."

"*Your* town house?"

"I did not think it appropriate for me to bring her here."

Cross was silent for a long while. "I confess, I am eager to meet this woman who looked into the face of marriage with cold, hard Bourne and did not run away."

She hadn't had a choice.

There was no way that she would have gone through with a wedding to him if he hadn't forced her to the parish vicar. If she'd had more time to think it through. He was everything that she was not, coarse and angry, with no hope of ever returning to the world into which he'd been born. Into which *she'd* been born.

Penelope . . . she was proper and perfectly bred for a life in that world. This world—filled with gaming and drink and sex and worse—it would scare her to death. *He* would scare her to death.

But she'd asked to see it.

And so he would show it to her.

Because he could not resist the temptation of her corruption. It was too compelling. Too sweet.

She didn't know what she asked. She thought adventure was a late-night walk in the woods surrounding her childhood home. The main floor of The Angel on any given night would send her into hysterics.

"The turn?" Cross said, leaning against the wall, arms crossed over his chest. "You said it did not go as planned."

"I agreed to match her sisters as well."

Cross's brows rose. "How many of them?"

"Two. Easy enough, I think." He met Cross's serious grey gaze. "You should know it was a love match. We married this morning. I couldn't bear being apart from her a moment longer."

A beat passed as Cross heard the lie. Understood its meaning. "Since you are so very much in love."

"Precisely."

"This morning," Cross tested the words. Bourne turned away and placed his hands flat on the roulette table, pressing them firmly into the plush green baize. Knowing what was to come even before the words were spoken. "You left her alone on your wedding night."

"I did."

"Is she horsefaced?"

No.

When she was in the throes of passion, she was stunning. He wanted to lay her down on his bed and make her his. The memory of her writhing against him in Falconwell Manor had him shifting to accommodate the way his breeches tightened against him.

He scrubbed one hand across his face at the lie. "I need some time in the ring with Temple."

"Ah. I see that she is."

"She's not."

"Then perhaps you should return home and consummate your marriage to this woman whom you love so very passionately. Lord knows it's a more pleasurable experience than having Temple serve you your ass in the ring."

Even if you deserve the pounding.

For a fleeting moment, Bourne considered the words. Played out the events that would occur if he returned home and sought out his innocent new wife. Imagined what it would be like to lay her down on his bed and stake his claim, to make her his. *To show her the adventure she did not even know she had requested.* Her silken hair would cling to the rough stubble on his chin, her full lips would part on a sigh as he stroked her soft skin, and she would cry out at the pleasure he wrung from her.

It was a wicked, wonderful temptation.

But she would not take the experience as it was given. She would ask him for more. More than he was willing to give.

His gaze returned to the roulette wheel, drawn, inexorably, to where the little white ball had found its seat.

Black.

Of course.

He turned back. "There is more."

"There always is."

"I agreed to return to society."

"Good God. Why?"

"The sisters need to be matched."

Cross swore, amazement in the single, vicious word. "Needham negotiated your reentry? Brilliant."

Bourne did not tell the truth—that it had been his wife who had negotiated the terms first. Most successfully. Instead, he said, "He has information that will ruin Langford."

Cross's eyes widened. "How is that possible?"

"We weren't looking in the right place."

"Are you sure it—"

"It will destroy him."

"And Needham will give it to you when the daughters are matched?"

"Shouldn't take long; apparently one of them is halfway to the altar with Castleton."

Cross's brows rose. "Castleton is a dimwit."

One of Bourne's shoulders lifted in a noncommittal shrug. "He's not the first aristocrat to marry a woman above his intelligence. Won't be the last, either."

"Would you let your unmarried sister marry him?"

"I don't have an unmarried sister."

"It sounds to me like you have two of them now."

Bourne heard the censure in the words . . . knew what

Cross was saying. Knew that marriage to Castleton would condemn any woman with a brain in her head to a lifetime of boredom.

And Penelope would suffer knowing that another one of her sisters had made a bad match. *I don't fool myself into thinking that they could find love. But they could be happy, couldn't they?*

He ignored the echo. "It's virtually done. It gets me one step closer to Langford. I'm not about to stop it. Besides, most women of the aristocracy have to suffer their husbands."

Cross raised a brow. "You have to admit . . . marriage to Castleton would be something of a trial. Particularly for a young lady hoping for say, conversation. You should introduce her to someone else. Someone with a thought in his head."

Bourne raised a brow. "Are you offering your services?"

Cross cut him a look. "Surely there is someone."

"Why look for someone else when Castleton is here, and ready?"

"You're a cold bastard."

"I do what it takes. Perhaps you're growing soft."

"And you're hard as you've ever been." When Bourne did not reply, he pressed on. "You may get some of the invitations without help, but for the rest—for a true return to society—you're going to need Chase. It's the only way you'll unlock all the doors you require."

Bourne nodded once, standing straight, taking a deep breath and adjusting the sleeves of his frock coat carefully. "Well, then I ought to find Chase." He met Cross's grey gaze. "You'll start putting it out that . . ."

Cross nodded. "You've been laid low by love."

There was a heartbeat of hesitation before Bourne nodded.

Cross saw it. "You shall have to do better than that if you want anyone to believe you." Bourne turned away, ignoring the words until Cross called him back. "And one other thing. If your revenge relies upon your marriage and your pristine reputation, you'll want to secure them both quickly."

Bourne's brows snapped together. "What are you saying?"

Cross smirked. "I'm merely suggesting you ensure that your wife hasn't grounds for annulment. Take the woman to bed, Bourne. Quickly."

Bourne did not have a chance to reply, as there was a sudden commotion in the main entryway to the club, beyond a wide oak door that stood half-open. "I don't give a damn that I'm not a member. You'll let me see him, or I shall make it my life's purpose to destroy this place . . . and you with it."

Bourne met Cross's gaze, and the taller man said casually, "Have you ever noticed that it's always the same promise, but never from one powerful enough to deliver?"

"Did your companion have a husband by chance?"

Cross went stone-faced. "That is one puddle in which I do not play."

"Not for you, then." Bourne headed for the door, pushing it open to find Bruno and Asriel, two of the door-men of the hell, holding a man of average height and average build face-first against the wall. "Gentlemen," he drawled. "What have you found?"

Asriel turned to him. "He's after you."

At the words, the man began to fight in earnest. "Bourne! You'll see me now, or you'll see me at dawn."

He recognized the voice.

Tommy.

It had been nine years since the last time he'd seen Tommy Alles, since the night his father had taken everything that Bourne had, with pleasure. Since Tommy had chosen his inheritance—*Bourne's inheritance*—over his friend.

Nine years, and still the hot betrayal coursed through him at the way his *friend* had turned his back. At the way he had been so complicit in his father's actions.

"Do not for one moment imagine that I would not gleefully meet you at dawn," he said. "Indeed, I would think very carefully before making the offer if I were you."

Tommy turned his head against the velvet-covered wall, facing Bourne. "Call off your dogs."

Asriel growled deep in his throat, and Bruno thumped Tommy into the wall. At his grunt, Bourne said, "Careful now, they do not take well to bad manners."

One arm went high between his shoulders, and Tommy winced. "This isn't their battle. It's yours."

Needham had likely warned Tommy of Bourne's plans and their arrangement. There could be nothing else that would bring Langford's son here to face Bourne and his anger. "What you seek is not here."

"I hope to hell she isn't."

She.

And with that single word, it all fell into place.

Tommy hadn't come for Needham's document. Likely didn't even know it existed.

He had come for Penelope.

He had come for Falconwell.

"Let him go."

Once released, Tommy shrugged back into his coat and cast a loathing glance at the two men. "Thank you." Bruno and Asriel stepped back but did not leave the small space, ready to leap to their employer's aid should he need them.

Bourne spoke first. "I shall be very clear. I married Penelope this morning and, in doing so, made Falconwell mine. Neither you nor your father will touch it. Indeed, if I discover that either of you ever sets foot on the land again, I'll have you arrested for trespassing."

Tommy wiped one hand across a swollen lip and laughed, the sound hollow and humorless. "You think I didn't know you'd come for it? I knew you'd do whatever was required to reclaim it the second it was out of my father's hands. Why do you think I tried to marry her first?"

The words echoed through the small room, and Bourne was grateful for the dim light that hid his surprise.

Tommy was the fiancé.

He should have seen it, of course. Should have imagined that Thomas Alles was still in Penelope's world. In her life.

Should have expected that he would have angled for Falconwell the moment it was removed from his inheritance.

So he'd proposed to her, and she'd accepted, foolish girl, likely thinking that she loved him—the boy to whom she'd been a friend for so long. Wasn't that what silly girls dreamed? To marry the boy they'd known since childhood? The simple, friendly companion, the safe friend who never demanded anything but laughter?

"Still bound by Papa's purse strings, Tom? Had to run off and marry a girl to get yourself an estate? *My estate?*"

"It hasn't been yours for a decade," Tommy spat. "And you don't deserve it. You don't deserve her."

A memory flashed. He, Tommy, and Penelope in a little boat on the middle of the lake at Falconwell, Tommy standing precariously on the bow of the craft, professing to be a great sea captain, Penelope laughing, her blond hair shining gold in the afternoon sunlight, all her attention on the other boy.

Watching her, Bourne had grasped the sides of the rowboat, rocking it once, twice, three times, and Tommy had lost his footing and fallen into the lake with a shout. *Tommy!* Penelope had cried, rushing to the edge of the boat as the boy came to the surface, laughing and gasping for air. She'd looked back, censure in her gaze, all her focus on Bourne. *That was unkind.*

He extinguished the memory, returning his attention to the present day, to toppling Tommy once more. He should be pleased that he'd snatched one more thing from Tommy's grasp, but it was not pleasure that coursed through him; it was fury.

Fury that Tommy had nearly had what was Bourne's. Falconwell. *Penelope.* His gaze narrowed. "Nonetheless, both the land and the lady are mine. You and your father are too late."

Tommy took a step toward him, coming up to his full height, a match for Bourne. "This has nothing to do with Langford."

"Don't fool yourself. This has everything to do with Langford. You think he did not expect me to come after Falconwell the moment Needham won it? Of course he did. And he must also know that I will not stop until I've ruined him." He paused, considering this man who had once been his friend. "And ruined you, in the process."

Something flashed in Tommy's gaze, something close to understanding. "You will take pleasure in it, I have no doubt. Pleasure in destroying her, as well."

Bourne crossed his arms over his chest. "My goals are clear—Falconwell and revenge on your father. That you and Penelope stand in the way of those things is unfortunate indeed."

"I shan't let you hurt her."

"How noble of you. What will you do, ferret her away? Guinevere to your Lancelot? Tell me, was he born on the wrong side of the blanket as well?"

Tommy went still at the words. "So that is your plan; you destroy my father by destroying me."

Bourne raised a brow. "His legacy for mine. His son for my father's."

"You've a faulty memory if you think he ever thought of me as a son of his heart." The words rang true—in all of their youth, Langford had never had a kind word for Tommy. He'd been a cold, hard man.

Bourne no longer cared. "It matters not what he thought. What matters is what the world thinks. Without you, he has nothing."

Tommy rocked back on one heel, his jaw setting square, a quiet echo of the boy he'd once been. "You're a scoundrel; I'm a gentleman. They'll never believe you."

"They will when I show them proof."

Tommy's brows knitted together. "There is no proof."

"You are welcome to test that theory."

Tommy's jaw clenched and he took a step forward, anger propelling him toward Bourne, who dodged the blow before Bruno came out of the darkness to stay the inevitable brawl.

The men stared down the bodyguard's massive arms at each other. "What do you want from me?" Tommy asked.

"There is nothing you have that I want." Bourne paused, letting the silence taunt his foe. "I've Falconwell and revenge and Penelope. And you've nothing."

"She was mine before she was yours," Tommy said, anger in his tone. "All those years without you . . . she still had me. And when she sees who you are . . . what you've become . . . she will turn to me again."

Bourne loathed the idea that Tommy and Penelope had remained friends, even after Bourne had lost everything, even after he'd been unable to return to Surrey and resume his place—the third point of their triangle. "You're a brave man to threaten me." He looked to Bruno. "See him out."

Tommy pulled out of the large man's grasp. "I can see myself out." He crossed to the exterior door, hovering there for the briefest of seconds before turning back to meet Bourne's gaze. "Return her to Surrey, Michael. Leave her alone. Before you destroy her with your anger and your vengeance."

He wanted to reject the premise. But he was not a fool. He would destroy her, of course. He would, because it was what he did. "If I were you, I would worry less about protecting my wife and more about protecting your name. Because when I am through with your father, you won't be able to show your face in London."

When Tommy replied, there was steel in his tone—conviction that Michael did not recognize from the boy he'd once known. "I don't fool myself into believing that I can protect myself from the scandal you plan to unleash, but I shall do everything I can to fight you—everything I can to protect Penelope. To remind her that there was a time when her friends would have done anything to keep her from harm."

Bourne raised a brow. "It appears you failed in that, didn't you?"

Regret flashed quick and unguarded on Tommy's face. "I did. But it was never supposed to be my role."

If he'd allowed it, the words would have stung. Instead, he mocked, "Take comfort, Tom, at least she will not have to deal with your scandal when I release it to the papers."

Tommy turned back, his knowing gaze finding Bourne's in the darkness before he spoke his parting words. "No, she won't have the scandal on her head . . . but she will have the regret of marrying you. Do not doubt that."

He did not doubt it in the slightest.

The heavy door closed behind Tommy, and Bourne turned away from the sound, anger and irritation and something else—something he did not wish to define—coursing through him.

Chapter Nine

Dear M—

I am writing to you from a carriage, where I have spent the last six days with all four of my sisters and my mother trundling through the North Country to visit Aunt Hester (whom you will remember from my last letter). I cannot imagine what would have possessed the Romans to continue their march north to build Hadrian's Wall. They must not have had sisters, or they would not have made it through Tuscany.

Yrs, persevering—P
Somewhere on the Great North Road, June 1816

No reply

He'd left her.

It had taken a quarter of an hour for Penelope to come to her senses, standing there in the entryway of Michael's London home, along with several piles of her belongings.

He'd left her, summarily, with a simple, "Good-bye."

She stared at the massive oak door through which he had departed for longer than she cared to admit, struggling with several key truths.

He had left her.

On her first night at his London home.

Without even introducing her to the staff before leaving.

On their wedding night.

She did not want to think too carefully about that bit.

Instead, she focused on the fact that she was standing like a fool in the foyer of her husband's town house, with no companions but two very young-looking footmen who seemed uncertain of their exact role in such an event. Penelope wasn't certain if she should take comfort in the idea that they were not often met with solitary females in this town house, or if she should be offended that they had not thought to put her in a receiving room while they devised a plan for her.

She forced a smile and addressed the older of the two—who could not have been more than fifteen—desperate to soldier on. "I assume the house has a housekeeper?"

She watched a wave of relief flood the young man and felt a bit envious. She wished she knew how to behave in this situation. "Yes, m'lady."

"Excellent. Perhaps you could fetch her?"

The footman bowed once, then again, obviously eager to do his best. "Yes, m'lady. As you wish, m'lady." He was off like a flash, his counterpart growing more and more uncomfortable by the minute.

She knew the feeling.

But just because she was in a state of complete uncertainty did not mean the poor boy standing in front of her was required to suffer as well. "You needn't remain here," she said with a little, encouraging smile, "I'm sure the housekeeper will be along presently."

The footman—far too young to be a footman, frankly—mumbled an agreement and disappeared, nearly instantly.

Penelope let out a long breath and considered the entryway of the town house, all marble and gilt, the height of fashion and expense—a touch too extravagant for her tastes, but she instantly understood the décor.

Michael might have lost everything in a now-infamous game of chance, but he'd earned it back twentyfold; anyone entering his home would see that.

Something clenched in her chest at the thought of the young marquess working so hard to restore his fortunes. What strength it must have taken . . . what commitment.

It was a shame he did not have the same commitment to his wife.

She pushed the thought aside, confronting the massive trunk that had arrived along with their carriage that evening. Well, if she wasn't to be put in a room, she might as well make herself comfortable. She unbuttoned her traveling cloak and sat on the luggage, wondering if, perhaps, she was to live here . . . in the foyer.

A commotion began at the back of the house . . . a smattering of fevered whispers punctuated by the clattering of footsteps, and Penelope could not help but smile at the sound. It seemed that none of the servants had been apprised of their master's taking a bride. She supposed she should not be surprised, as she herself had not expected such a thing until two days prior.

But she could not help but be slightly annoyed at her husband.

He could have at least taken a moment to introduce her to the housekeeper before heading off to whatever important business called to him at this point in the day.

On the day of his marriage.

She sighed, hearing the impatience and the irritation in the sound. Knowing that ladies did not display irritation.

She could only hope that the rule was not so steadfast if one was married to a fallen aristocrat.

Surely there was possibility for interpretation when one was sitting in one's new home, waiting to be shown to a room. Any room.

She inspected the palm of one glove and wondered how Michael might respond if he returned, hours from now, to discover her seated on a trunk, waiting for him.

The image of him, surprise in his eyes, made her chuckle.

It might be worth it. She shifted, ignoring the pain in her backside.

Marchionesses most certainly did not think of discomfort in their backsides.

"My lady?"

Penelope shot to her feet, spinning toward the words, tentative and curious, spoken from behind her, by the most beautiful woman she'd ever seen.

It did not matter that she wore a simple uniform—identifiable in any home across Britain as a housekeeper's frock—or that her flaming red hair was pulled back tightly into a neat, perfect knot. This woman, young and lithe, with the largest, most beautiful blue eyes Penelope had ever seen, was stunning.

Like a painting by a Dutch master.

Like no servant Penelope had ever seen.

And she lived in Michael's house.

"I—" She began, then stopped, realizing that she was staring. She shook her head, "I—yes?"

The housekeeper gave no indication that she had even noticed the odd behavior, instead coming forward and dropping into a curtsy. "I apologize for not greeting you immediately upon your arrival. But we didn't—" It was her turn to stop.

We didn't expect you. Penelope heard the words even as they weren't spoken.

The housekeeper tried again, "Bourne didn't—"

Bourne.

Not Lord Bourne. Just Bourne.

Emotion flared, hot and unfamiliar. *Jealousy.*

"I understand. Lord Bourne has been very busy for the past few days." She lingered on his title, noting the understanding in the other woman's gaze. "You are the housekeeper, I assume?"

The beautiful woman flashed a small smile and dipped another curtsy. "Mrs. Worth."

Penelope wondered if Mrs. Worth was married, or if the woman had come by the title with her position. The thought of Michael with a stunning, young, unmarried housekeeper did not sit well.

"Would you like to see the house? Or meet the staff?" Mrs. Worth seemed uncertain of what came next.

"I should like to see my rooms for now," Penelope said, taking pity on the other woman, who was certainly as surprised by her master's marriage as Penelope was. "We traveled much of the day."

"Of course." Mrs. Worth nodded, leading the way to the wide staircase that rose to what Penelope assumed were the private quarters of the house. "I'll have the boys bring your trunks up immediately."

As they climbed the stairs, Penelope could not help herself. "Is your husband also in the employ of Lord Bourne?"

There was a long pause before the housekeeper answered, "No, my lady."

Penelope knew that she should not press. "A nearby home, then?"

Another pause. "I have no husband."

Penelope resisted the unpleasant jealousy that flared with the pronouncement . . . and the urge to ask more questions of the beautiful housekeeper.

Mrs. Worth had already turned away, calmly opening the door to a dimly lit bedchamber. "We will start a fire immediately, of course, my lady." She moved forward with purpose, lighting candles around the room, slowly revealing a cozy, well-appointed bedchamber outfitted in lovely greens and blues. "And I shall have a tray made for you. You must be hungry." When she had completed her task, she turned back to Penelope. "We don't have a lady's maid on staff, but I would be happy to . . ." She trailed off.

Penelope shook her head. "My maid cannot be far behind."

Relief flashed across the other woman's face, and she

dipped her head in acquiescence. Penelope watched her carefully, fascinated by this beautiful creature who seemed to be both competent servant and not servant at all.

"How long have you been here?"

Mrs. Worth's head snapped up, her eyes finding Penelope instantly. "With Bou—" She stopped, catching herself. "With Lord Bourne?" Penelope nodded. "Two years."

"You're very young to be a housekeeper."

Mrs. Worth's gaze grew guarded. "I was very lucky that Lord Bourne found room for me here."

A dozen questions flashed through Penelope's mind, and it took all her energy to hold herself back from asking them—from uncovering the truth about this beautiful woman and how she had come to live with Michael.

But now was not the time, no matter how curious she was.

Instead, she reached up and unpinned her hat, moving to a nearby dressing table to set it down. Turning back, she dismissed the housekeeper. "My trunks and supper sound lovely. And a bath, please."

"As you wish, my lady." Mrs. Worth was gone instantly, leaving Penelope alone.

Taking a deep breath, Penelope turned in a slow circle, considering the room. It was beautiful—lushly appointed with silks on the walls and an enormous rug that had to have come from the East. The art was tasteful and the furniture perfectly wrought. There was a fire in the hearth, but the chill and the lingering smell of smoke on the air proved that the house had been unprepared for her arrival.

She crossed to the washbasin, set by a window that overlooked a wide, extravagant garden, poured water into the bowl, and set her hands to the white porcelain, watching as the water distorted their color and shape, giving them the appearance of being broken and unhinged. She took a deep breath, focusing on the place where the cool liquid gave way to the air of the room.

When the door opened, Penelope leapt back from the basin, nearly toppling the stand and splattering water on herself and the carpet. She turned to face a young girl—no older than thirteen or fourteen—who entered with a quick curtsy. "I've come to set the fire, milady."

Penelope watched as the girl crouched low with a tinderbox, and a vision flashed of Michael, only days earlier, in the same position at Falconwell. The kindling caught fire, and Penelope's cheeks heated as she remembered all that came that evening . . . and the morning after. The memory brought with it a pang of regret.

Regret that he was not there.

The girl stood, facing Penelope with her head dropped low. "Is there anything else you need?"

Curiosity flared again. "What is your name?"

The girl's head snapped up. "My—my name?"

Penelope tried for a comforting smile. "If you care to share it."

"Alice."

"How old are you, Alice?"

She dipped a half curtsy again. "Fourteen, milady."

"And how long have you worked here?"

"At Hell House, you mean?"

Penelope's eyes went wide. "*Hell House?*"

Dear Lord.

"Yes'm." The little maid rushed to answer, as though it were a perfectly reasonable name for a house. "Three years. My brother and me needed jobs after our parents . . ." She trailed off, but Penelope had no difficulty filling in the rest.

"Your brother works here as well?"

"Yes'm. He's a footman."

Which explained the unexpected youth of the footmen.

Alice looked extraordinarily nervous. "Is there anything else you'll be needing from me?"

Penelope shook her head. "Not tonight, Alice."

"Thank you, mum." She turned for the door and had almost reached freedom when Penelope called her back.

"Oh, there is one thing." The girl turned back, wide-eyed and waiting. "Could you tell me where the master's chamber is?"

"You mean, Bourne's rooms?"

There it was again. Bourne.

"Yes."

"Most of us use the next door down the hallway, but you've a door direct," Alice said, pointing at a door at the far end of the room, nearly tucked away behind the dressing screen.

A door direct.

Penelope's heart began to beat a bit faster. "I see."

Of course she'd have a direct passage to her husband's rooms.

He was, after all, her husband.

Perhaps he'd use it.

Something shimmered through her, something that she could not identify. Fear, possibly.

Excitement.

Adventure.

"I'm certain he won't mind you being in here, milady. He does not often sleep here."

Penelope felt heat wash over her cheeks again. "I see," she repeated. He slept somewhere else. *With someone else.*

"Good night, m'lady."

"Good night, Alice."

The girl was gone then, and Penelope stood staring at that door, unbearably curious about what was behind it. The curiosity remained as her trunks arrived, followed by her supper—a simple, sumptuous meal of fresh bread and cheese, warm ham, and lovely, rich chutney. It gnawed at her while she ate, and as her newly arrived maid unpacked her most vital pieces of clothing, and while the boys who had brought her trunks filled her bath, and while she bathed, and dried, and dressed, and tried desperately to write a letter to her cousin Catherine.

When the clock struck midnight, and she realized that her wedding day—and wedding night—had come and gone, the curiosity about what was behind that door turned into disappointment.

And then irritation. Her gaze was drawn to the adjoining

door once more. She eyed the mahogany, anger and not a little bit of embarrassment coursing through her. And in that split second, she made her decision.

She went to the door and yanked it open, revealing a great, yawning darkness.

The servants knew he did not plan to return that night, or they would have kept a fire lit for him. She was the only one who had expected him to return. The only one who thought, perhaps, their wedding night might be something . . . *more.*

Silly Penelope.

He hadn't wanted to marry her.

He'd married her for Falconwell. Why was that so difficult for her to remember? She swallowed around the knot in her throat, taking a deep breath. She would not allow herself to cry. Not tonight. Not in this new house, with its curious servants. Not on her wedding night.

The first night of the rest of her life.

Her first night as Marchioness of Bourne, with the freedoms that came with the title.

So, no, she would not cry. Instead, she would have an adventure.

Lifting a large candlestick from a nearby table, she entered the room, a pool of golden light following her, revealing a long wall of shelves filled to bursting with books and a marble fireplace with two large, lovely chairs arranged comfortably nearby. She paused at the hearth to investigate the enormous painting that hung above, lifting her candle to lend more light to the landscape.

Recognition flared.

It was Falconwell.

Not the house, but the land. The rolling hills that gave way to the stunning, glittering lake that marked the western edge of the lush, green property—the jewel of Surrey. The land that had once been his birthright.

He awoke to Falconwell.

When he slept in this room, that was.

The thought chased away any sympathy she might have

felt in that moment, and she spun away, irritation and disappointment flaring. Her candle revealed the end of a massive bed—bigger than any bed she'd ever seen. Penelope gasped at its sheer size, enormous oak posts at each of its corners, each more finely wrought than the last, the canopy above rising at least seven feet—maybe more. It was shrouded in fabrics the color of wine and midnight, and she could not stop herself from reaching out to run her fingers over the velvet draping.

It was lush and rich and extravagant in the extreme.

And devastatingly masculine.

The thought had her turning away to face the rest of the room, her gaze following the candlelight as it caught a large crystal decanter filled with dark liquid and a matching set of tumblers.

She wondered how often he poured himself a finger of scotch and took to his massive bed. Wondered how often he poured an equal amount of the liquor for a guest.

The idea of another woman in Michael's bed, dark and voluptuous, matching him in her beauty and her boldness, fueled Penelope's ire.

He'd left her there, in his home, on her first night as his wife.

And he'd gone off to drink scotch with a goddess.

It did not matter that she had no proof; it made her angry nonetheless.

Had their conversation in the carriage meant nothing? How were they to prove to London and to society that this sham of a marriage was nothing close to the scandal it was if he was off gallivanting with . . . with . . . ladies of the evening?

And what was she to do while he lived the life of a rakish libertine?

Sit here with needlepoint until he decided to grace her with his presence?

No.

She would not do it.

"Most definitely not," she vowed softly, triumphantly in the dark room, as though once the words were spoken aloud, they could not be rescinded.

And perhaps they couldn't.

Her gaze set upon the decanter once more, the deep cuts in the glass, the wide base, designed to keep the bottle from tipping over on rough seas. He *would* have a ship's captain's decanter in this decadent room, a den of fabric and sin that could have belonged to any self-respecting pirate.

Well. *She would show him rough seas.*

Before she could give it much thought, she was headed for the drink, setting down her candelabrum, turning over a tumbler and pouring more scotch into the glass than any decent woman should drink.

That she was not certain exactly how much scotch a decent woman could drink was irrelevant.

She took a perverse pleasure in the way the amber liquid filled the crystal, and she snickered as she wondered what her new husband would think if he arrived home to that moment—his proper wife, plucked from the path to spinsterhood, clutching a glass half-full of scotch.

Half-full of the future.

Half-full of adventure.

With a grin, Penelope toasted herself in the wide mirror mounted behind the decanter and took a long drink of the whiskey.

And nearly died.

She was not prepared for the wicked burn that seared down her throat and pooled in her stomach, making her retch once before she regained control of her faculties. "Blech!" she announced to the empty room, looking down into the glass and wondering why anyone—particularly the wealthiest men in Britain—might actually *choose* to drink such smoky, bitter swill.

It tasted like fire. Fire and . . . trees.

And it was foul.

As far as adventures went, this one was not looking at all promising.

She thought she might be sick.

She perched on the edge of the sideboard, bending over and wondering if it was possible that she might have actually done serious, irreversible damage to her innards. She took several deep breaths, and the burn started to subside, leaving behind a languid, vaguely encouraging warmth.

She righted herself.

It wasn't so bad, after all.

She stood again, lifting the candelabrum once more and heading for the bookshelves, tilting her head to read the titles of the leather-bound books that filled them to bursting. It seemed strange that Michael might have books. She could not imagine him ever stopping long enough to read. But here they were—Homer, Shakespeare, Chaucer, several German tomes on agriculture, and an entire shelf of histories of the British Kings. And *Debrett's Peerage.*

She ran her fingers across the gilded lettering of the volume—the complete history of the British aristocracy—its spine worn from use. For someone who was so happily absent from society, Michael seemed to peruse the volume quite a bit.

She pulled the book from the shelf, smoothing one hand across the leather binding before opening it at random. It fell open to a page, oft-viewed.

The entry for the Marquessate of Bourne.

Penelope ran her fingers across the letters, the long line of men who held the title before Michael. Before now. And there he was. *Michael Henry Stephen, 10th Marquess of Bourne, 2nd Earl Arran, born 1800. In 1816, he was created Marquess of Bourne, to him and the heirs male of his body.*

He might play at not caring for his title . . . but he felt connected to it in some way, or this book would not be so well used. Pleasure ripped through her at the thought, at the idea that he might still think of his time in Surrey, of his land there, of his childhood there, of *her.*

Perhaps he had not forgotten her—just as she had not forgotten him.

Her index finger ran along the line of text. *The heirs male of his body.* She imagined a set of gangly, dark-haired boys, dimples in their cheeks and mussed clothing.

Little Michaels.

The heirs male of her body as well.

If he ever came home.

She returned the book to its home and inched closer to the bed, investigating the enormous piece of furniture more closely, taking in that dark coverlet, wondering if it was velvet—if it matched the curtains around the bed. She set her light down and reached out, wanting to touch the bed. Wanting to feel the place where he slept.

The coverlet was not velvet.

It was fur. Soft, lush fur.

Of course it was.

She ran the flat of her hand across the fabric, and imagined, for one fleeting moment, what it might be like to lie in this bed, wrapped in darkness and fur.

And in Michael.

He was a rogue and a scoundrel, and his bed was an adventure in itself.

The soft fur beckoned to her, tempting her to climb up and bask in its warmth, its decadence. As quickly as the idea occurred to her, she was moving, letting her glass fall to the floor, unheeded, as she climbed onto the bed like a child on the hunt for biscuits, scaling the larder shelves.

It was the softest, most luxurious thing she'd ever experienced.

She rolled onto her back, spreading her arms and legs wide, loving the way the feathers and fur cradled her weight, allowing her to sink into the covers in pure, utter pleasure.

No bed should be this comfortable.

But, of course, his was.

"He is depraved," she said aloud to the room, hearing the lingering echo of the words as they faded into the darkness.

She lifted her arms, which seemed heavier than usual, and raised them straight up to the canopy above, wriggling deeper into the covers before closing her eyes, turning her cheek to one side, and rubbing against the fur.

She sighed. It seemed unfair that such a bed would go unused.

Her thoughts were slow, as though they were coming to her from underwater, and she was keenly aware of the weight of her body sinking into the mattress.

This glorious relaxation must be why people drank.

It certainly made her more open to the idea.

"It seems you have lost your way."

She opened her eyes at the words, low and soft in the darkness, to find her husband standing beside the bed, staring down at her.

Chapter Ten

Dear M—

Having received no reply from you in English, I thought perhaps you might respond to alternate languages. Be warned, there is (likely incorrect) Latin ahead.

Écrivez, s'il vous plaît
Placet scribes
Bitte schreiben Sie
Scrivimi, per favore
Ysgrifennwch, os gwelwch yn dda

I confess, I had one of the Welsh kitchen girls help with that last one, but the sentiment remains.

Please write—P
Needham Manor, September 1816

No reply (in any language)

As part-owner in London's most luxurious gaming hell, Bourne was no stranger to temptation. He specialized in sin. He was a personal acquaintance of vice. He knew the pull of emerald baize stretched across a billiard table, he understood the way the heart raced at the sound of hazard dice clattering in one's hand, he knew the precipice upon which a gamer teetered when waiting for that single card that would make—or lose—a fortune.

But he had never in his life experienced temptation as acute as this—the call to sin and wickedness that rang in his head as he watched his new, virginal wife writhe upon his fur coverlet in nothing but a linen shift.

Desire shot through him, thick and intense, and he fought to keep himself from reaching down and tearing her night rail in two, baring her to his eyes and his hands and his mouth for the rest of the night.

To claim her as his.

Anger lingered, now mixed in heady combination with desire as she blinked up at him, slow and languid in the flickering candlelight. The whisper of a smile she offered him made him want to strip bare and climb onto that bed with her to rub the fur coverlet across her pristine skin and show her precisely how glorious depravity could be.

She blinked again, and he thickened, his perfectly tailored trousers suddenly too tight. "Michael," she whispered, a hint of pleased discovery in her tone that did not help matters. "You are not supposed to be here."

And yet he was, a fox leaping into a henhouse. "Were you expecting someone else?" The words were harsh to his ears, filled with a meaning that she would not understand. "It remains my bedchamber, does it not?"

She smiled. "You made a joke. Of course it does."

"Then why am I not to be here?"

The question seemed to bother her. She wrinkled her nose. "You're supposed to be with your goddess." She closed her eyes and rocked into the fur again with a low hum of pleasure.

"My goddess?"

"Mmm. Alice told me that you do not sleep here." She tried to sit up, the fur and the feather bed making the movement difficult, and Michael watched as the edge of her nightgown slipped, devastatingly, beautifully, down the slope of one bare breast. "You are always so silent, Michael. Do you try to intimidate me?"

He willed his voice calm. "Do I intimidate you?"

"Sometimes. But not right now."

She crawled toward him, kneeling in front of him on the bed, one knee pulling the fabric taut, and Bourne found himself praying that her night rail would fall an inch more . . . half an inch. Just enough to bare one of her perfect pink nipples.

He shook off the thought. He was a man of thirty, not a boy of twelve. He had seen plenty of breasts in his day. He did not need to lust after his wife, swaying before him, testing the strength of her nightgown's fabric and his sanity, all at once.

Indeed, he had not returned in a fit of lust. He'd returned because he was angry. Angry at her for nearly marrying Tommy. For not telling him the truth.

She broke into his thoughts, and he caught her by the waist to steady her. "I am sorry that I am not perfect."

Right now, the only thing imperfect about her was the fact that she was clothed.

"What makes you say that?"

"We were married today," she said. "Or perhaps you do not remember?"

"I remember." She was making it impossible to forget.

"Really? Because you left me."

"I remember that, too." He had returned, ready to consummate the marriage. Ready to claim her as his and eliminate any doubt that they were married, that Falconwell was his.

That *she* was his. His, and not Tommy's.

"Brides do not expect to be left on their wedding night,

Michael." He did not reply, and she brazened on, raising her hands to his arms, clutching him through layers of clothing. "We do not like it. Especially when you forgo an evening with us for one with your . . . raven-haired beauty."

She wasn't making sense. "Who?"

She waved a hand. "They're always raven-haired, the ones who win . . ."

"Who win what?"

She was still talking. " . . . It doesn't matter if she's raven-haired or not, really. It just matters that she exists. And I don't like it."

"I see," he said. She thought he'd been with another woman? Perhaps if he'd been with another woman, he would not be here, wanting *her* so much.

"I don't think you do see, actually." She wavered, watching him carefully. "Are you *laughing* at me?"

"No." He at least knew *that* was the correct answer.

"Shall I tell you what else brides do not like on their wedding night?"

"By all means."

"We do not like to sit at home. Alone."

"I imagine that goes with not liking being left."

She narrowed her gaze and lowered her hands, swaying back, enough for him to tighten his grip and hold her steady—to feel the soft warmth of her beneath her shift, reminding him of the way she molded to his hands . . . to his mouth . . . to the rest of him. "You mock me."

"I swear I don't."

"We also don't like to be mocked."

He had to take control before he lost his mind. "Penelope."

She smiled. "I like the way you say my name."

He ignored the words and the unplanned flirtation in them. She did not know what she was doing. "Why aren't you in your own bed?"

She tilted her head, considering the question. "We married for all the wrong reasons. Or, all the right reasons . . .

if you're looking for a marriage of convenience. But, either way, we did not marry for passion. I mean, think about it. You didn't *really* compromise me at Falconwell."

A memory flashed of her writhing against him, pressing up into his hands, his mouth. The feel of her. The taste of her. "I am fairly certain that I did."

She shook her head. "No. You didn't. I know enough to understand the mechanics of the process, you know."

He wanted to explore that knowledge. In depth. "I see."

"I know there's . . . *more*."

So much more. So much more that he wanted to show her. So much that he had planned to show her upon his return home. But . . . "You have been drinking."

"Just a little." She sighed, looking over his shoulder into the darkness of the room beyond. "Michael, you promised me adventure."

"I did."

"A *nighttime* adventure."

His fingers tightened at her waist, pulling her to him. Or maybe she was simply swaying in that direction. Either way, he didn't stop the movement. "I promised you a tour of my club."

She shook her head. "I don't want that tonight. Not anymore."

She had the most beautiful, blue eyes. A man could lose himself in those eyes. "What do you want instead?"

"We were married today."

Yes. They were.

"I'm your wife."

He stroked his hands up her back until his fingers slid deep into golden curls, taking hold of her head and tilting her just so, perfectly, so he could lay claim to her and remind her that he was her husband.

He, and no one else.

He leaned in, brushing his lips across hers, light and teasing.

She sighed and pressed closer, but he pulled back, refusing to allow her to take over. She'd married him. She'd given him the chance to restore his name and his lands. And tonight, he wanted nothing more than to give her access to a world of pleasure as his thanks.

"Penelope."

Her eyes drifted open. "Yes?"

"How much have you had to drink?"

She shook her head. "I am not in my cups. It seems I drank just enough to find the courage to ask for what I want."

She'd had too much, then. He knew it, even as her words sent desire lancing through him, "And what is it you want, darling?"

She met his gaze head-on. "I want my wedding night."

So simple, so direct. So irresistible. He took her lips again knowing he shouldn't, and kissed her as though they had all the time in the world, as though he was not dying to be a part of her. To be inside her. To make her his. He sucked her full lower lip between his teeth, licking and stroking with his tongue until she moaned her pleasure at the back of her throat.

He released her mouth, kissing across her cheek, whispering, "Say my name."

"Michael," she said without hesitation, the word trembling at his ear, sending a shaft of pleasure straight through him.

"No. Bourne." He took the lobe of one ear into his mouth and worried it before releasing her and saying, "Say it."

"Bourne," she shifted, pressing against him, asking for more. "Please."

"There will be no turning back after this," he promised, his lips at her temple, hands reveling in her softness.

Her blue eyes opened, unbelievably light in the darkness, and she whispered, "Why would you think I would turn back?"

He stilled at the question, at the honest confusion in her words. It was the drink talking. It had to be. It was inconceivable to think that she did not understand what he meant.

That she did not see that he was nothing like the men who had courted her before.

"I'm not the man you had planned to marry." He should confront her with Tommy. But he did not want another man's name spoken in this moment. In this place.

She was already making him weak.

She smiled, small and perhaps sad. "You are the man I married nonetheless. I know that you don't care about me, Michael. I know that you only married me for Falconwell. But it's rather too late to look back, isn't it? We are married. And I wish to have a wedding night. I deserve it, I think, after all these years. Please. If you don't mind too much."

His hands moved to the collar of her nightgown, and, with a mighty tug, he rent the clothing in two. She gasped at the movement, her eyes going wide. "You ruined it." Bourne groaned at the wonder in the words. At the pleasure there.

He wanted to ruin more than the linen.

He brushed the night rail down her arms until it pooled at her knees, leaving her pale and naked in the candlelight. The too-dim candlelight. He wanted to see every inch of her . . . to watch the way her pulse raced at his touch, the way she quivered as he stroked the insides of her thighs, the way she clenched around him as he entered her.

As he claimed her.

He eased her back onto the fur, aching at the way she sighed as her back rubbed against the soft mink, as she learned the sheer decadence of skin against fur. He leaned over her, claiming her mouth until her hands were tangled in his hair, and she was pressing up against him. Only then did he lift his lips from hers and whisper, "I'm going to make love to you on this fur. You're going to feel it against every inch of you. And the pleasure I give you will be more than you've ever imagined. You will cry *my* name as it comes."

He left her then, removing his clothes, carefully arranging them in a neat pile on a chair nearby before returning to the bed to find that she had covered herself, one hand across her breasts, the other pressed to the triangle of curls that hid her most private parts. He stretched out on his side next to her, one hand propping up his head, the other smoothing over the soft swell of her thigh, up over the curve of her hip, across her rounded stomach. Her eyes were squeezed tightly shut, her breath coming in harsh little bursts, and Bourne could not help himself. He leaned down, licking the curve of one ear, nibbling at the lobe before asking, "Never hide from me."

She shook her head then, blue eyes wide. "I can't. I can't just . . . lie here. Bare."

He nipped her earlobe again. "I didn't say anything about just lying there, darling." He lifted the hand that was covering her breasts and slipped one finger into his mouth, licking the pad delicately before scraping it gently between his teeth.

"Oh . . ." She sighed, her gaze rapt on his lips. "You're very good at that."

He slowly extracted the finger and leaned down to kiss her, long and lush. "It's not the only thing I am good at."

Her eyelids flickered at the erotic promise in the words, and she said, softly, "I imagine you have had much more practice than I have."

It did not matter that he had been with other women in that moment. All he wanted was to learn Penelope. To be the one to show her pleasure. To be the one to teach her to take it for herself. "Show me where you want me," he whispered.

She blushed, closing her eyes and shaking her head. "I couldn't."

He returned her finger to his mouth, sucking carefully until her blue eyes opened, finding him, ethereal in the candlelight. She watched the movement of his lips, and the moment was so intense, he thought he might spend there and then. "Show me. Say, 'Please, Bourne,' and show me."

Courage flared in her eyes then, and he watched with keen pleasure as that finger, the one he'd made love to, trailed along her breast, circling the puckered, straining tip of it. He swiped the back of one hand across his lips as he watched the movement, as she tempted him beyond belief.

"Please . . ." She trailed off.

He lifted his head. "Please, who?"

"Please, Bourne." And he wanted to reward her for saying his name—his and no one else's. He leaned down, suckling her gently as her finger moved to her other breast and she exhaled on a long, shuddering, "Yes . . ."

His hand stroked over her stomach, lower, lower still before he removed it and nipped at the soft skin on the underside of her breast. "Don't stop now, darling."

She didn't, her finger wandering over the soft skin of her rounded stomach, into the curls that hid that magnificent place between her thighs. He watched, encouraging her with whispered guidançe as she explored for herself, as she tested her own knowledge, her own skill, until he thought he might die if he was not inside her.

He pressed a long, lingering kiss on the swell of her belly, then on her extended wrist, the hitch in her breath at the touch a reward in itself. He whispered his question to her skin. "What do you feel here?" One finger slid over the back of her hand, lingered at her knuckles. When she did not reply, he looked up to meet her gaze, reading the embarrassment there.

She shook her head, her words barely audible. "I can't."

He met her fingers in silken heat, and said, "I can." He pressed one finger into her, curling deep, and she gasped at the sensation. "You're wet, darling . . . wet and ready for me. For *me*. No one else."

"Michael," she whispered his given name, and the pleasure of the simple moment was nearly unbearable. With a shy, uncertain smile, she spread her thighs and welcomed him with such trust that he could hardly bear it. He moved against her, the smooth head of him cradled against the velvet opening of her body and hovering there, resting his weight on his arms, looking down at her face, a mix of relaxation and pleasure and bewilderment, and he could not stop himself from kissing her, his tongue stroking slickly against hers, before pulling back. It was the most difficult thing he'd ever done, pausing there on the precipice of what he knew would be a remarkable moment . . . easing against her gently, just barely pushing inside before pulling out.

He thought he might die from the pleasure of it.

Her eyes eased shut, and he whispered, "Open your eyes. Watch me. I want you to see me." When she did as she was told, he rocked into her smoothly, as gently as possible. She sucked in a short breath, pain flooding her gaze. He stopped, not wanting to hurt her. He leaned down, kissed her once—deeply—to regain her attention. "Are you all right?"

She smiled, and he recognized the strain there. "I am fine!"

He shook his head, unable to keep the smile from his voice. "Liar." He reached down to where she was so small and tight—marvelously tight—around the thickness of him. He found the hard, straining nub at the core of her and rubbed a slow circle there, watching as her eyes narrowed with pleasure. He continued the movement as he slid into her, slow and deep until she held all of him.

He stilled, aching to move against her. "Now?" She took a deep breath, and he sank deeper, surprising them both. He put his forehead to hers. "Tell me it's all right. Tell me I can move."

His innocent little wife slid her fingers into the hair at the nape of his neck and whispered, "Please, Michael."

And he could not resist the little plea. He took her lips with a wicked kiss, a growl rolling deep as he moved carefully, slowly pulling out until he was nearly gone from her, then rocking back into her gently, over and over, his thumb working against her, ensuring her pleasure even as he wondered if he would be able to hold his at bay.

"Michael," she whispered, and he met her gaze, worried that he might be hurting her. He stilled.

She arched her back. "Don't stop. Don't stop moving. You

were right . . ." Her eyes drifted closed, and she gave a moan of pleasure as he sank into her with one long stroke. He thought he might lose control at the sound of that moan, low and beautiful, at the back of her throat, but he did not stop.

She shook her head, her hands running over his shoulders and down his back, finally coming to rest on his buttocks, clasping in time to his movements, to the stroke of his thumb. "Michael!"

It was happening to him, too.

He'd never given much thought to timing his release to his partner's. He'd never cared to share the experience. But, suddenly, he could think of nothing but meeting Penelope there, on the edge of her pleasure, and letting it crash over both of them. "Wait for me," he whispered at her ear, thrusting against her. "Don't go without me."

"I can't wait. I can't stop it!" She convulsed around him, milking him in a rapid, stunning rhythm, his name on her lips sending him into oblivion, tumbling over the edge in a terrifying, extravagant climax that rivaled anything he'd ever experienced.

He collapsed against her, his breath coming in great, heaving bursts as he buried his face in the angle of her neck and allowed the extraordinary pleasure to wash over him in waves unlike anything he'd ever felt before.

Long minutes passed before, afraid that he would crush her with his weight, Bourne rolled away from Penelope, ran one hand down her side, and pulled her against him, not yet ready to release her.

Dear God. It had been the most incredible sex he'd ever had.

It had been mind-altering.

It had been more than he'd ever imagined it could be.

And the very idea that such an experience had come with Penelope spread cold fear through him.

This woman. This marriage. This evening.

It did not mean anything.

It *could not* mean anything.

She was a means to an end. The path to his revenge.

That was all she could be.

In his lifetime, Bourne had destroyed everything of value he'd ever held.

When Penelope realized that . . . realized that he was every kind of disappointment, she'd thank him for not allowing her too close. She'd be grateful for his releasing her to a quiet, simple world, where she had everything she wanted . . . and did not have to worry about him.

You do not deserve her.

Tommy's words echoed in his thoughts—those words that had sent him home, to his wife, to prove his place in her life. To prove that she belonged to him. That he could master her body in a way no other man had.

But it was he who had been mastered.

"Michael," she whispered against his chest, his name a lingering promise on her lips as one of her hands stroked up his torso. The long, lush touch sent another wave of pleasure through him, followed all too closely by desire when she whispered, soft and sleepy and tempting, "That was *splendid.*"

He meant to tell her not to become too comfortable in his bed.

Not to become too comfortable in his life.

He meant to tell her that the evening had been a means to an end.

That their marriage would never be the kind she required.

But she was already asleep.

Dear M—

I realize that you may not wish to reply to my letters, but I plan to send them nonetheless. A year, two, or ten—I would never want you to think I had forgotten you. Not that you would believe such a thing, would you?

It's your birthday next week. I would have embroidered a handkerchief for you, but you know that needlepoint and I do not exactly suit.

Remembering—P
Needham Manor, January 1817

No reply

The next morning, Penelope entered the breakfast room, hoping to see her new husband—the man who had changed everything in one glorious day and glorious night, the man who had made her realize that perhaps their marriage could be more. That perhaps their contrived love match could be less contrived and more . . . well . . . a love match.

For surely there was nothing so superb as the way he'd made her feel the prior evening in his bed. It was of little consequence that she had awoken not cloaked in decadent fur but in her perfectly pristine, perfectly pressed white linen sheets in the bedchamber she had been assigned.

In fact, she was rather touched that he might have moved her there in the night without waking her. He was obviously a kind, caring, loving husband, and their marriage, which had begun as such a disastrous farce, was destined for something much much more.

She hoped that he would join her as she took her seat at the lovely long table in the handsome and lavishly appointed breakfast room, wondering if he still enjoyed sausage at breakfast, as he had when he was very young.

She hoped that he would join her as she accepted a plate of egg and toast (no sausage in sight) from the young footman, who clicked his heels together in a rather extravagant manner before returning to his post in the corner of the room.

She hoped Michael would join her as she lingered over her toast.

As she sipped her fast-cooling tea.

As she eyed the newspaper, perfectly folded and placed to the left of the empty seat at the far end of the soon-growing-too-long table.

And, after a full hour of waiting, Penelope stopped hoping.

He was not coming.

She remained alone.

Suddenly, she was keenly aware of the footman in the corner of the room, whose job it was to simultaneously know immediately what his mistress might require and to ignore her altogether, and Penelope felt a blush rise high on her cheeks.

For, surely, the young footman was thinking terribly embarrassing things.

She slid a glance at him.

He was not looking.

But he was most definitely *thinking.*

Michael wasn't coming.

Stupid, stupid Penelope.

Of course he wasn't coming.

The events of the prior evening had not been magical to him. They'd been necessary. He'd officially taken her to wife. And then, like any good husband, he'd left her to her own devices.

Alone.

Penelope eyed her empty plate, where the bright yellow yolk of the egg she had eaten so happily had congealed, affixing itself rather grotesquely to the porcelain.

It was the first full day of her life as a married woman, and she was eating breakfast alone. Ironic, that, considering she'd always viewed breakfast with a husband who barely knew her as a lonely affair indeed. But now, she would, with pleasure, take breakfast with her husband over breakfast by herself, under the watchful eyes of a too-young footman who was doing his very best not to see her.

For it seemed that in her desire for a husband who wanted her for more than what was ordinarily requested of a wife, she'd found herself married to one who did not even want her for that.

Perhaps she'd done something wrong the evening before.

The flush had reached her ears, and she felt them burning, likely red as roses as she tried to think of what she might have done wrong, of how her wedding night might have gone differently.

But every time she tried to think, she remembered the young footman, now blushing himself, in the corner, not knowing what to say to his mistress and very likely wishing she would finish her breakfast and leave the room.

She had to leave this room.

She rose from the table with all the grace expected of a marchioness and, desperate to ignore the embarrassment, headed for the door. Blessedly, the footman did not meet her gaze as she moved across the room at a pace that could only be described as as-close-to-a-run-as-possible-without-being-unladylike-as-ladies-do-not-run.

But the door opened before she could get to it, and Mrs. Worth entered, leaving Penelope with no choice but to stop short, the skirts of her yellow day dress, chosen for beauty rather than sense on this frigid January day, swishing around her legs as she halted.

The stunning young housekeeper paused on the threshold of the room, not revealing any emotion as she dipped a quick curtsy, and said, "Good morning, my lady."

Penelope resisted the urge to do the same, instead clasping her hands tightly in front of her, and saying, "Good morning to you, Mrs. Worth."

Pleasantries behind them, the two women stared at each other for a long moment before the housekeeper said, "Lord Bourne asked me to inform you that you will be dining at Tottenham House on Wednesday."

Three days hence.

"Oh." That Michael had passed such a simple message to her via a servant made her realize just how misguided she had been about the events of the evening prior. If he could not find the time to tell his wife about a dinner engagement, he had little interest in his wife indeed.

She took a deep breath, willing disappointment away.

"He also asked me to remind you that the dinner will be the first you attend as husband and wife."

There was no need to will disappointment away, as it was almost instantly replaced by irritation. Penelope's attention snapped to the housekeeper. For a moment, she wondered if it was Mrs. Worth who saw fit to make such an obvious pronouncement, as though Penelope were some kind of imbecile and could not recall the events of the last day. As though she might have somehow forgotten that they had not yet been introduced to society.

But one look at Mrs. Worth's downcast gaze made Penelope absolutely certain of the identity of the irritant in this particular situation—her husband, who seemingly had little confidence in her ability to either reply to dinner invitations or understand the importance of the invitations themselves.

Without thinking, she raised a brow, met the housekeeper's eyes, and said, "What an excellent reminder. I had not realized that we've been married for less than twenty-four hours and that, during that time, I have not left the house. It is lucky, is it not, that I have a husband so willing to remind me of the simpler things?" Mrs. Worth's eyes widened at the sarcasm dripping from Penelope's words, but she did not reply. "It is a shame he could not remind me himself, at breakfast. Is he at home?"

Mrs. Worth hesitated before saying, "No, my lady. He has not been home since you returned from Surrey."

It wasn't true, of course. But what it told Penelope was that Michael had returned late last night and left immediately following their interlude.

Of course he had.

Penelope's anger burned hotter.

He'd come home to consummate the marriage and left again, almost instantly.

This was to be her life. Coming and going at his whim, doing his bidding, attending his dinners when the invitation included her and standing by, alone, when it did not.

What a disaster.

She met Mrs. Worth's gaze, registered the sympathy there. Loathed it.

Loathed him for making her feel so embarrassed. For making her feel so unfortunate. For making her feel so much *less.*

But this was her marriage. This had been her choice. Even as it had been his—there had been a small part of her that had wanted it. That had believed it might be more.

Silly Penelope.

Silly, poor Penelope.

Straightening her shoulders, she said, "You may tell my husband that I will see him Wednesday. For dinner at Tottenham House."

Chapter Eleven

Dear M—

Tommy said he saw you in town at the beginning of your holiday, but that you barely had time to speak to him. I am sorry for that, and so is he.

Pippa has adopted a three-legged dog, and (unflattering as it sounds) when I watch him gambol by the lake, his limp makes me think of you. Without you, Tommy and I are a three-legged dog. Dear God. This is the kind of metaphor to which I must resort without you to keep me quick-tongued; the situation grows dire.

Desperately—P
Needham Manor, June 1817

No reply

The trouble with lies was that they were too easy to believe.

Even if you were the one telling them.

Perhaps *especially* if you were the one telling them.

Three days later, Penelope and Michael were the guests of honor at dinner at Tottenham House—an event that provided them the perfect opportunity to tell the carefully developed story of their love match to several of the most vocal gossips of the *ton*.

Gossips who were very eager to live up to their name if the way they hung upon each of Penelope's and Michael's words was any indication.

Not to mention the *looks*.

Penelope hadn't missed them . . . not when they'd entered Tottenham House, several minutes early, having carefully planned their arrival to be neither too early nor too late, only to discover that the rest of the invitees had carefully planned *their* arrivals to be early—ostensibly to ensure that they wouldn't miss a single moment of the Marchioness and Marquess of Bourne's first evening in society.

Nor had she missed the looks when Michael had thoughtfully placed one large, warm hand at Penelope's back, shepherding her into the receiving room where the dinner guests waited for their meal to be served. The hand had been placed with such precision, paired perfectly with such a warm smile—one that she barely recognized—that Penelope had been hard-pressed to hide both her admiration for his strategy and her unexpected pleasure at the little movement.

Those looks had been followed with a fluttering of fans in the too-cool room, a cacophony of whispers that she pretended not to hear, looking up at her husband, instead, with what she hoped was a suitably doting look. She must have achieved it, because he had leaned close and whispered, "You're doing splendidly," low in her ear, sending a flood of pleasure through her even as she swore to resist his power over her.

She'd chided herself for the warm, treacly feeling.

She reminded herself that she hadn't seen him since their wedding night—that he'd made it quite clear that any husbandly interaction was all for show, but by that time the flush was high on her cheeks, and when she met her husband's eyes, it was to find a look of supreme satisfaction in them. He'd leaned in again. "The blush is perfect, my little innocent," the words fanning the flames, as though they were very much in love and utterly devoted to each other when quite the opposite was true.

They'd been separated for dinner, of course, and the real challenge had begun. The Viscount Tottenham had escorted her to her place, sandwiched between himself and Mr. Donovan West, the publisher of two of the most-read newspapers in Britain. West was a golden-haired charmer who seemed to notice everything, including Penelope's nervousness.

He kept his words for only her ears. "Do not allow them a chance to skewer you. They'll take it quickly. And you'll be done for."

He was referring to the women.

There were six of them dispersed around the table, with equal pursed lips and disdainful glances. Their conversation—casual enough—was laced with a tone that made each word seem to have a double meaning; as though all assembled were in on some jest of which Michael and Penelope had no knowledge.

Penelope would have been irritated if it weren't for the fact that she and Michael had a spate of secrets themselves.

It was near the end of the meal when the conversation turned to them.

"Tell us, Lord Bourne." The Dowager Viscountess Tottenham's words oozed along the table, too loud for privacy. "How was it, precisely, that you and Lady Bourne became affianced? I do love a love match."

Of course she did. Love matches were the best kind of scandal.

Second only to idyllic ruination.

Penelope pushed the wry thought aside as conversation came to a stop and those assembled hung on the silence, waiting for Michael's response.

His gaze slid to Penelope's, warm and rich. "I defy anyone to spend more than a quarter of an hour in my lady's company and not come away adoring her." The words were scandalous—not at all the kind of thing that well-bred, callous members of the aristocracy said aloud, even if they believed it—and there was a collective intake of breath, punctuating amusement and surprise. Michael seemed not to care as he added, "I was lucky indeed that I was there, on St. Stephen's. And that she was there—her laughter reminding me of all the ways I needed mending."

Her heart quickened at the words and the way the corner of his mouth lifted in a ghost of a smile.

Amazing, the power of words. *Even false ones.*

She could not stop herself from smiling back at him, and she had no need of faking the way she dipped her head, suddenly embarrassed by his attention.

"How lucky, also, that her dowry abuts land belonging to the marquessate." The words sailed down the table on a drunken burst from the Countess of Holloway, a miserable woman who took pleasure in others' pain and whom Penelope had never liked. She did not look to the countess, focusing, instead on her husband before taking her turn.

"Fortuitous mostly for me, Lady Holloway," she said, her gaze steadfast on her husband. "For without our being childhood neighbors, I am certain that my husband would never have found me."

Michael's gaze lit with admiration, and he lifted his glass in her direction. "At some point I would have realized what I was missing, darling. And I would have come looking for you."

The words warmed her to her core before she remembered that it was all a game.

She took a deep breath as Michael took control, spinning their tale, assuring those assembled that he had lost head, heart, and reason to love.

He was handsome and clever, charming and funny, with just the right amount of contrition . . . as though he were attempting to make amends for past ills, and he was willing to do whatever it took to return to the aristocracy—for the sake of his new wife.

He was perfect.

He made her believe that he'd been there, in the main room of the Coldharbour parsonage, surrounded by revelers and holly wreaths and a St. Stephen's feast. He made her believe that he'd met her gaze across the room—she could feel the knot in her stomach as she imagined the long, serious look that he would have given her, the one that made her breathless and light-headed, the one that made her believe that she was the only woman in the world.

And he captured her with his pretty words.

Just as he captured the rest of them.

" . . . Honestly, I've never danced a reel in my life. But she made me want to dance a score of them."

Laughter rang out around the table as Penelope lifted her glass and took a small sip of wine, hoping the alcohol would calm her roiling stomach, watching her husband as he regaled the roomful of diners with the tale of their whirlwind love affair.

"I suppose it was only a matter of time before I returned to Coldharbour and realized that Falconwell Manor was not the only thing I had left behind." His gaze found hers across the table, and she caught her breath at the sparkle in those eyes. "Thank heavens I found her before someone else did."

A collection of feminine sighs from around the table punctuated the racing of Penelope's heart. Michael was as silver-tongued as they came.

"It wasn't as though additional suitors were legion in number," Lady Holloway said snidely, laughing a touch too loudly. "Were they, Lady Bourne?"

Penelope's mind went blank at the cruel reference to her spinsterhood, and she searched for a cutting remark before her husband came to the rescue. "I couldn't bear the thought of them," he said, staring straight at her, all seriousness, until she was flushed with his attention. "Which is why we married so quickly."

Lady Holloway harrumphed into her wine as Mr. West

smiled warmly, and asked, "And you, Lady Bourne? Did your connection . . . surprise you?"

"Be careful, darling," Michael said scandalously, a sparkle in his grey-green eyes. "He shall quote you in tomorrow's news."

She could not take her eyes from Michael as laughter sounded around them. He captured her and held her expertly in his web. When she replied to the newspaperman's question, it was straight to her husband. "I was not at all surprised. If I were to tell the truth, it seemed as though I had been waiting for Michael to return for years." She paused, shaking her head, registering the attention around the table. "I'm sorry—not Michael. Lord Bourne." She gave a little, self-deprecating laugh. "I've known he would make a wonderful husband forever. I am very happy that he will be *my* wonderful husband."

There was a flash of surprise in Michael's eyes, there and instantly gone, hidden by his warm laugh—so unfamiliar. "You see? How could I fail to mend my wicked ways?"

"How indeed." Mr. West took a drink of wine, considering her over the rim of his glass and, for a moment, Penelope was certain that the man saw their falsehood as clearly as if she had embroidered *Liar* into her dinner dress, and knew that she and Michael had been married for a reason far removed from love, and that her husband had not shared a moment with her in the days since he'd carried her back to her bedchamber after consummating their marriage.

That he'd only touched her to ensure that their marriage was legitimate. And now he spent his nights away from her, with God knew whom, doing God knew what.

She made a show of eating her crème caramel, hoping that Mr. West would not press her for more information.

Michael spoke up, all charm. "It isn't true, of course. I'm absolutely rubbish at husbanding; I can't bear the thought of her being apart from me; I hate the idea of other men capturing her attention; and I warn you now, I shall be a veritable bear when it comes time for the season and I am required to relinquish her to dance partners and dinner companions." He paused, and Penelope noticed the skill with which he used the silence, eyes glittering with a humor she had not seen in him since he was a child. *Humor that wasn't there. Not really.* "You shall all be very sorry indeed that I've decided to dust off my title."

"Not at all," the Dowager Viscountess interjected, her normally cool eyes flashing with excitement. "We are thrilled to welcome you back into society, Lord Bourne. For truly, there can be nothing more cleansing than a love match."

It was a lie, of course. Love matches were scandals in themselves, but Michael and Penelope outranked her, and their invitation had come from the young Tottenham, so the old woman had very little control of the situation.

Michael smiled at the words nonetheless, and Penelope could not tear her eyes from him in that moment. Everything about him lightened with the smile—a dimple flashed in one cheek, and his wide, full lips curved, making him even more handsome.

Who was this man with his easy jokes and charming smiles?

And how could she convince him to stay?

"And a love match it must be . . . look at how your bride hangs upon your every word," Viscount Tottenham spoke up, obviously throwing his support behind them, and Penelope did not have to feign her embarrassment when Michael turned to face her, his smile fading.

The dowager pressed on, turning a pointed look on her son. "Now, if only you would take a cue from Bourne and find a wife."

The viscount gave a little laugh and made a show of shaking his head before settling his gaze on Penelope. "I fear Bourne has found the last ideal bride."

"She has sisters, Tottenham," Michael added, teasing in his tone.

Tottenham smiled graciously. "I shall look forward to meeting them."

Understanding dawned. There, as simply as taking sweets from a babe, Michael had expertly laid the groundwork for Olivia to meet Lord Tottenham and possibly marry him.

Her eyes went wide, and she turned her surprise on her husband, who took her look in stride, immediately redefining it. "I find that now that I am so very enamored by my own wife, I cannot help but encourage those around me to seek their own."

Such lies. So smooth.

So easy to believe.

The dowager chimed in, "Well, I, for one, think it a marvelous idea." She stood, the men assembled following her to her feet. "In fact, I think we shall leave the gentlemen to their discussion."

The rest of the attendees took their cue, the ladies peeling away from the table to retire to another room for sherry and gossip. Penelope had no doubt that she would be the center of attention for the last.

She followed the dowager viscountess with heavy footsteps to a lovely little salon, but had barely made her way inside when a large warm hand enveloped her own, and Michael's deep, familiar voice rumbled, "Excuse me, ladies, I've need of my wife for one, brief moment, if you don't mind. I told you, I cannot bear to be without her." There was a collective gasp as Michael pulled Penelope from the room and into the hallway, closing the door to the salon behind them.

Penelope wrenched her hand from his, looking both ways down the hall to ensure that they had not been seen. "What are you doing?" she whispered. "This is not done!"

"I do wish you would stop telling me what is and is not done," he said. "Don't you see it only makes me want to do it more?" He pulled her farther away from the door into a dimly lit alcove. "Gossip about how much I adore you is the kind of gossip we're looking for, darling."

"There's no need to call me that, and you know it," she whispered. "I'm not your darling."

He lifted a hand to her face. "You are when we are in public."

She swatted it away. "Stop it." She paused, then lowered her voice. "Do you think they believe us?"

He gave her an indignant look. "Why wouldn't they, my love? Every word of it is true."

She narrowed her gaze. "You know what I mean."

He leaned close, and whispered, "I know that the walls in houses like this have ears, love." And then he *licked* her. Actually licked her, a lovely caress on the lobe of her ear that had her clutching his arms at unexpected pleasure. Before she could respond, his lips were gone, and he returned his hand to her jaw, tipping her face up to his. "You were splendid in there."

Splendid. The word echoed through her on a flood of pleasure as he set a warm kiss to the place where her pulse beat frantically at her throat.

"I don't like the way they judge you," she whispered. "Especially Holloway."

"Holloway is a bitch." She gasped at the word, and he continued in her ear. "She deserves a thrashing. It's a shame that her earl is too feeble to do it."

Pleasure lanced through Penelope at the words, and she could not help her smile. "You seem to have few qualms about spanking women."

"Only those I like." He stilled and lifted his head, dark gaze finding hers in the close quarters.

She tried to ignore the silken promise in the words. Tried to remember that it wasn't real. That this night was all façade. That this strange man was not her husband. That her husband had done nothing but use her for his own gain.

Except, tonight wasn't about him. It was about her and her sisters. "Thank you, Michael," she whispered in the darkness, "I know that you did not have to honor this part of the arrangement. That you did not have to help my sisters."

He was silent for a long moment. "I do have to."

His willingness to keep his word surprised her even as it

reminded her of their agreement. "I suppose there is honor among thieves after all." She hesitated, then said, "And the rest of the agreement?"

One of his dark brows rose.

"When do I get my tour?"

"You're learning to drive a hard bargain."

"I've little else to keep me entertained," she replied.

"Are you bored, wife?"

"Why would I be bored? Staring at the walls of your town house is so fascinating."

He chuckled at her words, and the sound sent a shiver of heat through her. "Fair enough. Why not take your excitement now?"

"Because right now, we're trying to convince them that you have changed and our disappearing from the festivities will not help."

"Oh, I think my disappearing with my proper wife would help a great deal." He crowded closer. "More than that, I know you'll enjoy it."

"Hiding in the hallway of Tottenham House like a thief?"

"Not like a thief." He peeked around the edge of their hiding place before returning his attention to her. "Like a lady having a clandestine affair."

She gave a little snort of disapproval. "With her *husband*."

"Having an affair with one's husband is . . . He trailed off, his eyes darkening.

"Bourgeois?"

One side of his mouth twitched. "I was going to say it was an adventure."

An adventure.

She stilled at the word, looking up at him where he towered above her, his lips turned up in something akin to a smirk, his hands cupping her face, everything about him, his heat, his scent . . . *him,* surrounding her.

She should deny him. She should tell him that she found their wedding night as plain and uninteresting as dinner at Tottenham House.

Should put him in his smug place.

But she couldn't. Because she wanted it again. She wanted him to kiss her and touch her and make her feel all those glorious things she had felt before he'd left her as though he hadn't felt a thing.

He was so close and so handsome and so *male*. And as she looked up into the eyes of this man who was one moment exciting and entertaining and the next dark and dangerous, she realized that she would take adventure with him any way he offered it.

Even here, in the alcove of Tottenham's hallway.

Even if it was a mistake.

She placed her hands flat against his chest, feeling the hard, flat strength that coiled there beneath layers of perfectly fitted linen and wool. "You're so different tonight. I don't know who you are."

Something flashed in his eyes at the words, something there, then gone so fast that she could not identify it. When he spoke, his words were low and soft and liquid, with a hint of teasing. "Then why not get to know me a little better?"

Why not, indeed.

She lifted herself onto her toes, reaching up for him as he bent toward her and claimed her lips in a searing, nearly unbearable kiss.

He pressed closer to her, pushing her back against the wall, covering her with his body until she could do nothing but reach up and thread her arms around his neck, pulling him toward her until his lips, firm and silken, gave her what she had not even known she wanted, what she had not even known could be—a hard, possessing kiss that she would never, ever forget. She was consumed with the feel of him, his broadness, his strength, as his hands cupped her jaw and moved her to align her mouth more lushly, more perfectly to his own.

He licked at the seam of her lips, the feel of his tongue tempting her until she gasped, and he took advantage of the sound to capture her open lips and slide into her, pressing against her, tickling and tasting until she thought she might die from the excitement of it. Of their own volition, her fingers threaded into the curls at the nape of his neck, and she leveraged herself up to press against him, more firmly, *more scandalously . . . and she didn't care.*

She didn't care a whit . . . not as long as he didn't stop.

Not as long as he never stopped.

As she pressed closer, he shifted his grasp, his hands lowering in a long, torturous slide, pressing just barely at the outside of her breasts, just enough for her to ache in places of which she'd never thought, before sliding lower, lower still, until he clasped her bottom and pulled her tight against him with a force that both shocked and aroused.

He groaned his pleasure at the movement, and she pulled back at the sound, wondering at the very idea that he might be as consumed by the caress as she was, and he opened his eyes to meet hers once, fleetingly, before he captured her mouth again, delving more deeply, stroking more firmly, until she was overcome by the pleasure. By the adventure. By him.

Seconds passed. Minutes. Hours . . . it didn't matter.

All that mattered was this man. This kiss.

This.

It ended, and he raised his head slowly, placing one soft, lingering kiss on her lips before he reached up and untangled her arms from around his neck. He smiled down at her, something breathtaking in his gaze, and she realized that this was the first time he'd smiled at her—only at her—since they were children.

It was magical.

He opened his mouth to speak, and she was on tenterhooks, unable to control the anticipation that coursed through her as his lips formed words.

"Tottenham."

Confusion flared, and Penelope's brows shot together.

"Ordinarily, I frown upon gentlemen accosting ladies in my hallway, Bourne."

"How do you feel about husbands kissing their wives?"

"Honestly?" Tottenham's voice was dry as sand. "I think I might like it even less."

Penelope closed her eyes, mortification flooding her. He played her so well.

"You'll change your mind when you meet my sister-in-law, Olivia, I wager."

The words made her want to do him harm. Actual. Physical. Harm.

He'd done it on purpose.

It had all been for Tottenham's benefit.

To keep up the pretense of their love match.

Not because he could not keep his hands off her.

Would she not learn?

"If she's anything like her sister, I fear that is a wager I would not win."

Michael laughed, and she winced at the sound, hating it. Hating the falseness of it. "I don't suppose you can give us a moment?"

"I think I have to, or Lady Bourne might never be able to meet my eyes again."

Penelope was staring at the folds of Michael's cravat. She willed her voice calm, knowing that carefree was too far out of reach. "I am not sure a moment will change that, my lord."

He'd used her again.

Tottenham chuckled. "The brandy is poured."

And then he was gone. And she was alone.

With her husband, who seemed to make a practice of disappointing her. She did not look away from the crisp linen at his neck. "That was well played," she said, an edge of sadness in her voice. If he heard it, he did not show it.

When he spoke, it was as though they had been discussing the weather rather than kissing in the dark corner. "It will likely go a long way toward proving that we are matched for more than Falconwell."

She'd almost believed it herself.

Indeed, she seemed unable to learn her lesson. It wasn't fair that she was so angry with him. So hurt. The silly love match had been her idea, had it not? She had only herself to blame for the way it made her feel.

Cheap. Used. But her sisters would get their proper, unblemished matches from this. And that would be worth it. *She had to believe that.*

Penelope pushed her sadness aside. "Why are you doing this?" His brows rose in question and she continued, "Agreeing to this farce?"

He looked away. "I gave you my word."

She shook her head. "Don't you feel . . . as though I am taking advantage of you?"

One side of his mouth lifted in a wry smile. "Did I not take advantage of you when I married you?"

She'd not thought of it in such a stark way. "I suppose you did. And still . . ." *This feels worse,* she wanted to say. *I feel like everything I am, everything I have, it's all in service to others.* She shook her head. "It seems different. And I regret it, nonetheless, asking you to do this for them. For me."

He shook his head. "Never regret."

"Another rule?"

"Of scoundrels only. Gamers inevitably regret."

She supposed he would know.

"Well, I regret it, nonetheless."

"It's unnecessary. I've a good reason to join you in this farce."

She stilled. "You do?"

He nodded. "I do. We all receive something from the game."

"What do you receive?" He was silent, and uncertainty flared deep within her. "From whom do you receive it?" He did not reply, but Penelope was no fool. "My father. He had something else. What is it?"

"It's not important," he said, in a way that made her feel that it was very much important. "Suffice to say, you should not regret our agreement as I shall benefit well from it. I will walk you back to the rest of the ladies," he offered, reaching out to take her elbow.

And, perversely, the idea that he'd been playing their game for his own benefit made her feel worse. As though she, too, had been the victim of his lies.

Betrayal flared, hot and instant, and she pulled back almost violently at his touch. "Don't touch me."

His brows rose at the words, at their ire. "I beg your pardon?"

She did not want him near her. Did not want to be reminded that she, too, had been fooled. "We may be feigning a romance for them, but *I* am not them. Don't touch me again. Not if it's not for their benefit."

I don't think I can bear it.

He lifted both hands high, proof that he heard the request. Heeded it.

She turned away before she said anything else. Before she betrayed her feelings.

"Penelope." He called to her as she stepped into the dim hallway. She stopped, a flicker of hope deep in her, hope that he might apologize. That he might tell her that she was wrong. That he actually did care for her. That he did want her. "This is the most difficult part—with the ladies—you understand?"

False hope.

He meant that she would have to keep up their pretense. That the women would question her far more carefully in private than they had in public.

It would be a challenge.

But that he would call it the most difficult portion of the evening was almost laughable, for surely she had just experienced the most difficult portion of the evening.

"I shall manage the ladies, my lord, as we agreed. By the end of the evening, they shall be certain that you and I are very much in love, and my sisters will be on their way to having a sound season." She steeled her voice. "But you would do well to remember that you promised me a tour of your club, which I now see was not generosity but payment for my part in your ruse."

He stiffened. "So I did."

She nodded once, firmly. "When?"

"We'll see."

Her gaze narrowed at the words, the universal synonym for *no*. "Yes, I suppose we shall."

She turned her back and returned to the ladies' salon, head high, shoulders straight as she turned the handle and pushed the door open, rejoining the women.

Temper fraying, vowing to remain unmoved.

Chapter Twelve

Dear M—

Tommy was home for Michaelmas and we celebrated in grand style, even though we were sorely lacking our own Michael. Nevertheless, we soldiered on, picked the lingering blackberries and ate them until we were ill, as per tradition. Our teeth turned thoroughly troublingly greyish blue in the process—you would have been proud.

Perhaps we'll see you for Christmas this year? The St. Stephen's feast in Coldharbour is becoming a fine fête indeed.

We are all thinking of you, and miss you very much.

Always—P
Needham Manor, September 1818

No reply

She'd asked him not to touch her, and he granted the request.

Taken it a step further.

He'd left her completely alone.

He'd left her alone that night, when he'd returned her to Hell House and promptly left, without a word, headed to wherever it was that husbands went without their wives.

And again the next night as she ate her supper in the enormous, empty dining room under the watchful eyes of several mismatched, too-young footmen. She was getting used to them, at least, and was quite proud of herself for not blushing through the entire meal.

And again the night after, while she stood at the window of her bedchamber like a ninny, pulled in the direction of his carriage as though attached with a string as she watched it trundle away. As though, if she watched long enough, he would return.

And he would give her the marriage she wanted.

"No more windows," she vowed, turning away from the cold dark street and heading across the room to submerge her hands in the washbasin, watching the cool water pale and distort her hands beneath the surface. "No more windows," she repeated, quietly, when she heard a carriage pull to a stop outside the town house, ignoring the increased beat of her heart and the pull of the glass.

Instead, she dried her hands with impressive calm and moved to the door that adjoined her husband's bedchamber to her own, pressing her ear to the cool wood and listening for his arrival.

After long minutes that provided her with nothing but a rather irritating crick in her neck, Penelope's curiosity got the best of her, and she headed for the door to her bedchamber to sneak into the hallway and see if her husband had indeed, returned home.

She cracked the door—less than an inch—to look into the hallway.

And came face to face with Mrs. Worth.

She gave a little start and slammed the door shut, heart pounding, before she realized that she'd just made a fool of herself in front of her husband's unsettling housekeeper.

Taking a deep breath, she opened the door with a wide smile. "Mrs. Worth, you startled me."

The housekeeper dipped her head. "You have a visitor."

Penelope's brows snapped together. "A visitor?" It was past eleven o'clock.

The housekeeper extended a card. "He says it's very important."

He.

Penelope took the card.

Tommy.

Happiness thrummed through her. He was the first person to visit her here in this large, empty house—not even her mother had come, instead sending word that she would visit *once the newly wedded bloom was off the rose.*

Little did her mother know that such bloom had never even hinted at the rose.

But Tommy was her friend. And friends visited. She was unable to keep the smile from Mrs. Worth. "I shall be right down. Give him tea. Or . . . wine. Or . . . scotch." She shook her head. "Whatever it is that people drink at this hour."

She closed the door and righted her appearance before throwing herself down the stairs and into the front receiving room, where he stood at a large marble fireplace, dwarfed by the extravagant room. "Tommy!" she called, moving directly to him, thrilled to see him. "What are you doing here?"

He smiled. "I'm here to steal you away, of course."

It should have been a jest, but there was an edge to the words that she did not like, and it was in that moment that she realized Tommy should not be there—that Michael would be furious if he discovered Tommy Alles in his receiving room, with his wife. It would not matter that Tommy and Penelope had been friends for an age. "You shouldn't be here," she said as he turned to her, taking her hands and lifting them to his lips. "He shall be livid."

"You and I are friends still, are we not?"

She did not hesitate, her guilt over their last meeting still fresh. "Of course we are."

"And as a good friend, I'm here to make sure that you are all right. Hang him."

After the last interaction she had with her husband, she should have supported the *Hang him* strategy, but she couldn't. For some reason, the very idea of standing here in this room with Tommy made Penelope feel as though she was betraying her husband and their marriage.

She shook her head. "It is not a good idea for you to be here, Tommy."

Tommy looked down at her, uncommon seriousness in his gaze. "Tell me one thing. Are you all right?"

The words were soft with concern, and she wasn't expecting the emotion that crashed through her at them, the tears that sprang instantly to her eyes. It had been a week she'd been married in a tiny, rushed ceremony in Surrey, and no one had thought to ask after her. *Not even her husband.* "I—" she stopped, emotion closing her throat.

Tommy's normally friendly blue eyes darkened. "You're miserable. I'll kill him."

"No! No." She put one hand out, resting it on his arm. "I'm not miserable. I'm *not.* I'm just . . . I'm . . ." she took a deep breath, finally settling for, "It's not easy."

"Has he hurt you?"

"No!" She leapt to defend Michael before considering the question. "Not . . . no." Not in the way he meant.

He did not believe her. He crossed his arms. "Do not protect him. Has he hurt you?"

"No."

"What then?"

"I don't see him much."

"That is not a surprise," he said, and she heard the sting in his words. The emotion that came with friendship lost. She had felt it when Michael had left. When he'd stopped writing. When he'd stopped caring. Tommy was quiet for a long time before he said, "Do you wish to see him more?"

It was a question without an easy answer. She wanted nothing to do with one-half of Michael, with the cold, distant man who had married her for land. But the other half—the man who held her and cared for her comfort and did delicious, wonderful things to her mind and body—she wouldn't mind seeing him again.

Of course, she could not say that to Tommy. Could not explain that Michael was two men and that she was at once furious with and fascinated by him.

She could not say it because she barely wanted to admit it to herself.

"Pen?"

She sighed. "Marriage is a strange thing."

"Indeed it is. Doubly so if one is married to Michael, I'm guessing. I knew he'd come for you. Knew he'd be cold and heartless and devise a way to marry you quickly—for Falconwell." Belatedly, Penelope realized she should be protesting the words and telling Tommy their well-spun tale, but he was moving on, and it was too late. "I tried to marry you first . . . to spare you marriage to him."

Tommy's words from the morning of his proposal echoed in her mind. "That's what you meant. You wanted to protect me from Michael."

"He's not the same as he was."

"Why didn't you tell me that?"

He tilted his head. "Would you have believed me?"

"Yes." *No.*

He smiled, smaller than usual. More serious. "Penny, if you'd known he was coming for you, you would have waited." He paused. "It was always him."

Penelope's brow furrowed. It wasn't true. Was it?

A vision flashed—a warm spring day, the three of them inside the old Norman tower that stood on Falconwell lands. As they had explored, a staircase had given way beneath

Penelope, and she'd been trapped a level above Michael and Tommy. It hadn't been far, a yard or two, but far enough for her to be afraid of jumping. She'd called for help, and Tommy had been the first to find her. He'd urged her to jump, promised to catch her. But she'd been frozen in fear.

And then Michael had come. Calm, fearless Michael, who had looked up into her eyes and given her strength. *Jump, Sixpence. I shall be your net.*

She'd believed him.

She took a deep breath at the memory, at the reminder of her time with Michael, of the way he had always made her safe. She looked to Tommy. "He's not that boy any longer."

"No. He's not. Langford made sure of that." He paused, then said, "I wish I could have prevented it, Pen. I'm sorry."

She shook her head. "No apologies. He's cold and infuriating when he wishes to be, but he's built so much for himself—proven his worth tenfold. The marriage may be challenging, but I imagine most of them are, don't you?"

"Ours would not have been."

"Ours would have been a challenge in a different way, Tommy. You know that." She smiled. "Your poetry . . . it is abhorrent."

"There is that." His smile was there, then gone. He changed the conversation. "I've been thinking of India. They say there is a world of opportunity there."

"You would leave England? Why?"

He drank deep at the words, placing his empty glass on a nearby table. "Your husband plans to ruin me."

It took a moment for her to comprehend the words. "I'm sure that's not true."

"It is. He told me."

Confusion flared. "When?"

"On the day of your wedding. I came to Needham House to find you, to convince you to marry me, only to find that I was too late and that you'd already left for London with him. I followed you. Went straight to his club."

Michael hadn't said anything. "And you saw him?"

"Long enough for him to explain that he had plans for revenge against my father. Against me. When he's through, I shall have no choice but to leave Britain."

The words did not surprise her. Of course Falconwell would not be enough for her immovable husband. Of course he would want vengeance against Langford. But Tommy? "He wouldn't do that, Tommy. You have a past. A history. The three of us do."

Tommy smiled a small wry smile. "Our past does not weigh so heavily as revenge, I'm afraid."

She shook her head. "What could he possibly plan—"

"I am not . . ." He took a deep breath. "He knows . . ." Paused. Looked away. Tried again. "I am not Langford's son."

Her jaw dropped, along with her voice. "You cannot mean it."

He laughed a small, self-deprecating laugh. "I certainly would not lie about it, Pen."

He was right, of course. This was not the sort of thing one lied about. "You are not—"

"No."

"Who—"

"I don't know. I didn't know I was a bastard until a few years ago, when my—when Langford told me the truth."

She watched him carefully, registering the quiet sadness behind his eyes. "You never said anything."

"It's not something one says, really." He paused. "You do what you can to keep it a secret . . . and hope no one discovers."

But someone had discovered.

Penelope swallowed, turning her attention to a large oil painting on the wall—another landscape—this one in a wilderness too rugged and untouched to be anything but the North Country. She fixed her stare on a large boulder to one side of the artwork as understanding dawned. "It would ruin your father."

"His only child, a bastard."

Her gaze returned to his. "Don't call yourself that."

"Everyone else will, soon enough."

Silence. And in it, the keen awareness that Tommy was right. That Michael's plans included his ruin. *A means to an end.* He saw the moment she recognized the truth and took a step toward her. "Come with me, Penny. We can leave this place and this life and start fresh. India. The Americas. Greece. Spain. The Orient. Anywhere you choose."

Her eyes went wide. He was serious. "I'm married, Tommy."

One side of his mouth crooked up. "To *Michael.* You require escape as much as I do. Maybe more—at least my ruin at his hands will come swiftly."

"Be that as it may, I'm married. And you . . ." She trailed off.

"I am nothing. Not when he's through with me."

She thought of her husband, to whom she had vowed fidelity and loyalty, who had fought for so long to rebuild his fortunes without his name. He knew the importance of a name. Of an identity. She couldn't believe he'd do this.

She shook her head. "You're wrong. He wouldn't . . ." But even as she said the words, she knew they weren't true.

He would do anything for his revenge.

Even ruin his friends.

Tommy's jaw set, and she was suddenly nervous. She'd never seen him so serious. So driven. "I'm not wrong. He has proof. He's willing to use it. He's ruthless, Pen . . . no longer the friend we once knew." He was close, and he took one of her hands in both of his. "He doesn't deserve you. Come with me. Come with me, and we neither of us shall be lonely."

She was quiet for a long moment before she said softly, "He is my husband."

"He is using you."

The words, however true, stung. She met his gaze. "Of

course he is. Just as every other man in my life has done. My father, the Duke of Leighton, the other suitors . . . you."

When he opened his mouth to deny it, she shook her head and raised one finger. "Don't, Tommy. Don't try to make fools of us both. You might not be using me for land or money or reputation, but you are afraid of your life once the truth is out, and you think I will make a friendly companion—someone to keep the loneliness at bay."

"Is that so bad?" Tommy asked, desperation creeping into his voice. "What of our friendship? What of *our* past? What of me?"

She did not pretend to misunderstand the words and the ultimatum in them, born of distress. He was asking her to make a choice. Her longest-standing friend—the one who had never left, or her husband, her family, her life. It was no choice. Not really. "He's my husband!" she said. "Perhaps I would not have written this tale, but this is the tale, nonetheless."

She stopped, irritation and frustration taking her breath. Tommy watched her for a long moment, her words hanging between them. "And that is that." He smiled, sad. "I confess, I am not surprised. You always liked him best."

She shook her head. "That's not true."

"Of course it is. One day, you'll realize it." He lifted one hand to her chin in a brotherly gesture. That was the problem, of course, Tommy had always been more brother than beau. Not like Michael. There was nothing brotherly about Michael.

There was nothing kind about him, either. And while she might have chosen him in this strange, sad war, she would not stand by as he tore down Tommy. "I shan't let him ruin you," she vowed. "I swear it."

Tommy sliced one hand through the air, his disbelief palpable. "Oh, Penny . . . as though you could stop it."

The words should have made her sad. She should have heard the truth in them.

But instead, they made her angry.

Michael had taken her from her family, changed her life in a hundred ways, forced this farce upon her, and threatened her dearest friend. And he'd done it all while keeping her at a safe distance, as though she were an insignificant thing about which he need not worry.

Well, he had better begin to worry.

She lifted her chin, straightened her shoulders. "He is not God," she said, her voice firm. "He does not have the right to toy with us like little tin soldiers."

Tommy recognized her ire. He smiled, sad. "Don't do this, Pen. I'm not worth it."

She raised a brow. "I disagree. And even if you weren't, I am. And I am through with him."

"He will hurt you."

One side of her mouth twisted in a wry smile. "He'll likely hurt me anyway. All the more reason to face him." She headed for the door to the receiving room, pulling it open to let him exit. As he neared, his shining black Hessians soft on the lush carpet, sadness twisted through her. "I am sorry, Tommy."

He took her shoulders in his and pressed a warm kiss to her forehead, before he said, "I do want your happiness, Pen, you know that, don't you?"

"I do."

"You'll let me know if you change your mind?"

She nodded. "I will."

He stared at her for a long time before turning away, a shadow crossing his handsome face. "I shall wait for you. Until I can wait no more."

She wanted to tell him not to go. She wanted to tell him to stay. But whether from sadness or fear or a keen knowledge that her husband was a ship that would not be turned, instead she said, "Good night, Tommy."

He turned and walked through the open door into the foyer, and Penelope followed the line of his shoulders as he made his way to the exit to Hell House. The door closed behind him and she heard the clatter of carriage wheels in the silent space, punctuating her solitude. She was alone.

Alone in this mausoleum of a house, filled with things that were not hers and people she did not know. Alone in this quiet world.

There was a movement in the shadows at the far side of the foyer, and Penelope knew immediately that it was Mrs. Worth. She knew, as well, where the housekeeper's loyalties lay.

Penelope spoke in the darkness, "How long before he hears that I had a gentleman caller at eleven o'clock?"

The housekeeper came into the light but did not speak for a long moment. When she did, it was with all calm. "I sent word to the club upon Mr. Alles's arrival."

Penelope watched the beautiful woman, the betrayal—however expected—washing through her, stoking the fires of her ire. "You wasted your paper."

She headed for the central staircase of Hell House and began to climb. Halfway up, she turned back to face the housekeeper, standing at the foot of the stairs, watching her with her perfect hair and perfect skin and perfect eyes, as though if she stood sentry, she could prevent Penelope from doing anything else that might irritate her master.

And that only served to make Penelope more angry.

Suddenly, she was feeling quite reckless indeed.

"Where is the club?"

The housekeeper's eyes went wide. "I am sure I do not know."

"Funny, because I am sure that you do." She did not lower her voice, letting it call down to the other woman without remorse. "I am sure you know everything that goes on in this house. All the comings and goings. And I am sure that you know that my husband spends his evenings at his club instead of here."

For a long moment, Mrs. Worth did not speak, and Penelope wondered, fleetingly, if she had the authority to dismiss the insolent, beautiful woman. Finally, she waved one hand and began her climb once more. "Tell me or don't. If I must, I shall hire myself a hack and go looking for it."

"He would not like that." The housekeeper was following her now, down the long upper corridor to Penelope's bedchamber.

"No. He wouldn't. But I find I have little interest in his likes or dislikes." Indeed, her lack of interest in those things was rather freeing, she was discovering. She opened the door to her chamber and crossed the room to her wardrobe, from which she extracted a large cloak. Turning back, she met the lovely housekeeper's wide-eyed gaze.

And paused. Perhaps *this* was Michael's raven-haired goddess. Perhaps it was Mrs. Worth who held his heart and his mind and his evenings. And as she studied the housekeeper's porcelain face, measuring the woman's height, the way she would fit against Michael, the way she would suit him so much better than Penelope suited him, Mrs. Worth smiled. Not just a smile, really. A wide, welcoming grin. "Mr. Alles. He is not your lover."

The idea that a servant would say something so utterly inappropriate set Penelope back for a moment before she answered, in all honesty. "No. He is not." And, as the gloves were off, "And you are not Michael's mistress."

Surprise had the housekeeper speaking without thought. "Dear God, no. I wouldn't have him if he begged." She paused. "That is . . . I didn't mean . . . he's a good man, my lady."

Penelope exchanged her white kidskin gloves for navy blue suede. As she fitted the fingers to her hand, she spoke honestly. "He's a horse's bottom. And I am not entirely certain I would have him if he begged either. Except for the fact that I am married to him."

"Well, if you'll beg my pardon, you should absolutely *not* have him until he begs. He shouldn't be leaving you so . . ."

"Regularly?" Penelope filled in the gap, deciding that perhaps she had misjudged the housekeeper. "Unfortunately,

Mrs. Worth, I do not believe that begging is in my husband's repertoire."

The housekeeper smiled. "You are welcome to call me Worth. It's what all the others call me."

"The others?"

"The other partners in The Angel."

Penelope's brows snapped together. "How do you know my husband's partners?"

"I used to work at The Angel, scrubbing pots, plucking chickens, whatever needed to be done."

Curiosity flared. "How did you end up here?"

A cloud passed over the other woman's face. "I aged into my body. People began to notice."

"Men?" It didn't have to be a question. Penelope knew the answer. A face like Worth's could not hide for long even in the kitchens of a gaming hell.

"The employees did everything they could to keep the members from getting too close—not just to me—to all the girls." Penelope leaned forward, knowing what was coming. Loathing it. Wishing she could erase the words before they were spoken. "But I was careless. Powerful men can be persistent. Wealthy men can be a temptation. And the entire sex are pretty liars when they want to be."

Penelope knew it. Her husband was as silver-tongued as they came.

Worth's smile was sad. "Bourne found us."

Penelope watched as the other woman ran a finger across the gilded frame of a large oil painting on the wall. "He was furious," she said, knowing instinctively that—whatever his faults—her husband would never have stood for such behavior.

"He nearly killed the man." Penelope felt a surge of pride as Worth continued. "For all his darkness . . . for all his selfishness . . . he's a good man." She stepped back, assessing Penelope's garments. "If you're going to march into The Angel, you're going to have to enter through the owner's entrance. It's the only way you'll get onto the main floor. And you'll need a cloak with a larger hood if you're going to keep your face covered."

Penelope hadn't thought of that. She crossed the room, passing into the dimly lit hallway beyond. "Thank you."

"He'll be furious when you get there," Worth added. "My note will not have helped." She paused. "I am sorry about that."

Penelope cut Worth a look as they reached the foot of the stairs. "I shall collect on that debt," Penelope said, "but not tonight. Tonight, I shall simply tell you that your message was incomplete. And I intend to deliver the rest of it in person."

Dear M—

My birthday has come again, and this one more troublesome than any of those prior. My mother is ready to host a coming-out ball, and I am targeted as the fatted calf (It's not the most becoming of metaphors, is it?). At any rate, she's already making plans for March, if you can believe it—I'm certain I shan't last the winter.

Do promise you'll come to the fated event . . . I know that twenty is far too young for you to be attending balls or caring a bit about the season, but it would be nice to see a friendly face.

Always—P
Needham Manor, August 1820

No reply

"You should be at home with your wife."

Bourne did not turn away from his place at the window

overlooking the pit floor of The Fallen Angel. "My wife is tucked safely in her bed, asleep."

He knew how that would look, Penelope in her pristine, white linen nightgown, wrapped in a collection of blankets, curled on her side, her blond hair spread out like a wave behind her—sighing a sweet little sigh in her sleep, tempting him, even in fantasy.

Or, even better, in his bed, on his fur, lush and waiting to be discovered.

The days since she'd requested he not touch her had been interminable.

The night at Tottenham's had begun with a single, achievable goal—to lay the foundation of Bourne and Penelope's false love for the rest of society. But then she'd gone and stood strong in that viper pit of a dining room, bolstering his story, feigning fondness and devotion and, ultimately, defending him in her perfect, cultured way.

As much as he'd told himself that he had gone after her to further convince Tottenham's guests of his fascination with his new wife, he knew, deep down, that it wasn't true. The guests had been far from his mind, and his fascination had been nothing close to fraudulent. He'd had to touch her. He'd had to be close to her.

The moment he'd kissed her, he'd lost control of the situation—gasping for breath, clutching her to him, wishing that they were anywhere but there, in that hallway, in that house, with those people. He'd wanted to murder Tottenham for interrupting them, but God knew what would have happened if the viscount hadn't done just that, considering that Bourne had been seriously considering lifting his bride's skirts, lowering himself to his knees, and showing her precisely where pleasure could take them both when the viscount had cleared his throat—and Bourne's head.

She'd gone statue-still in his arms, and he'd known in that moment that she'd believed the worst of him. She'd believed it had all been concocted for Tottenham's benefit

. . . and it had—but Bourne hadn't expected it to go so far. And he'd never admit to her that he'd been just as carried away as she was.

So he'd told her the truth about the arrangement, knowing that the words would sting. Knowing she'd hate him more for deceiving her. And when she'd pronounced, with all the poise of a queen, that he was not to touch her again, he'd known it was best for them both.

Even if he'd wanted nothing more than to take her home and make her recant the words.

Chase tried again. "You've been here every night since your return."

"Why do you care so much?"

"I know women. And I know they do not like to be ignored."

Bourne did not reply.

"I hear that you're angling for one of the Marbury girls to become Lady Tottenham."

Bourne narrowed his gaze. "You hear."

Chase shrugged one shoulder and smirked. "I have my sources."

Bourne turned back to the window, watching Tottenham far below at the piquet table. "The unmarried young ladies Marbury are just today in town. That gives me a few days to secure the interest of the viscount."

"So the dinner was a success?"

"I dream of invitations arriving in droves."

Chase laughed. "Poor, sad Bourne. Forced to restore the only thing he doesn't want for the only thing he does." Bourne leveled Chase with a look, but he did not disagree. "You realize that the club has made you more money than you could ever spend, and that there's no reason at all for you to prove yourself by exacting your revenge, do you not?"

"It's not about the money."

"What is it about, then, the title? The way he cheapened it?"

"I don't care about the title."

"Of course you do. You're just like every other peer—consumed with the magical power of your title. Even if you resent it." Chase paused. "Not that it matters anymore. You've married the girl, and you're well down the road to revenge. Or is it resurrection?"

Bourne scowled through the red stained glass that marked a flame of hell, through which he could see the roulette wheel spinning far below. "I've no plans for resurrection. I shall do what is necessary to ruin Langford. And once that is done, I'm returning to my life."

"Without her?"

"Without her." *But he wanted her.*

He'd gone without things he wanted before. Survived.

"And how do you expect to explain that to the lady?"

"She doesn't need me to have the life she wants. She can live where she wants, the way she wants, on my land, with my money. I'm happy to leave her to it." He'd said it before, more than once, but it was becoming more difficult to believe.

"How do you envision that happening?" Chase fairly drawled. "You are married."

"There are ways for her to be happy nonetheless."

"And is that what you are looking for? Her happiness?"

He considered the words, heard the surprise in Chase's tone. He certainly had not begun this journey with any thought of Penelope's happiness. And still—even as he knew it made him the worst possible kind of husband—he would sacrifice her happiness for his revenge. But he was not a monster; if he could, he would keep her happy *and* ruin Langford.

As proof, he would honor her request not to touch her.

For he knew well enough that making a habit of taking his perfect, virginal bride to bed would be a mistake, as she was precisely the kind of woman who would want more.

Far more than he had to give.

So he would stay the hell away from her.

Even if he wanted her more than he could say.

"I forced her to marry me for a piece of land. The least I can do is think about what might make the lady content after our marriage has served its purpose. I'm sending her away the moment proof of Langford's fall is mine."

"Why?"

Because she deserves more.

He feigned disinterest. "I promised her freedom. And adventure."

Chase chuckled at that. "Did you? I'm sure she was thrilled to accept it. She's waited a long time since that first proposal—long enough to realize that most marriages aren't worth the paper on which the licenses are printed. So you'll honor the promise?"

Bourne did not look away from the pit floor. "I will."

"Any adventure?"

Bourne turned his head. "What does that mean?"

"I mean, in my experience, ladies with excitement in their reach are rather . . . creative. Are you prepared for her to travel the globe? To toss your money away on frivolities? To host raucous parties and scandalize the *ton*? To take a lover?"

The last was spoken casually, but Bourne knew Chase was deliberately taunting him. "She may do whatever she likes."

"So, should the lady choose, you'd allow her to cuckold you?"

He knew it was bait. Knew he should not rise. His fists clenched, nonetheless. "If she is discreet, it is not my concern."

"You don't want her for yourself?"

"No." *Liar.*

"An unsatisfying experience, was it? Best to let another handle her, then."

Bourne resisted the urge to put Chase straight into the wall. He hated the very idea of another man's touching her. Another man's discovering her eagerness, her passion—

more tempting than cards, than billiards, than roulette. She threatened his control, his tightly leashed desires, his long-hidden conscience.

He could not make her happy.

And it was only a matter of time before he would want to.

It was better this way.

For both of them.

The door to the owners' suite opened, and Temple saved Bourne from having to continue the irritating conversation. The third man's hulking silhouette blocked out the light beyond as he crossed the room. It was Saturday evening, and Chase, Cross, and Temple had a standing faro game.

Cross followed behind Temple, shuffling a deck of cards. He spoke, surprise in his tone. "Bourne is playing?"

Bourne ignored the temptation that flared at the question. He wanted to play. He wanted to lose himself in the simple, straightforward rules of the game. He wanted to pretend that there was nothing more to life than luck.

But he knew better.

Luck had not been on his side for a very long time.

"I'm not playing."

The three hadn't really expected him to join, but they always asked. Chase met his eyes. "Stay for a drink, then."

If he stayed, Chase would push him farther. Would ask him more.

But if he left, Penelope would haunt him, making him feel like a dozen kinds of fool.

He stayed.

The others had taken their seats at the owners' table, used only for this game—Temple, Cross, and Chase the only players. Bourne sat in the fourth chair, always at the table, never at the game.

Temple shuffled the cards, and Michael watched as they fanned through the big man's fingers once, twice, before they flew across the table, the rhythm of smooth paper against thick baize a temptation in itself.

They'd played two hands in silence before Chase's question came, clear and unyielding across the table. "And when she desires children?"

Temple and Cross hesitated in considering their cards, the question so unexpected that they could not help but show their interest. Cross spoke first, "When who desires children?"

Chase leaned back. "Bourne's Penelope."

Bourne did not like the possessive description.

Or perhaps he liked it too much.

Children. They would require more than a father in London and a mother in the country. They would require more than a childhood spent living in the shadow of a gaming hell. And if they were girls, they would require more than a father with a sordid reputation. A father who ruined everything he touched.

Including their mother.

Shit.

"She will want them," Chase pressed on. "She's the type to want them."

"How would you know?" Bourne asked, irritated that this was even a topic of discussion.

"I know a great deal about the lady."

Temple and Cross now swung their attention to Chase. "Honestly?" Temple asked, disbelief in his tone.

"Is she horsefaced?" Cross asked. "Bourne says she's not, but I think that must be the reason why he's here with us instead of home, showing her how entertaining the late-night experiences of the Marchioness of Bourne can be."

Irritation flared in Bourne. "Not all of us spend our evenings rutting like pigs."

Cross considered his cards once more. "I prefer rabbits," he said casually, drawing a bark of laughter from Temple before he looked to Chase once more. "Honestly, though. Tell us about the new Lady Bourne?"

Chase discarded. "She is not horsefaced."

Bourne gritted his teeth. *No. She isn't.*

Cross leaned forward. "Is she dull?"

"To my knowledge, no," Chase said, before turning to Bourne. "Is she dull?"

A vision flashed of Penelope traipsing through the snow in the dead of night with a lantern before announcing that she was in search of inland pirates, followed by a memory of her naked, spread across his fur coverlet. He shifted in his seat. "She is in no way dull."

Temple lifted a card. "Then what is wrong with you?"

There was a pause, and Bourne looked from one partner to the next, each wider-eyed than the last. "Honestly, you're all like gossiping, scandal-loving women."

Chase raised a brow. "For that, I'm telling them." There was a pause, as the others leaned forward, waiting. "What's wrong with him is that he's committed to sending the lady away."

Temple looked up. "For how long?"

"Forever."

Cross pursed his lips together and turned to Bourne. "Is it because she was a virgin? Really, Bourne. You can't fault her for that. I mean, Lord knows why, but most of the aristocratic nobs out there value the trait. Give her time. She'll learn."

Bourne clenched his teeth. "She did just fine."

Temple leaned in, all seriousness. "Did she not like it?"

Chase snickered, and Bourne narrowed his eyes to slits. "You are enjoying yourself, are you not?"

"Quite."

"Perhaps you could ask Worth for some advice," Cross offered, discarding.

Chase picked up the card. "I'm happy to share from my personal experience, if you like."

Temple grinned at his hand. "And I."

It was all too much. "I do not need advice. She enjoyed it immensely."

"I hear they don't all enjoy it right off the bat," Cross said.

"That is true," Chase said, all expertise.

"It's fine if she didn't, old man," Temple offered. "You can try again."

"She enjoyed it." Bourne's voice was low and tight, and he thought he might kill the next person who spoke.

"Well, one thing is for certain," Temple said, casually, and Bourne ignored the pang of disappointment that the enormous man was very likely the only one at the table he could not kill.

"What's that?" Chase asked, discarding.

"If she wants children, someone's going to have to do the deed."

If she wanted children, he would do the deed.

Cross discarded. "If you're sure she's not ugly, I'm happy to—"

He did not finish the sentence. Bourne lunged at him, and the two went tumbling to the floor, in a cacophony of broken chairs, laughter, and the sound of flesh hitting bone.

Temple sighed, throwing his cards down to the table. "These games never end the way cards are supposed to end."

"I thought good card games always end in a brawl," Chase said. Cross and Bourne rolled into a chair, toppling it over as Justin entered the suite. The bespectacled man ignored Bourne and Cross, tumbling across the floor, and leaned low to whisper something to Temple and Chase.

Temple entered the fray then, a stray fist grazing the high arch of one of his cheeks, eliciting a wicked curse before he yanked Cross from Bourne. Pulling out a handkerchief, Cross wiped the blood from a cut just above his eye and leveled a long, knowing look at Bourne. "If you're this high-strung on the first week of your marriage, you need to get that wife of yours into bed, or you need to get her out of your house."

Bourne wiped a hand along one swollen lip, knowing the words were true.

"I need her. Without her, I haven't got Langford."

And if I touch her again, I might not let her go.

And then he'd ruin her just as he'd ruined everything else of value he'd ever had.

Cross's eyes gleamed, one fast swelling shut, as though he'd heard Bourne's thought with crystal clarity. "That limits your options, then."

"Bourne," Justin said, drawing his attention, "you've a note from Worth."

A thrum of unease coursed through Bourne as he broke the seal of Hell House and read the few lines of text scrawled hastily across the paper. Disbelief and fury shot through him at the words.

Tommy Alles was in his house. With his wife.

He would kill him if he touched her.

He might kill him anyway.

With a wicked curse, Bourne was on his feet and headed for the door, halfway across the massive room before Chase spoke, "I'm told there's a problem at the roulette table as well."

"Bugger the roulette table," he growled, yanking open the door to the owner's suite.

"Well, considering your wife is down there, Cross might be willing, but—"

Bourne froze at the words, disbelief and dread settling in his gut as he registered his partners' smirks. Barely retaining his control, he headed for the window to look down on the casino floor, drawn immediately to a cloaked figure standing at one side of the roulette field, one delicate hand reaching out to place a single gold coin on the numbered baize.

"It appears the lady is taking the adventure you promised," Chase said, wryly.

No.

It could not be her. She would not have done something so foolish.

She would not have risked her sisters.

She would not have risked *herself.*

Anything could happen to her down there, in the pit of

vipers, surrounded by men who drank too much and wagered too much . . . men who were high on their winnings or driven to prove that they were in control of something, even if it was not their purse.

He cursed, dark and wicked, and set off for the door at a run.

A low whistle sounded, and Cross's words followed behind him. "If her face is half as fine as her courage, I'll happily take her off your hands."

Over his dead body.

Chapter Thirteen

Dear M—

Well, the Marchioness of Needham and Dolby is very proud indeed today. I had my coming out, presentation at court, vouchers to Almack's and all, and there's no question that I am a resounding success.

This should come as no surprise, as I've been officially on the marriage mart for nearly two weeks and I haven't had a single interesting conversation. Not one, would you believe it? My mother's angling for a duke, but it's not as though there is a glut of young, eligible ones on hand.

I confess, I had hoped I might see you—at a ball, or a dinner or some affair this week, but you've gone missing, and all I am left with is foolscap.

An apt name. Fool indeed.

Unsigned
Dolby House, March 1820

Letter unsent

The Fallen Angel was magnificent.

Penelope had never seen anything so stunning as this place, this marvelous, lush, place, filled with candlelight and color, teeming with people who called out obscene bets and rolled with laughter, who kissed their dice and cursed their bad luck.

She had announced herself quietly, not wanting to reveal her identity but knowing that if she did not tell the men guarding the entrance her name, she would not be allowed inside. Their eyes had gone wide as she'd spoken her identity, naming her husband and lingering in the shadows of the entryway, waiting for them to decide they believed her.

When one of the large men had grinned wide and knocked twice on the inner door to the club with a fist the size of a ham, the door had opened just barely. "Bourne's lady. Best let 'er in."

Bourne's lady.

A shiver of awareness shot through Penelope at the description—one she did not want and still could not resist. One she planned to use to her full advantage that night as she gave her husband a significant piece of her mind.

But the door opened all the way then, revealing a carnival of movement and sound, and Penelope forgot her immediate goal.

She pulled her cloak tightly around her, grateful for Worth's counsel and for the too-large hood casting her into shadow while she watched those around her hover over their cards, track the little ivory ball in the roulette wheel, follow their dice across the rich, green baize, as it tumbled in the winds of fate.

It was adventure in its basest, purest form.

And she loved every inch of it.

No wonder Michael spent so much of his time here; this was his goddess, his raven-haired beauty. And she could not blame him. It was a magnificent mistress.

The men in their stark, black coats and their perfectly pressed cravats, the butlers who traveled the floor of the casino with trays laden with scotch and brandy, and the women in their revealing bodices, each a more brilliant color than the last. They were painted and primped, coiffed and colored, and Penelope wanted to *be* them. For one, fleeting moment, to know what it was to hold fortune in her hand. To throw the dice and know the thrill of exploit.

But it was the stained-glass mural, massive and undeniably beautiful, that had her catching her breath. A great, stunning portrait of Lucifer, chain around his ankle wrapping twice around his leg before trailing off into the abyss, his scepter, snapped in half, still held in one hand, his crown in the other. The massive angel fell, his wings no longer able to keep him in flight, headfirst into the flames of hell.

It was at once beautiful and grotesque—the perfect backdrop for this den of vice.

She kept her head down and moved through the crowd, loving the way the bodies moved her through their mass. She allowed them to guide her, and she promised herself that she would stop at the first table she found along the path.

It was the roulette table, and her heart leapt to her throat in a mix of gratitude and excitement. She knew this game. Knew its rules. Knew it was pure, unbridled luck. And she wanted to try hers.

For suddenly she felt very lucky, indeed.

She met the eyes of the tablemaster, who raised a brow and waved his long rake above the field. "Gentlemen . . . lady," he intoned seriously, "your bets, please."

Her hand was already in her pocket, already toying with the coins there. She pulled out a shiny gold sovereign, running her thumb across its face, watching the others at the table place their bets. Coins were set on the rich green plush all along the field, and Penelope's eyes were drawn to a tempting, red space at the middle of the table.

Number twenty-three.

"We await the lady's wager."

Her eyes met the dealer's and she reached out, tentatively,

to place a coin on the baize, loving the way the gold glinted in the candlelight.

"No more bets, please."

And then the wheel was in motion, and the ball was spinning along the gutter, the sound of ivory against steel a temptation in itself. Penelope leaned forward, eager for an unobstructed view, her breath catching in her throat.

"They say that roulette is Lucifer's game." The words came at her shoulder, and she could not resist turning toward the voice even as she was careful to keep her cloak pulled low over her face. "Fitting, is it not?"

The stranger placed his hand on the edge of the table, close enough to touch her, and the lingering caress was too slow to be a mistake. She snapped her hand back from the unpleasant sensation.

"Fascinating," she said, edging away from her unwelcome companion, hoping that the single word would end their conversation. Her attention returned to the wheel, spinning in glorious red and black, too fast to keep track.

"There is a story of a Frenchman who was so caught up in the game, so tempted by the wheel, that he sold his soul to the devil to learn its secrets."

The wheel was beginning to slow, and Penelope leaned in, understanding that poor Frenchman's temptation. The man at her side slid one finger down the outside of her arm, sending a shiver of distaste through her and drawing her attention. "What would tempt you to sell your soul?"

She did not have the chance to reply, or to tell her neighbor to remove his hands from her person, as he was instantly yanked from his spot and tossed to the floor several feet away. She turned at the commotion to find Michael stalking the man as he scurried backward, like a crab, into the legs of a group of people who had stopped in the center of the casino floor to watch the drama unfold.

Her husband leaned down and grabbed the man by his cravat, his great hulk blocking the prone man's face. "You will never touch a lady in this hell again," her husband growled, raising his fist in a wicked threat.

"Goddammit, Bourne." The words were strangled from the man's throat as he lifted his hands to Michael's wrists. "Lay off. She's just a—"

Michael's hand wrapped around the other man's neck. "Finish the sentence, Densmore, and give me the pleasure of robbing your breath," he said, low and close to his prey. "If I see it, or hear of you laying a hand on another female here, your membership will not be the only thing you lose. Do you understand?"

"Yes."

"Say it." He looked ready to kill, and Worth's tale echoed through Penelope's memory.

"Yes. Yes, I understand."

Michael tossed him back to the floor and rounded on Penelope, who moved instinctively to push back her cloak. He reached out and grabbed one of her hands, pulling her into an alcove too poorly lit for anyone to see her, stepping close to shield her from prying eyes. "And you," he whispered, his fury unmistakable. "What the hell are you doing here?"

She met his gaze firmly, refusing to be cowed. It was time for her to act her part—the marchioness out for her adventure. "I was having a fine time before you arrived and caused a scene."

A muscle twitched in his jaw, and his fingers tightened around her wrists. "*I* caused a scene? Half of London is in this room, and you think a silly cloak will hide you from them?"

She twisted her hands in his grasp, trying to free herself. He did not release her. "It was doing just that. No one noticed me." He pushed her against the wall, farther into the darkness. "No one *recognized* me. *Now*, of course, they are all wondering who I am."

"They likely know." He gave a harsh laugh. "I recognized you the moment I saw you, you foolish woman."

He had? She ignored the thrum of pleasure that shot

through her and squared her shoulders, refusing to back down.

The roulette croupier appeared at the edge of the alcove. "Bourne."

Michael shot a look over his shoulder that could have stopped an army. "Not now."

"Well, considering I'm in full view of half of London, as you are so quick to point out, what's the worst that could happen?" she asked.

"Let's see," he said, his voice dripping with sarcasm, "you could have been abducted, mistreated, *revealed* . . .

Penelope stiffened. "And how would that have been different than my treatment at your hands?" she whispered, keeping her voice low enough so that only he could hear her, knowing she was pushing his limits.

His eyes flashed. "It would be immensely different. And if you can't see that—"

"Oh, please. Don't pretend you care a bit about me, or my happiness. It would be the same cell, a different jailer."

His teeth clenched. "Three minutes in private with that pig Densmore, and you would have seen that I'm a veritable saint compared to some scoundrels. I told you, you were not to come here. Not without me."

"I find I no longer care for being told what I am not to do." She took a deep breath, not knowing from where her courage had come, but hoping it would not fail her now, as he looked very, very angry.

And, she realized, very disheveled. His cravat was wrinkled beyond repair, his coat was not straight on his shoulders, and one of his cuffs had disappeared beneath its sleeve.

It wasn't normal. Not for Michael.

"What happened to you?" she asked.

"Bourne."

The third time the dealer said his name, Michael spun around. "Goddammit. What is it?"

"It's the lady."

"What about her?"

Penelope peeked around Michael, pulling her hood forward, making sure she could not be recognized. The dealer's brows lifted as he offered them both a half smile. "She won."

A beat, then Bourne said, "What did you say?"

"She won." The dealer could not mask his surprise. "Number twenty-three. Straight up."

Michael's gaze slid to the table, then to the wheel. "She did?"

Penelope's eyes went wide. "I did?"

The croupier gave her a silly smile. "You did."

"Send her winnings up to the suite." In a matter of seconds, Michael had pulled her through a well-guarded door nearby.

As they climbed a long, dark set of stairs, Penelope shored up her courage, prepared to face him. But first, she had to keep up with him. Her hand was tucked into his, and he showed no indication of releasing her as he pulled her down a long hallway and, ultimately, into a large room that would have been completely dark if not for the light from the main floor of the casino pouring through the stained-glass wall at one end of the room—casting the entire space into a mosaic of color.

"How gorgeous," she whispered, not noticing that he'd let her go before locking the door behind them. "From below, there is no indication that there is anything behind the glass."

"That's the point."

"It's stunning." She headed for the window, reaching one hand out to touch a golden panel that made up a lock of Lucifer's hair.

"What are you doing here, Penelope?"

She snatched her hand back at the question, turning to him, barely able to make him out in the shadows. He seemed to have faded away into the darkness at the far end of the room. Her heart began to pound, and she remembered why she had set out for the club. "There is a conversation we must have."

"It could not have waited for me to return to Hell House?"

"If I ever believed you would return to the house, my lord, I might have waited," she said tartly. "As I am unsure of your plans in that regard, I felt it best for me to attend you."

He crossed his arms across his wide chest, the fabric of his coat straining against his muscled arms. "I'm going to fire the coachman who brought you."

"Impossible. I came in a hack." She could not keep the triumph from her voice.

"If Tommy helped you in any way, I shall take great pleasure in destroying him."

She lifted her chin. "And so we come to it."

"You are not to see him again."

She did not care that he towered over her in the darkness, clearly angry with her. For she was angry with him, as well. "I am not so certain that I will follow that order."

"You will." He crowded her against the door. "See him again, and I'll destroy him. Let it be on your head."

It was the opening for which she had been waiting. "I am told that you plan to destroy him anyway." He did not deny it, and a sliver of disappointment shot through her. She shook her head. "It's amazing, how I continue to believe better of you only to be proven wrong." She spun away from him, heading for the window once more, staring out on the floor. "You're heartless."

"It's best you realize that now, before the days of our marriage grow any longer."

She spun back toward him, furious at the callous way he referred to their life. To her life. "Perhaps our sham of a marriage isn't long for this world anyway."

"What does that mean?"

She gave a little humorless laugh. "Only that you clearly care not a bit for it."

"Your precious Tommy asked you to run with him, didn't he?" It was her turn to remain silent. Let him believe what he wanted. He came closer. "Are you planning to go, Penelope? Planning to ruin our marriage and your reputation and your sisters' names with one selfish choice?"

She could not stop herself from replying. "*I* am selfish?" She laughed, and pushed past him toward the door. "That is amusing, coming from you—the most selfish man I've ever known—selfish enough to destroy your friends, and your *wife* in service to your own goals."

She reached for the door handle, gasping when his hand snaked out of the darkness to capture her wrist. "You are not leaving until this is through. Until you have given me your word that you will stay away from Tommy Alles."

Of course she wasn't going anywhere with Tommy. But she refused to allow him the satisfaction of knowing that. "Why? Wouldn't it be easier for you if I left with him? Then you could get your revenge and your freedom in one wide swath."

"You're mine."

She rounded on him. "You are unbalanced."

"That may be. But I am also your husband. You would do well to remember that fact. And the fact that you pledged to obey me."

She gave a little, humorless laugh. "And *you* pledged to *honor* me," she retorted. *And we both pledged to love the other. That hasn't worked out either.*

He stilled. "You think I have done you a dishonor?"

"I think you do me a dishonor every time you touch me."

He released her then, so quickly it was as though her skin had burned him. "What does that mean?"

She hesitated, uncertain, the argument suddenly moving in a direction with which she was not entirely comfortable.

"Oh no, my lady." He fairly spat the honorific. She realized she had offended him. "You will answer the question."

Yes. She would.

"Every time you touch me, every time you show me the slightest interest, it is for your benefit. Your goals. Your revenge, of which I want no part. There is nothing about it that is for me."

"No?" The words dripped with sarcasm. "Interesting, as you seem to have enjoyed my touch."

"Of course I've enjoyed it. You've done everything you could to ensure that I would follow you through fire in those instances. You've used your obvious . . . She paused, waving a hand in his direction, " . . . prowess in the bedchamber to further your own goals." The words were coming fast and furious now. "And you've done a remarkable job of it. I confess, I am impressed. By both your clever strategy and your impeccable performance. But pleasure is fleeting, Lord Bourne—fleeting enough that it is not worth the pain of being used." She set one hand to the door handle, eager to leave the room. And him. "Forgive me if I find myself unwilling to drop everything and remember my vows when you have so *misused* your own."

"You think it would have been different with your precious Tommy?"

Her gaze narrowed. "I shan't apologize for caring for him. There was a time when you cared for him as well. He was your oldest friend." The third of their trio. She let her disappointment edge into her tone.

Anger flashed in his eyes. "He was no friend at all when it was time to show himself."

She shook her head. "You think he did not regret his father's actions? You are wrong. He did. From the start."

"Not enough. But he will when I am through with him."

She became protective. "I shan't let you hurt him."

"You haven't any choice. Your dear Tommy will be ruined alongside his father. I vowed revenge nine years ago, and nothing will stand in my way. And you shall thank God you did not marry him, or I would level you with them."

Her gaze narrowed. "If you ruin Tommy, I promise I shall regret every moment of my marriage to you."

He laughed at that, humor absent in the sound. "I imagine you're already on that path, darling."

She shook her head. "Hear me. This misguided vendetta—should you follow through with it—it will prove that everything you ever were, all the good in you . . . it is gone."

He did not move. Did not even show he'd heard her.

He didn't care. Not about Tommy. Or about her. Or about their past, and the truth of it made her ache. She could not stem the tide of words. "He was devastated by the loss of you. Just as—" She stopped.

"Just as—?" he prompted.

"Just as I was," she spat, hating the words even as they came on a flood of memory, along with the aching sorrow she had felt when she'd heard the story of Michael's ruin. "He missed you just as I did. He worried about you just as I worried. He looked for you. Tried to find you. *Just as I did.* But you were gone." She took a step toward him. "You think *he* left *you*? It was you who left, Michael. You left *us*." Her voice was shaking now, all the anger and sadness and fear she had felt in those months, those years after Michael had disappeared.

"You left *me*." She put her hands to his chest, pushing him with all her might, with all her anger. "And I missed you so much." He took several steps back in the silence of the dark room, and Penelope realized that she had said more than she should have said—more than she ever would have imagined saying. She took a deep breath, pushing back the tears that threatened, so close. She would not cry. Not for him.

Instead, she whispered around the knot in her throat, "I missed you so much. I still do, damn you."

She waited there, in the darkness, for him to say something. *Anything.*

For him to apologize.

To tell her that he missed her, as well.

A minute passed. Two. More.

When she realized he was not going to speak, she spun away, wrenching open the door before he moved, his hand shooting over her shoulder to slam it shut again. She tugged at the handle, but he held the door closed with one, wide hand. "You're a brute. Let me out."

"No. Not until we finish this. I'm no longer that boy."

She gave a little, humorless laugh. "I know."

"And I'm not Tommy."

"I know that, too."

His hand came to her neck, his fingers tracing the corded muscle there, and she knew he could feel her pulse racing. "You think I did not miss you?" She froze at the words, her breath coming shallow, desperate for him to say more. "You think I did not miss everything about you? Everything you represented?"

He pressed against her, his breath soft against her temple. She closed her eyes. How had they found themselves here, in this place where he was so dark and so broken? "You think I did not want to come home?" His voice was thick with emotion. "But there was no home to which I could return. There was no one there."

"You're wrong," she argued. "I was there. I was there . . . and I was . . ." *Alone.* She swallowed. "*I* was there."

"No." The word was harsh and graveled. "Langford took it all. And that boy . . . the one you miss . . . he took him, as well."

"That may be, but Tommy *didn't.* Can't you see, Michael? He's just a pawn in your game . . . just like me . . . just like my sisters. You married me; you'll match them. But if you ruin him . . . you'll never forgive yourself. I know that."

"You're wrong," he replied. "I shall sleep well. Better than I have in a decade."

She shook her head. "It's not true. You think your revenge will not hurt? You think you will not ache with the impact of it? The knowledge that you destroyed another man in the systematic, horrible way that Langford destroyed you?"

"Tommy *was* an unfortunate casualty in this war. After today, after his attempt to take you away, I am not certain he will not deserve the punishment I mete out."

"I'll wager you for it." The words were out of her mouth before she had thought of them. "Name the game and your price. I'll play. For Tommy's secrets."

He stilled. "You have nothing I want."

She hated the words, and him for saying them. She had herself. She had their marriage. She had their future, none of it of value to him.

And that was the moment she realized that Tommy had been right—that it always had been Michael, that strong, sure boy she'd known. The one she'd laughed with and grown with and mourned for too long. The one who was gone, leaving in his place this dark, haunted man who was, in his own way, just as tempting.

The fight left her. "Let me go."

He pressed closer, speaking in her ear. "I will have my revenge. The faster you realize that, the easier our marriage will be."

She stayed quiet, silence her resistance.

"You want to leave?" he asked, the words raw and graveled.

No. I want you to want me to stay.

Why? Why must he have such an effect on her? She took a deep breath. "Yes."

He lifted his hand from the door and took a step back, and she missed his warmth almost instantly. "Go then."

She did not hesitate.

She fled into the hallway beyond, unable to shake the thought that something had just happened between them. Something that could not be taken back. She paused, leaning against the wall, breathing deeply as she was cloaked in the darkness and the muffled din from the casino beyond.

She wrapped her arms tightly around herself, closing her eyes against the thought—against the words they'd just shared, against the keen understanding that she'd waited eight years for a marriage that was about more than what she owned, or represented, or had been bred for, only to marry a man who saw her for nothing more than those things.

Worse, a man she had always thought would be different.

That man had never existed.

He'd never grown from the boy she'd known.

From the boy she'd loved.

She released one long breath and laughed harshly in the darkness.

Fate was cruel indeed.

"Lady Bourne?"

She started at the sound of her name—still so foreign to her—and pressed back to the wall as a very tall man materialized from the blackness. He was reed thin, with a strong, square jaw, and the expression in his eyes, a mix of sympathy and something else that she could not name, had her believing him more friend than foe.

He gave a short, barely there bow. "I am Cross. I have your winnings."

He held out a dark pouch, and it took Penelope a moment to understand what it was—to remember that she'd come here tonight for excitement and adventure and pleasure, and she was leaving with nothing but disappointment.

She reached for it, the heavy weight of the coins within surprising her.

He laughed, low and rich. "Thirty-five pounds is quite a bit of money," he said. "And on roulette? You're very lucky."

"I'm not at all lucky." *Not tonight, at least.*

A beat. "Well, perhaps your luck is changing."

Doubtful.

"Perhaps."

There was a long silence as he considered her before he dipped his head in a little nod, and he said, "Be careful on your journey home. That's enough blunt to make a thief's year." He turned away, and she transferred the pouch from one hand to the other, testing the weight of the coins inside, the sound they made as they rubbed against each other.

And then, before she could reconsider, she called after him, "Mr. Cross?"

He stopped, turning back. "My lady?"

"Do you know my husband well?" she blurted into the darkness, and, for a long moment, Penelope thought he might not reply.

And then he did. "As well as anyone knows Bourne."

She could not help her little laugh at the words. "Better than I do, to be sure."

He did not reply to the statement. He didn't have to. "Is there something that you want to ask?"

There were so many things she wanted to ask. Too many things.

Who is he? What happened to the boy she once knew? What made him so distant? Why wouldn't he give an inch to this marriage?

She could not ask any of them. "No."

He waited for a long moment for her to change her mind. When she didn't, he said, "You are exactly what I expected."

"What does that mean?"

"Only that the woman who sets Bourne so completely on edge must be something remarkable indeed."

"I don't set him on edge. He doesn't think of me beyond what I can do in service to his higher goals." She regretted the words instantly. Regretted their peevishness.

One of Cross's brows shot up. "I assure you, my lady, that is not at all the case."

If only it were true.

Of course, it wasn't.

"It seems you do not know him very well after all."

He seemed to understand that she was not interested in arguing the point. Instead, he changed the subject. "Where is he?"

She shook her head. "I don't know. I left him."

His teeth flashed white in the darkness. "I'm sure he adored that."

He'd forced her away. "I don't entirely care how he felt about it."

He laughed, then, the sound loud and friendly. "You're perfect."

She didn't feel perfect. She felt like a singular idiot. "I beg your pardon?"

"In all the years that I've known Bourne, I've never known

a woman to affect him the way you do. I've never seen him resist someone the way he does you."

"It's not resistance. It's disinterest."

One ginger brow rose. "Lady Bourne, it is most definitely *not* disinterest."

He did not know. He had not seen how Michael left her. How he stayed so very far from her. How he cared so little for her.

She did not wish to think on it. *Not tonight.* "Do you think you could help me hire a hack? I should like to go home."

He shook his head. "Bourne would murder me if he knew I'd let you return home in a hack. Let me find him."

"No!" she blurted before she could stop herself. She lowered her gaze to the floor. "I do not wish to see him."

He does not wish to see me.

She no longer knew which was more important.

"If not he, then I shall escort you myself. You are safe with me."

She narrowed her gaze. "How do I know you are telling the truth?"

One side of his mouth kicked up. "Among other things, Bourne would take visceral pleasure in destroying me if I harmed you."

She recalled the way Michael had tossed Densmore across the casino floor without breaking a sweat earlier in the evening. The way he stood over the sputtering earl, fist clenched, voice shaking with anger.

If there was one thing of which she was certain, it was that Bourne would never allow her to be hurt.

Unless, of course, he was doing the hurting.

Chapter Fourteen

Dear M—

I've heard about Langford, that beast of a man, and about what he's done. It's atrocious, of course. No one believes he could be so hateful—no one but Tommy and me. As for Tommy . . . he's been looking for you. I pray that he finds you.
Quickly.

Ever—P
Needham Manor, February 1821

Letter unsent

Temple's left hook was wicked and welcome.

And deserved.

It connected with Bourne's jaw, snapping his head back and sending him careening into a wooden post at the edge of the boxing ring in the basement of The Angel. Bourne caught himself before he fell to the sawdust-covered floor, his eyes meeting Chase's over the top rope of the ring before he pulled himself up and turned to face his sparring partner.

Temple danced from one foot to the other as Bourne advanced. "You're a fool."

Bourne ignored the words and the truth in them, throwing a punch that would have felled an oak.

Temple ducked and feinted away before flashing a grin. "You're a fool, and you're losing your touch. Perhaps with the ladies, as well?"

Bourne landed a quick blow to Temple's cheek, enjoying the sound of fist on flesh. "What do you have to say about my touch now?"

"Half-decent punch," Temple offered with a grin, swerving left, out of the way of Bourne's second blow. "But your wife did go home with Cross, so I can't speak to that."

Bourne swore and went after his friend, taller by several inches and wider by half a foot, but Bourne more than made up for the difference in speed and agility and, tonight, sheer will.

He attacked with no hesitation, his fists, wrapped in a length of linen, eager to connect with the larger man's bare torso. First left, then right. The movements were punctuated with Temple's short grunts before the larger man danced away.

"Don't tease him, Temple," Chase said from beyond the ring, shuffling through a pile of papers, only half paying attention to the sparring. "He's having a difficult enough evening as it is."

Lord knew it was true.

He'd let her go home. It had been the hardest thing he'd ever done.

Because what he'd really wanted to do was make love to her on the floor of the owners' suite, with the light from beyond the stained glass bathing her in a myriad of colors. He'd wanted to prove that he had never once intended to dishonor her.

Indeed, the idea that he had dishonored her made him feel like a dozen kinds of ass.

Temple's fist connected with his jaw in a perfect straight right, and Bourne rocked back on his heels.

"Why not go after her?" Temple asked, bending away from Bourne's fists and coming back to land a quick blow to his chest. "Take her to bed. That usually makes them feel better, no?"

Bourne could not tell his friend that taking his wife to bed had landed him in this predicament to begin with. "When you find yourself with a wife of your own, you can offer all the advice you like."

"By that time I won't have to. You'll have driven yours away for good." He dodged back. "I like the girl."

Sadly, so did Michael. "You don't even know her."

"Don't have to." Bourne's right hook would have knocked out a lesser man, but the blow had no effect on Temple. Unfortunately. He simply pressed on. "Anyone who sets you off the way she does deserves my admiration. She's garnered my loyalty for her part in tonight's entertainment alone. And I imagine that Cross will be half in love with her by the time he returns."

The words were meant to incite, and they did. With a growl, Bourne charged at Temple, who blocked two quick punches before getting in a jab to the stomach. Bourne cursed, and leaned into the other man, his breath coming as fast as his perspiration for one second, two. Five. Finally, Temple pulled back, and before Bourne had a chance to move, the larger man jabbed once, twice, sending Bourne reeling into the ropes, blood pouring from his nose.

This time, he was not fast enough to catch himself. He landed on his knees.

"That's the round," Chase called, and Bourne swore wickedly as Temple came forward to help him up.

"Leave it," he snapped, coming to his feet and making his way to the chair at one corner of the ring, marked by a green handkerchief. "Thirty-eight seconds," he said, ripping the cloth from the post, holding it to his nose, and tilting his head back. "I suggest you prepare your next counterattack."

Temple accepted a drink from Bruno, his second in command, and drank deep before leaning against the ropes, widespread arms—each sporting a wide-banded tattoo across the massive biceps—covering nearly half the length of the ring. Temple might have been born into the aristocracy, but this was his kingdom now. "What did she say that has you so eager to take a beating?"

Bourne ignored the question, the explosion of pain in his cheek not doing its job, failing to take away all thought of what had happened earlier with his wife. Of how her blue eyes had flashed as she'd accused him of using her body to secure his interests. Of how she'd squared her shoulders and defended her own honor—something he should have done for her.

Of how she'd looked at him, truth and tears in her eyes, and told him that she'd missed him.

The words had taken his breath away—the idea that pure, perfect Penelope had thought of him, had worried about him.

Because he had missed her, too.

It had taken him years to forget—years that were erased in one moment of honesty, when she'd looked into his eyes and accused him of leaving her.

Of dishonoring her.

And there, in the pit of his stomach, still unmasked by the pain of Temple's beating, was the emotion he'd feared since the beginning of this charade.

Guilt.

She'd been right. He'd misused her. He'd treated her as less than she deserved. And she'd defended herself with strength and pride. Remarkably.

And even as he'd tried to let her go, to push her from him, he'd known that he wanted her. He didn't fool himself into thinking that the desire was new. He'd wanted her in Surrey, when she'd stood in the darkness with nothing but a lantern to protect her. But now . . . want had become something more serious. More visceral. More dangerous. Now, he wanted *her*—his strong, intelligent, kindhearted wife, who became more tempting every day as she shifted and blossomed into someone new and different than the girl he'd met on that dark Surrey evening.

And now, he was married to her, virtually bound by laws of God and man to take her. To lay her down and worship her. To touch her in every wicked way he could imagine.

To claim her as his.

And she wanted nothing to do with him.

He fisted his left hand, enjoying the stinging ache beneath the linen strips—the feel of the fight he'd just had, the promise of the one yet to come—and lowered the handkerchief. His nose had stopped bleeding.

If she had not decided to push him away today, it would have come eventually—perhaps after it was too late, when he was unwilling to release her. "I need someone to watch her."

Chase looked to him. "Why?"

"Alles asked her to flee with him when I drag him through the mud."

The other men shared a look before Temple said, "And you wish to pay someone to make certain it does not happen?"

He wanted to believe it would not happen. That she would choose him.

That she would fight for him the way she fought for Tommy.

A long-buried memory came unbidden—young Penelope, hands outstretched at a garden party, playing blind man's buff. Children were scattered everywhere, calling out to her, and she lurched and lunged, laughing at the silly game. He and Tommy had crept toward her and simultaneously whispered her name. She'd spun toward him, capturing him easily, her hands coming to settle on his cheeks, her smile wide and lovely. "Michael," she'd said softly, "I've caught you."

He ran his hands down his face and looked to his feet, covered in sawdust. "I think it's best."

Chase was the first to respond. "It might not be the best way to endear yourself to the lady, Bourne, having her followed."

He came to his feet. "I am open to less villainous ideas."

Temple smirked and said, "Why not leave the ring and go to her? Give her the words she's looking for, take the girl to bed, and remind her why you're better than Alles in all ways that count?" He bounced back into the ropes several times in a foul approximation of coitus. "A different fight, but far more pleasurable."

Bourne scowled and came to his feet, shaking out his hands and testing his weight on tired legs.

"How long has it been since you've slept?" Chase asked.

"I sleep." *Not much.*

He took a step toward the center of the ring, feeling the room sway just barely. Temple did not pull his punches. Ever. It was what made him such a stellar opponent on those days when one wanted nothing but oblivion.

"How long since you've slept more than an hour here and there?"

"I do not require a mother."

Chase lifted a brow. "Perhaps a wife, then?"

Bourne wished Chase were in the damn ring, too.

The sound of Temple's drawing a line in the wood shavings at the center of the ring echoed through the dark, cavernous room. "Come to scratch, old man. Let me give you the beating you richly deserve. We'll send you home to your marchioness in desperate need of her care and concern."

Bourne headed for the center of the ring, ignoring both the words and the unpleasantness that settled in his heart at the idea that his marchioness was no longer willing to provide him with either care or concern.

After another round of boxing, Bourne exited the ring, barely able to see out of his left eye. Temple remained in the box, stretching against the ropes, watching as Bourne accepted a side of raw beef from the icebox at Bruno's feet and took the seat next to Chase, leaning back and placing the meat over his swelling eye.

Minutes went by—several of them—before Chase broke the silence. "Why did she leave without you?"

Bourne released a long breath. "She's furious with me."

"They always are," Temple said, beginning to unwrap the length of linen he had wrapped around his knuckles before the fight.

"What did you do?" Chase asked.

There were a hundred reasons why she was furious. But only one mattered, and it came quick and clear, like a blow from one of Temple's massive fists. "I'm an ass."

Bourne expected instant agreement from his partners, so when no one spoke, he wondered if, perhaps, they'd left him alone in the room. He lifted the piece of beef from his eye and looked up, only to discover that Chase, Temple, and Bruno had all gone wide-eyed, watching him. "What?" he asked.

Chase found words first. "Only that in the five years I've known you—"

"Much longer for me," Temple interjected.

"—I've never known you to admit that you were wrong."

Bourne slid his gaze from Chase to Temple to Chase again. "Sod off." He returned the steak to his eye and leaned back again. "I can't give her what she wants."

"Which is?"

It was easier to speak to them without having to look at them. "A normal marriage. A normal life."

"Why not?" Chase prodded.

"All I succeed at is sin and vice. She is the opposite of those things. She will want more. She will want . . ." He trailed off.

Love.

The one thing he could not buy her. The one thing he could not risk giving her.

Chase's papers rustled. "And therein, the fear of Alles."

Bourne stiffened. "Not fear."

"Of course not," Chase revised in a tone laced with humor. "Following the lady, Bourne, is not the answer. It's giving her the things she wants. It's being the husband she deserves."

Damn him, he wanted to be that husband. She was slowly destroying him with her strength and her spirit. It wasn't supposed to be like this. It was supposed to be easy and clean—a quick abduction, an easy marriage, and a tranquil parting of ways that served them both.

Except, nothing about his wife seemed easy or tranquil.

Michael flexed his fingers, feeling the ache in the knuckles from the fight. "It's not that easy."

"It never is, with women," Chase continued. "You can say all you like that you'll toss her away after your revenge is meted out, but you shan't be able to. Not entirely. You'll still be married."

"Unless she goes with Alles," Temple taunted from inside the ring.

Michael cursed him wickedly. "She doesn't need Alles for the life she wants. I'll give it to her. Everything she wants."

"Everything?" Chase asked. Michael did not reply. "It's no longer all for the land and the revenge, is it? You care for the lady."

He should not. He had lost everything he had ever cared for. He had ruined everything good that he had ever touched. His care was a harbinger of her destruction.

But he defied any man in Britain to spend a day with his wife and not care for her.

"At the very least, he wants her," Temple interjected. "And you can't blame him. Her courage tonight would tempt a saint."

"*Did* tempt a saint," Chase replied. "*Cross* escorted her home."

Anger flooded through Michael at the words. "Cross won't touch her."

"No. He won't. But not because she's not tempting; because he's Cross," Chase said.

"And if he weren't, he wouldn't touch her because she's yours," Temple added.

God help him, he wanted her to be his.

"She's not mine. I can't have her."

She wants nothing to do with me. He'd ruined any chance of that, just as he had ruined everything else that was good and right in his life.

"But Bourne," Temple said, "you *do* have her."

There was a long silence as the words echoed around the room. They weren't true, of course. They weren't right. If he had her, he wouldn't be so afraid of going home to her. If he had her, he wouldn't be here, stinking of sweat and raw meat. If he had her, she wouldn't have left him.

Finally, he said, "I'm married to her. That's not the same thing."

"Well, it's a start, I'd think." Chase stood at that, lifting the sheaf of papers and adding, "She's yours, bought and paid. And since you are stuck with each other—God help her—perhaps it's time you attempt a marriage that does not end as awfully as it began."

The idea—the possibility that she might someday care for him—that they might someday have more than a shell of a marriage, it tempted him more than cards, more than the wheel.

Tempted him to be the husband she deserved.

Dear M—

Her Grace, Duchess of Leighton. It seems a glut of young, eligible dukes was unrequired. One was enough. The Duke of Leighton has expressed a desire to court me, my father has agreed, and my mother is utterly overcome with glee.

There is much to recommend him, of course. He is handsome and intelligent, powerful and wealthy, and as Mother likes to remind me at every opportunity—he is a DUKE. If he were horseflesh, there would be a run on Tattersalls, no doubt.

Of course, I will do my duty. This will be a marriage for the ages. It's hard to believe I shall be a duchess—the holy grail of the eldest, aristocratic daughter. Huzzah.

I have not missed you so much in a long time. Where are you?

Unsigned
Dolby House, September 1823

Letter unsent

The next morning, Penelope sent a note round to the newly inhabited Dolby House to invite Olivia and Philippa to join her for the day—her first in which she stopped waiting for her husband and began to live her life once more.

She was going ice-skating.

She was very much in need of an afternoon with her sisters to remind her that there was a reason for the arguments with Michael and her own discontent, and for keeping up this foolish ruse—ensuring that her marriage appear to be real and not the tragic sham that it was.

She needed to remind herself that her scandal would be theirs in no time if it were allowed to get out, and Philippa and Olivia deserved their chance at better. At more.

She gritted her teeth at the word, at everything it had meant on that fateful night when she'd allowed herself to be caught up in the adventure of marriage—of Michael. Pushing the thought from her mind, she nodded to her maid, who helped her to step into her clothes, tightening corset strings and tying bows, fastening tapes and buttons.

Penelope knew that she would be scrutinized beyond the walls of Hell House, and she dressed carefully for the eyes of all of London—at least, all of those who were in residence in London in January—who would be watching, searching for the chink in the armor of the new Marchioness of Bourne.

The woman who they believed had captured the heart of the wickedest partner in The Fallen Angel, convincing him to restore his title and return to their ranks.

The woman he avoided at all costs.

She selected a bright green wool dress, thinking it warm and festive for the outing, and paired it with the navy blue cloak that she had worn that fateful evening when she'd crossed Needham and Falconwell lands and met Michael, now Bourne, in the cold, dark night.

It could have been a nod to that evening, to the moment she'd unlocked this strange new future, to the hope that she might find more, despite a husband who wanted nothing to do with her. She would have her adventure in this cloak, with or without him.

A fur-lined bonnet and gloves rounded out her outdoor dress, and in perfect time; she descended the wide central stairs of Hell House to the sounds of her sisters' chattering in the foyer below, their conversation rising to fill the empty space that seemed to loom everywhere in her husband's home.

Her home, she supposed.

As she hurried across the first-floor landing, eager to reach her sisters and leave the house, the door to Bourne's private study opened and he strode out, papers in hand, frock coat unbuttoned, his white linen shirt pulling taut across his broad chest. He came up short at the sight of her and instantly reached to button his coat.

She stilled, her eyes dragging over his face, taking in the mottled discoloration at one eye, the wicked-looking cut on his lower lip. She stepped forward, one gloved hand rising of its own accord, unable to stop herself from reaching for his battered face. "What happened to you?"

He retreated from the touch, his gaze flickering over her. "Where are you going?"

The abrupt change in conversation did not give her a chance to decide if she wanted him to hear the truth. "Ice-skating. Your eye . . ."

"It's nothing." He lifted a hand to the bruise.

"It looks awful." He raised a brow, and she shook her head. "I mean . . . oh, you know what I mean. It's all black and yellow."

"Is it disgusting?"

She nodded once. "Quite."

"That's what I was hoping for." *Was he teasing her?* "Thank you for the concern." There was a long pause, during which she would have thought Michael was uncomfortable if she had not known better. Ultimately, he added, "You saw that I accepted an invitation to the Beaufetheringstone Ball."

She could not help her response. "I did. You do know that it is usually the wife who accepts social invitations, do you not?"

"When we are more adept at receiving them, I shall happily relinquish the task of accepting them. I was surprised we were invited at all."

"I would not be. Lady B enjoys a scandal more than most. Especially if it's in her ballroom."

A cacophony of laughter rose from the ground floor, saving her from having to answer, and Michael edged toward the banister to look down into the foyer. "The young ladies Marbury, I presume?"

Penelope tried her best to look away from the gash on his lip. She really did.

That she failed was not of import.

"They have returned to town." She paused, unable to keep the edge from her tone when she added, "Sure to be matched soon enough . . ."

He snapped his attention back to her. "Ice-skating?" There was surprise in the words.

"You don't remember skating on the pond when we were children?" The words were out before she could stop them, and she wished that she'd said something else . . . anything else . . . anything that did not remind her of the Michael she'd once known. Once understood.

It was as though he had erased the memory of her. She hated the way that made her feel. "I am late." She spun away from him, heading for the staircase, not expecting him to say anything. He was so good at remaining silent; she'd given up thinking he would speak without prodding. And she was through prodding him.

So, when he did speak, she was shocked. "Penelope."

The sound of her name on his lips shocked her. She turned back instantly. "Yes?"

"May I join you?"

Penelope blinked. "I beg your pardon?"

He took a deep breath. "Ice-skating. May I join you?"

Her gaze narrowed. "Why? Do you think Lord and Lady Bourne will receive an inch or two in the papers if we are seen hand in hand, gliding across the Serpentine?"

He raked a hand through his dark curls. "I deserved that."

She would not feel guilty.

"Yes. You did. And more, too."

"I should like to make it up to you."

Her eyes widened. *What was this?*

He was likely manipulating her and their future and this time, she would not be swayed. She would not be fooled.

She knew better. She was tired of the ache that settled in her chest whenever he was near—whenever he was not near. She was tired of the battles, the games, the falsehoods. She was tired of the disappointments.

He could not possibly imagine that one small offer of companionship would make up for everything that he'd done . . . everything that he'd threatened. Steeling herself and her voice, she said, "I don't think so."

He blinked. "I should have expected that."

After the way they'd left each other the evening before? Yes. He should have. She turned away, heading for the stairs leading down to her sisters.

"Penelope." He stayed her with her name, low and lovely on his lips.

She could not help but turn back. "Yes?"

"What would it take? To join you?"

"What would it *take*?"

"Name your price." He paused. "One afternoon with my wife without the specter of the past or future with us. What would it take?"

She replied without hesitation, straight and serious. "Don't ruin Tommy."

"Always asking for others. Never for yourself."

"And you, always doing for yourself and never for others."

"I find I prefer the outcome." He was an infuriating man. He came closer, spoke low, sending a thrum of awareness through her. "What would it take for me to have you for an afternoon?"

Her breath quickened as the words conjured up a variety of images that had nothing to do with ice-skating or her sisters and everything to do with the fur coverlet in his luxurious bedroom.

He reached out and trailed one finger down her cheek. "Name your price."

God help her, he so easily managed her.

"One week," she said, voice shaking. "One week of safety for him." *One week to convince you that you are wrong. That revenge is not the answer.*

He did not immediately agree, and she forced herself to turn back to the staircase, disappointed by her utter lack of power over him. As she set foot on the top step, Philippa noticed her. "Penny!" she announced. "And Lord Bourne!"

Penelope looked back at Michael, and whispered, "You need not escort me. I assure you I am quite capable of finding my way to the front door."

"You have a deal," he said quietly at her elbow. "One week."

Success coursed through her, heady and exciting. They had reached the bottom of the stairs before she could say anything, and Olivia pounced. "Have you seen *The Scandal Sheet* today?"

"I haven't, I regret," Penelope teased, pretending not to notice that Michael was uncomfortably close behind her. "What scintillating gossip have you heard?"

"No gossip *for* us," Pippa replied. "Gossip *about* us . . . well, about *you,* at least."

Oh, no. Someone had discovered the truth of their marriage. Of her ruination in the country. "What kind of gossip?"

"The kind in which all of London is envious of your gorgeous, unbearably romantic marriage!" Olivia cried.

It took a moment for the meaning of the words to register.

"We did not know that you met on St. Stephen's, Penelope," Olivia said. "We did not even know that Lord Bourne had been in Surrey over Christmas!"

Pippa met Penelope's gaze, all seriousness. "No. We didn't."

Pippa was no fool, but Penelope forced a smile.

"Read it, Pippa," Olivia demanded.

The youngest Marbury pushed her glasses farther up her nose and lifted the paper. "*The last days of January are not always the time for the ripest fruits of gossip, but this year we have a particularly juicy treat in the newly returned*

Marquess of Bourne!" She looked up at Michael. "That's you, my lord."

"I suspect he knows that," Olivia said.

Pippa ignored her sister and pressed on. "*Certainly our discerning readers*—I'm not sure that readers of *The Scandal Sheet* are precisely 'discerning,' are you?"

"Really, Philippa. Keep reading!"

"*Certainly our discerning readers have heard that the marquess has taken a wife.*" Philippa looked up at Penelope, but before she could say anything, Olivia groaned and snatched the paper from her hands.

"Fine. *I* shall read it. *We hear that Lord and Lady Bourne are so entirely encompassed with each other that they are rarely seen apart. And, a delicious addendum! It seems that it is not only Lord Bourne's eyes that follow his wife . . . but hands and lips as well! In public, no less!* How excellent!"

"That last bit was Olivia editorializing," Pippa interjected.

Penelope thought she might die of embarrassment. Right there. On the spot.

Olivia continued. "*Not that we expect anything less of Lord Bourne—husband or not, he remains a rogue! And that which we call a rogue, by any other name would scandalize as sweet!*"

"Oh, for heaven's sake." Penelope did roll her eyes at that, looking to Michael, who looked . . . pleased. "You're *complimented*?"

He turned innocent eyes on her. "Should I not be?"

"Well," Philippa added thoughtfully, "anything Shakespearean must be at least a *vague* compliment."

"Precisely," Michael said, gifting Pippa with a smile that made Penelope more than a little envious of her younger sister. "By all means, continue."

"*Suffice to say, readers, we are very pleased with this winter's tale—*"

"Do you think they meant the second Shakespearean pun?" Philippa interrupted.

"Yes," said Olivia.

"No," said Penelope.

"—and we can only hope that the arrival of the final duo of Ladies Marbury—"

Pippa pushed her glasses back on her nose, and said, "That's us."

"—will make for excitement enough to keep us all warm in these cold days. Isn't that the most salacious item you've ever heard?" Olivia asked, and Penelope resisted the urge to tear the ridiculous newspaper article to shreds.

It had not occurred to her that her sisters might not know the truth.

That her marriage was a fraud.

It made sense, of course. The fewer people who knew—the fewer young women with a penchant for gossip who knew—the easier it would be for them to be matched. Bourne slid one arm around her waist. Her sisters eyed that arm, the way his hand snaked, warm and direct, across her body, resting on the curve of her hip as though it belonged there. As though *he* belonged there.

As though she belonged with him.

She stepped away from his touch.

She might have agreed to lie to half of Christendom, but she would not lie to her sisters.

She opened her mouth to deny the article, to tell them the truth.

And stopped.

The love match might be a farce, Michael might be in it for his own mysterious purposes, but Penelope had a reason. She'd had a reason from the beginning. Her sisters had lived in the shadow of her ruin for too long. She would shade them no longer.

He was already speaking, silver-tongued. "With the advent of this article, you'll be needing protection from the droves of suitors who will almost certainly come swarming."

"You must join us!" Olivia said, and Penelope resisted the

urge to scream at the way that her sisters played right into his hands.

His gaze flickered to her, and she willed him to refuse, to remember what she had said abovestairs. "I'm afraid I cannot."

She should have been pleased, but up was too often down when it came to her husband, and instead, she found herself so pleasantly surprised that he had honored her request that she was wishing that he had agreed to join them.

Which was ridiculous, of course.

Men were vexing indeed.

And her husband, more than most.

"Oh, do," Olivia pressed, "it would be lovely to come to know our new brother."

Pippa chimed in. "Indeed. You married so quickly . . . we never had a chance to properly reacquaint ourselves."

Penelope's gaze shot to her sister. Something was off. Pippa knew. She had to.

He shook his head again. "I'm sorry, ladies, but I haven't any skates."

"We've extra skates in the coach," Olivia said. "Now you've no reason not to come."

Penelope was instantly suspicious. "Why would you have extra skates in the coach?"

Olivia smiled, bright and beautiful. "One never knows when one might meet someone with whom one wants to skate."

Penelope turned surprised eyes on Michael, who appeared to be having difficulty holding back a smile. She raised a brow as he said, "An excellent adage. It seems I have no choice but to play chaperone."

"You may not make the best chaperone, Bourne," Penelope said through her teeth. "What with you being such a *rogue*."

He winked at her. Actually winked at her! *Who was this man?*

"Ah, but who better than a rogue undergoing reformation to identify the same? And I confess, I would like the chance to skate with my wife again. It's been too long."

Lie.

He didn't remember skating with her. He'd virtually admitted it earlier, upstairs.

She did not think she could suffer an outing with all of them, with him constantly touching her, asking after her well-being, teasing her, *tempting her.*

Not after last night, when she'd been so strong. When she'd been so sure of herself.

Of what she wanted.

Suddenly, by day, this kinder, gentler Michael did not seem so resistible.

And that was a very bad thing indeed.

Chapter Fifteen

Dear M—

By now you've heard the news, even from wherever you are. I'm ruined. The duke did everything he could to save me from embarrassment, but this is London, and such an effort is, of course, futile. He married again within a week—in a love match, no less. Mother is (no surprise) beside herself, keening and wailing like a chorus of mourners.

Is it wrong that I feel as though something of a weight has been lifted? Probably.

I wish you were here. You would know what to say.

Unsigned
Dolby House, November 1823

Letter unsent

Penelope sat on a wooden bench, looking out toward the frozen Serpentine, where half of London appeared to teem.

The winter's uncommon cold had resulted in the thickest ice in nearly a decade, leaving the little lake packed to the gills with people eager to spend their afternoon ice-skating.

There was no escaping the watchful eyes of the *ton.*

Once their skating party had alighted from the carriage and crested the hill that sloped gently down to the Serpentine Lake, they took turns sitting to attach the wood-and-steel blades to the soles of their walking boots. Penelope waited as long as possible to take her seat and strap on her blades, keenly aware of the fact that ice-skating with Michael would be a challenge, as he would likely take the opportunity to show all of London how very much in love they were.

For the hundredth time, Penelope cursed the ridiculous farce and watched her sisters make their way down the hill, hand in hand, reminding her of the greater purpose of her frustration.

Her distraction made it difficult to slide the ice blades onto her feet, and after her third try, Michael tossed his own blades to the side and crouched before her, taking one of her feet by the ankle before she realized his intentions. She yanked her foot back, sending him tipping backward to catch himself on his hands in the snow and drawing the attention of a nearby cluster of young women. "What do you think you are doing?" she whispered, leaning forward, not wanting to cause any more of a scene.

He looked up at her, all handsome angles and falsely innocent eyes, and said, simply, "Helping you with your skate."

"I don't need your help."

"Forgive me, but it seems that you do." He lowered his voice to a level only she could hear. "Let me help you."

He was not helping her for her. He was helping her for *them,* those watchful others who would love the scene and no doubt fall over themselves in a frenzy to tell their friends and families all about how the Marquess of Bourne was the most solicitous, kindhearted, wonderful man ever to walk the banks of the Serpentine Lake.

But she *wouldn't* love it.

She would put on her own damned skates.

"I'm fine. Thank you." And she promptly slid the contraptions over her walking boots, carefully tightening the straps to ensure a snug fit. "There." She looked up at Michael, watching her carefully, something strange and unidentifiable in his gaze. "Perfect."

He came out of his crouch then, reaching down to help her up. "At least let me do this, Penelope," he whispered, and she couldn't resist the soft words.

She placed her hands in his.

He lifted her to her feet and held her as she regained her balance on the blades. "If I remember correctly, you were never as good at walking on your blades as you were at skating on them."

She blinked up at him, nearly tipping over with the movement and clasping his arms carefully as she regained her balance. "You said you didn't remember."

"No," he said, quietly, guiding her down the hill and toward the lake. "*You* said I didn't remember."

"You do, though."

One corner of his mouth lifted in a small, sad smile. "You'd be amazed by all that I remember."

There was something in the words, a softness that was foreign to him, and she couldn't help her suspicion. "Why are you behaving like this?" Her brow furrowed. "Another chance to prove our love match?"

Something flickered in his gaze, there then gone. "Any chance to prove it," he said, softly before he looked away. She followed the line of his gaze to find Pippa and Olivia, hand in hand, helping each other toward the ice. Any chance to match her sisters.

"I should join them," she said, lifting her face to him, meeting his beautiful hazel eyes. It was only then that she realized how closely he held her, and how the gentle incline of the hill brought her almost eye to eye with him.

One side of his mouth twitched. "Your cheeks are like cherries."

She tucked her chin into the fur cowl at her neck. "It's cold," she said, defensively.

He shook his head. "I am not complaining. I think they're rather charming. They make you look like a winter nymph."

"I am hardly nymphlike."

He lifted a hand and pressed one finger to her raised brow. "You never used to do that. Never used to be so sardonic."

She pulled away from the warm touch. "I must have learned it from you."

He looked at her for a long moment, all seriousness, before he leaned close and whispered in her ear, "Nymphs should not be cynical, love."

Suddenly, it did not seem so cold.

He pulled back, shaking his head. "What a pity."

"What is?"

He bent his head toward her, nearly touching her forehead with his. "I am almost certain that you are blushing. But the cold makes it impossible to tell."

Penelope could not help her smile, enjoying the banter, forgetting, for one fleeting moment, that it was not real. "How sad that you shall never know."

He lifted her hands to his lips, kissing first one set of kidskin-covered knuckles, then the other, and she wished that she were not wearing gloves. "Your ice awaits, my lady. I shall join you presently."

She looked past him to the crowded lake, where her sisters had joined the revelers in their circles on the lovely, smooth surface, and suddenly standing here with him seemed far more exciting than anything that could happen on the ice. But standing with him was not an option. "So it does."

Michael saw her down to the lake's edge, where she pushed off and disappeared into the crowd, soon finding her sisters. Olivia looped one hand through Penelope's arm, and said, "Bourne is wonderful, Penny. Tell me, are you ecstatic?" She sighed. "I would be ecstatic."

Penelope looked down at her feet, watching them glide

across the ice, peeking out from beneath her dress. "*Ecstatic* is one way to describe it," she said. *Frustrated and impossibly confused would be another.*

Olivia made a show of looking around the lake. "I wonder if he knows any of these unattached lords?"

If he was to be believed, half of them owed The Angel money. "I imagine he does, yes."

"Excellent!" Olivia added, "Well done, Penny. I think he shall be the brother-in-law worth his salt! And handsome, too, isn't he? Oh! I see Louisa Holbrooke!"

She waved furiously across the ice and was off to visit with her friend, leaving Penelope to say quietly, "Yes. He's handsome," grateful for one moment during which she did not have to lie.

Her gaze moved to the spot on the hill where they'd stood mere moments ago. He stood stock-still, all attention on her. Her hand itched to wave. But that would be silly, wouldn't it?

It would be.

As she was considering the action, he made the decision unnecessary. He raised one long arm and waved to her.

It would be rude to ignore him.

So she waved back.

He lowered himself to the bench and began to strap on his skates, and Penelope gave a little sigh, forcing herself to turn away before she did something even more foolish.

"Something's happened."

For a moment, Penelope thought that Pippa had noticed the strange interactions between Michael and her. Mind racing, she turned to face her younger sister. "What do you mean?"

"Castleton has proposed."

Penelope's eyes went wide at the unexpected announcement, and she waited for Pippa to acknowledge the fact that they had spent much of the morning together, and Pippa had only just decided to mention the proposal.

When Pippa said nothing, calmly gliding forward as

though they were discussing the weather and not her future, Penelope could not stop herself. "You do not sound very happy about it."

Pippa kept her head down for a few long minutes. "He's an earl. He seems friendly enough, he doesn't mind that I hate dancing, and he has a handsome stable of horseflesh."

Penelope would have smiled at the simplicity in the words, as though the four character traits were enough to make a satisfactory marriage, if not for the hint of resignation in them.

It occurred to Penelope that Pippa might have chosen her moment to share the proposal because there were so many people around—so many eyes watching and ears listening—too many to allow for a serious conversation.

Nonetheless, Penelope clasped one of her sister's hands and drew her to a halt there at the center of the lake. She leaned in and said, softly, "You don't have to say yes."

"Will it matter if I say no?" Pippa replied, smiling broadly as though they were discussing some amusing event from the morning instead of her future. Her dreams. "Won't there just be another man around the bend looking to capture my dowry? And another after that? And another? Until my choices disappear. He knows I'm smarter than he is, and he's willing to let me run his estate. That's something." She faced Penelope. "I know what you did."

Penelope met her sister's knowing gaze. "What do you mean by that?"

"I was there on St. Stephen's, Penny. I think I would have noticed Bourne's return. As would have half the vicarage."

Penelope nibbled on one lip, wondering what she should say.

"You needn't tell me I'm right." Pippa saved her. "But know that I see what you've done. I appreciate it."

They skated along in silence for a while, before Penelope said, "I did it so you would not have to accept Castleton, Pippa. Michael and I . . . the story was for your benefit. Yours and Olivia's."

Pippa smiled. "And that's sweet of you. But it's silly to

think we'll have love matches, Penny. They don't come along every day. You know that better than most."

Penelope swallowed around the knot in her throat at the words, at the reminder that her own marriage was nothing near a love match. "Others marry for love," she pointed out, adjusting her fur-lined gloves and looking out over the little lake. "Consider Leighton and his wife."

Pippa cut her a look, eyes large and owl-like behind her spectacles. "That's the best you can do? A scandalous marriage from eight years ago?"

It was the example she carried closest to her heart.

"The number of years does not matter. Nor does the scandal."

"Of course it does," Pippa said, standing and tying her own bonnet beneath her chin. "A scandal like that would send Mother into hysterics. And the rest of you into hiding."

"Not me." She was emphatic.

Pippa considered the words. "No, not you. You've a scandalous husband of your own."

Penelope considered her husband, far across the lake, her eyes lingering over the enormous bruise on one side of his face. "He is a scandal."

Pippa turned to face her. "Whatever the reason for your match, Penny . . . he does seem to care for you."

Drury Lane is missing a great talent, surely. She did not say that. Pippa did not need to hear it.

"I might as well marry Castleton," Pippa said. "It will make Father happy. And I shall never have to see the inside of a season again. Think of all the visits to the dressmaker I can forgo."

Penelope smiled at the jest, even as she wanted to open her mouth and scream at the unfairness of it all. Pippa did not deserve a loveless marriage any more than the other Marbury girls did. Any more than Penelope did.

But this was London society, where loveless marriages were the norm. She sighed but said nothing.

"Don't worry about me, Penny," Philippa said, pulling

Penelope into the throngs of skaters once more. "I shall be fine with Castleton. He's a good enough man. I don't think Father would have allowed his suit if he weren't." She leaned closer. "And don't worry about Olivia. She hasn't any idea that you and Lord Bourne are . . ." She trailed off. "She's too focused on trapping herself a handsome peer."

Penelope was not comforted by the idea that she might have fooled her youngest sister into believing that her marriage was a love match. It made her terribly uncomfortable. Olivia, *The Scandal Sheet,* the rest of society's believing that Michael loved her—that she loved Michael—only served to prove the worst . . . that Penelope was losing herself to this charade.

If her sisters barely questioned her feelings for Michael, who was to say that she wouldn't soon believe the pretense herself?

Then where would she be?

Alone again.

"Penelope?" Pippa's question pulled her from her reverie.

She forced a smile.

Pippa watched her for a long while, seeming to see more than Penelope wished, and she looked away from the scrutiny. Finally, her sister said, "I think I shall join Olivia and Louisa. Will you come?"

Penelope shook her head. "No."

"Shall I stay with you?"

Penelope shook her head. "No. Thank you."

The younger Marbury smiled. "Waiting for your husband?" Penelope instantly denied it, and Pippa's smile turned knowing. "I think you like him, sister. Against your best judgment. There's nothing wrong with that, you know." She paused, then said matter-of-factly, "I should think it would be rather nice to like one's husband."

Before Penelope could reply, Pippa was gone. Without thinking, she sought Michael once more, now gone from the spot on the hill where she'd seen him last. She scanned the lake and located him, just on the edge of the ice, in conversation with Viscount Tottenham.

She watched for a long moment before Michael looked out across the ice, his serious gaze finding hers almost instantly. Nervousness shot through her and she turned away, unable to stand firm with half of London between them. She tucked her chin into her muff and skated, head down, through a nearby crowd to the far end of the lake, where she stepped off the ice and hobbled toward a chestnut vendor who had set up shop on the rise there.

She'd barely taken a step when she heard the chatter.

"Can you believe Tottenham is willing to give him the benefit of the doubt?" The question came from behind her, and Penelope paused, knowing instantly that someone was discussing her husband.

"I can't even imagine how Tottenham would be acquainted with someone like *him*."

"I hear that Bourne is still managing that scandalous club. What do you think that says?"

"Nothing good. Bourne is wicked as sin, just like the men who frequent that club." Penelope resisted the urge to turn around and tell the gossipers that they were very likely sired by or espoused to men who would give their left arms for a chance to wager at The Fallen Angel.

"They say he's angling for invitations this season. They say he's ready to return to the *ton*. They say *she's* the reason why."

Penelope leaned closer as the wind picked up, and the words became more difficult to hear. "Lady Holloway told my mother's cousin that he could not stop touching her at dinner last week."

"I heard the same—and did you see *The Scandal Sheet* this morning?"

"Can you believe it? A love match? With *Penelope Marbury*? I would have sworn he married her for her reputation, poor thing."

"And don't forget Falconwell—it was the seat of the marquessate before—"

The words were lost in the wind, but Penelope heard them anyway. *Before he lost it.*

"One does wonder how someone as pristine as Penelope Marbury can care for someone as wicked as the Marquess of Bourne."

Far too easily, Penelope feared.

"Nonsense. Look at the man. The real question is how someone like *him* could tumble into love with someone as boring as she! She couldn't even keep cold, boring Leighton."

The two dissolved into giggles, and Penelope closed her eyes at the high-pitched sound. "You're terrible! Poor Penelope."

God, she hated that name.

"Well really. Wicked as sin and twice as handsome—even with that eye. Where do you think he got it?"

"I am told there are fights at the hell. Brawls that rival those of the gladiators." Penelope rolled her eyes. Her husband was many things, but a modern-day gladiator was not one of them.

"Well, I confess, I would not refuse to tend to his wounds . . ." The voice trailed off on a sigh.

Penelope resisted the urge to show the wicked women just what kind of wounds could be inflicted on a person.

"Perhaps Penelope would give you some tips—you could try to catch one of the other members."

Their cruel laughter faded into the distance. She turned to watch them go, fists clenched, unable to recognize them from the rear. Not that she would have done anything if she had.

Of course they found the story worthy of gossip. It was laughable that she and Michael had a love match. That their marriage might be anything more than a business arrangement.

That someone like him could love someone like me.

She sucked in a deep breath at the thought, the cold sting of the air combating the knot of emotion in her throat.

"Lady Bourne." She spun toward the still-strange title only to find Donovan West scant feet away, headed for her. There was no indication that the newspaperman had overheard the women, but Penelope could not help but think that he had.

"Mr. West," she said, pushing thoughts of boredom aside and matching his smile. "What a surprise."

"My sister required my chaperon," he said, pointing to a group of young girls several yards away. "And I confess to a weakness for winter sport." He offered her an arm and indicated the vendor nearby. "Would you care for some chestnuts?"

She followed his gaze, the smoke from the chestnut cart obscuring its owner's face. "I should like that very much, thank you." They moved slowly toward the stall, Penelope hobbling along on her blades, Mr. West too gentlemanly to mention her lack of coordination. "I, too, have sisters." She thought of Pippa's resignation—her decision to marry Castleton despite her disinterest, for all the wrong reasons.

"Troublesome creatures, are they not?"

She forced a smile. "As a sister myself, I must refrain from answering."

"A fair point." The blond man paused, adding teasingly, "I imagine that a marriage to Bourne would make any sister somewhat troublesome."

She smiled. "Consider yourself lucky that you are not my brother."

He paid the vendor and passed a bag of roasted nuts to Penelope, waiting for her to try one before saying, "You are doing very well."

Her attention snapped to his shrewd brown gaze. *He knew.* She did her best to sound unmoved when she spoke, deliberately misunderstanding his words. "I've skated for my whole life."

He tilted his head, acknowledging the way she avoided his words. "Well, your technique shows more skill than would be expected of a lady."

They were not discussing skating, that much she knew,

but was he referencing the gossip about her and Bourne? Or their farcical marriage? Or something even more damning?

She nibbled on a chestnut, savoring the sweet meat as she considered her response. "I'm always happy to surprise those around me."

"Performing with such finesse takes a great deal of strength."

She raised a brow and leveled the newspaperman with a frank look. "I've had years of practice."

He smiled warmly then. "Indeed you have, my lady. And may I say how very lucky Bourne is to have finally secured you. I look forward to seeing you throughout the season—surely you'll be the most talked about couple in London. I know my columnists are already thrilled to have you in town."

Clarity came like icy wind. "Your columnists."

He dipped his head, smiling secretly, "*The Scandal Sheet* is one of mine."

"The item today . . ." she trailed off.

"Shall pale in comparison to the one about your skating skills."

She pursed her lips. "So unexpected."

He laughed. She was not trying to be amusing.

"Penelope has been able to skate rings around me since we were barely old enough to stand." Michael's words startled her, and she spun to face him, her surprise at his appearance upsetting her precarious balance on her blades and tipping her into his waiting arms, as though he'd planned the whole thing. She gave a little squeak as he pulled her against him.

"As indicated by my extraordinary grace in this particular moment," Penelope offered, eliciting a warm laugh from Michael that rumbled through her all-too-pleasantly. She pulled back to meet his gaze.

He did not look away from her as he said, "It's one of the many reasons I married her. I'm sure you can't blame me, West."

A blush flooding her cheeks, Penelope turned to face the newspaperman, who dipped his head, and said, "Not in the slightest. It's a lucky match indeed." He winked at Penelope. "She's obviously committed to you." He looked off to the distance then before tipping his hat and giving Penelope a short bow. "I have neglected my sister for too long, I think. Lady Bourne, it has been an honor to skate with you."

She dropped a tiny curtsy. "The pleasure was mine." When he skated away, she turned to face Michael again, lowering her voice to a whisper. "That man knows that there is more to our marriage than a love match."

He leaned in, matching her volume. "Don't you mean *less* to our marriage?"

Her eyes narrowed. "You are avoiding the point."

"Of course West knows," he said casually. "He's one of the smartest men in Britain. Possibly *the* smartest man in Britain, and one of the most successful, as well. But he will keep our secrets."

"He's a *journalist,*" she reminded him.

He laughed then, a lovely, honest laugh that made him infinitely more handsome. "You needn't say it as though he is an insect under glass." He paused, watching the man in question charm his sister and her gaggle of friends. "West knows better than to speculate on our marriage in print."

She did not believe him. The truth of their marriage would make for incredible scandal. "How do you know him?"

"He likes hazard."

"It seems like the smartest man in Britain would not enjoy a game of chance so very much."

"He would if he had the luck of the devil."

"You don't seem worried that he knows."

"That is because I am not. I know too many of his secrets for him to share any of mine."

"But he'll happily share Tommy's?"

Michael slid her a look. "Let's not talk about that."

She pressed on. "Are you still planning to ruin him?"

"Not today."

"When, then?"

He sighed. "At least a week from now, as promised."

There was something there, in the soft, resigned way that he spoke, something she wished she could identify. Was it doubt? Regret? "Michael—"

"I have bought and paid for this afternoon, wife. No more." He reached into her bag of chestnuts and popped one, whole, into his mouth. Instantly, his eyes went wide, and he sucked in a long breath. "Those are scalding!"

She should not have taken pleasure in his pain, but she did. "If you had asked for one before simply taking what you wanted, I would have warned you."

One of his brows rose. "Never ask. Take what you want, when you want it."

"Another rule of scoundrels?"

He dipped his head to acknowledge the quip. "It is part of the fun."

The words sizzled through her as the memory came—unbidden—of his tossing her over his shoulder on that first night . . . the night that had changed everything.

She raised her chin, refusing to be embarrassed. "Yes, I discovered as much last night at your club when I won at the wheel." His brows shot up, and Penelope was rather proud of herself. *A direct hit.*

"It's a game of chance. It requires no skill."

"No skill but luck," she quipped.

He smiled, more handsome than one man should be. "Come, wife. Let's around the lake."

He took the bag from her hands, stuffing it into his coat pocket before he guided her to the ice, and she returned the conversation to secrets. "Is that the way of it? You trade in secrets?"

"Only when I must."

"Only as a means to an end." The words were more for herself than for him.

"I know I have been out of the aristocracy for a decade, but this remains London, does it not? Information is still the most valuable commodity?"

"I suppose it is." She did not like how simple it was to him. How callous he was. How easily he kept secrets. How easily he used them to punish those around him. She forced a smile, knowing that all of London watched them. Hating being on display. "And that is the way of it with you and Langford?"

Michael shook his head. "No Langford either, today. We made our deal."

"I never agreed."

"Your not tossing me from the carriage on the way here was tacit agreement," he said dryly. "But if you'd like to formally agree, I will accept your marker in good faith."

"I don't have a marker of my own."

"All is well," he smiled. "You may borrow mine."

She cut him a look. "You mean I may *return* yours."

"Semantics."

She could not hide her small smile as she reached into the pocket of her cloak, where she carried the guinea he'd given her and extracted the coin. "One afternoon," she said.

"For one week," he agreed.

She dropped the coin in his outstretched palm, watching as he deposited it inside his coat pocket. She turned away, watching Pippa laughing across the pond with a group of young women. "Lord Castleton has proposed to Pippa."

He did not move. "And?"

"And she will say yes." He did not respond. Of course he didn't. He didn't understand. He *wouldn't* understand. "They are not a good match."

"Is that so strange?"

No. No, it wasn't. But he didn't have to be so callous about it.

She began to skate faster. "She deserves a chance at more."

"She need not say yes."

She cast him a sidelong glance. "I'm surprised you would say such a thing. Don't you want her married as quickly as possible?"

He looked away, focusing on his skating for long minutes. "You know I do. But I have no interest in forcing her hand."

"It is only my hand that you were interested in forcing?"

"Penelope," he began, and she pulled ahead of him, skating faster, feeling the cold wind on her cheeks, wishing that she could keep going, wishing that she could glide away from this strange, forced life that she was living. She edged past a large group of people, and he was beside her again, his hand on her arm, slowing her. "Penelope," he said again. "Please."

Perhaps it was the word. The softness of it. The strangeness of it on his tongue. The way he said it, as though she could ignore him and he would let her go.

But she stopped, her skates digging deep into the ice as she turned to face him. "I was supposed to stop this," she said, knowing there was too much emotion in her words. "I was supposed to make it so that they could have a different life. Marriages that were built on more than . . ."

"More than a handsome dowry."

She looked away from the words. "They're supposed to have a better chance than us. You gave me your marker."

"And at least one of them will." He pointed to the far end of the lake and she followed the line of sight to where Olivia and Tottenham stood in conversation, a blush on Olivia's perfect cheeks and a wide grin on Tottenham's face. "He's worth a fortune, and his reputation is clean enough to make him prime minister someday. If they suit, it could be a tremendous match."

"They are alone? Together?" She began to skate again, toward them. "Michael, we must go back!"

He reached for her hand, slowing her pace. "Penelope, they are not alone on a balcony at a ball. They are standing, quite happily, on the lakeshore, conversing."

"*Sans chaperone.*" She said, "I'm serious. We must return!"

"Well, if you say it in French, it must be very serious indeed." His face was turned away, so she couldn't exactly tell, but she thought he was teasing her. "It's all entirely aboveboard." He reached out and took her hand, turning her to skate in a different direction even as she tried to pull away. "You owe me an afternoon, wife." When he held her firm, she stopped resisting, and he orbited her until she couldn't help but follow him, facing him the entire way.

And then he pulled her into his arms as though they were dancing, and they skated back in an approximation of a waltz, until they were a fair distance from anyone overhearing them.

"Everyone is watching."

"Let them watch." He held her tightly, whispering low at her ear, "Don't you remember what it was like to spend those first, breathless minutes alone with a suitor?"

"No." She tried to pull away. "Michael, we must go back."

Suddenly, it wasn't for Olivia that she felt she must return. It was for herself. For her sanity. Because being in his arms, like this, with his voice at her ear, was not good for her convictions.

He twirled them in a slow circle. "We shall return to them in a few minutes. For now, answer the question."

"I did answer it." She tried to pull back, but he held her firmly. "This isn't proper."

"I'm not letting you go. If anyone sees us, they'll simply see the Marquess of Bourne doting on his lovely wife. Now answer the question."

Except, he wasn't doting on her. It wasn't real.

Was it?

"I've never been courted. Not to breathlessness." She couldn't believe she'd admitted it to him.

"Didn't your duke do his best to woo you?"

Penelope couldn't help it. She laughed. "Have you ever met the Duke of Leighton? His is not the most wooing of dispositions." She paused, a memory of the duke stopping a ball for his future wife flashing through her mind, before adding, "At least, it was not with me."

"And the others?"

"Which others?"

"The other suitors, Penelope. Surely one of them did his best to . . ."

She shook her head, looking around them, searching for her sisters, afraid of being seen. Philippa was standing with a group of girls at the center of the glittering ice. "I've never been rendered breathless by a suitor."

"Not even Tommy?"

No. She should have said it, but didn't want to. Didn't want to betray her friend. Didn't want Michael to know she'd been a means to an end for all of them . . . even Tommy. "I thought we weren't discussing Tommy."

"Do you love him?" There was urgency in his tone, and she knew he would not relent until she answered him.

She lifted one shoulder. "He is a dear friend. Of course I care for him."

His eyes grew dark. "That isn't what I mean, and you know it."

She did not pretend to misunderstand. Instead, she told him the truth, knowing the confession would give him power. Not caring, because she wanted something in their relationship to be real. "He did not make me breathless either."

A small child—no older than four or five—skated past, followed by his apologetic father and a laughing mother who turned to dip a curtsy to them. Penelope smiled and waved away the apology before she said, softly, "Perhaps that is the problem, though. Perhaps I waited too long for breathlessness and missed . . . well . . . everything else."

When he said nothing, she looked up at him to find him tracking the same family she had been watching. Finally, he looked down at her very seriously, and she could not look away as they turned and turned in the momentum of the waltz, neither of them forcing movement, but spinning nonetheless. Something shifted in the air between them.

"I'm very happy that you did not marry Leighton or Tommy or any of the woefully lacking others, Sixpence."

No one but Michael had ever called her Sixpence, a silly nickname he'd given her a lifetime ago, assuring her that she was worth far more than a penny to him. They had been sweet words at the time, a lovely little idea that had been sure to make her smile, and her response now was no different.

Warmth spread through her at the name, followed by a question far more serious than the name. "Is that honesty? Or is it false honesty? Who are you, right now? The real you? Or some approximation of the man you think they want you to be? Don't tell me it doesn't matter, because now . . . in this moment . . . it matters." Her voice grew soft. "And I'm not even sure why."

"It's the truth."

And maybe it made her a fool, but she believed him.

They stood there for a long moment, his eyes flecked with greys and golds and greens and so intent upon her, as though they were alone on that lake—as though all of London were not swaying and gliding around them—and she wondered what might happen if all of London weren't there. If all of London did not matter.

He was so close, the heat of him so real and tempting, and she thought he might kiss her there.

No.

She pulled away before he could.

She had to.

She couldn't bear the idea of him using her again.

Snow had begun to fall, dusting the brim of his pin-striped cap and the shoulders of his beautifully tailored coat. "I should go to Olivia before she and Tottenham decide to elope." She paused. "Thank you for the afternoon."

She turned and left, skating away, feeling the loss of him keenly. It was wrong that he could make her want him so much, so quickly, with a single soft smile or kind word. She was weak when it came to him.

And he was so very strong.

"Penelope," he called out to her, and she turned back to meet his gaze, something altogether dangerous sparkling in his brown eyes. "The afternoon is not over."

And, for a brief instant, Penelope thought she might be breathless.

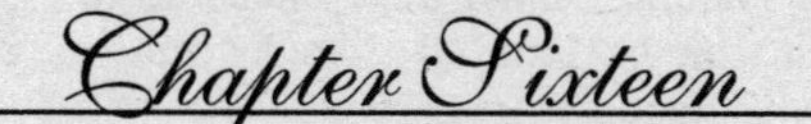

Chapter Sixteen

Dear M—

I had absolutely no doubt that this season would be horrid, but it's worse than I thought. Oh, I can suffer the gossip, the whispers, the way that I have become invisible to those eligible bachelors who used to ask me to dance, but seeing the duke and his new, beautiful duchess—that is difficult.

They're so very much in love; they don't even seem to notice the chatter that follows them. And then, yesterday, I heard tell in a ladies' salon that she is increasing.

It is so strange to see someone else live the life you might have had. Stranger still to ache for it and exalt in the freedom of not having it all at once.

Unsigned
Dolby House, April 1824

Letter unsent

It was a strange thing indeed, wooing one's wife.

He would have expected such a thing to involve candlelight, a quiet bedchamber, and an hour or two of salacious whispering. And yet it appeared that the wooing of *his* wife would involve her sisters, her somewhat ridiculous mother, five of her father's hounds, and a game of charades.

It was the first time he'd played charades since he'd left Surrey for school eighteen years earlier.

"You needn't remain here, you know," Penelope said, sotto voce, from her place next to him on the Dolby House drawing-room settee.

He leaned back, crossing one ankle over the other. "I enjoy a good round of charades as much as the next man."

"And it is my experience that men do adore parlor games," she said wryly. "The afternoon is past, you know."

The words were a not-so-subtle reminder that she'd paid him in full . . . that his time was up. He met her blue gaze. "It's still past the hour of noon, Sixpence." He lowered his voice. "By my count, I've at least five more hours with you—well into the night."

She blushed, and he resisted the urge to make love to her right there—to strip her out of her too-becoming frock and lay her down bare on the very settee on which they sat.

Her family would likely not have approved.

It was not the first time that he'd considered stripping her of her clothes that day, nor was it the tenth. Nor, likely, the hundredth.

Something had happened on the ice, something for which he had not been prepared.

He'd enjoyed himself.

He'd enjoyed Penelope.

He'd enjoyed skating with her, and teasing her, and watching her with her sisters, each charming in her own right. And he'd been so tempted to reach out and claim his wife. But when he'd tried, she'd turned from him—filled with glorious strength—chin high, lovely, refusing to settle for less than what she deserved.

He'd been riveted as she left him, so proud of her as she crossed the Serpentine, and it had taken all his control not to follow her and keep her there, in that place that seemed so far from where their marriage actually existed. He'd luxuriated in the feel of her in his arms as they'd skated, exalted in the way she smiled up at him when he'd stolen a chestnut from her paper sack, and when she'd asked him, wide-eyed, for the truth—he'd been happy to answer her with honesty.

His honesty had not been enough, though. *A well-learned lesson.*

She'd expected him to refuse the invitation to charades, he knew, and he likely should have. But he found he was not ready to leave her—indeed, he found he did not like the idea of ever leaving her. And so here he was, in a drawing room, playing charades in family idyll.

Her sisters tumbled into the room, Philippa carrying a bowl filled with slips of paper, followed by a large brown dog that trotted over to the settee and pushed his way up to sit between him and Penelope, turning twice before settling, chin on Penelope's thigh, hindquarters shoved against Michael's hip. He shifted, making room for the hound, as her hands moved to idly stroke the dog's ears.

Jealousy flared as the dog sighed and burrowed into the touch. Michael cleared his throat, irritated at his canine envy, and asked, "How many dogs are there in this house?"

She wrinkled her nose, thoughtfully, and he was struck by the expression—a vestige from their youth that made him want to reach out and run his finger down the creases in the pert little slope. "Ten? Eleven?" She shrugged, small and sweet. "I've honestly lost count. This is Brutus."

"He appears to like you."

She smiled. "He likes attention."

Michael decided that foolish or not, he would happily turn over his stake in The Angel to have her hands on him in such a lovely, soothing way.

"Did you see how *tall* Tottenham is? And so handsome!" Olivia gushed, coming over to take the chair next to Michael, leaning in to speak to him. "I had no idea that a brother-in-law with a reputation like yours would have access to such a tremendous potential husband!"

"Olivia!" The Marchioness of Needham and Dolby looked as though she might perish with embarrassment. "One does not discuss such things with *peers*!"

"Not even one's brother-in-law?"

"Not even him!" Lady Needham's voice had risen several octaves. "An apology would not be out of hand!"

Pippa looked up from where she had set the large bowl of charades clues and pushed her glasses higher on her nose. "She doesn't mean that your reputation is *bad,* my lord. Just that it's . . ."

Michael raised a brow, wondering how she would finish the sentence.

"Really, Pippa. He's not addlepated. He knows he's a scandalous reputation. I'd wager he enjoys it." She smiled at him, all teeth, and he decided he liked these girls. They were entertaining, if nothing else.

"All right. That's enough," Penelope interjected. "Shall we play? Olivia, you first."

Olivia seemed more than willing to begin the game, and she headed for the large fireplace to take her turn. Selecting a slip of paper from the bowl, she read, pursing her lips, ostensibly considering her strategy.

Instead of pantomiming the item on the paper, however, she looked up, and said, "Do you think Tottenham will buy me a very large betrothal ring?"

"*The Marriage of Figaro,*" Penelope said, matter-of-factly.

"Yes!" Olivia said. "How did you know?"

"How indeed," Penelope replied.

"What a clever girl!" the marchioness announced.

Michael couldn't help it. He laughed, drawing his wife's attention, her brow furrowed in confusion as though he were a strange specimen of flora that she'd just discovered. "What is it?" he asked.

"Nothing . . . I just . . . you don't laugh much."

He leaned in, as close as he could get with the dog between them. "Is it unbecoming?"

She laughed, the sound like music. "No . . . I . . ." She blushed again, and he would have given his fortune for her thoughts at that moment. "No."

"Olivia," Pippa said, "try again."

Olivia reached into the bowl once more, but not before looking straight at Michael and announcing, "I've always liked rubies, Lord Bourne. I believe they complement my complexion. In case it should arise in conversation. With anyone."

Tottenham was in a great deal of trouble, indeed.

"Oh, I'm certain that it will," Penelope said, dryly, "what with all the talk of jewels and ladies' complexions that men like Bourne and Tottenham must have."

"You would be surprised," he said to his wife, all seriousness, and she laughed again. "I shall endeavor to remember your preference for rubies, Lady Olivia."

She smiled. "See that you do."

"I'm not sure jewels complement a complexion," Pippa said smartly. "A play."

"Philippa, we've invited Lord Castleton to luncheon tomorrow," the marchioness announced. "The two of you shall have time in the afternoon for a walk, I hope."

"That would be fine, Mother." Pippa's attention did not waver. "Five words."

"Tottenham wasn't invited to luncheon," Olivia said with a pout.

"You're not supposed to talk, Olivia," Pippa said. "Though that was five words, so well done."

Michael smiled at the clever retort, but did not miss the disinterest in his sister-in-law's response. She did not wish to marry Castleton. Not that he could blame her; Castleton was an idiot. It had taken only a few hours for Bourne to discover that Pippa was smarter than most men and that Castleton would make her a terrible match. Of course, Castleton would make anyone a terrible match, but Philippa would find her marriage particularly soul-destroying.

And Penelope would hate him for not putting a stop to it.

He looked to his wife, who was watching him carefully. She leaned in. "You do not like the match."

He could have lied. The faster Philippa and Castleton were matched, the faster Michael had his revenge, the faster he could live his life out from beneath the cloud of anger and fury that had shadowed his last decade. Nothing had changed.

Except, something had.

Penelope.

He shook his head. "I do not."

Something lit in her beautiful blue eyes, something that could become his addiction. Hope. Happiness. It made him feel ten times a man to be the reason for it. "You will stop it?"

He hesitated. Would he stop it?

It would make Penelope happy.

But at what price?

He was saved from having to reply by Philippa, turning to face them. "What on earth? Do you see this?"

He had not been paying attention, but Olivia was now alternately pantomiming cracking a whip, and screwing up her face, eyes tightly closed, teeth bared, with her fingers splayed out at either edge of her mouth.

"Driving a squid! Whipping the sunshine!" the marchioness called out, pride in her tone, drawing laughter from the rest of the room.

"*Driving a Squid* is a play I would dearly love to read," Philippa said on a giggle, turning back to Penelope. "Penny, really. We could use your help."

Penelope watched Olivia for a long moment, and Michael had difficulty looking away from her—entranced by her focus. He wondered what it would be like to be the recipient of such interest. Of such contentment. Jealousy flared again, and he scolded himself. No grown man should be envious of dogs or sisters-in-law. "*The Taming of the Shrew.*"

Olivia stopped. "Yes! Thank you, Pen. I was beginning to feel foolish up there."

"I can't imagine why," Pippa said, dryly. "I don't think shrews are blind, Olivia." This, from Philippa.

"Oh, tosh. I should like to see you do it better. Who is next?"

"It's Penny's turn. She guessed the last."

Penelope stood and smoothed out her skirts, and Michael watched as she made her way to the makeshift stage, withdrawing a slip of paper and unfolding it. She considered the phrase for a long moment before an idea dawned, and her face lit up. He shifted in his seat, suddenly uncomfortable, suddenly wanting to hurry her from the room and the house, home, to his bed.

But the round had begun, and he would have to wait.

She held up three fingers, and he imagined the feel of them on his jaw, his lips, his cheeks.

"Three words!"

She stiffened her posture and saluted her sisters, then marched stiffly around the stage, her full breasts straining at the edge of her gown. He leaned forward, elbows on his knees, and watched, enjoying the view.

"Marching!"

"Soldiers!"

She made an encouraging sign with her hands.

"Napoleon!"

She mimed firing a rifle, and his attention lingered at the place where her shoulder and neck met, the soft, shadowed indentation there that he ached to kiss . . . the place he would kiss in another time and place, if they were married and he were a different man.

If he were a man she could love.

If theirs was a marriage built on something other than revenge.

Do not touch me. The words whispered through him, and

he loathed them. Loathed what they represented—the way she thought of him, the way she believed he would treat her. The way he *had* treated her.

The way he was treating her.

"Hunting!"

"Father!"

"Father hunting Napoleon!" Olivia's silly guess pulled Penelope from her mime with a laugh. She shook her head, then pointed at herself. "Father hunting you!"

Pippa looked at Olivia. "Why on earth would that be in the charades bowl?"

"I don't know. Once, I had *Aunt Hester's wig*."

Pippa laughed. "I put that one in!" Penelope cleared her throat. "Right. Sorry, Pen. What were you not saying?"

Penelope pointed to herself.

"Lady?"

"Female?"

Wife. His wife.

"Girl?"

"Daughter?"

"Marchioness!" The Marchioness of Needham and Dolby interjected her first guess with such exuberant glee that Michael thought she might topple from her settee.

Penelope sighed and rolled her eyes before meeting his gaze, eyebrows raised as if to say, *Help?*

Something startlingly akin to pride exploded in his chest at the request—at the idea that she might come to him for assistance. He found he wanted to be the man to whom she turned. He wanted to help her.

For chrissake's, Bourne, it's charades.

"Penelope," he said.

Her eyes lit. She pointed at him.

"Penelope? You're a part of the clue?" Olivia looked skeptical. Penelope began to mime again. "Sewing?"

She grinned and pointed at Olivia, then mimed pulling a thread out of needlepoint quickly. "Unsewing?"

She pointed at Olivia again, then to herself, then mimed

sewing and unsewing once more before she looked to Pippa, clearly the sister she really expected to be able to put all the clues together.

He did not want Pippa to win. He wanted to win. To impress her.

"*The Odyssey,*" he said.

Penelope smiled, broad and beautiful, clapping her hands and jumping up and down, enjoying the fleeting triumph, then mimed firing a rifle and marched around the little stage once more. Penny spun around, pointing directly at Michael, all her attention on him, and he felt like a hero when he guessed, "The Trojan War."

"Yes!" Penelope announced on a great sigh of breath. "Well done, Michael."

He couldn't stop himself from preening. "It was, rather, wasn't it?"

"I don't understand," Olivia said. "How did Penny sewing and unsewing make for the Trojan War?"

"Penelope was Odysseus's wife," Philippa explained. "He left her, and she sat at her loom, sewing all day, and unraveling all her work at night. For years."

"Why on earth would someone do that?" Olivia wrinkled her nose, selecting a sweet from a nearby tray. "*Years?* Really."

"She was waiting for him to come home," Penelope said, meeting Michael's gaze. There was something meaningful there, and he thought she might be speaking of more than the Greek myth. Did she wait for him at night? She'd told him not to touch her . . . she'd pushed him away . . . but tonight, if he went to her, would she accept him? Would she follow the path of her namesake?

"I hope you have more exciting things to do when you are waiting for Michael to come home, Penny," Olivia teased.

Penelope smiled, but there was something in her gaze that he did not like, something akin to sadness. He blamed himself for it. Before him, she was happier. Before him, she smiled and laughed and played games with her sisters without reminder of her unfortunate fate.

He stood to meet her as she approached the settee. "I would never leave my Penelope for years." He said, "I would be too afraid that someone would snatch her away." His mother-in-law sighed audibly from across the room as his new sisters laughed. He lifted one of Penelope's hands in his and brushed a kiss across her knuckles. "Penelope and Odysseus were never my favored mythic couple, anyway. I was always more partial to Persephone and Hades."

Penelope smiled at him, and the room was suddenly much much warmer. "You think they were a happier couple?" she asked, wry.

He met her little smile, enjoying himself as he lowered his voice. "I think six months of feast is better than twenty years of famine." She blushed, and he resisted the urge to kiss her there, in the drawing room, hang propriety and ladies' delicate sensibilities.

Missing the exchange, Olivia announced, "Lord Bourne, I make it your turn."

He did not look away from his wife. "It grows late, I am afraid. I think I should take my wife home."

Lady Needham came to her feet, toppling a small dog from her lap with a little yelp. "Oh, do stay a little longer. We are all so enjoying your visit."

He looked at Penelope, wanting to snatch her away to his underworld but allowing her to make their decision. She turned to her mother. "Lord Bourne is right," she said, sending a thrill through him. "We have had a long afternoon. I should like to go home."

With him.

Triumph surged, and he resisted the impulse to toss her over his shoulder and carry her from the room. She would let him touch her tonight. She would let him woo her.

He was sure of it.

Tomorrow remained a question, but tonight . . . tonight, she would be *his*.

Even if he did not deserve her.

Dear M—

Victoria and Valerie were married today in a double wedding to mediocre husbands indeed. I've no doubt that their choices were limited because of my scandal, and I can barely swallow back the anger and the unfairness of it all.

It seems so unfair that some of us get such a life—filled with happiness and love and companionship and all the things we are taught never to even dream of because they are so rare and not at all the kind of things to expect from a good English marriage.

I know envy is a sin, and covetousness, as well. But I cannot help wanting what others have. For me, and for my sisters.

Unsigned
Dolby House, June 1825

Letter unsent

She was falling in love with her husband.

The startling realization came as he handed her up into the carriage, knocking twice on the roof before settling in beside her for their return home.

She was falling in love with the part of him that ice-skated, played charades, teased her with wordplay, and smiled at her as though she were the only woman in the world. She was falling in love with the kindness that lurked beneath his exterior.

And there was a part of her, dark and quiet, that was falling in love with the rest of him. She did not know how she could manage being in love with all of him. He was too much.

She shivered.

"Are you cold?" he asked, already moving to pull a blanket over her.

"Yes," she lied, clutching the wool to her, trying to remember that this man, the kind solicitous man who asked after her comfort, was only a fleeting part of her husband.

The part that she loved.

"We shall be home soon enough," he said, coming close, wrapping one arm around her shoulders, a band of warm steel. She loved his touch. "Did you enjoy your afternoon?"

The word simmered through her like a promise, and she could not keep the flush from her cheeks, even as she did her best to distance herself from him and the emotions he inspired. "I did. Charades with my sisters is always amusing."

"I like your sisters very much." The words were soft, a rumble of sound in the darkness. "I was happy to be a part of the game."

"I think they are happy to have a brother they enjoy," she said, thinking of her brothers-in-law. "Victoria's and Valerie's husbands are less . . ." She hesitated.

"Handsome?"

She smiled. She couldn't help it. "That as well, but I was going to say—"

"Charming?"

"And that, but—"

"Utterly enthralling?"

Her brows rose. "Utterly enthralling, are you?"

He feigned affront. "Have you not noticed that about me?"

The frightening thing was that she had. Not that she would tell him that. "I hadn't. But I can see that you are also infinitely more modest than the others."

It was his turn to laugh. "They must be very difficult, indeed."

She grinned. "I see you know your limitations."

Silence fell again, and she was surprised when he broke it. "I enjoyed charades. It was as though I was a part of the family."

The words were so honest and unexpected, so honest, and tears came, unbidden, to prick at Penelope's eyes. She blinked them back, saying simply, "We are married."

He searched for her gaze in the darkness. "Is that all it takes? The exchange of vows in front of Vicar Compton, and a family is born?" When she did not reply, he added, "I wish it were so."

She tried to keep the words light. "You are welcome to my sisters, my lord. I am certain that they would both enjoy having you for a brother . . . what with your friendship with Lord Tottenham and . . ." She stopped.

"And?" he prompted.

She took a breath. "And your ability to keep Pippa from becoming Lady Castleton."

He sighed, leaning his head back against the seat. "Penelope . . . it is not so easy."

She stilled, then pulled away from his embrace, the cold attacking instantly. "You mean it does not serve you."

"No. It does not."

"Why do their quick marriages matter?" He hesitated, and she filled the silence. "I have tried to understand, Michael . . . but I cannot see it. How does one serve the other? You already have proof of Tommy's illegitimacy . . ." And suddenly, she understood. "You don't though, do you?"

He did not look away, but neither did he speak. Her mind spun as she tried to make sense of the arrangement, of how it must have been organized, of the parties who must have been involved, of the logic of the situation. "You don't have it, but my father does. And you will pay him handsomely for it in married daughters. His favorite commodity."

"Penelope." He leaned forward.

She pressed against the door of the coach, as far away as she could get. "Do you deny it?"

He stilled. "No."

"And so it goes," she said bitterly, the reality of the situation filling the small space of the carriage, threatening to suffocate her. "My father and my husband conspiring to manage both my sisters and me. Nothing changes. That's the choice, is it? My sisters' reputations or my friend's? One, or t'other?"

"At first, it was a choice," he conceded. "But now . . . I would not allow your sisters to be ruined, Penelope."

She raised a brow. "Forgive me if I do not believe you, my lord, considering how much you have threatened those same reputations since our meeting."

"No more threats. I want them happy. I want you happy."

He could make her happy. The thought whispered through her, and she did not doubt it. Not at all. This was a man who had singular focus, and if he set his mind to giving her a lifetime of happiness, he would succeed. But that was not in the cards. "You want your revenge more."

"I want both. I want everything."

She turned away from him, speaking to the street beyond the carriage window, suddenly irritated. "Oh, Michael, whoever told you that you could have everything?"

They rode in silence for an age before the coach stopped, and Michael descended, turning back to help her from the conveyance. As he stood there in the dim shadows of the coach, one hand extended, she was reminded of that night at Falconwell, when he'd offered her his hand and his name and his adventure, and she'd taken it, thinking he was still the boy she'd once known.

He was not. He was nothing of that boy . . . now entirely a man with two sides—kind protector and vicious redeemer. He was her husband.

And, God help her, she loved him.

All those years she'd waited for this moment, for this revelation, sure that it would change her life and cause flowers to bloom and birds to sing with its euphoria.

But this love was not euphoric. It was painful.

It was not enough.

She lowered herself from the carriage without his aid, avoiding his strong, gloved hand as she climbed the steps and entered the town house foyer, empty of servants. He followed her, but she did not hesitate, instead heading straight for the stairs and beginning her climb.

"Penelope," he called from the foot of the stairs, and she closed her eyes against her name, against the way its sound on his lips made her ache.

She did not stop.

He followed, slowly and methodically, up the stairs and down the long, dark hallway to her bedchamber. She had left the door open, knowing that he would find entry even if she locked herself inside. He closed the door behind him as she moved to her dressing table and removed her gloves, draping them carefully over a chair.

"Penelope," he repeated, with a firmness that demanded obedience.

Well, she was through obeying.

"Please, look at me."

She did not waver. Did not reply.

"Penelope . . ." He trailed off, and from the corner of her eye, she saw him rake his fingers through his hair, leaving a path of glorious imperfection there—so handsome, so uncharacteristic. "For a decade, I have lived this life. Revenge. Retribution. This is what has fed me—nourished me."

She did not turn back. Could not. Did not want him to see how he moved her. How much she wanted to scream and rail and tell him that there was more to life . . . more to *him* . . . than this wicked goal.

He would not hear her.

"You're wrong," she said, moving to the washbasin at the window. "It has poisoned you, instead."

"Perhaps it has."

She poured cool, clear water into the bowl and submerged her hands, watching them pale and waver against the porcelain, the water distorting their truth. When she spoke, it was to those foreign limbs. "You know it will not work, don't you?" When he did not reply, she continued. "You know that once you've meted out your precious revenge, there will be something else. Falconwell, Langford, Tommy . . . then what? What comes next?"

"Then life. Finally," he said, simply. "Life out from beneath the specter of that man and the past he gave me. Life without retribution." He paused. "Life with you."

He was close when he said it, closer than she expected, and she lifted her hands from the water and turned around even as the words stung—even as they made her ache. They were words she had desperately wanted to hear . . . since the beginning of their marriage . . . perhaps since before that. Perhaps since she began writing him letters, knowing he'd never receive them. But no matter how much she wanted to hear those words, she found she could not believe him.

And it was belief—not truth—that mattered. He had taught her that.

He stood less than an arm's length away, serious and stark, his hazel eyes black in the shadows of the room, and she could not stop herself from speaking even as she knew she would never make him see the truth. "You're wrong. You shan't change. Instead, you shall remain in the darkness, cloaked in revenge." She paused, knowing that the next words were the most important for him to hear. For her to say. "You shall be unhappy, Michael. And I shall be unhappy with you."

His jaw steeled. "And you are such an expert? You with your charmed life, tucked away in Surrey, never a moment risked, not a single mark on your perfect, proper name. You don't know the first thing about anger, or disappointment, or devastation. You don't know what it's like to have your life ripped from under you and want nothing more than to punish the man who did it."

The quiet words were like a cannon in the room, echoing around Penelope until she could no longer hold her tongue. "You . . . selfish . . . man." She took a step toward him. "You think I do not understand disappointment? You think I was not disappointed when I watched everyone around me—my friends, my sisters—marry? You think I was not devastated the day I discovered that the man I was to marry was in love with another? You think I was not angry every day that I woke in my father's home knowing that I might never have contentment . . . and that I would never find love? You think it is easy to be a woman like me, tossed from one man to another to control—father, fiancé, now *husband*?"

She was advancing on him, pressing him back toward the door of the room, too irritated to enjoy the fact that he was retreating along with her. "Need I remind you that I have never, ever had a choice in the direction of my life? That everything I do, everything I am, has been in service to others?"

"That is your fault, Penelope. Not ours. You could have refused. No one was threatening your life."

"Of course they were!" she exploded. "They were threatening my safety, my security, my future. If not Leighton or Tommy or *you,* what? What was to happen when my father died, and I had *nothing*?"

He came toward her then, taking her shoulders in his hands. "Except it was not out of self-preservation, was it? It was out of guilt and responsibility, and a desire to give your sisters the life you could not have."

Her gaze narrowed. "I will not apologize for doing what was right for them. We are not all you, Michael, spoiled and selfish and . . ."

"Don't stop now, darling," he drawled, releasing her and crossing his arms over his broad chest. "You were just coming to the good bit." When she didn't reply, he raised a brow. "Coward. Like it or not, you made your choices, Sixpence. No one else."

She hated him for using the nickname with her now. "You're wrong. You think I would have chosen Leighton? You think I would have chosen Tommy? You think I would have chosen—"

She stopped herself . . . wanting desperately to finish the sentence, to say *you*. Wanting to hurt him. To punish him for making everything so much more difficult. For making it impossible to simply love him.

He heard the word anyway. "Say it."

She shook her head. "No."

"Why not? It's true. If I were the last man in Britain, it would never have been me. I'm the villain in this play, the one who snatched you from your perfect country life, all vengeance and wrath, far too hard and cold and undeserving of you. Of your feelings. Of your company."

"Your words. Not mine." Except they weren't true. Because, of all the things she'd done, of all the matches she'd almost made, he was the only one she'd really wanted.

He took a step backward, raked a hand through his hair, and gave a short huff of laughter. "You have learned to do battle, haven't you? Poor Penelope no longer."

She squared her shoulders and took a deep breath, promising herself that she would put him—and the fact that she loved him—from her mind. "No," she finally agreed. "Poor Penelope no longer."

Something shifted in him, and for the first time since their marriage, she did not question the emotion in his gaze. Resignation. "So that's that, is it?"

She nodded once, every inch of her resisting the words, wanting to scream at the injustice of it all. "That's that. If you insist upon revenge, you do so without me at your side."

She knew the ultimatum would never be met, but it was no less of a blow when he said, "So be it."

Chapter Seventeen

Dear M—

I was at the theater tonight, and I heard your name. A handful of ladies were discussing a new gaming hell and its scandalous owners, and I could not help but listen when I heard them mention you. It's so odd to hear you referred to as Bourne—a name I still associate with your father, but I suppose it's been yours for a decade.

A decade. Ten years since I've seen you or talked to you. Ten years since everything changed. Ten years, and I still miss you.

Unsigned
Dolby House, May 1826

Letter unsent

Michael climbed the steps to Dolby House one week later, responding to the summons from his father-in-law that had arrived at Hell House that morning, as he'd stood in his study and tried to keep himself from rocketing through the house to take hold of his wife and prove once and for all that they were married and that she was his.

It had come to this . . . the embarrassing truth that he spent most of his time at home listening for her footstep beyond the door, waiting for her to come to him, to tell him that she'd changed her mind, to beg him to touch her.

Just as he wished her to touch him.

For six nights, he had spent evenings at the house, avoiding his wife even as he stood on his side of that cursed adjoining bedchamber door, listening as servants filled her bath and chatted with her, then as she'd slid into the water, the sounds of her movement in the water making him ache with temptation.

With desire to prove himself to her.

The experience was torturous. And he deserved it, punishing himself by refusing to enter that room, pull her from her bath and lay her out on her bed, lovely and lush, to ravish her. As he'd turned away from the door that taunted him with the secrets that lay beyond, it was regret he felt.

She was becoming everything he wanted, and she had always been more than he deserved.

Last night had been the worst—she'd been laughing with her maid about something, and he'd stood, one hand on the door handle, the sound of her lyric laughter a siren's call. He'd pressed his forehead to the door like a fool and listened for long minutes, waiting for something to shift.

Finally, he'd turned away, aching to go to her, to find Worth standing at the far end of the room, just inside the closed door.

He'd been embarrassed and irritated. "Is knocking no longer done?"

Worth raised one ginger brow. "I did not think it necessary, as you are rarely home at this hour."

"I am home tonight."

"You are also an idiot." The housekeeper had never been one to mince words.

"I should sack you for insolence."

"But you won't. Because I'm right. What is wrong with you? You clearly care for the lady, and she clearly cares for you."

"There's nothing clear about it."

"You're right," the housekeeper said, setting a stack of towels down near the washbasin. "It's perfectly obscure—the reason why both of you spend so much time on opposite sides of that door, listening for the other."

Michael's brows pulled together. "Does she—"

Worth shrugged one shoulder. "I suppose you'll never know." She paused. "Dammit, Bourne. You've spent so much of your adult life protecting others. Who will protect you from yourself?"

He turned away from the housekeeper. "Leave me."

That night, he'd listened intently, waiting for Penelope to step from her bath and come to the adjoining door. He swore that if he even caught a hint of her standing on the opposite side, waiting, he would open it, and they would have it out. But instead, he watched the light beneath the door extinguish, heard the rustle of blankets as she climbed into bed, and fled to The Angel, where he spent the evening in the pit, watching as tens of thousands of pounds were wagered and lost, reminding him of the power of desire, of weakness. Reminding him of what he had conquered.

Of what he had lost.

Still wearing his coat and hat, Bourne followed a footman through the maze of Dolby House—one of the few estates within the borders of London—and out onto a large balcony that led down to the snow-covered lands of the property. There was a set of human footprints leading away from the house, surrounded by a collection of paw prints.

A rifle's report echoed in the silence, and Michael turned to the footman, knowing he was expected to follow the sound. He followed the track, the freshly fallen snow muffling his footsteps, toward his father-in-law.

A brisk wind blew, and he slowed, turning his head away

from the gust, baring his teeth at the bitter cold. A hunting rifle sounded from beyond a small hill, and trepidation flared. He was not in the market for being shot by the Marquess of Needham and Dolby, at least, not *accidentally.*

Considering his options, he stopped, cupped his hands around his mouth, and called out, "Needham!"

"Huzzah!" A rich cry sounded from beyond the ridge, punctuated with a half dozen different barks and howls.

Bourne took it as a sign to approach.

He paused as he crested the rise, looking at the wide spread of land that stretched down to the Thames. He took a deep breath, enjoying the feel of the cold air in his lungs, and directed his attention to Needham, who was shielding his eyes from the morning sun.

Halfway down the rise, Needham called up, "I wasn't sure you'd come."

"I find that it behooves one to respond to the summons of one's father-in-law."

Needham laughed. "Especially when the man in question holds the only thing you want."

Michael accepted Needham's firm handshake. "It's bloody cold, Needham. What are we doing out here?"

The marquess ignored him, turning away with a loud "Ha!" and sending the dogs into the brush twenty yards away. A single pheasant was flushed into the air. Needham lifted his shotgun and fired.

"Damn! Missed it!"

A shock, certainly.

The two men walked toward the bushes, and Bourne waited for the older man to speak first. "You've done a fine job of keeping my girls out of your mud." Michael did not reply, and Needham continued, "Castleton has proposed to Pippa."

"I heard that. I confess, I'm surprised you agreed."

Needham grimaced as the wind tore past them. A dog barked nearby, and Needham turned back. "Come on, Brutus! We're not finished!" He resumed walking. "Dog can't hunt worth a damn." Bourne resisted the obvious retort. "Castelton's a simpleton, but he's an earl, and that makes the wife happy." The dogs flushed another pheasant, and Needham fired and missed. "Pippa's too smart for her own good."

"Pippa is too smart for a life with Castleton." He knew he shouldn't say it. Knew that he shouldn't care who the girl married as long as the betrothal ended with the means for Langford's revenge in his hands.

But he couldn't stop thinking of Penelope, and the way Pippa's uninspired match had upset her. He didn't want her upset. He wanted her happy.

He was going soft.

Needham didn't seem to notice. "The girl accepted. I can't call it off. Not without a decent reason."

"And the fact that Castleton is a muttonhead?"

"Not good enough."

"What if I find you another reason? A better one?" Surely there was something in the files at The Angel—something that would condemn Castleton and end the betrothal.

Needham cut him a look. "You forget, I am keenly aware of the punishment for broken engagements. Even the ones with good reason damage girls. And their sisters."

Like Penelope.

"Give me a few days. I shall find something to end it." Suddenly, it was critical that Bourne find Pippa a way out of her engagement. It did not matter that he could taste revenge, so close and sweet.

Needham shook his head. "I've got to take the offers that come, or I'll have another Penelope on my hands. Can't afford that."

Bourne gritted his teeth at the words. "Penelope is a marchioness."

"She wouldn't have been if you hadn't come after Falconwell, would she? Why do you think I attached the land to her in the first place? It was my last chance."

"Your last chance at what?"

"I don't have a son, Bourne." He looked toward Dolby House. "When I die, this house and the manor shall be passed down to some idiot cousin who doesn't care a whit for them, or the land on which they sit. Penelope's a good girl. She does what she's told. I made it clear to her that she had to marry to keep her sisters valuable. She couldn't decide to be a spinster and spend the rest of her days languishing in Surrey. She knew her duty. She knew that Falconwell would go to her children, and with it, some of the history of the Needham land."

A little row of towheaded girls appeared in his thoughts.

Not memory. Fantasy.

Her children.

Their children.

The thought consumed him, as did the desire that came with it. He'd never considered children. He'd never imagined he'd want them. Never thought he'd be the kind of father they deserved. "You wanted something of your past to give to your future."

The marquess turned back toward the house. "Something you understand, I'd wager."

How strange that he'd never really thought of it in such a way. Not until this moment. He'd been so focused on regaining Falconwell that he'd never thought of what he would do with it. Of what would come next. Of *who* would come next.

In his mind, nothing had come after the restoration of Falconwell. Nothing but revenge.

Except, now there was something more, beyond the hulking shadow of the house and his past.

Something that revenge would kill.

He pushed the thought aside.

"I confess, when Langford offered Falconwell as his stake in the game, I knew you'd come after it. I was happy to win it, knowing that it would summon you."

Michael heard the self-satisfaction in them. "Why?"

Needham lifted one shoulder in a small shrug. "I'd always known that she'd marry you or Tommy Alles and, between us, I'd always hoped it would be you—not for the obvious reason—Alles's illegitimacy—though that was a bit of it; I always liked you, boy. Always thought that you'd come back from school and be ready to take the title and the land and the girl. When Langford paupered you, and I had to hunt for Leighton, I was not a small bit put out, I'll tell you."

Michael would have found the selfishness of the statement amusing if he weren't so shocked by the idea that Needham had always wanted him for Penelope.

"Why me?"

Needham looked out over the Thames, considering the question. Finally, he said, "You were the one who cared the most for the land."

It was true. He'd cared for the land and its people. So much, that when he'd lost it all, he hadn't had the courage to come back to face them. *To face her.*

And now it was too late to fix those mistakes.

"That," Needham went on, "and you were the one she liked best."

A thrum of excitement coursed through him at the words, at the truth in them. She had liked him best. Until he'd left. And she'd been alone. And she'd stopped trusting him. She was right not to, of course. He'd made his goals clear, and in securing the only thing he'd ever wanted, he would lose her.

She was the sacrifice he had planned to make from the beginning. Not so much sacrifice then—now, too much to think on.

It was expected, of course—he'd ruined everything of value he ever held.

"It doesn't matter now," Needham went on, unaware of the cacophony of Michael's thoughts. "You've done well. This morning's paper extolled the virtues of your marriage . . . I confess, I am surprised by the effort you've put into spinning your tale—chestnut eating and waltzing on ice and spending afternoons with my girls and other ridiculousness. But you've done well . . . and West seems to believe it. The papers swear yours is a love match. Castleton wouldn't have proposed if our name was in any way tainted by a scandalous marriage."

It should be you who opposes the match, not Castleton. Pippa would be better off with a man who was half otter. Michael opened his mouth to say just that when Needham said, "At any rate, you've fooled them. Revenge is yours, as agreed."

Revenge is yours. The words he'd waited a decade to hear.

"I've the letter in the house, ready for you."

"You don't want to wait for Olivia to be betrothed as well?" The question was out before he could stop it . . . before he could consider the fact that he was reminding his father-in-law that Michael's end of the bargain had not been officially completed.

Needham lifted his rifle, pointing it in the direction of a low-lying hedge at the bank of the river. "Tottenham's invited her to ride today. The boy will be prime minister one day; Olivia's future appears bright." He fired, then looked to Michael. "And, besides, you've done well by the girls. I keep my promises."

But he'd not done well by them, had he? Philippa was to marry an imbecile, and Penelope—Penelope had married an ass. He shoved his hands into his pockets, bracing against the wind, and turned back to look up at the looming Dolby House. "Why give it to me?"

"I've five girls, and, though they drive me to drink, if something were to happen to me, I would want to know that their guardian—the man I appointed to the deed—would care for them as I did." Needham turned back toward the house, retracing his tracks. "Langford ignored that code. He deserves everything you give him."

Michael should have felt triumph. Should have felt pleasure. After all, he'd just been given the thing he'd wanted most in the world.

Instead, he felt empty. Empty save a single, incontrovertible truth.

She would hate him for this.

But not as much as he would hate himself.

Billiards tonight.

A carriage will collect you at half eleven.

Éloa

The small ecru square, stamped with a delicate female angel, arrived just after luncheon, delivered by Worth with a knowing smile. Penelope unfolded the letter with trembling hands and read the dark, mysterious promise on the note.

The promise of adventure.

She looked up from the summons, color springing to her cheeks, and asked the housekeeper, "Where is my husband?"

"He has been out all day, my lady."

Penelope lifted the paper. "And this?"

"Arrived not five minutes ago."

She nodded, considering the invitation and its implications. She had not seen Michael since the day they'd ice-skated and argued, and she'd realized that she loved him. He'd left her bedchamber that night and never returned—even as she'd waited, knowing better than to hope he might decide to give up on his quest for vengeance and choose life with her instead.

Was it possible that the invitation was from him?

The thought had her breath catching in her throat. Perhaps it was. Perhaps he had chosen her. Perhaps he was giving her an adventure and giving them both a new chance at life.

Perhaps not.

Either way, the note was a temptation she could not resist—she wanted her chance at adventure, at billiards, at a night at The Angel. And she would not lie, she wanted her chance to see her husband again. Her husband, for whom she ached even as she knew it was pointless.

She might have committed to avoiding him, to keeping her distance from his temptation, to protecting herself from the way he made her feel, but she could not resist him.

It was all she could do to wait for nightfall, then, in the darkness, for the appointed hour to come. She dressed carefully, wishing she didn't care so much for what he might think, for how he might see her, choosing a deep, salmon silk, entirely inappropriate for early February, but a color she'd always thought flattered her pale skin and made her seem less plain and more . . . *more.*

The carriage had arrived at the servants' entrance of Hell House, and it was Mrs. Worth who came to fetch her, eyes light with a knowledge that had Penelope flushing with anticipation.

"You'll need this," the housekeeper whispered as she pressed a domino of plain, black silk, adorned with scarlet ribbons, into Penelope's hand.

"I shall?"

"You'll enjoy your evening much more if you are not concerned with discovery."

Penelope's heart began to race as she stroked the mask, loving the feel of the silk—its promised thrill. "A mask," she whispered, more to herself than to the housekeeper. Anticipation flared. "Thank you."

The housekeeper smiled, quiet and knowing. "It's my pleasure." She paused, watching as Penelope lifted the mask to her eyes, tying it back, and adjusting the silk against her brow. "May I say, my lady, how happy I am that he chose you?"

It was presumptuous and not at all the kind of thing housekeepers said, but Worth was not at all the kind of housekeeper one had usually, so Penelope smiled, and said, "I am not certain he would agree with you."

Something lit in the other woman's eyes. "I think it is only a matter of time before he does." Worth nodded her approval, and Penelope was through the door and into the waiting coach, heart in her throat, before she could turn back.

Before she could stop herself.

The carriage did not deliver her to the main entrance to The Angel, but instead to a strange, unimpressive entrance accessible through the mews that ran alongside the building. She ascended in near darkness, clutching the hand of the coachman who had come to help her down and guide her to a blackened steel door. Nervousness flared.

She was at Michael's club once more, this time, by invitation, in what she believed was her prettiest gown, for a game of billiards.

It was extraordinarily thrilling.

The driver knocked for her and stepped away as a little slot in the door slid open and a pair of eyes—black as coal—appeared. No sound came from behind the door.

"I . . . I received an invitation. To billiards," she said, lifting one hand to check that her mask was secure, hating the movement and the hitch in her throat, the way her nerves held the high ground.

There was a pause, and the slot slid shut, leaving her standing alone in the darkness in the middle of the night. Behind a London gaming hell.

She swallowed. *Well. That hadn't gone exactly as expected.*

She knocked again. The little slot opened once more.

"My husband is—"

The slot closed.

"—your employer," she said to the door, as though it might open on its own with the proper encouragement.

Alas, it remained firmly shut.

Penelope pulled her cloak around her and looked over her shoulder to the coachman behind, just pulling himself up onto his seat. He noticed her predicament, thankfully, and said, "Usually there's a password, milady."

Of course. The strange, final word of the invitation.

Whoever needed a password to do anything? It was like something from a gothic novel. She cleared her throat and confronted the enormous door once more.

Knocked again.

The slot slid open with a click, and Penelope smiled at the eyes.

No sign of recognition.

"I have a password!" she announced triumphantly.

The eyes were not impressed.

"Éloa," she whispered, not knowing how the process worked.

The slot closed again.

Honestly?

She waited, turning back to the carriage and throwing a nervous glance up at the driver. He shrugged his shoulders as if to say, "I haven't any idea."

And just as she was about to give up, she heard the clicking of a lock and the scrape of metal on metal . . . and the massive door opened.

She couldn't help her excitement.

The man inside was enormous, with dark skin and dark eyes and an immovable countenance that should have made Penelope nervous, except she was far too excited. He was dressed in breeches and a dark shirt, the color of which she could not make out in the dim light, and wore no coat. She might have thought him inappropriately attired, but she quickly reminded herself that she had never entered a gaming hell through a mysterious, password-requiring door, and so she supposed she knew very little about the appropriate dress of a man in such a situation.

She waved the paper that had been delivered earlier that day. "Would you like to see my invitation?"

"No." He stepped aside to let her in.

"Oh," she said, slightly disappointed, as she pushed past him into the little entryway, watching as he closed the door behind her with an ominous thud. He did not look at her; instead, he sat on a stool perched near the door, lifted a book from a nearby shelf, and began to read by the light of a wall sconce.

Penelope blinked at the tableau. Apparently he was a man of letters.

She stood quietly for a long moment, uncertain of her next move. He seemed not to notice.

She cleared her throat.

He turned a page.

Finally, she said, "I beg your pardon?"

He did not look up. "Yes?"

"I am Lady—"

"No names."

Her eyes went wide. "I beg your pardon?"

"No names on this side." He turned another page.

"I—" She stopped, uncertain of what to say. *This side?* "All right, but I . . ."

"No names."

They remained in silence for a little longer until she could not bear it a moment more. "Perhaps you could tell me if I am to stand here all night? If so, I would have brought a book of my own."

He looked up at that, and she took pleasure in the way his black eyes widened ever so slightly, as though she'd surprised him. He pointed to the far end of the entryway, where another door loomed in the darkness. She hadn't seen it earlier.

She moved toward it. "Billiards is through here?"

He watched her carefully, as though she were a specimen under glass. "Among other things, yes."

She smiled. "Excellent. I would ask for your name so I might thank you properly, sir, but . . ."

He returned to his book. "No names."

"Precisely."

She opened the door, letting in a shock of light from the corridor beyond. She looked back at the strange man, impressed by the play of golden light across his dark skin, and said, "Well, thank you just the same."

He did not reply, and she stepped into the brightly lit hallway, closing the door firmly behind her, leaving her alone in the new space. The hallway was wide and long, spanning in both directions, and the candles lit every few feet blazed against the gilded décor, making the entire space warm and bright. The walls were covered in a paisley pattern of scarlet silk and wine-colored velvet, and Penelope could not help but reach out to touch them, loving the way the plush gave beneath her touch.

A burst of feminine laughter came from one end of the hallway, and she headed for it instinctively, not knowing what she would find, but feeling strangely prepared for whatever was to come next. She edged down the hallway, her fingers trailing along the wall, tracking her movement past one closed door after the next. She paused before an open door, the room beyond empty save for a long table, and she stepped inside without thinking to get a closer look.

There was a green baize field set deep into the table—several inches down—and the soft fabric was embroidered in crisp, clean white thread with a grid of numbers that ran its length and breadth. Penelope leaned over to inspect the confusion of carefully wrought text—the mysterious combination of numbers, fractions, and words.

She reached out to run one gloved finger along the word *Chance*, a thrum of excitement coursing through her as she traced the curve of the C and the looping H.

"You've discovered hazard."

She gasped in surprise and spun toward her name, hand at her throat, to find Mr. Cross standing in the doorway of the room, a half smile on his handsome face. She stiffened, knowing that she'd been caught. "I'm sorry. I didn't know where to . . . There was no one in the . . ." She trailed off, deciding silence a better choice than carrying on like an imbecile.

He laughed and came forward. "No need to apologize. You're a member now and can move about freely."

She tilted her head. "A member?"

He smiled. "It is a club, my lady. Membership is required."

"I'm only here for billiards. With Michael?" She hadn't meant for it to come out as a question.

Cross shook his head. "With me."

"I—" She stopped, her brows knitting together. *Not with Michael.* "The invitation was not from him."

Cross smiled, but Penelope was not comforted. "It was not."

"Is he not here?" Would she not see him here, either?

"He's here, somewhere. But he does not know *you* are here."

Disappointment flared.

Of course he didn't.

He was not interested in spending the evenings with her.

On the heels of that thought came another. *He was going to be furious.*

"It came from you."

He tilted his head. "It came from The Angel."

She considered the words, and their mystery. *The Angel.*

"It's more than an invitation isn't it?"

Cross lifted one shoulder. "You know the password now. That makes you a member."

A member.

The offer was tempting—access to one of the most legendary clubs in London, and all the adventure that she'd ever wanted. She thought of the excitement that had come with the invitation to billiards, of the wonder that had come when she'd stepped through the door into the warm, brilliant hallway of this mysterious club. Of the thrill that had coursed through her as she'd watched the roulette wheel spin during her first visit.

But she'd thought her next visit—tonight—would be with him.

She was wrong.

He wanted no part of her. Not like this.

He reminded her of that every time they pretended their love affair. Every time he touched her to ensure her participation in their farce. Every time he left the house instead of spending the night with her. Every time he chose vengeance over love.

She pushed the knot of emotion in her throat away.

He would not give her marriage . . . *And so she must take adventure instead.*

She was too far down this path to be able to walk away from it, after all.

She met Cross's quiet grey gaze and took a deep breath. "Billiards, then. Do you intend to make good on that promise?"

Cross smiled and waved a hand toward the doorway. "The billiards room is across the hall." Her heart began to pound. "May I take your cloak?"

"You look lovely," he said as black wool gave way to salmon satin—the dress she'd worn for a different man, one who would not see it and who, if he did see it, wouldn't care at all how she looked.

She put the thought from her mind and met Cross's friendly grey gaze, smiling when he produced a white rose, offering the lovely stem toward her. "Welcome to the Other Side," he said, when she accepted the bloom. "Shall we?"

He indicated the hallway beyond, and Penelope led the way from the room. Before she could open the door to the billiards room, a collection of chatter came from down the hall. She turned, thankful for her simple disguise as a group of women, similarly masked, hurried toward them.

They dipped their heads as they passed, and curiosity surged through Penelope. Were they members of the aristocracy as well? Were they women like her? Searching for adventure?

Did their husbands ignore them, too?

She shook her head at the thought, errant and unwelcome before one of the women stopped to face Cross, her blue eyes glittering behind her pink domino.

"Cross . . ." she fairly drawled, leaning forward to gift

him with a first-rate view of her bosom. "I'm told you are sometimes lonely in the evenings."

Penelope's jaw dropped.

Cross raised a brow. "Not this particular evening, darling."

The lady turned to Penelope, gaze lingering on the rose in her hand. "First night? You may join us, if you like."

Penelope's gaze went wide at the words. "Thank you, but no." She paused, adding, "Though I'm quite . . . flattered." It seemed like the right thing to say.

The woman tilted her head back and laughed, the sound loud and without hesitation, and Penelope realized that she did not think she'd ever heard the honest laughter of a woman to whom she was not related. *What was this place?*

"Run along, love," Cross said with an encouraging smile. "You pretties have a fight to watch, do you not?"

The smile turned into a perfect moue, and Penelope resisted the temptation to try the expression herself. Some women made flirtation seem so very easy. "We do, indeed. I hear Temple is in fine form tonight. Perhaps he'll be lonely after the match."

"Perhaps he will," Cross said in a way that made Penelope think there was no question whatsoever that Temple would be lonely after the match.

The masked lady raised a finger to her lips. "Or maybe Bourne . . . she said thoughtfully.

Penelope's brows snapped together.

Absolutely not Bourne.

The very idea of this woman with her husband made Penelope want to tear the mask from her eyes and give her a fight to witness in wicked proximity. She opened her mouth to tell her just that when Cross interjected, seeming to understand the direction in which the conversation was moving. "Doubtful Bourne will be available this evening, darling. You'll miss the beginning if you don't rush."

That seemed to spur the other woman into motion. "Drat. I must go. Will I see you at Pandemonium?"

Cross dipped his head gracefully. "I would not miss it."

She hurried off, and Penelope watched her for a long moment before turning to him. "What is Pandemonium?"

"Nothing with which you need concern yourself."

She considered pressing him on the issue as he reached for the door to the billiards room. If the other woman was planning to attend this event, Penelope wanted to as well, if for no other reason than to find the courage to call off the jezebel.

Not that Penelope was much different.

After all, she was wearing a mask, about to receive a lesson in billiards from a man who was not—

"It's about bloody time you showed up. I don't have time to wait for you and your ladies tonight. And what on earth are we doing playing on this side? Chase will have our heads if—"

—her husband. Who was leaning against the billiard table in question, cue in hand, looking very very handsome.

And very very angry.

He came to his full height. "Penelope?"

So much for the mask.

"This side makes it easier for the lady to play," Cross said, clearly amused.

Michael took two steps toward them before coming to a halt, hands fisted at his side. His gaze found hers, glittering green in the candlelight. "She's not playing."

"I don't believe that you have a choice," she said, "as I have an invitation."

He seemed not to care. "Take off that ridiculous mask."

Cross closed the door, and Penelope reached up to remove the domino, unmasking in front of her husband more difficult than stripping bare in front of all of Parliament.

Nevertheless, she squared her shoulders and removed the mask, facing him head-on. "I was invited, Michael," she said, hearing the defensiveness in her voice.

"How? Did Cross offer you an invitation when he escorted you home in the dead of night? What else did he offer you?"

"Bourne," Cross said, his words filled with warning as he stepped forward to defend himself.

To defend her. She did not need his defense. She had done nothing wrong. "No," Penelope said, steel in her tone. "Lord Bourne knows precisely where I've been and with whom for the duration of our short, disastrous marriage." She stepped toward Michael, her offense making her bold. "Home, alone. Instead of here, where the female half of London is apparently wishing they had the password to his bed." His eyes went wide.

"I would appreciate it if you would leave, Michael," she added, tossing the mask and the rose to the billiard table. "You see, I've been looking forward to this billiards lesson. And you are making it very difficult to enjoy."

Chapter Eighteen

Dear M—

I wish I had the courage to come to your club and announce myself as your old friend, but of course I don't. It is probably for the best, however, as I'm not certain which I'd like to do more: hit you or hug you.

Unsigned
Dolby House, March 1827

Letter unsent

She was running him ragged.

Gone was the soft, sweet wife he'd thought he was getting, snow dusting her bonnet as she confessed past courtships, one errant flake landing and melting almost instantly on the tip of her nose as she smiled up at him.

And in that woman's place was an Amazon, standing at the center of his club, in the heart of the London underworld, placing bets on roulette while the city watched, demanding the safety of her friends and the reputation of her sisters, and scheduling billiards lessons with one of the most powerful and feared men in the city.

And now, she stood in front of him, and bold as brass, suggested he leave her alone.

He should do just that.

He should walk away from her and pretend they'd never married.

Return her to Surrey or, better, ship her to the North Country to live out her newfound scandalous desires far from him. He had Falconwell, and the tools for his revenge, and it was time to chase her from his life.

But he did not want to give her up.

He wanted to throw her over his shoulder and take her home to bed. Hell. The bed wasn't even necessary. He'd wanted to throw her down on the snowy banks of the Serpentine or the floor of her father's drawing room or the too-narrow seat of his coach and strip her bare, leaving her unprotected from his hands and lips, and that desire had not changed.

The billiard table was sturdy enough to hold them both, he guaranteed.

"I'm not going anywhere until you tell me why you are here." He growled, not trusting himself to move closer, uncertain of his ability to be near her without railing against her, without explaining to her, very clearly, that this was not a place for her.

That she was not welcome here.

That it would ruin her.

The final thought pushed him over the edge. "Answer me, Penelope. Why are you here?"

She met his gaze, her blue eyes firm. "I told you. I'm here to play billiards."

"With Cross."

"Well, to be fair, I thought it might be with you."

"Why would you think that?" He would never have invited her to his gaming hell.

"The invitation was delivered by Mrs. Worth. I thought you sent it."

"Why would I send you an invitation?"

"I don't know. Perhaps you'd realized you were wrong and did not want to admit it aloud?"

Cross gave a little snort of laughter from his position at the door, and Michael considered killing him. But he was too busy dealing with his difficult wife. "You thought wrong. Tell me you hired a hack again."

"No," she said, "a carriage came to fetch me."

His eyes went wide. "A carriage owned by *whom*?"

She tilted her head, thinking. "I'm not certain."

He honestly thought he might have gone mad. "You accepted transportation in a strange carriage to the back entrance of the most notorious gaming hell in London—"

"Which my *husband* owns," she said, as though it should make a difference.

"Wrong answer, darling." He took a step back, forcing himself to lean on the billiard table. "You came here in a strange carriage."

"I thought you had sent it!"

"Well, I didn't!" he thundered.

"Well, that's not my fault!"

They both went silent, her furious retort echoing around the little room, their breath coming hard and fast.

He was not going to let her win. "How the hell did you get in here?"

"My invitation included a password," she said, and he heard the pleasure in her voice. She was enjoying his surprise.

She came closer, and he was drawn to the way her skin glistened in the light. He took a deep breath, telling himself it was meant to be calming and not because he was desperate to catch her delicate scent—like the violets that grew in Surrey summer. "Did anyone see you come in?"

"No one but the coachman and the man at the door who took the password."

The words did not appease. "You shouldn't be here."

"I had no choice."

"Really? No choice but to leave our warm, comfortable home in the dead of night and come to my place of business—a place to which I expressly told you never to come? A place that is not at all the kind of place that women of your ilk should be?"

She stilled, her blue eyes glittering with something he did not recognize. "First of all, it is not *our* home. It is *your* home. Though I can't imagine why you even have it considering how little time you spend there. It's most certainly not *my* home, though."

"Of course it is." What was she talking about? He'd virtually handed the house over to her.

"No. It isn't. The servants answer to you. The post comes to you. For heaven's sake, you won't even let me reply to social invitations!" He opened his mouth to retort but found he had no defense. "We're supposed to be *married,* but I haven't any idea of how that house operates. Of how you live. I don't even know your favorite pudding!" The words were coming faster and more furious now.

"I thought you didn't want a marriage based on pudding," he said.

"I don't! At least, I didn't think I did! But since I know virtually nothing else about you, I would settle for pudding!"

"Figgy pudding, darling," he mocked. "You've made it my favorite."

Her gaze narrowed on him. "I should like to drop a figgy pudding on your head."

Cross snickered, and Michael remembered that they had an audience. He slid a look at his partner. "Out."

"No. He invited me here. Let him stay."

Cross raised a brow. "It's hard to say no to a lady, Bourne."

He was going to murder the ginger-topped beanpole. And he was going to enjoy it. "What are you doing inviting my wife out of her home in the dead of night?" he asked, unable to keep himself from taking one menacing step toward his former friend.

"I assure you, Bourne, I am so enjoying watching your wife run you in circles that I wish it *had* been me who had sent the invitation. But it wasn't."

"I beg your pardon?" Penelope interjected. "You did not send the invitation? If not you, then who?"

Bourne knew the answer. "Chase."

Chase was unable to stay out of the affairs of others.

Penelope turned on him. "Who is Chase?"

When Bourne did not answer, Cross did, "Chase is the founder of The Angel, my lady, who brought us all into partnership."

Penelope shook her head. "Why would he invite me to billiards?"

"An excellent question." He turned to Cross. "Cross?"

Cross crossed his arms and leaned back against the door. "It seems Chase feels the lady is owed a debt."

One of Bourne's brows rose, but he did not speak.

Penelope shook her head. "Impossible. We've never met."

Michael narrowed his gaze on Cross, who smiled, and said, "Sadly, Chase is always one step ahead of the rest of us. If I were you, I would simply accept payment."

Penelope's brows rose. "In visits to a gaming hell?"

"It seems that is the offer."

She smiled. "It would be rude to refuse."

"Indeed it would, my lady." Cross laughed, and Michael despised the familiarity in the sound.

"She'll accept invitations to The Angel from Chase, or anyone else, over my dead body," he growled, and Cross seemed, finally, to recognize that he was serious. "Get out."

Cross looked to Penelope. "I shall be just outside should you need me."

The words set Bourne further on edge. "She won't need you."

I shall give her everything she needs.

He did not have to say it, as Cross was already gone, and Penelope was speaking. "I have put up with a great deal from men over the years, Michael. I have suffered betrothal to a man who cared not a whit for me and everything for my reputation, and a broken engagement that echoed through ballrooms for two complete seasons—while my fiancé married his love and birthed his heir, and no one seemed to mind."

She ticked off the items on her fingers as she spoke, moving toward him. "After that came five years of courting from men who saw me as nothing more than my dowry—not that avoiding *those* marriages helped a whit, as I seem to have landed myself in a marriage that has nothing to do with me and everything to do with my connection to a piece of *land*."

"What about Tommy, your dearest love?"

Her eyes flashed with fire. "He's not my dearest love, and you know it. He wasn't even my fiancé."

He could not conceal his surprise. "He wasn't?"

"No. I lied to you. I pretended he was so you would stop your insane plans to abduct me into marriage."

"I didn't stop."

"No, you didn't. And by that point, I did not feel much like telling the truth." She stopped and collected herself. "You were just like all the others, so why should I have? At least the engagement to Leighton involved some aspect of my own character—even if it was the boring, proper aspect of it."

Michael held his tongue as she advanced. There was nothing boring or proper about this Penelope, standing in a gaming hell as though she owned it, absolutely livid. She was vibrant and magnificent, and he'd never wanted anything in the world the way he wanted her in that moment.

She pressed on. "As you care not a bit about my wishes, I have decided to take my own pleasures in hand. As long as I receive invitations to adventure, I shall accept them."

Not without him, she wouldn't.

It was his turn to advance upon her, not knowing where to begin, pressing her back toward the billiard table. "Do you realize what could happen to you in a place like this? You could have been attacked and left for dead."

"People are rarely attacked and left for dead in Mayfair, Michael." She gave a little laugh. An *actual* laugh, and he considered strangling her himself. "Unless I was at risk of accosting by your literary door-man, I think this place is quite safe, frankly."

"How would you know? You don't even know where you are."

"I know I'm on the other side of The Angel. That's how the man at the door referred to it. How Cross referred to it. How *you* referred to it."

"What password were you given?"

"Éloa."

He sucked in a breath. Chase had given her carte blanche at the club. Access to any room, any event, any adventure she wanted, without chaperone.

Without him.

"What does it mean?" she asked, registering his surprise.

"It means I'm going to have words with Chase."

"I mean, what does Éloa mean?"

He narrowed his gaze, answered her literally. "It's the name of an angel."

Penelope tilted her head, thinking. "I've never heard of him."

"You wouldn't have."

"Was he a fallen angel?"

"She was, yes." He hesitated, not wanting to tell her the story, but unable to stop himself. "Lucifer tricked her into falling from heaven."

"Tricked her how?"

He met her gaze. "She fell in love with him."

Penelope's eyes widened. "Did he love her?"

Like an addict loves his addiction. "The only way he knew how."

She shook her head. "How could he trick her?"

"He never told her his name."

A beat.

"No names."

"Not on this side, no."

"What happens on this side?" She leaned back against the billiard table, her hands clutching the side cushions.

"Nothing you need think about."

She smiled. "You can't keep it from me, Michael. I'm a member, now."

He didn't want her to be. He didn't want her touched by this world. He moved toward her slowly, unable to resist. "You shouldn't be."

"What if I want to be?"

He was close to her now, close enough to reach out and touch her, to run his finger down the pale, smooth skin of her cheek. When he lifted his hand to do that, she edged away, turning and running one gloved hand along the green baize.

Do not touch me.

Her words whispered through his mind, and he stopped himself from following her.

"Michael?" His name pulled him from his reverie. "What happens here?"

He met her blue eyes. "This is the ladies' side of the club."

"There are women on the other side, too."

"Not ladies. Those women come with men . . . or leave with them."

"You mean they are mistresses." Her fingers found a white billiard ball, and she rolled it to and fro beneath her hand, and he was transfixed by the way her hand moved, capturing and releasing, rolling and stopping.

He wanted that hand on him.

"Yes."

"And on this side?"

She was directly across from him now, six feet of slate and felt between them. "On this side, there are ladies."

Her eyes went wide. "*Real* ladies?"

He could not help his dry tone. "Well, I am not certain how much they deserve the adjective, but yes. They bear the titles, for the most part."

"How many of them?" She was fascinated. He couldn't blame her. The idea that any number of aristocratic females had access to vice and sin on a moment's notice was scandalous indeed.

"Not many. One hundred?"

"*One hundred?*" She laid her hands flat on the table and leaned forward, and his eyes were drawn to the swell of her breasts rising and falling rapidly beneath the edge of her dress. The fabric was fastened with a long white ribbon, the silk ends begging to be unfastened. "How does this remain a secret?"

He smiled. "I already told you, love, we deal in secrets."

She shook her head, admiration on her face. "Amazing. And they come here to gamble?"

"Among other things."

"*What* things?"

"Everything men do. They gamble, they watch fights, they drink extravagantly, they eat extravagantly . . ."

"Do they meet lovers here?"

He did not like the question, but he knew he should answer it. Perhaps it would scare her away. "Sometimes."

"How exciting!"

"Do not get any ideas."

"About taking a lover?"

"About any of it. You're not to make use of The Fallen Angel, Penelope. It's not for women like you." *And certainly not with a lover.* The idea of another man touching her had Michael itching to strike something.

She watched him in silence for a long while before she moved, easing back around the table toward him. "You keep saying things like that. *Women like me.* What does that mean?"

There were so many ways to answer the question—women who were innocent. Women who were perfectly behaved, with perfect backgrounds and perfect upbringings, and perfect lives. Women who were perfect. "I don't want you touched by this life."

"Why not? It's your life, too."

"That's different. It's not for you."

It's not good enough for you.

She stopped at the near corner of the table, and he saw the hurt in her eyes. Knew she was bothered by his words. Knew, too, that it was best for both of them if she remained hurt. And stayed away from this place.

"What's so wrong with me?" she whispered.

His eyes widened. Had he had a year to think of what she might say in this situation, the idea that she would perceive his forbidding her to come to The Fallen Angel because there was something wrong with her would never have occurred to him.

God, there was nothing wrong with her. She was perfect. Too perfect for this.

Too perfect for him.

"Penelope." He stepped toward her, then stopped, wanting to say the right thing. With women across Britain, he knew what to say, but he never seemed to know what to say with her.

She released the billiard ball, letting it roll across the table to send another careening off in a new direction. When it came to a stop, she looked back at him, her blue eyes gleaming in the candlelight. "What if I weren't Penelope, Michael? What if the rules were in effect here? What if there really were no names?"

"If there really were no names, you would be in serious danger."

"What kind of danger?"

The kind that ends with another angel fallen.

"It's irrelevant. There are names. You are my *wife*."

Her lips turned up in a wry smile. "Ironic, is it not, that beyond that door, one hundred wives of the most powerful men in England are taking what they want with whomever they want, and in here, I can't even persuade my husband to show me what might be. My husband, who *owns* the club. Who loves it. Why not share it with me?" The words were soft and tempting, and there was nothing that Michael wanted more in that moment than to show her every inch of this decadent life.

But for once in his life, he was going to do the right thing.

So he said, "Because you deserve better." Her eyes went wide as he tracked her across the room, backing her away from the table. "You deserve better than a billiard room in a gaming hell, than roulette with a handful of men who think you're, at best, someone's mistress and, at worst, something far less flattering. You deserve better than a place where at any moment a brawl might begin, or a fortune might be wagered, or an innocence might be lost. You deserve to be kept far from this life of sin and vice, where pleasure and devastation are red and black, in and out. You deserve better," he repeated. "Better than me."

He kept coming, watching as her eyes widened, as their blue darkened with fear or nervousness or something more, but he couldn't stop himself. "There hasn't been a single valuable thing in my life that I haven't ruined when I touched it, Penelope. And I will be damned if I allow the same to happen to you."

She shook her head. "You won't ruin me. You wouldn't."

He lifted his hand to her cheek, running his thumb across the impossibly smooth skin there, knowing even as he did that he was making it harder to let her go. He shook his head. "Don't you see, Sixpence? I already have. I've already brought you here, exposed you to this world."

She shook her head. "You didn't! I brought myself here. I made this choice."

"But you wouldn't have if not for me. And the worst part is—"

He stopped, not wanting to say any more, but she lifted her hand and covered his, holding him to her cheek. "What is it, Michael? What is the worst part?"

He closed his eyes at the touch, at the way she made him burn.

It wasn't supposed to be this way.

She wasn't supposed to affect him like this.

He wasn't supposed to want her so very much.

He wasn't supposed to be so very drawn to this adventurous, exciting woman who had evolved from the woman he'd married.

And yet he was.

He pressed his forehead to hers, aching to kiss her, to touch her, to throw her down and make love to her. "The worst part is that if I don't send you back, I'm going to want to keep you here."

Her eyes were so blue, so lovely, framed with full, golden lashes the color of autumn wheat, and he could see desire in them. She wanted him.

Her hand moved to his chest, settling for a long moment before it slid up and around to the nape of his neck, her fingers twining in his hair with a beautiful, unbearable touch. Time slowed as he savored the feel of her against him, the warmth of her in his arms, the scent of her trapping his thoughts, the knowledge that she was soft and flawless and *his* for that moment.

"And you'll hate me for it." He closed his eyes and whispered, "You deserve better."

So much better than me.

"Michael," she said softly, "there's no one better. Not for me."

The words crashed through him, and she tilted her head, came up on her toes, and pressed a kiss to his lips.

It was the most perfect kiss he'd ever experienced, her lips firmly on his, soft and sweet and utterly mesmerizing. He'd ached for her for days and she laid claim to him with the caress, taking his lower lip between hers and stroking once, twice, until he opened for her, and she stole his breath with the tentative exploration of her tongue—a silken slide against his. He wrapped her in his arms, pulling her tightly against him, loving the way she felt, soft where he was hard, silk where he was steel.

When she finally pulled back from the kiss, her lips were swollen and pink, and he could not keep his gaze from them, parted sweetly before they curved around her words. "I do not wish to learn about billiards tonight, Michael."

His gaze flickered up from those lips, meeting her gaze. "No?"

She shook her head slowly, the movement a sinful promise. "I should much rather learn about you."

She kissed him again, and he could not resist her. There wasn't a man alive who could. His hands were on her, pulling her tightly against him.

He was lost.

His wife stood before him like temptation incarnate, asking him to make love to her—risking her reputation and everything for which he'd been working.

And he found he didn't care.

He reached past her, throwing a hidden switch and swinging the wall away to reveal a staircase beyond, steps stretching up into a great, yawning darkness. He extended his hand to her, palm up, allowing her to make the choice to ascend with him. He did not want her to ever think that he had forced her into this moment. Into this experience. Indeed, it felt just the opposite, as though this courageous, female explorer were calling to him.

And when she settled her hand in his without hesitation, without remorse, desire shot through him, quick and nearly unbearable.

He pulled her to him, kissing her thoroughly before leading her into the dark stairwell, closing the door behind them, plunging them into blackness.

"Michael?"

She whispered his name, and the sound, soft and decadent, was a siren's call. He turned toward her, his hand squeezing hers, pulling her to stand on the first step with him, feeling his way to her waist, loving the way her body felt beneath his hands, the roundness of her hips, the soft swell of her stomach.

Her breath hitched as he lifted her to stand on the step above him. Her lips were even with hers now, and he stole a kiss, stroking deep, loving the taste of her, a drug of which he could never have enough.

He pulled away, just barely, and she sighed, the sound of her pleasure making him want her more than he'd ever imagined. He took her mouth again, and her hands came to his hair, her fingers tangling in his curls, tugging at them, making him wish they were naked, and she was guiding his mouth to where she wanted it most.

He growled at the fantasy and pulled away, grasping her hand in his and saying, "Not here. Not in the darkness. I want to see you."

She kissed him, pressing her breasts to his chest, robbing his breath, making him desperate for her, for her skin, her touch, the little cries that made him harder than stone. When she released him from the intoxicating caress, he found he'd lost his patience.

He wanted her that moment.

Immediately.

Without hesitation.

So he lifted her in his arms and carried her up the stairs. Up to decadence. Up to pleasure.

Chapter Nineteen

Dear M—

Today, I am twenty-six.

Twenty-six and unmarried—growing older and more wizened by the hour, despite what my mother likes to say in her high-pitched moments.

Eight years of seasons, and not one decent match . . . a shabby record for the eldest daughter of the House of Needham and Dolby. This morning, over breakfast, I saw the disappointment in all their gazes.

But, knowing what my options have been, I found I couldn't bring myself to agree with their censure.

I am a bad daughter, indeed.

Unsigned
Needham Manor, August 1828

Letter unsent

The stairs led to the owners' suite.

Michael set her on her feet just inside the secret doorway

that opened at the top of the passage, closing it securely behind them before moving with quick grace to the main door to the room. She followed him closely, eager for what was to come next, not wanting to miss a moment of this. Of him.

She had thought he would take her to bed—for surely in this massive club, where men came to explore wickedness and pleasure, there was a place where he slept. Where she might sleep with him.

Where they might do other things, as well, before they had to return to reality and remember all the reasons their marriage was in shambles and their lives were all wrong.

When he locked the door and turned back to her, she stilled in the room, lit by the warm light of a trio of fireplaces and the large golden window that looked out onto the floor of The Angel.

Realization coursing through her. *He meant for them to . . . Here.*

She backed away instinctively, and he followed, slow and steady, a silken promise gleaming in his eyes. "Where are you going?" he asked, and she caught her breath at the deep gravel in his voice.

She took a step back. "We'll be discovered."

He shook his head. "We won't be disturbed."

"How do you know?"

He raised a brow. "I know."

She believed him. Her heart pounded in her ears as he stalked her across the large, dark room, toward the window, his intent clear.

He would have her. And it would be glorious.

And suddenly, she was not backing away from him out of nervousness or concern or embarrassment. She was backing away because it was unbearably exciting to be pursued by him. He was beautiful and sleek, and he moved with a purpose lacking in lesser men. It was that single-mindedness that drew her to him, that made him so tempting. His pursuit of those things he wanted was relentless.

And right now, he wanted her.

Anticipation thrummed through her and she stilled. In the next heartbeat, he was upon her. He reached for her, cupping her cheek, tilting her face up to his, capturing her gaze with such attention. Such focus.

All on her.

She was consumed with excitement at the realization. With breathlessness.

"What are you thinking?" His thumb stroked along the line of her jaw, leaving heat in its wake.

"The way you look at me," she said, unable to look away from him. "It makes me feel . . ." She trailed off, uncertain of her words, and he leaned down to press a kiss to the base of her throat, where her pulse raced.

He lifted his head once more. "How does it make you feel, love?"

"It makes me feel powerful."

She hadn't realized it until the words were spoken, and one side of his mouth lifted in the hint of a smile, his fingertips tracing over her skin, brushing across her collarbone, running along the edge of her silk dress, sending pleasure rippling across her skin. "How so?"

She took a deep breath at the pleasure he wreaked, at the way his eyes tracked his fingers along her skin, and said, "You want me."

Hazel darkened to brown, and his voice turned to smoke. "I do."

"It makes me feel like I could have anything."

He tugged gently at the bow that kept the bodice of her dress tight across her breasts, the movement loosening the ribbon and causing the fabric to gape. His finger dipped below the hem of the fabric, hinting, teasing there. "I would give you anything you want. Anything you ask."

Love me.

Not that. That, she knew, he wouldn't give her.

But before she could trace the thought, he was lifting her hands and unbuttoning her gloves, sliding them off slowly, the lush stroke of kidskin against flesh ensuring that she would never again be able to think of the donning or doffing of a glove as anything other than a sexual act.

He slipped one hand into her gaping bodice, beneath the edge of her chemise, to cup one breast and lift it from the fabric. She gasped at the sensation, and he leaned in to capture the sound with his kiss. "I want to lay you down in the light of The Angel and make love to you." The words were punctuated with the rough stroke of his thumb across one nipple, and the scrape of his teeth down her neck. "And I think you want it, too."

She could not stop her nod. Or her confession. "I do."

As long as it is with you.

He released her, turning her to face the massive painted-glass window. She looked out on the floor of The Angel, teeming with people, as he worked at her buttons, releasing them methodically. "Tell me what you see," he whispered, his lips pressing hot and soft along the curve of her shoulder.

"There are . . . men . . . everywhere." Penelope gasped and clutched the fast-loosening fabric to her chest.

He reached her corset and made fast work of the laces, releasing her from the bone-and-linen prison. She sighed at the sensation, and his hands stroked across the cotton chemise, soothing the skin beneath. One hand came up to the window to hold her steady at the sensation, so welcome against her worried skin.

He seemed to understand the sound, and he licked at her ear, his hands sliding beneath dress and corset, stroking, leaving a path of pleasure in their wake. "Poor love," he whispered, the words like fine brandy. "You've been neglected."

And it felt like she had been. It was as though her skin ached for his touch alone. For his kiss. For the long, warm strokes that brought her nearly excruciating pleasure.

"Only men?" he whispered, snapping her attention back to the room through the mottled glass that defined Lucifer's beautiful, corded neck.

His hands came around to cup her breasts over her chemise, lifting them and shaping them with his warm palms before he took the aching tips between his fingers and pinched just barely, just enough to send a spear of pleasure straight through her. She gasped. "Answer me, Penelope."

She forced herself to focus on the tableau before her. "No. There are women."

"And what are they doing?"

She focused on one woman in a lovely periwinkle silk, her black hair piled high on top of her head, curls falling down around her. "One is sitting on a gentleman's lap."

He pressed against her then, rocking his hips into her bottom, and Penelope wished they were not separated by layers and layers of clothing. "What else?"

"She has her arms around his neck."

He took the hand that braced her against the window and wrapped it behind her, around his neck, affording him better access to her lovely curves. "And?"

"And she's talking in his ear."

"Coaching his card game?" His fingers pinched again, and she gasped, closing her eyes and turning toward him.

"Michael," she whispered, wishing he would kiss her.

"I love the way you say my name. You're the only one who calls me Michael," he said, before he gave her what she wanted, his tongue stroking deep and smooth until she was squirming in his arms, pressing her breasts into his magic hands.

"You hated it," she protested.

"You've worn me down." He sucked gently at the soft skin of her neck. "Tell me more about the woman."

Penelope turned back to the window, struggling to focus once more. She watched the woman lean forward, allowing her partner a view straight down her bodice. He smiled, leaning in to press a kiss on her collarbone before one of his hands slid over her thigh and along her calf before finally disappearing beneath the hem of her dress.

Penelope arched back, against Michael. "Oh, he's touching her . . ."

His fingers lightened at the words, the caress barely there, its softness making Penelope wish they were both naked in the dark room. "Touching her where?"

"Beneath her—" She paused as Michael's hand moved downward, toward the place where she ached for him. She sighed the next word as his fingers found her core, stroking softly. "—skirts."

"Like this?" Despite the fabric of her skirts, Michael's knee found its way between her thighs, spreading her wider as his hand slid into the heat there, the heel of his palm rocking against her.

Her head fell back against his shoulder. "I don't know."

"What do you think?"

"For her sake, I hope so," she whispered, as he stroked her.

He laughed, the sound a low rumble behind her. "And I for his."

She closed her eyes as his hands moved in concert, one at her breast, toying, tempting, there and the other between her thighs, stroking masterfully. The caresses went on for several long moments before Penelope sighed, relishing the feel of him against her, pressing herself back to fit as perfectly as possible to him. He rocked into her movements, hissing at her ear. "If you keep up with that, darling, you shan't be able to watch them much longer."

"I don't want to watch them, anymore, Michael."

"No?" The question was curious at her shoulder, where his teeth were scraping across her skin.

She shook her head, tilting to afford him better access. "No," she confessed. "I want to watch you." His fingers did something wonderful between her thighs, and she sighed. "Please."

"Well," he said, and she heard the teasing smile in the words. "Since you asked so nicely . . ."

He turned her to face him, his eyes flickering over the place where she still held the fabric of her dress to her chest. "Let go of the dress, Penelope," he ordered, the words liquid smoke, and her grip tightened.

"What if—"

"No one can see you."

"But . . ."

He shook his head. "You cannot imagine I would let anyone see you, my glorious darling. You can't imagine I'd allow that and not murder them."

The words were so possessive, she could not help the pleasure that coursed through her at them. No one had ever called her glorious. No one had ever seemed the least bit interested in possessing her.

But in this moment, Michael wanted her.

She watched him carefully for a long moment, loving the way his eyes begged her to bare herself to him, before she released her grip on the fabric, letting it drop to the floor, leaving her bare, save for her stockings, to the dim light of the room . . . and to her husband.

He went still, his eyes roaming over her body, finally settling on her face before he said, reverently, "You are the most beautiful thing I've ever seen."

He was at her feet, removing her boots and pantalets, leaving her in nothing but her stockings. He stroked up her legs along her stockings, lingering at the place where silk met skin. When she gasped at the sensation, he licked at the skin there. "I have a weakness for stockings, love. Smooth and silk, like the softest part of you."

She blushed, not wanting to admit that she loved the feel of them against her skin, not wanting to tell him that since their wedding night, she'd savored the stroke of the satin along her legs, pretending that it was his touch.

"You like them, too, I see," he teased, and she felt the curve of his lips against her thigh.

"I like *you,*" she whispered, one of her hands settling on the back of his head, her fingers stroking through his soft curls.

He stood at that, leaving her stockings on, kissing her, rough and wonderful. "You're all perfect curves and soft skin," one hand stroked up, palmed the underside of her breast, "so lovely and full."

His words were destroying her sanity. They were more damaging than even his touch. She arched toward him, into his kiss, and he stole her breath and words and thought, his lips and tongue stroking along hers, promising more pleasure than she could possibly imagine. When he stopped the kiss, she sighed, forgetting her protest and watching as he stepped back, removed his clothes in quick, economical movements, and stood to face her, the light from the casino beyond the window turning him into a mosaic of color and texture, all long legs and corded muscle, lean hips and broad shoulders and . . .

No. She should not be looking at that.

It did not matter that she wanted to. That she was unbelievably curious.

Just one, quick look.

Oh, my.

Penelope went instantly shy, her hands moving to cover her nudity. "We cannot . . . I was not . . . This isn't what I expected."

He smiled then, a rare wolfish smile. "Are you nervous?"

She knew she should pretend not to be—he'd likely done this with a dozen other women. But, she *was* nervous. "A little."

He lifted her, carrying her to a low chaise on one side of the room and settling her onto his lap for a deep, searching kiss that stole her breath, and her inhibitions. She licked his lower lip, sucking it gently, and he pulled back with a harsh breath.

Her eyes went wide.

"I'm sorry . . . the lip. Temple's jabs have a tendency to linger."

She pulled back, lifting one hand to smooth back his hair and search his face for additional wounds. "You shouldn't let him hit you," she whispered, pressing one soft kiss next to the wound.

"It was the only way to take my mind off the fact that I could not go home and take you to bed." He drew one hand down her arm in a long, lush stroke. "You terrify me." His lips twisted into a wry smile as his fingers stroked and teased at the soft skin of her wrist, her elbow, her shoulder.

"How is that possible?"

"I can't take small tastes of you, love. I can only gorge on you. You're irresistible." He pressed a kiss to her shoulder, his tongue coming out to lave the skin there. "You're like the rattle of dice. The shuffle of cards. You call to me until I ache with desire for you." The words were a whisper of breath at the base of her neck. "I could easily become addicted to you."

The words set her heart pounding. "And that is bad?"

He chuckled, the rumble of laughter vibrating against her stomach and breasts. "For me, yes. Very very bad." He kissed her, long and slow. "And for you, too. You asked me not to touch you. I wanted to respect your wishes."

Except they hadn't been her wishes. Not really.

She'd always wanted him to touch her, even when she'd told him not to.

She'd always wanted him, even when she told herself she did not.

He was her weakness.

He saved her from having to speak by touching her, his fingers playing at the crest of one breast until she sighed at the sensation, her hands sliding into his hair. She pulled back and met his dark, lovely eyes. "Michael," she whispered.

He did not move his gaze from hers as he shifted her, lifting her as though she weighed nothing, running his hand down one thigh, urging her to spread her legs.

The very idea was a scandal.

A dream.

She hesitated only a fraction of a second before she followed his silent instructions, straddling him.

There was pride and pleasure in his voice when he said, "My adventuresome beauty . . ."

She knew it was an exaggeration. She was no beauty. But tonight she *felt* beautiful, and she did not even consider ignoring his request. The new position gave her access to all of him, to his broad, firm shoulders, to the wide chest that rose and fell with his breath, and she could not help placing her hands upon him, this marvelous, handsome man who was her husband.

He groaned his pleasure at her touch and lifted her until her breasts were at the level of his mouth, and he was blowing air across their tips in one long, steady stream. She followed the direction of his gaze, so intent upon her, watching as her nipples tightened—first one, then the other—unbearably hard and aching.

She wanted his mouth on her.

"Touch me," she whispered.

He was already there, licking and sucking at her until she thought she might die from the wicked, wonderful pleasure of it. Her hands threaded through his hair, holding him to her until he pulled back and set his mouth to the other, neglected breast, licking in long, lovely strokes before closing his lips around her and giving her precisely what she wanted.

She writhed in his arms, in time to the pull of his lips, the lick of his tongue, the scrape of his teeth. Dear heaven. He wielded pleasure like a master, with art and skill. And she never ever wanted it to end.

He pulled back, finally, lifting her higher, closer to him, placing one warm kiss to the soft skin of her torso before sliding her down his body and taking her mouth once more. His knees came up beneath her, holding her tightly to his chest as his fingers tunneled into her hair and sent pins flying this way and that, lost to the floor of the decadent room.

His mouth moved to her neck, where he licked at the delicate skin above one pulse point, and she sighed his name once more, feeling drugged with pleasure.

Pleasure she hadn't known existed before him.

Pleasure she would never have found if not for him.

"*Michael.*" She sighed his name.

He smiled, a self-satisfied, utterly masculine smile, one hand moving from behind her back, sliding between them.

She turned her gaze to that wicked, marauding hand, transfixed by its movement, then his fingers were brushing against her, at the core of her, ever so lightly, as though they had an infinite amount of time to explore her. She had never wanted anything so much in her life.

His fingers fluttered against her, and she squirmed against him, one of her hands tumbling down his torso to rest, tentatively, on the part of him about which she was so curious. He sucked in a breath as her hand settled on the hot steel of him. "Penelope . . ." The word was lost in a groan.

She wanted to touch him, to learn him, to give him all the pleasure that he was giving her. "Show me how. Teach me."

His eyes were black with pleasure, and he moved his other hand to guide her, showing her just how to touch, just how to stroke. When he groaned, long and lovely, she leaned forward and kissed his cheek softly, whispering against his skin, "This is much more interesting than billiards."

He laughed harshly at the words. "I couldn't agree more."

"You're so smooth," she said, stroking his length, marveling at the feel of him. "So hard." He closed his eyes as she touched him, and she watched his face, enjoying the play of pleasure across it.

She rubbed one thumb firmly across the tip, and he gasped, his eyes opening to slits. "Do that again."

She did, and he pulled her to him to kiss her long and deep as she continued her exploration, his hands on hers, showing her how to move, where to linger, how much pressure to exert. His head tilted back, and his breath came in short, pained spurts. "Is this all right?"

He groaned at the question. "It's perfect. I never want

you to stop." She was not interested in stopping. She loved watching him take pleasure. Finally, he pulled her away from him, the movement rough. "No more. Not before I'm inside you again." The words sent a blush across her cheeks, and he laughed, low and lovely. "Does the fact that I want to be inside you embarrass you, beautiful?"

She shook her head. "The fact that I want you to be inside of me embarrasses me. Ladies don't think such things."

He kissed her roughly. "I never want you to silence your salacious thoughts. In fact, I want to hear every single one of them. I want to make them all come true."

His fingers were moving firmly, doing wonderful things between her thighs, and she was gasping. "Michael. More."

"More what, beautiful?" The tips of his fingers slid against the place she wanted him, a tease more than a touch. "More here?"

She gasped at the sensation and he moved away before she repeated his name, hearing the pleading in her tone. "Or perhaps more here?" One long finger slid deep, and she moaned at the sensation.

"Everywhere."

"What a greedy, greedy woman I've married." He teased, kissing her, licking deep, holding her still as he explored her mouth, all the time, his fingers moving in wicked little circles, just barely touching her. He raised a brow, and a second finger joined the first on a slow, long slide of pleasure. "Here?"

"Yes," she gasped; he was close.

"Here?" He moved.

Closer. She bit her lip. Closed her eyes. "Yes."

"Here?"

So. Close.

She held perfectly still. Not wanting him to stop.

"I love touching you here, Penelope," he whispered, as his wicked hand explored. "I love discovering your shape, the feel of you, how wet you are for me." Those fingers stroked once more, his whispers continuing. He twisted his hand, circled just so, threatening that marvelous place. "I love searching you."

"Find it . . ." she whispered, unable to keep quiet.

"Find what, love?" He was all innocence. A wicked liar.

She met his gaze, feeling powerful. "You know what."

"Let's find it together."

It was too much. She reached between them, grasping his hand and finally, finally, pushing him against her. She leaned over him, meeting his eyes, seeing the dark pleasure in him, the tightly leashed need. His fingers slid through her soft curls, parting her secret folds, twisting, circling, guided by her hand at his wrist. His thumb stroked long and slow in a wicked loop that made her question her own sanity.

He watched her as she struggled under the weight of the pleasure, teasing her with his words as much as his fingers. "There, love? Is that where it feels good?"

She was lost to his wicked, encouraging words and his wicked, encouraging fingers, and she whispered her response, moving against him. And then he was touching her just as she wanted, circling her perfectly, stroking with exactly the right amount of pressure. It was as though he knew her body better than she did. It was as though her body belonged to him.

And perhaps it did.

One of his beautiful long fingers slid deep inside of her, the heel of his palm rocking against a point of acute, almost unbearable pleasure, and she called out his name, rocking against his touch, knowing that something incredible was about to happen.

"Michael," she whispered his name, wanting more. Wanting everything.

She was filled with desire and greed and she wanted him to never ever stop touching that most secret part of her. The part that now belonged to him.

"Wait for me," he whispered, and he was widening her legs. He pressed closer to her, his fingers leaving her, replaced with the soft, broad tip of him, and as he rubbed against her, he gave a long sigh at her ear, before whispering, "God, Penelope . . . You're like fire. Like the sun. And I can't help but want you. I want to be inside you and never to leave. You're my new vice, love . . . more dangerous than any I've ever had."

He slid deeper, gritting his teeth as the tip of him settled against the entrance to her, where she felt so empty . . . where she needed him. She edged closer to him, loving the feel of him against her. Wanting him deeper.

He stilled. "Penelope." She opened her eyes, meeting his serious black gaze. He leaned down and took her lips in a long, slow, promise-filled kiss. "I'm so sorry you ever felt dishonored, love . . . in this moment, there is nothing about you that I do not find utterly precious. Know that."

Tears came to her eyes at the words, stunning and filled with truth.

She nodded. "I do."

He would not release her gaze. "Do you? Do you see how much I value you? Do you feel it?" She nodded again, one tear spilling over, rolling down her cheek and dropping to the smooth skin of his shoulder. One of his hands slid to her cheek, thumb brushing away the salted track. "I adore you," he whispered. "I wish I could be the man you deserve."

She lifted her own hand to capture his at her cheek. "Michael . . . you can be that man."

He closed his eyes at the words, pulling her to him for a deep, soul-shattering kiss before he reached between them to seek and find that wonderful place where pleasure seemed to pool deep within her. He stroked and circled for long minutes, over and over in perfect, nearly unbearable rhythm until she was pushing against him, and she could feel her pleasure cresting. He stilled before she could reach the edge, letting her come back to earth before pushing her once more and hesitating again. She cried out her frustration. "Michael . . ."

He kissed the side of her neck, whispered in her ear. "Once more. Once more, and I'll let you take it. I'll let you take me."

This time, when she reached the edge, just as she was about to tip over, he slid deep into her in one long, smooth stroke, stretching her. Filling her. Gloriously. And she was lost, over the precipice, safe in his arms as they rocked together and she cried his name and she begged for more, and he gave it to her over and over until she could not breathe and could not speak and could do nothing but collapse in his arms.

He held her for an age, his hands stroking along her back, the movement soft and generous and patient.

She would never stop loving him.

Not for the immense pleasure he'd given her but for the almost unbearable softness he offered her now. For the way he stroked her gently and whispered her name as though he had all the time in the world, while he remained seated to the hilt in her, hard and unsatisfied. He had waited to take his own pleasure, wanting to be certain that she'd had hers first.

He worked so hard to hide this side of him, but here it was, all tenderness.

She loved it.

She loved *him.*

And he would never accept it.

She froze at the thought, lifting her head, afraid to meet his gaze, worried that he might sense her thoughts. His hands tightened around her. "Did I hurt you?" The question was hoarse, as though he couldn't bear the idea.

She shook her head. "No . . ."

He moved beneath her, trying to pull himself from her. "Penelope . . . let me . . . I don't want to hurt you."

"Michael."

And then, because she was too afraid to speak—too afraid that if she allowed herself to speak she might tell him something that he did not wish to hear—she rocked against him, lifting herself barely and sinking back onto him, loving the way his head tilted back, eyes narrowed to slits, teeth clenched, neck corded with unyielding control. She repeated the motion, and whispered, "Touch me."

At the words, he released his control and finally, *finally* moved.

She sighed at the movement, and he stroked deep, beautifully deep, all pleasure and perfection. They moved together, his hands on her hips, guiding her, as her hands settled on his shoulders, and she leveraged herself above him. "More . . ." she whispered, knowing, somehow, unquestionably, that there was more for him to give.

And he gave it in longer, deeper strokes. "Beautiful Penelope . . . so hot and soft and glorious," he whispered at her ear. "When I watched you come apart in my arms, I thought I might die with the pleasure of it. You're beautiful in ecstasy. I want to bring you there again . . . and again . . . and again." His words were punctuated by his thrusts, by his hands stroking along her back, across her shoulders, down again to cup her bottom and guide her, beautifully, on him.

"Michael, I . . ." And then his hands were on her, between them, and he was so deep, and she could not finish the sentence . . . because that strange, remarkable edge of pleasure was there again, looming up in front of her, and she'd never wanted anything so much as she wanted to reach it.

"Tell me," he whispered harshly, thrusting harder, faster, giving her everything she did not know she wanted. Needed.

I love you.

Somehow, she stopped herself from saying the words as pleasure rocketed through her. He tumbled over the edge with her, shouting her name in the dark room.

Chapter Twenty

Dear M—

I'm in a bit of a reflective mood—it's been six years to the day since "The Leighton Debacle" as my father likes to refer to it, and I've turned down three proposals—each less appealing than the last.

Nonetheless, my mother continues to ferry me about to modistes' shops and ladies' teas, as though she could somehow erase the past with a few yards of silk or a whiff of bergamot. This cannot go on forever, can it?

Worse, I continue to write letters to a specter and imagine that, one day, replies will arrive in the post.

Unsigned
Dolby House, November 1829

Letter unsent

"Gooseberry fool."

Penelope did not lift her head from where it lay on Michael's shoulder, her blond hair spread around them. "I beg your pardon?"

He stroked one warm hand down her spine, sending a shiver of pleasure through her. "So polite." He leaned over the edge of the chaise, not wanting to disentangle himself from her just yet but knowing that she would grow cold in the large room if he didn't do something. He grabbed his frock coat from where he'd left it in a pile on the floor in his rush to get to his wife, and pulled the navy wool over them both.

She cuddled against him under the coat and he caught his breath at the feel of her, soft and silk against him. "Gooseberry fool," he repeated.

"That's not a very nice thing to call your wife," Penelope said with a little smile, without even opening her eyes. "Though after what we just did, I might be a bit of a gooseberry fool over you."

It was incredibly silly, and Michael could not help his laugh.

How long had it been since he'd laughed at something so silly?

A lifetime.

"Funny girl," he said, tightening his arms around her. "Gooseberry fool is my favorite pudding."

She stilled at that, her fingers pausing the lovely swirling in the hair on his chest. He took her hand in his and brought her fingers up to his lips, kissing them quickly. "I like raspberry fool, as well. And rhubarb, too."

She lifted her head, her blue eyes searching his, as though he'd just made an earth-shattering confession. "Gooseberry fool."

He began to feel idiotic. She didn't really care about his favorite pudding. "Yes."

She smiled then, wide and beautiful, and he did not feel

idiotic anymore. He felt like a king. She laid her head upon his chest once more, her breasts rising and falling against his chest in a tempting rhythm.

Then she said, simply, "I like treacle," and he wanted to make love to her again.

How was it possible that conversation about dessert could be such an aphrodisiac?

His hand trailed down her spine again, curving over her rounded bottom, and he pulled her against him, loving the feel of her. He kissed her temple. "I remember that." He hadn't remembered until the moment she mentioned it, when a vision of young Penelope in the Falconwell kitchens, round face covered in treacle, had come fast and clear. He smiled at the sticky memory. "You used to convince our cook to let you lick the bowl."

She rolled her face into his chest in embarrassment. "I did not."

"Yes, you did."

She shook her head, her silken hair catching in the stubble on his unshaven cheek. "Spoons, maybe. But never the bowl. Ladies do not lick bowls."

He laughed at the proper correction, the deep rumble surprising them both. It felt good to lie there and laugh with her. Better than he had felt in a long, long time. Even as he knew that this moment was all they had, the last quiet moment before all hell broke loose, and he ruined the little goodwill she had for him.

He wrapped a second arm around her, holding her tight against him as the thought echoed through his head.

For now, she was his.

"It appears that your adventure was a success."

She lifted her head, setting her chin on her stacked palms and looking at him, her blue eyes glittering with teasing. "I am looking forward to the next one."

His hand slipped down one thigh, toying with the top of her silk stocking. "Why do I hesitate to ask?"

"I want to play hazard."

He imagined Penelope kissing the ivory dice before tossing them across the plush green baize in one of the hazard rooms downstairs. "You know hazard is a game you cannot win."

She smiled. "They say that about roulette, too."

He matched her smile. "So they do. You were simply lucky."

"Number twenty-three."

"Unfortunately, the dice only add up to twelve."

She gave a little shrug, his coat slipping off her pale, perfect shoulder. "I shall persevere."

He leaned his head forward to place a kiss on her bare skin. "We'll see about hazard. I'm still recovering from tonight's adventure, vixen." *And tomorrow, you shall remember all the reasons you don't want me near you.*

She closed her eyes and sighed with remembered pleasure, and the sound had him shifting beneath her to hide his thickening desire.

He wanted her again.

But he would control himself.

They should rise.

He could not bring himself to move.

"Michael?" When her eyes opened again, they were blue as the summer sky. A man could lose himself forever in those eyes. "Where did you go?"

"Where did I go when?"

"After you . . . lost everything."

A shiver of distaste ran through him. He did not want to answer her. Did not want to give her more of a reason to regret their marriage.

"I didn't go anywhere. I stayed in London."

"What happened?"

What a question. So much had happened. So much had changed. So much he did not want her to know. So much he did not want her to be a part of.

So much he wished he had not been a part of.

He took a deep breath, his hands to her waist to move her, to rise. "You don't want to hear about that."

She pushed herself up over him, hands flat on his chest, staying his movement. "I *do* want to hear about it." She stared down at him, refusing to let him up.

To let him retreat.

He lay back, resigned. "How much do you know?"

"I know you lost it all in a game of chance."

She was so close, her blue eyes so intent, and regret rocketed through him. He hated that she knew his mistakes. His shame. He wished he could be someone else for her. Someone new. *Someone worthy of her.*

But perhaps if he told her the tale, if she knew everything, it would keep her from coming too close. Perhaps it would keep him from caring too much.

Too late.

He steeled himself from the thought, barely a whisper. "It was *vingt-et-un.*"

She did not look away. "You were young."

"Twenty-one. Old enough to wager everything I owned."

"You were young," she repeated emphatically.

He did not argue. "I gambled everything. Everything that was not entailed. Everything that wasn't pinned down by generations. Like a fool." He waited for her to agree. When she didn't, he pressed on. "Langford pushed me to wager more and more, goading me, taunting until everything I had was on the table, and I was certain I would win."

She shook her head at that. "How could you know?"

"I couldn't, could I? But I'd been hot for the evening—I'd won hand after hand. When you are on a winning streak it's . . . euphoric. There comes a point when everything shifts, and reason flees, and you think it is impossible to lose." The words were coming freely now, along with the memories that he'd long kept locked away. "Gaming is a sickness for some. And I had it. The cure was winning. That night, I could not stop winning. Until I stopped winning and lost everything." She was watching him, her attention rapt. "He led me into temptation, convincing me to wager more and more . . ."

"Why you?" There was a furrow between her brows and anger in her voice, and Michael reached up to smooth the wrinkled skin there. "You were so young!"

"So quick to defend me without all the information." His touch followed the slope of her nose. "He'd built it. The lands, the money, everything. My father was a good man, but when he died, the estate was not as successful as it could be. But, there was enough there for Langford to work with, to make it prosperous, and he did. By the time I inherited, the marquessate was worth more than his own lands; he didn't want to relinquish it."

"Greed is a sin."

As is vengeance. He paused, thinking back on the long-ago game that he'd relived hundreds of times, thousands. "He told me I'd thank him, eventually, for taking everything from me," he said, unable to keep the derision from his tone.

She was quiet for a long moment, her blue eyes serious. "Perhaps he was right."

"He wasn't." Not a day went by that Michael did not resent the very air that Langford breathed.

"Well, perhaps gratitude is a bit much. But think of how you rose in spite of his obstacles. Think of how you faced his odds. Conquered them."

There was an urgent breathlessness in Penelope's voice, and Michael at once adored and loathed it. "I told you once not to make me a hero, Penelope. Nothing I did . . . nothing I am . . . is heroic."

She shook her head. "You're wrong. You are so much more than you think."

He thought of the papers in his coat pocket, of the plan he'd set in motion that morning. Of the vengeance for which he had waited all these years. She would see soon enough that he was no hero.

"I wish that were true."

For you.

The thought haunted him.

She leaned closer, her gaze serious and unwavering. "Don't you see, Michael? Don't you see how much more you are now than you would have been? How much stronger? How much more powerful? If not for that moment, for the way it changed you, the way it changed your life . . . you would not be here." Her voice dropped to a whisper. "And neither would I."

He tightened his arms around her. "Well, that is something."

They lay there for a long while, lost in their thoughts, before Penelope changed the subject. "And after the game? What happened then?"

Michael looked up to the ceiling, recalling. "He left me a guinea."

She lifted her head. "Your marker."

His intelligent wife. "I wouldn't spend it. I wouldn't take anything from him. Not until I could take *everything* from him."

She was watching him carefully. "Revenge."

"I had nothing but the clothes on my back and a handful of coins in my pocket—Temple found me. We'd been friends at school, and he was fighting anyone who would pay him for a match. On nights when he wasn't boxing, we were running dice games on the street in the Bar."

Her brow furrowed. "Wasn't that dangerous?"

He saw the worry in her eyes, and a part of him ached for her softness, for her sweetness. Her presence there, in his arms as he told this tale, was a benediction. It was as though she could, with her worry and her care, save him.

Except, he was long past saving, and she didn't deserve this life, filled with sin and vice. She deserved so much more. So much better. He shrugged one shoulder. "We learned quickly when to fight and when to run."

One of her hands came up to his face, and she touched his healing lip gently. "You still fight."

He smiled, his voice turning dark. "And it has been a long time since I have run."

Her gaze flickered to the glass window, where the night was growing long, and the candles in the chandeliers beyond were fading. "And The Angel?"

He lifted a hand and took a long lock of blond hair in hand, threading it through his fingers, loving the way it clung to him. "Four and a half years later, Temple and I had perfected our business . . . our dice games moved from place to place depending upon the players, and one night, we had twenty or thirty men, all betting on the outcome. I had a stack of money in hand, and we knew that it was a matter of time before we would have to end the game or risk being robbed." He released her hair and rubbed his thumb across her cheek. "I was never good at knowing when to stop. I always wanted one more game, one more roll of the dice."

"You wagered on the games?"

He met her gaze, wanting her to hear the words. The promise in them. "I haven't placed a bet in nine years."

Understanding flared in her gaze. Pride, too. "Not since you lost to Langford."

"It doesn't change the way the tables call to me. Doesn't make the dice less tempting. And when the roulette wheel spins . . . I always make a guess at where it will stop."

"But you never wager."

"No. But I love to watch others do it. That night, Temple said it several times—that we should leave. That the game was getting cold, but I could have gone another hour, another two, and I kept putting him off. One more roll of the dice. One more round of bets. One more main." He was lost to the memory. "They came out of nowhere, and we should be grateful that they had clubs and not pistols. The men rolling the ivories ran at the first hint of trouble, but they would have been fine even if they'd stayed."

"They wanted you." Penelope's words were a whisper.

He nodded. "They wanted our take. A thousand pounds. Maybe more."

More than anyone should have on a street in Temple Bar.

"We fought as well as we could, but it was two on six . . . felt like nine." He laughed, the sound barely there. "Nineteen, more like."

She was not amused. "You should have given them the money. It wasn't worth your life."

"My clever wife. If only you'd been there." Her face had gone white. Michael brought her mouth down to his for a quick kiss. "I'm here. Alive and well, unfortunately for you."

She shook her head, her urgency doing strange things to his gut. "Do not even jest. What happened?"

"I thought we were done for when a carriage careened in from God knows where, and a battalion of men Temple's size and larger exited. They joined our side, vanquished the foes, and when the scoundrels had run off, tails tucked between their legs, Temple and I were tossed into the carriage to meet our savior."

She was ahead of the tale. "Chase."

"The owner of The Fallen Angel."

"What did he want?"

"Business partners. Someone to run the games. Someone to handle security. Men who understood both the glitter and the vulgarity of the aristocracy."

She let out a long breath. "He saved your life."

Michael was lost in the memory of that first meeting, when he'd realized he might have a chance to regain everything he'd lost. "Indeed."

She leaned up and kissed him on his swollen lip, her tongue coming out to lick the bruise there. "He is wrong."

His attention snapped back to her. "Chase?"

She nodded her head. "He thinks he owes me a debt."

"So it seems."

"It is I who owe him one. He saved you. For me."

She kissed him again, and he caught his breath, telling himself it was in response to the caress, when it was her words that threatened his strength. His hands came up to burrow into her hair as he tasted her gratitude, her relief, and something else he could not place . . . a wonderful temptation.

Something he was certain he did not deserve.

He fisted one hand in her hair and pulled back from the kiss, wishing, desperately, that he could continue it. But he couldn't allow her—couldn't allow himself—another moment without reminding her of precisely who he was . . . what he was. "I lost everything, Penelope. *Everything.* Land, money, the contents of my homes . . . *of my father's homes.* I lost everything that reminded me of them." There was a long silence. Then, softly, "I lost you."

She tilted her head, fixing him with her gaze. "You've rebuilt it. Doubled it. More."

He shook his head. "Not the most important part."

She stilled, as though she'd forgotten his plans. Their future. "Your revenge."

"No. The respect. The place in society. The things that I should have been able to give my wife. The things I should have been able to give you."

"Michael—" He heard the censure in her tone, ignored it.

"You are not listening. I am not the man for you. I've never been that man. You deserve someone who has never made the mistakes I've made. Someone who can cloak you in titles and respectability and decency and more than a little perfection." He paused, loathing the way she stiffened in his arms at the words, resisting their truth. He forced her to look into his eyes, forced himself to say the rest. "I wish I were that man, Sixpence. But I'm not. Don't you see? I have none of those things. I have nothing deserving of you. Nothing that will keep you happy."

And Dear Lord, I want you to be happy. I want to make you happy.

"Why would you think that?" she asked. "You have so much . . . so much more than I would ever need."

Not enough.

He'd lost more than he could ever regain.

He could have a hundred houses, twenty times as much money, all the riches he could amass, and it would never be enough. Because it would never erase his past, his recklessness, his failure.

It would never make him the man she deserved.

"If I hadn't forced you into marrying me—" he started, and she cut him off.

"You didn't force me into doing anything. I chose you."

She couldn't believe that. He shook his head.

"You really don't see it, do you? How remarkable you are." He looked away at the words. At the lie in them. "No. Look at me." The words were firm, and he couldn't help but heed them, her eyes so blue. So honest. "You think somehow you lost all respectability when you lost your fortune. But what was that fortune but money and land cobbled together by generations of other men? It was *their* accomplishment. *Their* honor. Not yours. You—" He heard the reverence in the word. Saw the truth of her feelings in her eyes. "—you have built your own future. You've made yourself a man."

A lovely sentiment, romantic, but wrong. "You mean a man who stole his wife from the dead of night, forced her to marry him, used her for land and vengeance and then . . . tonight . . . stripped her bare in London's most legendary gaming hell?" He heard the disdain in his tone, and he looked away, toward the blackness that shrouded the high ceiling of the room, feeling like he belonged in the gutter. He wanted her dressed and far from him. "God. I swore I would never dishonor you again. I'm so sorry, Penelope."

She refused to be cowed. Placing one hand on his chin, she forced him to meet her gaze once more. "Don't make it sound filthy. I wanted it. I *enjoyed* it. I am not a child to be coddled. I married you to *live,* and this . . . you . . . all of it is *living.*" She paused and smiled, bright and beautiful, and the pleasure and regret that single smile wrought was a physical blow. "There was not a moment tonight during which I felt dishonored or misused. Indeed, I felt quite . . . worshipped."

That was because he had worshipped her.

"You deserve better."

Her brows came together. She pulled herself and rose from the chaise like a phoenix, wrapping herself in his coat. "It is *you* who is not listening. I hate that you place me up on some high shelf where you keep the things of value that you don't want broken. But I don't want that place of honor. I loathe it there. I loathe the way you leave me there for fear of hurting me. For fear of breaking me, as though I'm some kind of porcelain doll with no strength. With no character."

He stood, moving toward her. He'd never thought she had no character. Indeed, if she had any more character, she'd make him mad. And as for strength, she was Atlas. A small, lovely Atlas, clad in nothing but his coat.

He reached for her and she took a step backward. "No. Don't. I'm not through. I have character, Michael."

"I know you do."

"A great deal of it."

More than he'd ever imagined.

"Yes."

"I'm not perfect. I gave up perfection when I realized that the only thing it would ever get me was a lonely marriage with an equally perfect husband." She was shaking with anger, and he reached for her, wanting to pull her into his arms; but she pulled back, refusing to allow him to touch her. "And as for your not being perfect, well, thank God for that. I had a perfect life in my reach once, and it was a *crashing bore*. Perfect is too clean, too easy. I don't *want* perfect any more than I want to *be* perfect. I want imperfect.

"I want the man who tossed me over his shoulder in the woods and convinced me to marry him for the adventure of it. I want the man who is cold and hot, up and down. The one who runs a men's club and a ladies' club and a casino and whatever else this incredible place is. You think I married you in spite of your imperfections? I married you *because* of your imperfections, you silly man. Your glorious, unbearably *infuriating* imperfections."

It wasn't true, of course. She'd married him because she'd had no choice.

But he was not about to let her go.

Not after he'd just discovered how wonderful it was to have her in his arms.

"Penelope?"

She dropped her hands, and his coat opened, baring one long, narrow strip of skin from neck to knee. "What?" He would have laughed at the peevishness in her tone if he had not been overwhelmed by the way she looked in her stockings and his coat and nothing else. She took a deep breath, the fabric threatening to reveal her glorious breasts.

"Are you through?"

"Maybe," she said, reserving the right to say more.

"You can be very difficult when you want to be, you know."

One of her pretty blond brows rose. "Well. If that is not the pot calling the kettle black, I don't know what is."

He reached for her, and she let him catch her this time. Let him pull her into his arms, pressing her lush, curving body to his. "I am too imperfect for you," he whispered at her temple.

"You are perfectly imperfect for me."

She was wrong, but he did not want to think on it anymore. Instead, he said, "You are naked in a gaming hell, love."

Her reply was muffled against his chest, and he felt the words more than heard them. "I can't believe it."

One of his hands stroked down her back, over the fabric of his coat, and he smiled at the idea that she was wearing his clothes. "I can, my sweet, adventuresome lady." He kissed the top of her blond head, sliding a hand inside the coat to palm one lovely breast, adoring the shiver that coursed through her at the touch. "I should like for you to be naked beneath my clothes every day."

She smiled. "You know I am naked beneath my own clothes every day, do you not?"

He groaned. "You should not have said such a thing. How am I to do anything but think of you naked from now on?"

She pulled away with a laugh, and they began to dress, Penelope swatting at Michael's hands every time he reached for her.

"I am helping."

"You are hindering."

She righted the little cream bow at the front of her dress while he tied his cravat without a looking glass.

He could happily dress with her every day, for the rest of eternity.

But he wouldn't.

Not once she discovers your lies. The whisper echoed through his mind.

"Is this water?" She pointed to a pitcher standing in the corner next to a washbasin.

"Yes."

She poured water into the bowl and submerged her hands to the wrists. Not washing them, simply, settling them into the cool liquid. He watched her for a long moment as she closed her eyes and took a deep breath. Two. Three.

She removed her hands and shook off the liquid, turning back to face him. "There's something I feel I should tell you."

In nine years running dice and cards and every other kind of gaming there was, Michael had learned to read faces. He'd learned to identify nervousness and exhilaration and cheating and lying and rage and every other point on the spectrum of human emotion.

Everything but the emotion that filled Penelope's gaze—the emotion that lurked beneath the nervousness and the pleasure and the excitement.

Oddly, it was because he'd never seen it before that he knew precisely what the emotion was.

Love.

The thought robbed him of breath and he straightened, consumed all at once with desire and fear and something that he did not want to think on. Did not want to acknowledge.

He'd told her not to believe in him.

He'd warned her.

And for his own sanity, he could not let her tell him that she loved him.

He found he wanted it too much.

So he did what he did best. He resisted temptation, approaching her and pulling her into his arms for a quick kiss—a kiss he was desperate to prolong. To enjoy. To turn into something as powerful as the emotion coursing through him. "It's getting late, darling. No more talk tonight."

The love in Penelope's gaze gave way to confusion, and he was filled with self-loathing.

Sadly, that, too, was coming to be a familiar emotion.

A knock sounded on the door, saving him. Michael checked the clock; it was nearly three in the morning, far too late for visitors, which meant only one thing. *News.*

He crossed the room quickly and opened the door, reading Cross's face before the other man had a chance to speak.

"He is here?"

Cross's gaze flickered over Michael's shoulder to Penelope, then back to Michael, grey and inscrutable. "Yes."

He couldn't look at her. She was close, close enough for her delicate scent, to wrap around him, likely for the last time.

"Who is here?" she asked, and he didn't want to answer, even as he knew that she had to know. And that once she did, he would lose her forever.

He met her gaze, trying his best to be calm and unmoved. Remembering the singular goal that he had set for himself a decade earlier.

"Langford."

She stilled as the words crashed through the room. "One

week," she said softly, recalling their agreement before shaking her head. "Michael. Please. Don't do this."

He couldn't stop himself. It was all he'd ever wanted.

Until her.

"Stay here. Someone will take you home." He left the room, the sound of the door closing behind him echoing like a gunshot in the dark, empty hallway beyond, and with every step he took, he steeled himself against what was to come. Oddly, it was not facing Langford—the man who had ripped his life from him—that required the added strength.

It was losing Penelope.

"Michael!" She had followed him into the hallway, and the sound of his name on her lips had him turning back, unable to ignore the anguish there. Wanting desperately, instinctively, to protect her from it.

To protect her from himself.

She was racing toward him, fast and furious, and he could not do anything but catch her, lifting her in his arms as her hands clasped his face, and she stared into his eyes. "You don't have to do this," she whispered, her thumbs stroking across his cheeks, leaving agonizing tracks. "You have Falconwell . . . and you have The Angel . . . and more than he could ever dream. So much more than anger and vengeance and fury. You have me." She searched his gaze before finally saying, achingly soft, "I love you."

He'd told himself that he did not want the words, but once said, the pleasure that coursed through him at their sound on her lips was nearly unbearable. He closed his eyes and kissed her, deep and soul-searching, wishing to remember the taste of her, the feel of her, the smell of her—of this moment—forever. When he released her lips and returned her to her feet, he took a step back, breathing deep, loving the way her beautiful blue eyes flashed when he touched her.

He had not touched her enough.

If he could go back, he would have touched her more.

I love you.

The whisper echoed through him, all temptation.

He shook his head. "You shouldn't."

He turned away, leaving her in the dark hallway, heading to face his past, refusing to look back. Refusing to acknowledge what he was leaving.

What he was losing.

Chapter Twenty-one

Dear M—

No. No more of this.

Unsigned
Needham Manor, January 1830

Letter destroyed

Bourne had imagined this moment hundreds of times—thousands of them.

He'd played the scene over in his mind, entering a private card room where Langford sat, alone and on edge, dwarfed by the sheer size and power of The Angel, the kingdom over which Michael reigned.

Never once, in all that time, had he imagined he would feel anything but triumph in this moment, when nine years' worth of anger and frustration finally came to an end. But it was not triumph Michael felt as he opened the door to the luxurious private suite set far from the main floor of the club and met the emotionless gaze of his longtime enemy.

It was frustration. And anger.

For even now, nine years later, this man was still fleecing Michael. Tonight, he had robbed him of his future with his wife.

And it could not be allowed to continue.

Langford had always loomed large in his memory—bronze skin, white teeth, wide fists—the kind of man who took what he wanted without hesitation. The kind of man who ruined lives without looking back.

And nearly a decade later, Langford had not changed. He was just as healthy and hale as he'd always been, with a bit more grey hair, but the same thick neck and wide shoulders. The years had been kind to him.

Michael's gaze flickered to the place where Langford's left hand lay flat against the green velvet of the table. He remembered the mannerism, the way that hand would fist and knock against the wood to demand additional cards or to celebrate a win. When Michael was a young man, just learning the tables, he would watch that hand and envy its utter control.

He sat in the chair directly across from Langford and waited silently.

Langford's fingers twitched against the baize. "I object to being forced here in the dead of night by your henchmen."

"I did not think you would answer an invitation."

"You were correct." When Michael did not reply, Langford sighed. "I assume you've called me here to gloat about Falconwell?"

"Among other things." Michael reached into his coat pocket, removed the evidence of Tommy's birth, running the paper through his fingers.

"I confess, I was surprised you'd stoop to marrying the Marbury girl, even for Falconwell. She's not exactly a prize." He paused. "But the land was the goal, was it not? Well-done. The ends justify the means, I suppose."

Michael's teeth clenched at the words, so close to the way he'd described their marriage at the beginning of this journey. He hated the echo, the reminder that he was just as much of a beast as Langford.

Don't do this. Penelope's words echoed through him, a pleading request, and he stilled, feeling the aging edges of the paper against the pad of his thumb. *You are so much more than you think.* Michael turned the square of paper over in his hand, considering the words, his wife's blue eyes pleading with him to be more. Better. *Worthy.*

I love you. Her last weapon against his revenge.

Curiosity made Langford impatient. "Come on, boy. What is it?"

And with the quick, curt words, Michael was twenty-one again, facing this man, wanting to crush him. Only this time, he had the power to do so. With a flick of a wrist, he let the letter fly across the table with perfect aim.

Langford captured it, unfolded, read. He did not look up. "Where did you get this?"

"You may have my lands, but you do not have my power."

"It will ruin me."

"That is my dearest hope." Michael waited for the moment of victory. For surprise and regret to flash across the other man's face before he looked up from the paper and admitted defeat. But when Langford met Michael's gaze over the yellowed parchment, it was not defeat that shone in his eyes.

It was admiration. "How long have you been waiting for this moment?"

Michael shuttered his gaze, forcing himself to lean back in his chair, shielding his surprise. "Since you took everything from me."

"Since you lost everything to me," Langford corrected.

"I was a child then, with only a handful of games behind me," Michael said, anger rising. "No longer. I know now that you pushed the game. That you threw it, let me win until it was all there in one enormous bet."

"You think I cheated?"

Michael's gaze did not waver. "I know you did."

A ghost of a smile—enough to prove Michael right—

crossed Langford's lips before he returned his attention to the damning paper. "So now you know. The child was my brother's whelp, born of a local farmer's daughter. The woman I married was useless—large enough dowry but unable to birth a child. I paid the girl and took the child as my own. Better false heir than none at all."

Tommy had always been different from this man, never as cool, never as calculating. Now it all made sense, and Michael found that somewhere, deep within, buried where he did not think there was emotion to be found, he felt sympathy for the boy who had once been his friend—the boy who had tried so hard to be a son to his father.

The viscount went on. "There were only a handful of people who were close enough to recognize that my wife never bred." He lifted the note, a small smile on his lips. "I see now that even they were not to be trusted."

"Perhaps they decided it was you who was without honor."

One of Langford's brows rose. "You continue to blame me?"

"You continue to deserve it."

"Come now," Langford scoffed. "Look around you. You built this place; you rebuilt your life, your fortunes. What would you do if you were forced to give them away? To pass them off to someone who'd never had a hand in their growth? In their success? Are you saying you would not do the very same thing I did?" The older man set the paper to the table. "It would be a lie. You have as little conscience as I, and there's the proof."

He leaned back in his chair. "It's a shame I was saddled with Tommy and not you; you would have made me a fine son, with how well you learned the lessons I taught you."

Michael resisted the urge to recoil at the words, at the implication that he and Langford were similar, even as he recognized their truth. And loathed it.

His gaze flickered to the note on the table, its weight at once immense and nothing at all. There was a roar in his ears as he registered the importance of what he had done. Of what he was doing.

Unaware of Michael's thoughts, Langford said, "Let us come down to business. I still have the rest—everything your father passed to you. Your entire past. You think I didn't expect you to do something like this?" He reached into the pocket of his coat and withdrew a sheaf of papers. "We're cut from the same cloth, you and I." He set the stack on the table. "Is *vingt-et-un* still your game? My legacy against yours."

And when Michael saw it there, laid out on the green baize in calculated clarity, understanding rocketed through him. He'd replayed that fateful night hundreds of times—thousands of them—watching the cards flip over and slide across the baize into their seats, counting the ten, fourteen, twenty-two that had marked the end of his inheritance and his youth.

And he'd always thought it was the moment that marked the end of everything that was good about him.

It wasn't.

But this would be.

He thought of Penelope in his arms, her lips soft against his, the hitch in her breath as she begged him not to come here. Not to do this. The way she'd looked him straight in the eye and asked him not to give away his final chance at good—the last vestige of his decency.

Not to let revenge overshadow love.

He reached for the stack of deeds on the table, sifting through them, spreading them across the felt. Wales, Scotland, Newcastle, Devon—a collection of houses amassed by generations of marquesses—once so vitally important to him . . . now a collection of brick and mortar.

Only the past. Not the future.

Nothing without Penelope.

What had he done?

Dear God. He loved her.

The realization struck him like a blow, utterly out of place, and more powerful than anything else. And he hated himself for not having had the chance to tell her.

And, as though he'd conjured her up, suddenly she was

there, her voice rising from outside the door. "You may attempt to stop me with your silence and your . . . enormity . . . but make no mistake about it, I *will* enter that room!"

Michael stood to watch the door of the room spring open, revealing a confused Bruno and, just behind him, an irate Penelope. The guard lifted his hands in a helpless expression that would have amused Michael if they were in a different time and place. Bruno did not seem to understand what to do with this small, strange woman who had the strength of ten men. Of twenty.

She pushed past him and into the room, chin up, shoulders square, anger and frustration and determination on her lovely face.

And he'd never wanted her so much in his life.

But he did not want her anywhere near Langford. He approached her, pulling her aside, and saying quietly, "You shouldn't be here."

"Neither should you."

He turned to Cross, who had appeared in the doorway next to Bruno. "You were to take her home."

Cross lifted a shoulder in a lanky shrug. "The lady is rather . . . unbiddable."

Penelope turned a smile on the tall, ginger-haired man. "Thank you. That might well be the nicest thing anyone has ever said about me."

Michael had the distinct impression that this entire evening was about to get out of hand. Before he could say any more, Penelope moved past him, farther into the room. "Lord Langford," she acknowledged, looking right down her nose at the man.

"Penelope," the older man said, unable to keep the surprise from his gaze.

"It's Lady Bourne to you." The words were cool and cutting, and Michael was sure she'd never been more beautiful. "Come to think of it, it was always lady to you. And you never referred to me as such."

The older man's gaze narrowed in irritation, and Michael

had an intense urge to put a fist into the viscount's face for the look.

It was not necessary. His wife was more than able to care for herself. "You don't like that, I see. Well, let me tell you what I don't like. I don't like insolence. And I don't like cruelty. And I most definitely don't like you. It is time you and I have it out, Langford, because while you might have stolen my husband's lands and funds and reputation, and you might have been a truly horrendous father to my friend, I absolutely refuse to have you take another thing from me, you despicable old man."

Michael's brows went up at the words. He should stop her, he knew.

Except, he found he didn't want to.

"I do not have to listen to this." Langford turned a mottled, unpleasant shade of red and shot up from his chair in irate disbelief. He looked to Michael. "Control your female before I am forced to do it for you."

Michael came forward, fury roaring through him at the threat. Penelope turned to face him before he could get to the viscount, strong as steel. "No. This is not your battle."

He was struck dumb at the words though he should not be surprised; his wife kept him in a perpetual state of speechlessness. *What in hell was she talking about? This was absolutely his battle.* As if he'd not been waiting for this moment for almost a *decade,* Langford had just threatened the only thing he held dear.

He stilled at the thought. *The only thing he held dear.*

It was true. There was Penelope, and there was everything else. All the land, the money, The Angel, the revenge . . . none of it was worth even a fraction of this woman.

This marvelous woman who had turned her back on him once more.

She faced his enemy and waved a hand at the door, where Bruno and now Cross stood, looking very serious and very frightening. "Would you care to attempt escape before I am through?"

Michael couldn't help it. He grinned. She was a warrior queen.

His warrior queen.

"You have lived a life too free of consequence, Langford, and, while I assure you that I would dearly enjoy your losing everything you care for in one fell swoop, I fear that it would take too great a toll on those I love."

She looked to the table, taking in the papers there, immediately understanding the situation. "It's to be a wager, then? Winner take all?" She looked at Michael, her eyes wide with emotion for a fraction of a second before she shuttered her gaze. He recognized it anyway—disappointment. "You were going to wager?"

He wanted to tell her the truth, that he'd decided before she entered that it wasn't worth it . . . that none of it was worth risking her happiness. Their future.

But she'd already turned to the door. "Cross?"

Cross straightened. "My lady?"

"Bring us a deck."

Cross looked to Bourne. "I don't think—"

Bourne nodded once. "The lady wants a deck."

Cross went nowhere without his cards, and he crossed the room, withdrawing them, and extending the deck to Penelope.

She shook her head. "I intend to play. We require a dealer."

Michael's gaze snapped to her as Langford sneered, "I will not play cards with a *woman*."

She took the seat at one side of the table. "I usually will not play cards with men who rob children of their inheritance, but tonight appears to be one for exceptions."

Cross looked to Michael. "She is incredible."

Possessiveness flared as he took his seat, eyes on his wife. "She is mine."

Langford leaned toward Penelope, fury in his gaze. "I don't play cards with women. And I certainly don't play them with women who have nothing I want."

Penelope reached into her bodice and withdrew a paper

of her own, setting it on the table. "On the contrary, I have something you desperately want." Michael leaned forward to get a better look at the paper, but Penelope covered it with her hand. When he looked up, her cool blue gaze was on the viscount. "Tommy is not your only secret, is he?"

Langford's gaze narrowed, furious. "What do you have? Where did you get it?"

Penelope raised a brow. "It seems that you'll be playing cards with a woman after all."

"Anything you have will ruin Tommy as well."

"I think he'll be fine if it is allowed out. But I assure you, you will not be." She paused. "And I think you know why."

Langford's brows snapped together, and Michael recognized the frustration and anger on the other man's face as he turned to Cross. "Deal the cards."

Cross looked to Michael, the question in his gaze as clear as if he'd spoken it aloud. Michael had not wagered in nine years. Had not played a single hand of cards, as though he'd been waiting all that time for this night, this moment, when he would wager against Langford again . . . and this time, win.

But as he watched his wife, proud and glorious, take on the man he'd spent so much of his life hating, he realized that the wicked desire that had gnawed at him for the last decade every time he thought of Langford and the lands he'd stolen was gone, lost along with his desire for revenge.

They were his past.

Penelope was his future.

If he could deserve her.

"The lady plays for me." He lifted the proof of Tommy's legitimacy from where it sat in front of him and placed it on the table in front of her. She snapped her attention to him, her eyes clear and blue and filled with surprise as she registered the meaning of the move. He would not ruin Tommy. Something flashed across her face . . . a mix of happiness and pride and something else, and he made the decision in that moment to bring it back again and again, every day. It was gone in an instant, replaced by . . . sudden trepidation.

"You have what you want, love. It is yours." He raised a brow. "But I would not stop if I were you. You're on a winning streak."

She looked to Langford's wager—Michael's past—and he wanted to kiss her thoroughly for the emotion that showed on her face . . . nervousness and desire . . . desire to win.

For him.

She nodded to Cross, who took the change in stride, shuffling the deck with quick, economical movements. "One hand of *vingt-et-un*. Winner take all."

Cross dealt the cards, one down, one up, and it occurred to Michael that the game was not for ladies. While the rules were deceptively simple, Penelope had likely never played, and without a very good stroke of luck, she would find herself crushed by a veteran player like Langford.

As Michael considered the possibility—that after all this time he would have come so close to destroying Langford and restoring the lands of the marquessate, and failed—he realized that for too long he'd considered those things to be the markers of his redemption. Now, however, he knew the truth.

Penelope was his redemption.

In front of her, facing up, was the four of clubs. He watched as she lifted the corner of the other card, looking for any indication of what she might have. Nothing impressive, he was guessing. He turned to Langford, facing a ten of hearts, left hand flat on thc table, as ever.

Cross looked to Langford, who tapped his flat palm once on the table. "Hold." A decent hand.

Langford had likely come to the same conclusion as Michael—that Penelope was a novice, and like all novices, she would overhit.

Cross looked to Penelope. "My lady?"

She nibbled at her lower lip, drawing Michael's attention. "May I have another?"

One side of Michael's mouth lifted in the hint of a smile. So polite, even as she wagered for more than a million pounds' worth of real estate in the most exclusive of London's gaming hells.

Cross dealt another card, the three of hearts. *Seven*. Michael willed her to hold, knowing that the next hit would likely bring her over twenty-one. It was the easiest of mistakes, to wager on a pair of low cards.

"Another, please."

Cross hesitated, knowing the odds and not liking them.

"The girl asked for another," Langford said, all smugness, knowing he was about to win, and Michael vowed that, while the older man might leave the club without losing a thing, he'd leave having felt the full force of Michael's fist.

The six of hearts slid into place beside the other cards. *Thirteen.*

Penelope bit her lip and checked the facedown card again—proof that she was a novice at the game. If she had twenty-one, she would not have looked. She met Cross's gaze, then Michael's, worry in her eyes, and Michael would have wagered his entire fortune that she'd gone over. "Is that it?"

"Unless you'd like another."

She shook her head. "No."

"The girl is over. A blind man could see it." Langford revealed his second card with a smirk. A queen. *Twenty.*

The viscount was the luckiest man in London tonight.

And Michael didn't care.

He simply wanted this evening over, so he could bring his wife home and tell her that he loved her. *Finally.*

"I am, indeed, over twenty," Penelope said, revealing her final card.

Michael leaned forward, sure he was mistaken.

The eight of diamonds.

Cross could not keep the surprise from his voice. "The lady has twenty-one."

"Impossible." Langford leaned forward. "Impossible!"

Michael could not help himself. He laughed, drawing her attention with the sound. "My magnificent wife," he said, pride in his words as he shook his head in disbelief.

There was a movement behind her, then all hell broke loose.

"You cheating *bitch*." Langford's heavy hands were on her shoulders, yanking her out of her chair with furious anger, and she cried out and stumbled before he lifted her from the floor and shook her violently. "You think this a game? You cheating *bitch*!"

It couldn't have lasted more than a second or two before Michael reached her, but it felt like an eternity before he extracted her from Langford's grasp and passed her to Cross, already there, waiting to keep her safe.

And then Michael went after Langford with visceral intent. "I don't have to ruin you, after all," he growled. "I shall kill you instead." And then he had the other man's lapels in hand, and he was spinning him toward the wall, thrusting him into it with all his might, wanting to punish him over and over again for daring to touch Penelope.

For daring to hurt her.

He wanted this man dead. Now.

"You think I am still a boy?" he asked, pulling Langford away from the wall and pounding him back into it. "You think you can come to *my* club and threaten my *wife* without repercussions? You think I would let you *touch* her? You aren't fit to breathe her *air*."

"Michael!" she cried from across the room, where Cross kept her from entering the fray. "Stop it!" He turned to her, saw the tears running down her cheeks and stilled, torn between hurting Langford and comforting her. "He's not worth it, Michael."

"You married her for land," Langford said, sucking air into his lungs. "You might have fooled the rest of London. But not me. I know Falconwell matters more to you than anything in the world. She was a means to an end. You think I don't see that?"

A means to an end. The echo of the words—so oft repeated at the beginning of their marriage—was a blow, in part because they were true, but mostly because they were so very false. "You bastard. You think you know me?" He slammed Langford into the wall again, the force of the emotion making him more furious. "*I love her.* She is the *only* thing that matters. *And you dared to touch her.*"

Langford opened his mouth to speak, but Michael cut him off. "You don't deserve mercy. You've been a disgrace as a father and a guardian and a man. You owe the fact that you remain able to walk entirely to the generosity of the lady. But if you come within a mile of her again, or if I ever hear a whisper of your speaking ill of her, I shall take pleasure in tearing you limb from limb. Is that clear?"

Langford swallowed and nodded quickly. "Yes."

"Do you doubt I would do it?"

"No."

He thrust the viscount toward Bruno. "Get rid of him. And send for Thomas Alles." Michael was already moving across the room, sure that his bidding would be done, crushing Penelope in his arms.

She pressed her face to the curve of his neck. "What did you say?" she whispered to the skin there, her voice shaking as his hands ran over her back clasping her to him. She lifted her head, blue eyes glistening with tears, and repeated, "What did you say?"

It was not the way he would have planned to tell her, but nothing about their marriage had happened in a traditional manner, and he supposed this moment should be no different than all the rest. So there, standing in the middle of an overturned card room in a gaming hell, he met his wife's gaze, and said, "I love you."

She shook her head. "But, you chose him. You chose vengeance."

"No," he said, leaning against the card table, pulling her to stand between his thighs, taking her hands in his. "No. I choose you. I choose love."

She tilted her head, searching his gaze. "Is that true?"

And suddenly, the truth mattered more than he could ever have imagined. "God, yes. Yes, it's true." He cupped her face in his hands. "I choose you, Penelope. I choose love over revenge; I choose the future over the past; I choose your happiness over all else."

She was silent for a long while, long enough for him to worry. "Sixpence?" he asked, suddenly terrified. "Do you believe me?"

"I—" She started, then stopped, and he knew what she was about to say.

Wished he could stop it.

"I don't know."

Chapter Twenty-two

Penelope did not sleep that night. She did not even try.

And so, when Tommy called the next morning, it did not matter that it was at an hour far too early for callers. He was standing at the fireplace, greatcoat on, hat and cane in hand, when she entered the receiving room.

He turned, met her red eyes, and said, all tact, "Dear God. You look as awful as he does."

That was all it took. She burst into tears.

He came toward her, "Oh, Pen. Don't. Ah—dammit. Don't cry. I take it back. You don't look awful at all."

"Liar," she said, wiping away tears.

One side of his mouth kicked up. "Not at all. You look entirely fine. Not in the least bit like a simpering female."

She felt like a fool. "I can't help it, you know."

"You love him."

She took a deep breath. "Terribly."

"And he loves you."

Tears threatened again. "He says he does."

"You don't believe him?"

She wanted to. Desperately. "I can't . . . I don't understand why he would. I don't understand what about me would have changed him. Would have moved him. Would have made him love me." She shrugged one shoulder and looked down at her feet, the toes of her green slippers peeping out from beneath the hem of her dress.

"Oh, Pen . . ." He sighed, pulling her into a warm, brotherly embrace. "I was an idiot. And so was Leighton. And all the others. You were better than any of us. Than all of us combined." He stepped back and took her shoulders, firmly, looking straight into her gaze. "And you're better than Michael, too."

She took a deep breath, reaching out to smooth the lapel of his greatcoat. "I'm not, you know."

One side of his mouth kicked up in a wry smile. "And that is the reason why he doesn't deserve you. Because he's a royal ass, and you love him anyway."

"I do," she said softly.

"I saw him last night, you know, after you left him." She looked up. "He gave me the proof of my scandal. Told me you'd won it back from him."

"He gave it to me," she corrected. "I didn't have to wager for it. He wasn't going to ruin you, Tommy. He stopped it."

Tommy shook his head. "*You* stopped it. You loved him enough to show him that there was more to life than revenge. You've changed him. You've given him another chance to be the Michael we knew instead of the cold, hard Bourne he became. You've moved the mountain." He lifted one hand to tap her on the chin. "He adores you. Anyone with eyes can see it."

I choose you. I choose love.

The words she'd played over and over in her mind throughout the night suddenly made sense. And, as though a candle had been lit, she knew, without doubt, that they were true. That he loved her.

The realization made her giddy. "He loves me," she said, quietly first, letting the words echo through her, testing the way they felt on her tongue. "He loves me," she repeated, on a laugh, this time to Tommy. "He really does."

"Of course he does, you silly girl," Tommy said with a

smile. "Men like Bourne do not falsely profess love." He lowered his voice to a conspiratorial whisper. "It's not exactly in keeping with his character."

It wasn't, of course. The great, dangerous Bourne, all cold and cruel, the man who ran a gaming hell and abducted women in the dead of night and lived his life for revenge was not a man who fell in love with his wife.

But somehow, he had.

And Penelope knew better than to spend another moment asking how or why . . . when she could simply spend the rest of her life loving him back.

She smiled up at Tommy, and said, "I have to go to him. I have to tell him I believe him."

He nodded once, satisfied, straightening his greatcoat. "Excellent plan. But, before you rush off to save your marriage, do you have a moment to say good-bye to an old friend?"

In her eagerness to get to Michael, she didn't understand the words immediately. "Yes, of course." She paused. "Wait. Good-bye?"

"I'm for India. The ship leaves today."

"India? Why?" Her brows knitted together. "Tommy, you don't have to go now. Your secret . . . it is yours again."

"And for that I shall be eternally grateful. But I've passage booked, and it would be a shame to let it go to waste."

She watched him carefully. "You really want this?"

He raised a blond brow. "You really want Michael?"

Yes. God, yes. She smiled. "It's to be adventure for both of us, then."

He laughed. "Yours more challenging than mine, I suspect."

"I shall miss you," she said.

Tommy dipped his head. "And I you. But I shall send your children treats from faraway lands."

Children. She wanted to see Michael. Immediately.

"See that you do," she said. "And I shall regale them with tales of their uncle Tommy."

"Michael will love that," he replied with a great laugh. "I

expect them to follow in my footsteps, becoming remarkable fishermen and mediocre poets. Now, go fetch your husband."

She grinned. "I believe I shall."

Michael took the steps to Hell House two at a time, desperate to get to his wife, berating himself for not locking her in a room at the club the night before and refusing to allow her to leave until she believed that he loved her.

How could she not believe him? How could she not see that she was wreaking havoc on his mind and body, that she had destroyed his calm and devastated him with her love? How could she not see that he was desperate for her?

The door opened as he reached the top step, and the object of his thoughts came barreling out of the house, nearly toppling him down the stairs. She pulled up short, her green cloak swirling around her, brushing against his legs, and they stared at each other for a long moment.

He caught his breath at the sight of her. How was it possible that he'd ever thought her plain? She was a jewel in the cold, grey mid-February sleet, all rosy cheeks and blue eyes and lovely pink lips that made him want to carry her to the nearest bed. To their bed. For it was time they had a bed. He was going to knock down the wall between their bedchambers so he never had to stare at that godforsaken door again.

She broke into his thoughts. "Michael—"

"Wait." He cut her off, not wanting to risk hearing what she had to say. Not before he said his piece. "I'm sorry. Come inside. Please?"

She followed him inside, the sound of the great oak door closing behind them echoing through the marble foyer. Her gaze flickered to the package in his hand. "What is that?"

He'd forgotten he had it. His weapon.

"Come with me." He took her hand, wishing they weren't wearing gloves, wishing he could touch her, skin to skin, and climbed the stairs to the first floor of the house, pulling her into the dining room and setting the parchment-wrapped bundle on the long, mahogany table.

"It's for you."

She smiled, curious, and he resisted the urge to kiss her, not wanting to rush. Not wanting to scare her. She opened the paper carefully, peeling it back just enough to peer inside. She looked up, brow furrowed in confusion before she removed the parchment. "It's . . ."

"Wait." He reached for a match, then set the item on fire.

She laughed, and he relaxed slightly at the sound—music in the big empty room. "It's a figgy pudding."

"I don't want it to be a lie, Sixpence. I want it to be the truth. I want us to have fallen in love over a figgy pudding," he said, his voice catching. "In you I see my heart, my purpose . . . my very soul."

There was a moment of complete stillness as she recalled the first time he'd said the words, and he thought, fleetingly, that he might be too late. That this silly pudding was too little.

But then she was in his arms, kissing him, and he put all his love, all his emotion into that caress, loving the way her hands came up to play in the hair at the base of his neck, loving her little gasp as he worried her lower lip with his teeth. She pulled away and opened her beautiful blue eyes to meet his gaze, but he was not ready to release her, and he stole another kiss before vowing, "I am yours, my love . . . yours to do with as you will. When I stole you in the dead of night and claimed you for my own, how could I have known that now—tonight—forever—it would be I who am claimed? My heart that is stolen?

"I realize that I am unworthy of you. I realize that I have a lifetime of ruin for which I must make amends. But I swear to you, I shall do everything I can to make you happy, my love. I shall work every day to be a man deserving of you. Of your love. Please . . . please give me that chance."

Please believe me.

Her eyes glistened with tears, and when she shook her

head, he lost his breath, unable to face the possibility that she might refuse him. That she might not believe him. Silence stretched between them, and he was desperate for her words.

"For so long, I have ached," she whispered, her fingers at his face, as if to convince herself that he was there. That he was hers. "I have ached for more, dreamed of love. I have ached for this moment. I have ached for *you.*" A tear spilled over, tracking down one of her lovely cheeks, and he lifted his hand to wipe it away. "I think I have loved you since we were children, Michael. I think it was always you."

He placed his forehead to hers, pulling her to him, wanting her near. "I am here. I am yours. And dear God, Penelope, I have ached for you as well. So very much."

She smiled, so beautiful. "How is that possible?"

"How could it not be?" he asked, the words harsh and graveled with emotion. "For nine years, I thought it was vengeance that would save me, and it took you—my strong, beautiful wife—to prove that I was wrong and that love was my salvation. You are my redemption," he whispered. "You are my benediction."

She was crying in earnest, and he sipped at the tears before taking her mouth in one long, lush kiss, pouring all his love into the caress, stroking deep until they were both gasping for breath. He lifted his head. "Tell me you believe me."

"I believe you."

He closed his eyes against the wave of relief that coursed through him at the words. "Say it again."

"I believe you, Michael."

"I love you."

She smiled. "I know."

He kissed her, deep and quick. "It is customary for the lady to return the sentiment."

She laughed. "Is it?"

He scowled. "Tell me you love me, Lady Penelope."

"It's Lady Bourne, to you." She wrapped her arms about his shoulders and let her fingers tangle in his hair. "I love you, Michael. I love you quite desperately. And I'm very happy that you've decided to love me back."

"How could I not?" he asked. "You are my warrior. Facing down Bruno and Langford to fight."

She smiled shyly. "I could not leave. I would not be your fallen angel. I would follow you into hell . . . but only to bring you back."

The words humbled him. "I don't deserve you," he said, "But I am afraid I cannot let you go."

Her serious blue gaze did not waver as she asked, "Do you promise?"

With everything he was. "I do." He wrapped her in his arms, resting his chin upon her head, before he remembered the other item he'd brought for her. "I brought your winnings, love." He extracted the papers from the card game the previous evening and set them next to the pudding.

"Your property."

He pressed a kiss to her neck, and smiled against the skin when she sighed at the caress. "Not mine. Yours. Won handily."

She shook her head. "There is only one thing from last night's winnings that I want."

"What is that?"

She leaned up to kiss him thoroughly, robbing him of breath. "You."

"I think you might regret that win, Sixpence."

She shook her head, all seriousness. "Never."

They kissed again, lost in each other for long minutes before curiosity flared and he lifted his head. "What did you have on Langford?"

She gave a little laugh and curled around him to reach for the wager, sifting through the pile of papers to retrieve the small square of paper. "You forgot to teach me the most important rule of scoundrels."

"Which one is that?"

She unfolded the paper carefully and handed it to him. "When in doubt, bluff."

It was her invitation to The Angel.

Surprise gave way to laughter, then to pride. "My wicked, gambling wife. I believed you had something truly damning."

She smiled, bold and brilliant, and he found he'd had enough of talking.

Instead, he lowered his wife to the floor of his dining room and stripped her bare, worshipping every glorious inch of skin he revealed. And as her laughter gave way to sighs, he reminded her again and again of how very much he loved her.

For years, when children and grandchildren inquired about the round black mark on the Hell House dining-room table, the Marchioness of Bourne would tell tale of a figgy pudding gone wrong . . . before the marquess would interject that in his opinion, it had gone rather perfectly.

Epilogue

Dear Sixpence,

I saved them all, you know. Every letter you ever sent, even those to which I never replied. I'm sorry for so many things, my love: that I left you; that I never came home; that it took me so long to realize that you <u>*were*</u> *my home and that, with you by my side, none of the rest mattered.*

But in the darkest hours, on the coldest nights, when I felt I'd lost everything, I still had your letters. And through them, in some small way, I still had you.

I loved you then, my darling Penelope, more than I could imagine—just as I love you now, more than you can know.

Michael
Hell House, February 1831

One week later

Cross woke as usual, on a makeshift pallet inside his office at The Fallen Angel, wedged between an overflowing bookcase and a massive globe, surrounded by papers.

Not as usual, however, there was a woman sitting at his desk.

Strike that. Not a woman. A lady. A young, blond-haired, bespectacled lady.

She was reading the ledger.

He sat up, ignoring the fact that he was not wearing a shirt and that, conventionally, gentlemen did not greet ladies half-naked. Hang convention. If the woman hadn't wanted to see him half-naked, then she should not have invaded his offices in the night.

That most men did not make a practice of sleeping in their offices was of little import.

"May I help you?"

She did not look up. "You've miscalculated column F."

What in hell?

"I have not."

She pushed her glasses up her nose and tucked a stray strand of blond hair behind her ear, entirely focused on the ledger. "You have. The proper calculation should be one hundred and twelve thousand, three hundred forty-six and seventeen pence."

Impossible.

He stood, moving to look over her shoulder. "That's what it says."

She shook her head, placing one long finger on the tabulation line. He noticed the tip of the finger was slightly crooked, leaning a touch to the right. "You've written one hundred twelve thousand, three hundred, forty-*five* and seventeen pence. You—" She looked up at him, eyes owl-like behind her spectacles as she took in his height and his bare chest. "You—You've lost a quid."

He bent over her, deliberately crowding her and enjoying the way her breath caught at his nearness. "That *is* a six."

She cleared her throat and looked again. "Oh." She leaned in and checked the number again. "I suppose you've lost your handwriting skills, instead," she said dryly, and he chuckled as she reached for a pencil and repaired the number.

He watched, riveted to the callus at the tip of her second finger, before he whispered low in her ear, "Are you an accounting fairy sent in the dead of night to check my figures?"

She leaned away from the whisper and turned to look at him. "It's one o'clock in the afternoon," she said, matter-of-factly, and he had an intense desire to take her spectacles from her face and kiss her senseless, just to see what this odd young woman would say.

He quashed the desire.

Instead, he smiled. "Sent in the dead of day, then?"

She blinked. "I am Philippa Marbury."

His eyes went wide, and he took an enormous step backward, knocking into a hat stand and turning to rescue it before realizing that he absolutely could not be standing in his office, in a gaming hell, shirtless, with Bourne's sister-in-law. Bourne's *betrothed* sister-in-law.

He reached for a shirt. It was wrinkled and worn, but it would do. As he searched fruitlessly for the opening in the linen, he backed away again. Farther.

She stood and came around the desk toward him. "Have I upset you?"

Why didn't the shirt have an opening? As a last resort, he held the clothing in front of him, a shield from her enormous, all-seeing eyes. "Not at all, but I do not make a practice of having clandestine meetings with my partners' sisters, half-nude."

She considered the words before tilting her head to one side, and saying, "Well, you were asleep, so you really couldn't have prevented it."

"Somehow, I doubt that Bourne would see it that way."

"At least give me an audience. I came all the way here."

Cross knew he should refuse. Knew, with the keen sense of a lifelong gambler, that he should not continue this game. That it was unwinnable. But there was something about this young woman that made it impossible to stop himself. "Well, since you came all the way *here* . . . how may I be of service, Lady Philippa?"

She took a deep breath. Released it. "I require ruination. And I hear you are an expert in the subject."

NEW YORK TIMES BESTSELLING AUTHOR

SARAH MACLEAN

Nine Rules to Break When Seducing a Rake

978-0-06-185205-3

Lady Calpurnia Hartwell has always followed the rules of being a lady. But now she's vowed to live the life of pleasure she's been missing. Charming and devastatingly handsome, Gabriel St. John, the Marquess of Ralston, is a more than willing partner.

Ten Ways to Be Adored When Landing a Lord

978-0-06-185206-0

Nicholas St. John has been relentlessly pursued by every matrimony-minded female in the *ton*. So when an opportunity to escape presents itself, he eagerly jumps—only to land in the path of the most determined, damnably delicious woman he's ever met!

Eleven Scandals to Start to Win a Duke's Heart

978-0-06-185207-7

Bold, impulsive, and a magnet for trouble, Juliana Fiori is no simpering English miss. Her scandalous nature makes her a favorite subject of London's most practiced gossips . . . and precisely the kind of woman the Duke of Leighton wants far *far* away from him.

Give in to your Impulses!

These unforgettable stories only take a second to buy and give you hours of reading pleasure!

Go to ***www.AvonImpulse.com*** and see what we have to offer.

Available wherever e-books are sold.